THE FATE OF THE MALOUS

and

ACCOUNT UNSETTLED

*

SIMENON

THE COMPANION BOOK CLUB
LONDON

Made and printed in Great Britain
for The Companion Book Club (Odhams Books Ltd.)
by Odhams (Watford) Limited
Watford, Herts.
S.264.UB

CONTENTS

*

THE FATE OF THE MALOUS

translated from the French by

DENIS GEORGE

CHAPTER ONE

GABRIEL, the waiter, had nothing to do. With his napkin in his hand, he stood facing the street, a section of which was framed in the slightly misted windows of the café.

It was three o'clock in the afternoon and it was dark, inside as out. Inside, there was a rich subdued glow from the rich patina of the panelling which covered the walls and the ceiling, the richness of the purple velvet on the settles, and the reflection of the few electric lights already lit in the liquid depths of the bevelled mirrors.

Outside, was the Rue de Moulins, in fact the main street, too narrow, with its cars, trams, shops and Prisunic with its brash exterior; it was three o'clock and it was winter, without rain, without snow, with a cold dampness hanging in the air under the twilit sky.

Gabriel saw the long black limousine stop noiselessly beside the kerb, recognized Arsène who got out from his seat to open the door, Eugène Malou, looking congested as usual, who jumped out on to the pavement and proceeded to give orders to his chauffeur.

Mechanically, Gabriel wiped his napkin over the varnished wood of a table, Malou's table, the best, well in evidence, in the left-hand corner where it commanded the café and the street.

The car moved off. Malou entered. He was the same as ever. Despite what had been written about him that morning in the newspaper, he behaved exactly the same as ever.

"Armagnac, Gabriel . . ."

He put some papers, a whole bundle of them, on the table. He always had a lot of papers about him. He remained standing, slightly tilted back his grey felt hat.

"Bring me a coin for the phone . . ."

"Shall I get the number for you, Monsieur Malou?"

It was the only unusual detail: ordinarily, when he wanted to use the phone, he told the waiter to get him the number and only left his place when his correspondent was at the other end of the line.

It was at that moment that Gabriel looked at the time. It was two minutes past three. The cashier was knitting. The only customer, a commercial traveller, had been writing for more than half an hour without looking up.

Malou could dimly be seen in the half-light of the telephone booth. He did not speak for long. The click of the receiver was heard and he came out, went up to his table, drank, standing, a mouthful of Armagnac, then, without asking how much he owed, dropped twenty francs on the table.

After that, there was a gap in the time-table of Eugène Malou. Gabriel saw him go off on foot towards the left. A few shop windows were already lit. It was the most dismal hour of the day in a provincial town, and Gabriel went and leaned on the counter to chat to the cashier.

At four o'clock Eugène Malou was again in the Rue de Moulins and turned to the right into a sloping street, less commercial, where there were only one or two shops squeezed, as it were, between large private houses. He walked about fifty yards and lifted the brass knocker of one of those houses with old stone carving on them and a flight of five steps leading up to the door.

It was the town house of the d'Estiers. Everybody in town knew it. Its façade was reproduced in the folder put out by the town's publicity bureau.

A manservant in a white jacket came to admit him, then the door closed again.

From outside, two windows, ruddy with light, could be seen, one at street-level and the other on the first floor, but people passing by paid no attention, for, with the coming of night, the cold was becoming sharper; noses were red and men thrust their hands into the pockets of their overcoats.

It was November. In the main road higher up, where the trams swept by, the doors of Prisunic, continually swinging open, released a raucous music broadcast by a loud-speaker.

Just opposite the d'Estiers' house, there was a tiny chemist's shop, of the old-fashioned kind with a black shop front, two dingy windows enthroning two huge glass jars, green in one window and yellow in the other. Women went in from time to time, almost all of them of the working class, also in black, some of them dragging a child by the hand, and they could be seen talking to the chemist who wore a skull cap on his head and had a pepper and salt goatee beard.

It may have been a quarter past four, perhaps twenty past four, when the handle of the door of the d'Estiers' house turned. It turned without the door opening. It turned as it might, when someone has grasped the handle and is waiting impatiently for his visitor to be so good as to leave.

Probably the two men were standing in the wide hall which was lit by a lantern of Venetian glass. The door half-opened, closed again, was half-opened once more and someone who was walking quickly by heard raised voices, but did not look round.

The door opened wide, throwing a yellowish rectangle into the dark of the street. A very tall, middle-aged man was holding the door, and another, shorter and stouter, who was talking as he retreated backwards, almost missed the step and tumbled backwards down the flight.

The taller man was Count Adrien d'Estier, the other Eugène Malou. Did the Count really attempt to close the door again when Malou tried to prevent him once more?

There was an explosion which made the customers in the chemist's shop turn round. Next door, a woman who kept a draper's shop and also sold newspapers, ran to her doorstep and leaned out, clutching her shawl across her chest.

No one could say exactly what had happened, not even Count d'Estier who, at the time of the shot, had already more than half closed the door.

One of the women from the chemist's affirmed, however:

"He didn't fall straight away. He came down the steps backwards, almost bent double, and it was only at the bottom that he collapsed on the pavement . . ."

People had stopped, at the street corner, and were waiting to see if it was worth their while to go out of their way.

Before coming out of his house, Count d'Estier turned back inside and called somebody, his butler probably, for it was a man in a white coat whom they saw come down the steps first, cautiously, and bend over while the Count remained standing at the porch.

The chemist crossed the road and bent over in his turn. When he straightened up, there was already a circle of inquisitive people around him.

13

"A doctor," he exclaimed . . . "Someone go and fetch Doctor Moreau who lives ten doors further down . . . Quickly . . ."

People moved away, turned their heads aside, advised women who were coming up:

"Don't look . . ."

"What is it?"

"A man shot himself in the head . . ."

The revolver had fallen on to the flagstones. They avoided touching it. They looked at it in silence. A policeman in uniform arrived.

"We must carry him across to my place . . ." the chemist said.

And there were men willing to help him. There was also someone to pick up Eugène Malou's pearl-grey hat off the pavement.

He was moaning. It was a monotonous, mournful noise that none of those people had ever heard, a wailing so regular it had nothing human about it, it made one think of certain animal cries at night, or the grinding of some piece of machinery.

"Did he miss?"

The doorway of the chemist's shop was narrow.

"Make room there . . ." cried the policeman. "Everybody outside . . . Come along . . . Make room, for heaven's sake . . . We're not at the theatre . . ."

Nonetheless people packed into the corners. They laid the body flat on the floor, the head near the enamelled weighing-machine. A woman who had wanted to see, fainted.

It was ugly. Had Malou been too agitated to aim straight? Had his hand trembled? Had he meant to miss? Anyway the bullet apparently penetrating near his chin, at the corner of his mouth, had literally carried away part of his jaw.

He still had his eyes open. That was the most striking thing. He continued to see people coming and going about him. He saw them from the ground upwards, and one of his eyes had come almost entirely out of its socket.

"What about the doctor?"

"I have been there, monsieur . . . He's not at home."

"Someone telephone elsewhere . . . And to the hospital . . . But, for God's sake, let's have some room here . . ."

The chemist had ripped open some packets of cotton-wool

14

wadding. He was using it to staunch the blood which was already forming a sticky pool on the dust of the floor.

And still Eugène Malou did not die. It seemed impossible that he should live in the state he was in; everyone was secretly wishing that it would be quickly over, so that they should no longer see his eyes, no longer hear his continuous moaning.

The policeman had thrust back the major part of the on-lookers, and was standing outside the door, in front of a crowd getting steadily thicker, faces that could be seen looming out of the darkness, lit in yellow and green by the light from the glass jars.

Someone to the right of the counter was telephoning to all the doctors of the neighbourhood, but it was the time when the majority of them were on their rounds.

"It's Malou . . ." someone said in the crowd.

"How did it happen?"

"He was coming out of the Count's house, so it seems . . ."

Count d'Estier was still standing, quite alone, at the foot of his steps.

And then, in the street, in the whole neighbourhood wherever the news spread, there was a feeling of embarrassment.

Everybody had read the articles which had been appearing for several days in the *Phare du Centre*. Everybody had read the most threatening, almost triumphant one that had appeared that very morning:

MALOU'S END

Everybody had acclaimed it, for everybody was keenly in-volved in this battle that had been going on for so long.

"We'll get him in the end . . ."

Now they had got him! Eugène Malou was there, on the floor of a little chemist's shop, half his face torn away, the shoulder of his overcoat stuck in his own blood. And little by little the people fell back. They wanted to know, but they preferred not to see.

What had its birth in the street and was going to spread gradually throughout the town was something like a feeling of collective shame, and some people from now on began to look reproachfully at the figure of Count d'Estier who, still alone on the pavement, was smoking a cigarette.

Sometimes excited urchins chase a mangy cat and throw

stones at it. And when they have managed to hit it, to wound it without killing it, then you see them keeping their distance, ashamed of what they have done, moved by the blood flowing, by the agonized spasms of the animal that none of them has the courage to finish off.

If only Malou could die quickly! The white overall of the little chemist with the goatee beard could be seen going and coming, bending over, straightening up. He could be seen opening bottles, disappearing into his dispensary, returning with a syringe. And despite the closed door, they could still hear—or thought they could hear—the fluctuating moan which, in the end, set their nerves on edge.

"Go and play farther off, you children!"

A car, at last: a doctor's; he dashed inside taking off his coat as he entered.

Would he save Malou? That would be worse. People would have to see him about again with his deformed face, and, knowing him, he would be quite capable of walking about the streets like that, of taking his place again at the Café de Paris, of becoming a sort of living reproach.

That is why people hoped secretly that he would die. They were waiting for a signal from inside which would bring relief, the signal that all was over.

At that moment, three boys, three young men of about sixteen to seventeen, turned the corner of the Rue de Moulins. They were coming from school. Each had books and exercise books in his hand. The one in the middle was the tallest, the slimmest, and his dark overcoat, which hung straight down, seemed to make his figure longer still.

They were talking as they walked with long easy strides. They followed the left-hand pavement, the one past the d'Estiers' house. A voice could be heard saying:

". . . I told the English beak that since he kept on at me . . ."

They were recognized. It was they now who everybody looked at, the one in the middle particularly, who, in turn, was vaguely looking at the crowd gathered outside the chemist's shop.

Probably all three of them were going to cross the road to find out, to have a look for themselves? The people mechanically moved closer together, as though to block their path.

"Monsieur Malou . . ."

A dark patch of pavement, a half-open door at the top of the flight of five steps, Count d'Estier, who still had his cigarette in his hand and was advancing towards the boys.

"May I ask you to step in for a moment?"

The young man, astonished, looked at his questioner and at the chemist's shop in turn.

"Excuse me . . ." he said to his friends.

They were seen mounting the steps, the Count and the youth together. The door was not shut completely and once again the handle began to turn. It could not last for long. People had now begun to count the seconds. They wondered if the moaning was getting weaker, they could see Doctor Fauchon straighten up and move behind the counter to wash his hands.

An ambulance appeared at the corner of the street. It was not hard to guess its destination. What were they doing opposite? The crowd moved back on the pavement to give room for the vehicle with the red cross.

Finally the door opened. The young man came down the steps of the porch, and it was plain that he was not hurrying overmuch. He made a vague gesture to his friends, excused himself to the people he disturbed as he made a path for himself.

When they heard the bell ring as he pushed open the door of the chemist's shop, the doctor came forward to meet him as though to stop him. They could see everything, from outside, the doctor taking his hand and holding it in his own as he spoke to him earnestly. The words could not be heard, but the movements of the lips could be followed. There was the feeling that the young man was trying to free himself to approach the prostrate body, that the speaker, for his part, was still trying to gain a little time.

And if he had to gain time it must be because it was too painful to see, because it was not all over, because it was probably a question of minutes. The proof was that the two ambulance orderlies who had brought out the stretcher were kept waiting.

Finally Doctor Fauchon released the hand of the young man, who awkwardly took a step forward, then another, with a strange shyness, his eyes on the ground. They saw him bend over, stretch out his arm, then immediately straighten up again and remain motionless, tall and thin, with his two hands holding his hat on his stomach.

17

"He's dead . . ." said someone outside.

And they believed him. There were men who, until then, had hesitated to light their pipes or their cigarettes, and women who —at last—led their children away.

Count Adrien d'Estier, all alone on his stretch of the pavement, was still walking up and down and there was a face behind the curtains of the lighted window on the first floor.

"He's dead . . ." said a customer to Gabriel at the Café de Paris. And those who overheard, glanced at Eugène Malou's table. "He took a long time dying . . . It was grim . . ."

In the chemist's shop, the doctor put on his heavy overcoat and seized the young man by the arm. The latter, after a moment's resistance, submitted. Fauchon led him out of the shop, guiding him through the crowd.

His two classmates were there. Malou's son recognized them as he went by, for they were standing apart, under a lamppost, and he waved his hand to them.

"We must warn your mother before they come with the body . . ."

The doctor appeared to be supporting him, but the young man did not need it, he walked quickly, as though lost in a dream.

So much so that the doctor decided not to take his car. It's true it was only a short step. The road ran downhill, getting steadily darker, for shops were becoming scarcer. At the bottom there was only a furnishing establishment whose owners did not trouble to light the front windows.

Then they turned to the left, into a similar, narrower street. At that moment they were lifting the body of Eugène Malou into the ambulance and the police superintendent, who had not been at his desk when they telephoned, was arriving quite out of breath.

"You must be very brave in front of your mother . . ."

Alain Malou did not reply, perhaps was not listening. He had not wept. He had not yet said anything.

And they reached a small square, paved with round cobbles, with a pretty renaissance fountain in its centre. With the coming of night, a slight mist had appeared, which softened still more the old stonework of the large private houses.

The houses here, the five or six houses that surrounded the square, all had large gateways, with stone posts dating from the

18

days when carriages were used. The lights behind the few illuminated windows were so shaded that one might have thought there was still the gleam of candles as in former days. Footsteps ran on the ground, and were multiplied by the echoes.

The two men stopped at a door; the doctor rang, and the young man waited as though it were not his own front door, as though he were paying a visit.

"Perhaps there's nobody at home . . ." he murmured, when there was no immediate answer.

The doctor rang again, and finally footsteps could be heard in the house, a door slammed, someone was walking under the archway, a chain clanked, the heavy gate opened slightly.

"Is it you, Monsieur Alain?"

The man was wearing the black suit and white tie of a butler.

"I beg your pardon . . . You are not alone . . ."

The doctor enquired:

"Is Madame Malou in?"

"She went out about two hours ago . . ."

The young man stood there, without knowing what to do.

"I don't think it will be long before she is back. She went to her hairdresser . . ."

The doctor took charge of the practical details.

"You had better open both sides of the gate, so that the ambulance can get in."

"Has something happened?"

"Monsieur Malou is dead."

The ambulance was already turning into the square, and once again all was confusion. First of all the doors had to be opened. The doctor asked the butler quietly:

"Where are we going to put him?"

There must have been huge drawing-rooms on the ground floor. A double-twist staircase, of carved wood, led up to the first floor.

"We cannot leave him downstairs," the manservant whispered.

He had only turned on a few lights. Even so the doctor could see that red seals had been affixed to the doors.

"Upstairs?"

"The bailiffs left us three rooms . . ."

The orderlies carried the stretcher upstairs, which someone had covered with a sheet. The house seemed empty, abandoned.

The butler walked on ahead and switched on the lights as he came to them.

Alain and the doctor followed behind. He was not the family doctor. He had only been called to the house two or three times, by chance, for emergencies.

"The best thing's to put him in his room . . ."

But was it still the dead man's room? Here, too, seals were ranged all over the antique cupboards. Paintings, objects of all kinds, were piled in a corner. It was hard to imagine that a few hours earlier a family was still living there. One could search in vain for any sign of their habitation.

"What about your sister?" asked the doctor.

"She's due to return from Paris today . . ."

"And your brother Edgar?"

"Of course . . . We can ring him up at his office, at the County Hall . . ."

"If you'll come this way . . ." said the butler.

The body of Eugène Malou was stretched on his bed, still covered with a sheet. The orderlies were waiting for something. The doctor very nearly said to the young man: "You must tip them . . ."

But he eventually took a note from his pocket himself and slipped it into the hand of one of them.

There were other rooms in disorder, as if in preparation for moving house, baskets which probably contained linen or silverware, trunks, packing-cases. A dining-room was nearly intact, where the butler lit the chandelier.

"Your mother will be back at any moment. . . . Do you know who her hairdresser is?"

"Francis . . ."

"Perhaps it would be better to telephone so that someone can prepare her . . . ?"

"Do you think so?"

"Shall I try to get her on the phone?"

The doctor telephoned. He was able to speak to her where she sat, doubtless with a shell-shaped dryer above her head.

"Madame Malou? . . . Your son Alain wants to speak to you . . ."

"Mother?"

His voice was dry without warmth.

20

"Yes, Alain speaking . . . I'm at home . . . My father is dead . . ."

He listened for a moment longer, hung up and looked away, anywhere, as though he were a stranger in his house, in his family.

The doctor, who liked to do things thoroughly, telephoned to the County Hall, managed to get in touch with Edgar Malou, the elder son.

"You speak to him . . ."

"Is that you, Edgar? . . . Yes, this is Alain . . . Father's dead . . . What did you say? . . . You knew about it? . . . Yes, he's here . . . They've just brought him home . . . I've phoned Mother who was at the hairdresser's . . . If you like . . . I don't know . . . He didn't speak to me . . ."

The sound of a car in the square. Without waiting for the knock on the door, the butler went downstairs. There was lengthy whispering on the stairs. The steps and voices came nearer.

"Where is Alain?"

"In the small dining-room, Madame . . ."

A perfume which could be caught before she came into view. A fur coat thrown about her shoulders; hair set in a permanent wave.

"Oh! I beg your pardon, doctor . . ."

"It is I who beg your pardon, Madame . . . I was called to the chemist's shop and I thought I had better come on here . . ."

"How is it you were there, Alain?"

"I was going by on my way back from school . . ."

"Did you see him before? Did he speak to you? Where have they put him?"

"He is in his room, Madame . . . At the moment, it would be better if you did not insist on seeing him . . ."

She looked frail, with the indeterminate features of a woman of forty-five who takes care of herself, and yet she had not given way for a moment.

After an anxious look around her, she asked:

"What will happen now?"

"I don't know, Madame. I think the police superintendent will soon be here for a few formalities . . ."

"Where did he do it?"

21

"In the street . . . To be exact, outside the d'Estiers' front door . . ."

"Do you understand it, Alain?"

Then, nervously:

"Did he die immediately?"

"Almost immediately . . ."

"He didn't suffer?"

Alain looked down without saying a word.

"Sit down, doctor. . . . Has Joseph offered you anything?"

"I don't want anything, I assure you . . ."

"Joseph . . ."

Joseph had understood and put a carafe and glasses on the table.

"Is he an ugly sight?"

She had put a cigarette between her lips and was searching for her lighter in her handbag.

"You should make a fire, Joseph . . ."

Her nerves were on edge.

"And with Corine in Paris . . . Did you tell your brother?"

There was a ring downstairs. It was Edgar, the elder son, who had had time to take a taxi home and get his wife. It also looked as if they had had time to put on mourning, for they were dressed in black from head to foot.

They, too, were talking as they came upstairs, questioning the servant. The same question:

"Where have they put him?"

Then, solemnly, Edgar, who was twenty-seven, came towards Madame Malou, whom he took in his arms and held to him for some while in silence.

"My poor Mother . . ."

"My poor Edgar . . ."

Madame Malou's eyes moistened, and she sobbed, two or three times, after which it was the turn of her daughter-in-law to throw herself into her arms.

"Be brave, Mother . . ." she said.

"Does anyone even know how it happened?"

Edgar turned to his brother, Alain.

"You were there, weren't you?"

"I arrived when it was all over . . . Count d'Estier told me about it . . ."

"Will you excuse me? . . ." murmured Doctor Fauchon, who began to feel he was in the way.

They thanked him.

"Another drop of brandy, doctor?"

But he was in a hurry to make his departure, to breathe the air outside.

"Tell us . . ." Edgar said to his brother.

"Can't you guess?"

"It doesn't matter. Tell us . . . We ought to know the truth, there will be enough lies about. . . ."

"May I, Mother?" said his wife, as she took off her coat. Alain still maintained his somewhat distant attitude.

"What did d'Estier tell you?"

"Father went to see him . . ."

"I'd guessed that much. Then what?"

"He asked for more money . . ."

The elder brother, who was the head of an office at the County Hall, curled his lip. "Of course. And then?"

"He said he had had enough, that it was all too silly, that it was heartbreaking to see how people couldn't understand, and that since he was being pushed to the limit, he would prefer to blow his brains out . . ."

"Do you believe that?" his elder brother asked ironically.

The younger son fell silent, still standing by the table, and he was the only one who had not taken off his overcoat.

"Come on, speak up . . . You know as well as I do what I mean . . . It's not the first time . . ."

"He died . . ."

"I know that . . . But how?"

"It seems that he had taken his revolver from his pocket . . ."
Alain spoke almost reluctantly, his eyes wandering.

"The Count pushed him outside and tried to close the door . . . Father had put his foot in . . . d'Estier wasn't looking when he fired."

"It's a fine thing for us . . ."

"Father is dead . . ."

"And you are all in trouble . . . I'm wondering about myself at the County Hall . . ."

A glance from his wife, who was pink and chubby, made him fall silent. He went on almost immediately:

23

"What are you going to do, Mother?"

"How do I know!"

"Have you any money left?"

"You all know very well I haven't . . ."

"Your jewels . . . ?"

"They were pledged long ago . . ."

"I wonder how we're going to manage to pay for the funeral," said Edgar. "It costs a lot, a great deal . . . Marthe and I have had a lot of expenses this year, moving into the new house, and we haven't been able to save anything . . . Where is Corine?"

"She went to spend two days in Paris with a friend. She should be back today, if it isn't like last time . . ."

"What's going to happen to her?"

"And me . . . ?" the mother flashed back.

Someone had rung at the door a few seconds earlier. Joseph, the butler, came and announced:

"It's the police superintendent asking to speak to Madame."

Where could they receive him? There were seals everywhere. The house was no longer a house.

"Here . . ." she said.

She quickly swallowed a mouthful of brandy and threw her cigarette into the fireplace, where a few logs were blazing.

"Please excuse me, Madame."

"Of course, Superintendent. It is so unexpected, so terrible . . ."

"Please accept my sincere condolences . . . For you and your family in your great misfortune . . . I find I'm obliged . . ."

"I know . . . I was at my hairdresser's, Francis, when Alain phoned me . . . I don't think he realizes . . . He's young . . ."

Alain blushed and turned to the fireplace.

"You know all about the campaign that was being waged against my husband by certain people . . . He was used to a fight . . . I felt sure that he would come through it once more."

"Did you know he carried a revolver on him?"

"I've always known that that was his custom . . . At night, he put it within reach. . . . I've tried in vain to cure him of the habit . . . I used to ask him what he was frightened of . . ."

"This is the weapon, isn't it?"

"I think so . . . Yes . . . I admit I've never paid much attention to it, I have a horror of anything that can kill . . ."

"You admit the possibility and even the probability of suicide?"

"He must have been momentarily depressed . . . He has been gloomy, worried, these last few days."

"Because of this campaign in the *Phare du Centre*?"

"I don't know. . . . I suppose so."

"When the seals were affixed here . . ."

"That was this morning . . . I remember how charming he was to the bailiff, and that he went himself to the cellar to fetch a vintage bottle to offer him a drink. . . . He said to him: "'This is not the first time and no doubt will not be the last.' He also said something else to him, I remember:

" 'You know, if there weren't people like me on the earth, you would never earn your living . . . In fact, I suppose we are the best friends of you bailiffs . . .'

"He was showing off, I suppose . . . He always put a bold front on it . . . That's why I didn't expect this to happen."

She was weeping quietly, restrainedly.

"Now they stop me seeing him, on the grounds that the sight would be too much for me . . . What's going to happen, Superintendent . . . I'm left alone with my children . . . I've nothing of my own . . . There are seals everywhere . . . I haven't even got a penny to bury him . . ."

The superintendent turned to Edgar, who spoke to him in an undertone:

"I shall come and see you . . . We must have a conversation . . ."

Weren't they both civil servants? Didn't they both belong more or less to the same building?

"I don't know yet how things will turn out, Madame. For the moment, I have only to deal with the report. Believe me, I am very distressed to have had to . . . to have had to . . ."

Enough! It was over as far as he was concerned. He retired backwards, with a glance of complicity at Edgar.

The family remained alone; Marthe, the daughter-in-law, declared:

"Mother really must eat something . . . I'll go and see Joseph about it . . . Has the cook . . . ?"

"Julie left yesterday . . ."

"I'll go and see about it with Joseph."

Eugène Malou was all alone in the room with the seals on the cupboards, all alone under the sheet which hid his disfigured face.

"I wonder, Mother . . ."

"Sit down . . . You know very well I hate talking to someone who is always walking to and fro . . ."

"I wonder if the insurance policy . . ."

"Your father sold it back last month, so we have nothing to count on."

Alain went out silently. Nobody took any notice of him. The other two, Madame Malou and Edgar, were seated in armchairs in front of the hearth, and Madame Malou had lit a fresh cigarette.

Alain crossed the corridor, went into the bedroom where he was struck by the cold, for the central heating had not been working for three days now owing to lack of coal.

He didn't attempt to uncover his father's face. He sat on a low chair, near the bed, crossed his hands on his knees and remained motionless, looking at nothing, not even at the sheet under which the shape of the dead man could be seen.

A long while afterwards he heard the bell, footsteps. But it was part of another world and he paid no attention. A new female voice, that of his sister. It was all the same to him. He did not realize that she had just got home off the seven-twenty train and that she, in her turn, was being told everything.

They called him through the empty rooms:

"Alain! . . . Alain!"

Someone opened and closed the door of his old room, and his sister-in-law announced:

"He's not there."

So, to avoid their coming to look for him where he was, he got up, straightened his thin body, remained standing motionless for a moment, at the foot of the bed, his lips moving as though he were pronouncing words under his breath, then, opening the door, he called to them:

"I'm coming . . ."

Dinner was served in the dining-room, and when there was a moment's silence, the fountain could be heard flowing in the little square.

CHAPTER TWO

"ALAIN ... Alain ..."

It seemed to him that he had hardly fallen asleep, and yet, without raising his eyelids, he knew that it was already daylight. He knew too that it was pouring with rain, for, not far from his bedroom window, lower down, was a zinc lean-to on which the drops were rattling hard.

"Why did you go to bed fully dressed?"

He had to resign himself to leave the depths of sleep and to return to reality. It was his sister who called him in that way, who was sitting on the foot of his bed, and, when he opened his eyes, he saw with ill humour—he could have betted on it moreover—that she was sitting with her legs crossed, her dressing-gown open. Could she not understand that it embarrassed him to see her always half naked? It was like a mania with her. She had no modesty. In the morning she would come out of the bathroom with nothing on her body, and she would put on her stockings in front of him, holding up her legs one after the other while he did not know where to look.

Corine was beautiful. Everybody said she was beautiful, all the men ran after her. Her flesh was rich, her skin close-grained, her figure shapely. Her whole body was curved. She was all flesh and curves. She was a female, whereas Alain would have preferred a sister, like some of his school friends had, a real young lady whom you couldn't even imagine naked.

She smelt like a female. Even now he was conscious of her odour, for she had just got out of bed; she had slept in a little silken slip, very short and crumpled, which had pulled up over her white belly, and she didn't take the trouble to draw the skirts of her dressing-gown over herself.

"Joseph has gone ..." she announced.

"I know ..."

He realized straight away that he'd made a mistake, that he would have done better to keep quiet.

"How do you know? Did he tell you?"

He knew because in a manner of speaking he had not really slept that night.

And to begin with, he had gone to bed fully dressed without taking off his tie, because he was frightened. He could not have exactly said of what, but he was frightened. All alone in his room, he appeared incapable of undressing and perhaps there was something of modesty in his feelings. Wasn't his father's body, all alone, two rooms away, all alone in the darkness?

He had got into his four-poster bed. And he did not dare, even in thought, call it the catafalque, as he usually did.

It was practically a museum piece, black and gold, and loaded with carvings, coats of arms. The house was full of that kind of furniture bought at sales, particularly sales at large country houses. The chimney piece too was emblazoned, and also the wardrobe in which six people could have been shut and whose doors were closed by the bailiff's seals.

"How do you know he's gone?"

"I heard him."

It was in the middle of the night. His eyes were open. The bedroom of Joseph, the butler, was just above his. For a long while he had listened to the servant, coming and going, in his stockings, then the footsteps had moved to the staircase. Joseph was leaving, that was certain. All the other servants had left one after the other, despite the money that was owed them.

There was something else that Alain had heard: Joseph, who looked like an unfrocked priest, had gone into the room where the body was and had stayed there ferreting around for a good while.

Alain hadn't dreamed it, he was sure of it. His throat was tight, there was sweat on his forehead, but he hadn't dared move and he was relieved when finally he had heard the distant slam of the door, then footsteps on the pavement.

"There's nothing to eat in the house . . . You must go out and get something . . ."

Always he, of course! It was always Alain's name that was shouted through the house when there was some unpleasant job to perform.

He got up, glanced slyly at her.

"Have you got any money?" he asked.

"I'll go and ask mother . . . She feels very tired and is staying in bed . . ."

As usual too. In the mornings she was invariably tired and remained in bed until midday. In the times when there had been servants in the house, she enjoyed having them all parade in front of her.

28

He went into his mother's bedroom, after having run a comb through his hair and rinsed his face in water. His suit was crumpled and his tie twisted.

"Joseph has left . . ." she told him in her turn.

"I know, Corine told me."

"There's nothing to eat in the house. Just a piece of stale bread."

"Have you any money?"

That question was well known in the house. It had been repeated enough times for them to know it! Even his father who, sometimes, used to ask Alain to lend him his savings for a few hours.

"There should be some in the wallet."

He understood her meaning, for she glanced towards the room of the dead man. He also understood that his mother and sister hadn't wanted to go in there themselves.

It needed an effort. It wasn't the same thing as the evening before, in the dusk, with the rain trickling down the windows. He almost asked Corine to accompany him but his pride prevented him.

He remembered the visit that Joseph had paid to the room in the night and he was relieved to see the corpse in its place on the bed under the sheet. The jacket was on a chair, and he searched the pockets, but didn't find the wallet until he noticed it a second later, lying open on the carpet.

He picked it up and went out quickly, threw it on his mother's bed.

"I think it's empty . . ."

"Why?"

"Because it was on the floor. I bet it's Joseph."

And it was true. Had Joseph found any money in the wallet? At all events, in that case, he had taken it away with him.

"I have a little money in my handbag . . . Pass it to me . . . Buy some bread, butter, milk . . .When Edgar comes presently, I'll ask him for a little money . . . Although we must find some before then . . . Do you know who rang at the door?"

"Did someone ring?"

"About eight o'clock this morning, then a second time half an hour later . . ."

It was then he had fallen asleep at last, and he had heard nothing.

29

"Go and see if anything has been left in the letter box. I wonder what we're going to do without anybody . . ."

But she didn't get up.

"And then someone's got to do something about . . ."

A glance towards the dead man's room. Do something about the funeral, of course. Alain put on his overcoat, went downstairs, crossed the still freezing entrance and opened the little wicket door in the gate. He nearly went without the key, forgetting that there were no servants to let him in. He found it on a hook.

Outside, he put up the collar of his long overcoat. He had no hat. He never wore one. His blond hair was sprinkled with beads of rain, drops of water trembled at the end of his nose. The little square was empty. There was a dairy less than a hundred yards away, in an alley, but the woman had already sworn at him once in front of everybody because they were several months behind with their account.

He went further on. He nearly bought a paper which probably carried the story of his father. He went into a shop and saw clearly that the people looked at him with embarrassment and pity both at once.

Bread, half a pound of butter and a bottle of milk like the poor housewives. He carried them in his arms as he walked quickly.

When he got back to the flat, the two women were having an argument. Corine was no more dressed than when she had woken her brother. She was walking to and fro around her mother's bed.

"Of course I can't ask him for that . . . I don't know what you're thinking about, or what you take me for."

"I could take you for what you are . . ."

"What does that mean?"

"Don't be an idiot! . . . You realize this time it's for us . . . It's not for a fur coat, is it?"

"I forbid you to speak of . . ."

"Don't shout, please."

"Because of the servants, I suppose?"

"Because you're speaking to your mother . . ."

"My mother who wants me to go and ask a man for money . . ."

"Haven't you finished, the pair of you?" grumbled Alain, who contented himself with putting the food on his mother's dressing table.

30

"Your brother's just phoned . . ."

"What did he have to say?"

"That he's enquired about the funeral, that it will cost at the very least about twenty thousand francs and that he hasn't any money . . . He will be here presently, after going to the office, he claims he's got to go to the office . . . In other words: Manage by yourselves . . . I've asked your sister to phone Fabien . . ."

Alain blushed and turned towards the window. Couldn't they, on a day like this, have avoided speaking of that? Haven't women any sense of decency?

Fabien was a surgeon, the leading surgeon of the town, who owned a magnificent private nursing home. He was a youngish man, of about forty, good looking, with a taste for good living. He was married and had three children, but he was never seen with his wife.

At the theatre, at concerts, it was Corine who was with him, and, when, practically every week, he went to operate in Paris, she was almost certainly to be seen getting on the same train. It was in Paris that she had been on the previous evening. Supposedly with her friends the Manselles. It was her friends the Manselles, too, who were very rich, who had let her have the mink coat of which she was so proud for practically nothing.

"If Fabien is really a friend, as I am prepared to believe . . ."

"That will do, Mother," Corine cut in.

"That will do indeed," added Alain disgustedly.

"Is there nobody to make a cup of coffee?"

Brother and sister looked at each other. Corine opened her mouth, but she saw quite clearly Alain's stubborn expression, and knew that this time he would not let himself be imposed upon.

"I don't even know how to light the gas stove . . ." she grumbled as she went away.

"Pass me the telephone, Alain . . ."

"What are you going to do?"

"Have we or have we not got to bury your father?"

Once again, he turned to the window, moved the net curtains apart and stood lost in contemplation of the square.

"Hallo! Is that Count d'Estier's residence . . . ? Hallo! It's Madame Malou speaking . . . Yes, Malou . . ."

She was getting impatient and said bad-temperedly:

31

"Please be good enough to tell Count d'Estier that Madame Malou is on the phone and would like to speak to him . . ."

Corine, coffee pot in hand, had come and planted herself in the doorway and was listening.

"Hallo! . . . Count d'Estier? . . . Madame Malou, yes . . . I understand . . . Of course, I quite understand . . ."

Alain began to chew on a cigarette that he hadn't lit.

"I think that you, for your part, should understand the position . . . It is more serious than you imagine, for, at this moment, I don't know how I am going to manage to bury my husband decently . . . As a crowning misfortune, our butler went off in the night taking with him the contents of the wallet . . . I'm listening . . . Yes . . . I hear you quite distinctly . . ."

And he spoke for a long while, while Madame Malou sat motionless, the receiver in her hand, the instrument on her bed.

"I quite agree with you and it is quite understood that I shall not make any other demands on you . . . What? . . . I don't know yet . . . I know absolutely nothing . . . Put yourself in my place . . . And there's the children . . . Yes . . I'm grateful to you . . . for me and for him . . ."

She hung up and removed the instrument.

"That's settled," she said in conclusion.

"How much is he going to send you?" Corine asked.

"He didn't tell me. He is going to send a cheque round this morning, on condition that it's quite clearly understood that this is the last time . . . As if he hadn't made enough money with your father! . . . There's the bell, Alain . . ."

"I heard it . . ."

They kept forgetting that they had to open the door themselves.

"What about the coffee, Corine? . . ."

"The water's heating . . ."

Alain went downstairs, opened the door and found himself facing a little old woman who was holding a dripping umbrella in her hand, one of those enormous umbrellas that countryfolk carry when they go to market in the trap. She was dressed as a countrywoman too, with skirts which hung down to her heels, man's shoes, a funny little bonnet of black silk with the ribbons tied under her chin.

32

"I would like to speak to Madame Malou . . ."

"My mother is still in bed . . ."

"Well, it's urgent and I've come a long way."

"I fear that in view of what's happened . . ."

"Exactly . . . Tell your mother it's Madame Tatin . . . I'll be surprised if she hasn't heard of me . . . She must have seen me in any case, she has often had to go to houses where there's been a death . . . Colonel Chaput for example, it was I who watched by him . . . And the Baroness Beaujean too . . . I'm used to it, you understand . . . Generally the relations don't know what to do . . . But I know all about watching by the dead, for I've been doing nothing else for forty years . . ."

Was it a good idea? It seemed to Alain that she smelt of death, that she trailed the musty smells of holy water, boxwood and chrysanthemums around with her in the folds of her skirts.

"Come in for a moment . . ."

He didn't leave her in the entrance, where there was an icy draught. She stood on the mat in the hall, while he ran up the stairs four at a time.

"It's an old woman who watches over the dead . . ."

Madame Malou did not understand at first.

"It seems she's used to it, that she's done it in all the big houses in the town . . . She mentioned some names . . ."

"Perhaps it would be better to have her . . . Show her up . . . I'm going to go and speak to her . . ."

And the little old woman waited on the landing, while Madame Malou was dressing. They discussed the matter for a long while, both of them speaking in low voices, then the old woman was shown into the dead man's bedroom of which she took immediate possession.

"There are a few things that I shall need . . ."

"You can ask my daughter for anything you want . . ."

It was still raining, the square was empty, with its fountain in the middle, the windows in all the houses looking like black holes.

"Help me, Alain . . . Find me the number of the undertakers. The old woman said that it was surprising they haven't come by themselves, because generally they don't wait to be asked . . ."

She phoned, announced afterwards that the men were going to come.

"I must see the solicitor, the lawyer . . . There's one thing I'm wondering . . . Have we got to let Maria know? . . . I don't know where she lives . . ."

Maria, Eugène Malou's first wife, Edgar's mother, was a woman they never spoke of. She belonged to the distant past, of which little was known, and which they preferred not to mention.

A common woman, moreover, who had lived Heaven knows how or on what, who had written several times on abominable cheap paper, in a skivvy's handwriting with spelling mistakes even in the address.

She was supposed to be living in Marseilles or somewhere in the Midi.

"Edgar will know possibly . . ."

"Edgar won't be too keen to see her arrive here . . ."

Edgar's name was mentioned in the house in a peculiar way. Of course he was a Malou, since he was the son, indeed the elder son of Eugène Malou.

But not even Eugène Malou, in his lifetime, looked on him as he did on the other members of the family.

To start with he lacked spirit, a big effeminate chap and perpetually earnest. After a moderately successful school career, his immediate ambition had been to get himself an absolutely safe job.

His father's financial juggling terrified him. He had gone into Local Government, married the daughter of his office chief and become an office chief in his turn.

He lived in a quiet part of the town, on the outskirts: nothing but little houses of clerks, officials and retired people. He was buying the house by yearly payments and he was certainly putting money away; he had savings books in the names of his three children.

He was now probably ashamed, probably worried about his job, about the respect that he wanted people to feel for him, ashamed also at what his parents-in-law, who were very strict people, might think.

In the dead man's room, old Tatin was moving about as though she were at home, speaking to herself in a murmur. From time to time, she opened the door to call for sheets, or candlesticks, or matches.

The next ring at the bell was that of the undertaker's representative, whom Madame Malou received in the dining-room where there were still bowls of coffee and bread on the table.

"Mother . . ." Corine called from the landing.

Corine, who was still half naked, who didn't mind whether or not she showed her large white thighs. Behind the door she whispered:

"Perhaps it would be better to wait for the cheque before you decide anything . . . Since you don't know how much it will be for . . ."

Another ring at the bell, and still Alain on duty. There was still the rain, the empty square, a dark shape framed in the doorway. The man took off his soaking cap for he had no umbrella.

"I am sorry to disturb you, Monsieur Alain . . ."

"It's you, Monsieur Foucret . . ."

"I would have come earlier if my wife hadn't pointed out to me that it wasn't very tactful . . ."

"Please come in . . ."

A man of between fifty-five and sixty, tall, bony, who was certainly more at ease on a building site than here.

"Do you want to speak to my mother?"

"I'd just as rather speak to you, Monsieur Alain, since I've known you since you were a little boy . . ."

They couldn't go to the dining-room which was occupied. The majority of the rooms were sealed.

"Come to my room . . ."

The man with his clumsy shoes was frightened of making the place dirty. He passed respectfully before one door, which he guessed to be that of the dead man's room.

"Is he in there?" he whispered. "Do you know that I still can't believe it? I can't get rid of the idea that things went on that we don't know about. You see, Monsieur Alain, he spoke freely to me. You know what he was like. People thought they understood him but they were kidding themselves. To begin with he was the finest man on this earth and whoever dares to say he wasn't . . ."

"Thank you, Monsieur Foucret . . ."

"People have tried to insinuate a lot of things . . . That I was an idiot, a dupe, that he took advantage of me . . . Do you know anybody else who would have bought me a house, yes, Monsieur

35

Alain, who would have given it to me just like that, saying:

" 'Foucret, old chap, your idea's worth money . . . I haven't got any money at the moment but I shall have, because I shall take out the necessary patents, and I shall see some Americans about it and we shall be rich . . . It will take time . . . In the meanwhile, here is a house for you and your wife, since your children are married . . . I'm putting you near the sites, but not so as you shall work . . . You do what you like. You can walk round overseeing if it pleases you, or you can go fishing if you would rather and, at the end of each month, you will still draw your paypacket just the same . . .'

"That's what he said to me, Monsieur Alain, perhaps you didn't know it . . . And he kept his word . . . Even when there wasn't any money for the wages, he always found some for me, sometimes only a little, sometimes more . . .

"I knew very well he would succeed and that, when the patent started to bring in money, he would not forget me, as some people have tried to make me believe . . .

"That's why I've come to see you . . . To tell you in my turn:

"I knew your father . . . At the moment things are perhaps a bit hard for you . . . I haven't got much money, but I can always mortgage the house . . ."

He looked at the room, the four-poster bed; the seals on the furniture.

"Things have got to be done decently, haven't they? Certain people are only too glad to be rid of him . . . I wonder if they are not beginning to feel a bit ashamed . . . Even the dirty newspaper that attacked him every morning, which even yesterday was calling him all kinds of names, doesn't know what to write today . . . Look . . ."

He drew a soaking newspaper from his pocket.

"The distressing accident which . . . Well! Monsieur Alain, I've got something on my mind and it's got to come out . . . When I read the word accident, it struck me. Because, between us, I don't think your father did away with himself on purpose . . . I'm sorry . . . I knew him too well . . . You see, he loved life so much . . . He had serious troubles, I agree . . . But he had got over others, hadn't he? . . . You know that the only thing those money problems did was to make him laugh . . . I've listened to people talking . . . I've read the newspapers . . .

36

"He had probably gone to ask the Count for money . . . He would have done better to give him some . . . For, after all . . . without your father, how much would he have sold his château and woods for? . . . Not even a million francs, possibly half a million! Whereas with the Malouville housing estate, despite the snags at the moment, he must have collected three millions at least . . . Is that true or isn't it? . . .

"So my idea is that your father wanted to frighten him . . . It happened once that he asked someone for money in front of me . . . He looked tragic, but, when he wasn't being watched, he winked at me quickly and, when the chap had gone, he burst out laughing . . .

"Possibly he thought the revolver wasn't loaded. Or else he didn't mean to pull the trigger . . . Or perhaps, and this is really what I think, he only tried to wound himself . . . But here I am keeping you when you must have a lot to do . . . I've brought you this in case . . ."

He held out an envelope containing a few thousand franc notes.

"Thank you, Monsieur Foucret . . . I shall not forget your gesture, but, at the moment, we have all we need . . ."

"That's true, isn't it? . . . You're not doing it out of pride?"

"I assure you . . ."

Foucret opened his mouth to ask a question, but didn't dare, and Alain guessed that the question was—Whom have you asked?——

As he saw him down stairs, he noticed his sister making vigorous signs to him that he tried not to understand. Someone rang just as he was going to open the door. It was a gentleman's valet who held out a letter to him saying:

"For Madame Malou . . . Urgent . . ."

Had Foucret recognized Count d'Estier's valet? He shook his head like a man hurt.

"Well . . . Goodbye, Monsieur Alain . . . If you need me for anything at all, don't hesitate . . ."

Corine upstairs was on the watch for him, trying to catch a glimpse of the envelope.

"How much?"

"I haven't opened it."

"Give . . ."

She ripped it open, saying:

37

"You weren't very clever with old Foucret! . . . Why on earth didn't you take it? . . . Do you think it's going to be easy for us to manage? . . . Good . . . Fifty thousand . . . Let me tell mother . . ."

She went into the dining-room and slipped the cheque under the eyes of her mother, who was examining the undertaker's catalogue. The salesman saw the cheque too, tried vainly to read the amount upside-down, but was at any rate reassured.

There were other comings and goings on that day. Madame Malou went out at about eleven o'clock to cash the cheque, after having rung for a taxi. Corine had a long conversation on the phone, which Alain preferred not to hear, and two or three times he happened to hear a gurgle which sounded suspiciously like a laugh.

The solicitor Carel, small and tubby, pink and shining, smartly dressed, had to wait a long while in the dining-room for Madame Malou's return.

"What are we going to eat, Alain? We must at least have something to eat . . ."

"I went to do the shopping this morning. It's your turn . . ."

"What a gentleman you are! . . . I've an idea . . . I'll go and ask the old woman . . ."

So it was Mother Tatin, when Madame Malou returned with the money, who slipped out quickly to do the shopping. She was still talking to herself, and God knows what she had to say about that family that seemed so little like the others.

"Can you leave us alone for a minute, Alain, dear?"

Since she had had the money in her handbag, Madame Malou had regained her vitality and her self assurance. It had always been so. There had been times when everybody was at low water, the women particularly, and the servants, because there wasn't a single thousand franc note in the house and they did not know where to turn to get necessities on credit. At those times, Madame Malou spent the best part of her time in bed, complaining of her health, while Corine managed to disappear.

When money flowed in, and life returned, they stopped snapping, complaining and bickering with each other.

"Monsieur Carel and I must have a serious conversation. If Maître Desbois arrives, show him in. He will be a help to us."

They were still in the dining-room, with the dirty cups and the lighted chandelier which had been burning, forgotten, since the evening before.

Alain had to go down again to open the door to the undertaker's men. Since the rooms on the ground floor, still under seals, could not be used, the lying in state had necessarily to be arranged in the dead man's room, where they started hammering.

There were already a few cards, in the letter box, bearing condolences. The lawyer's car pulled up beside the kerb and gave a little more life to the front of the house.

Now, people were walking past, not many, under their umbrellas, who must have been going out of their way—for the square led nowhere—to come and look at the house. Curtains could be seen moving at the windows too, and faces which rapidly disappeared.

They were talking in the dining-room. The ear could distinguish the deep muffled voice of the solicitor, the slightly higher pitched voice of Maître Desbois and finally, from time to time, for a direct question, Madame Malou's, who had earlier slipped out for a moment to get some paper and a pencil.

When they left, a little after midday, her eyes were red and she walked through the rooms critically.

"What are you waiting for—to get dinner ready for us?" she asked her daughter, who had opened a book and curled up in an armchair.

"For old Tatin to come back with the shopping."

"Couldn't you have gone yourself?"

"And order a taxi, as you did to go to the bank which is only a step away?"

"You'll have to get used to the idea of getting around without a car, nevertheless . . . I want to warn you here and now that, when the funeral's taken place, it will leave us absolutely nothing."

"What do you want me to do about it?"

"You think that you will always be able to manage, don't you? I'm quite sure that it won't be by working . . ."

"What about you?"

"Is that all you find to answer?"

She was still crying, went and shut herself in her room to cry, while Alain wandered about without knowing where to settle.

He had a visitor himself, a little red-headed boy, Peters, one of

39

his two companions of the evening before, when, on returning from school, they had been stopped by the crowd in front of the chemist's shop.

He nearly didn't see him, for Peters didn't dare ring. He stood in front of the house, in the rain, his books under his arm, and stared at the windows in the hope of seeing his friend.

Alain went downstairs, opened the door to him, but the other wouldn't come in. Possibly he was frightened of death?

"Listen, Alain, I've come on behalf of your friends . . . We didn't dare disturb you today, but at the same time we wanted to let you know . . . to tell you. . . ."

"Thank you . . ."

"We wondered too if you would be coming back to school . . . It's the last year and . . ."

"I don't think so . . . I don't think so . . ."

"We shall still see each other, won't we? . . . Some people say that you are going to leave town . . ."

"Really . . ."

"Is it true?"

"I don't think I shall leave . . ."

"I understand! . . . You're a good chap . . ."

And, indeed, they both looked as though they understood each other. They were standing in the draught in front of the door; they had to move out of the way to let Madame Tatin through, loaded with parcels.

"I know her. . . . She came for one of my aunts who died last year . . . Doesn't she make you feel frightened?"

Then Alain smiled wanly. Was he still frightened? He had been frightened in the night. He was still a little bit afraid in the morning.

Now it had gone. He felt himself much older than Peters, who nevertheless was the same age as he was.

"She doesn't frighten me," he said, not without a trace of pride and superiority.

If there were only mother Tatin!

"You know that we'll all be there? . . . We've asked for the time off . . ."

"For the funeral, yes."

"Goodbye, Malou . . ."

"Goodbye, Peters . . ."

40

Why did closing the heavy door make him go cold this time? It was no longer a door of solid oak, but a wall that he was slowly building himself, of his own free will, between him and the others.

Peters went off home relieved, yes, relieved, as one always is at that age after discharging such a painful duty. He was probably putting his tongue out to catch the raindrops, as he always did; and he was thinking about the lunch waiting for him, the ritual remark that he would deliver from the threshold: "I'm hungry."

The entrance, the hall with its double twist staircase, that staircase suddenly so difficult to climb. They were still hammering. Something was spluttering in the kitchen, and a smell of onion was spreading through the rooms.

"Who was it?"

Corine, who had finally dressed herself, questioned him.

"A schoolfriend, Peters . . ."

"That reminds me that no one's come to see me yet . . . Perhaps it's too early . . . They'll begin in a little while . . ."

And indeed it began, practically at the same time as the rain stopped falling, about three o'clock. By that time, everything was ready to receive people, there was a mortuary chapel with candles burning on either side of the dead man who had been washed and shaved, a spring of boxwood in a bowl of holy water, and mother Tatin kneeling in the shadows muttering her way through her rosary.

The corpse was now a real corpse.

CHAPTER THREE

ON the morning of the funeral, in the mortuary chapel, the men were grouped in something like hierarchical order. First of all came Edgar Malou, by right, as the eldest child. They had hardly seen him for three days, but on that morning, he had arrived while everybody was still asleep, in his anxiety to make sure that nothing should go wrong. If he had bought no new black clothes since his wedding, which was five years ago, he had hardly worn the old ones and he was very careful with his

41

things; yet he had put on a bit of weight—he had become more flabby—and his suit, which fitted a little too tightly everywhere looked as though it had come from a cheap ready-made tailor.

A curious thing that morning was that Edgar's eyes were red, and he kept them so during the whole ceremony; he was the only one who was continually putting a handkerchief to his face. He was really pale and, when he looked at people who shook him by the hand, he seemed hardly to recognize them, he thanked them with all the effusiveness of a very unhappy person, for whom the slightest consolation is balm.

Besides him, Alain seemed taller and slimmer than ever in his suit of black cheviot tweed; after him came the husband of their aunt, Jules Dorimont.

The Dorimonts had arrived on the evening before, and they had had to put up beds for them in the house. Jeanne, Madame Malou's sister, had wept for the greater part of the evening, over her sister's misfortunes and her own both at once.

If one examined them closely, the two sisters resembled each other feature for feature. Except that with Jeanne, everything was coarser, commoner, which made her appear like the caricature of her sister.

For example, Madame Malou's hair was slightly mahogany in colour while Jeanne's was an unpleasant copper tint, and already there were a few grey threads. Both had big eyes, but Jeanne's protruded. What, with one, was nothing more than a slight thickening was clearly a double chin with the other, and finally no one could understand how Jeanne—Aunt Jeanne as the children called her—could possibly make herself up so badly, by turning her mouth into a red gash whose contours did not follow her lips and sketching two half moons in a curious pink colour on her cheekbones.

Aunt Jeanne was always complaining and pitying everybody. She had a tiny husband who looked like a collector's piece with his slim and pink woman's face topped by silky silver-grey hair. He had been a tenor in light opera. They had toured the provinces together before Dorimont had lost his voice. Afterwards, Eugène Malou had taken him in with him.

There was a time, when Alain was tiny and they lived at Bordeaux, that they shared house and board with the Dorimonts. Eugène Malou had finally tired of his sister-in-law's whinings. He even went as far as to say that she had the evil eye. And as they were in the money then—it was the time of the château in Dordogne—he had set him up in a little book-shop and lending library in Paris.

They had a son, Bertrand, nine months younger than Alain, who stood fourth in line, opposite the coffin lighted by candles. Bertrand looked like his mother. He had a great horselike face, and all his suits hung badly on him. They hadn't provided him with new clothes for the occasion and he wore a grey suit, on which had been stitched a black armband.

It was when the Dorimonts were there that one could see that the Malous were almost aristocrats. And it was the same in the dining-room where the women were.

When François Foucret, the foreman, had arrived to offer his condolences, Alain had leaned towards him, had whispered something. Foucret had made a half gesture of protest, but had gone and posted himself at the end of the line all the same.

Only the women could find out what was going on outside, for they were able to peep through the slats of the shutters. It was drizzling. Small groups had gathered in the square, men who smoked their pipes or cigarettes while watching the house and waiting for a few more to join them before going to pay their last respects. When a certain number of friends were gathered together, they could be seen putting out their cigar-ettes, straightening their ties, walking solemnly towards the entrance, and a moment later they could be heard tramping on the stairs.

The owner of the Café de Paris came among the first and ex-cused himself for going off again immediately. A quarter of an hour later, just time for his employer to get back, Gabriel ap-peared in his turn and waited for the body to be carried out.

There were tradespeople, even those who hadn't been paid and who never would be. They made up a group on their own in the square, a group of well-to-do people, used to this kind of ceremony.

Count d'Estier came too at the last minute. His car stopped in the square. He walked through the crowd, entered the mor-tuary chapel with dignity, shook Edgar by the hand at length and excused himself from going to the cemetery, being obliged to catch a train at eleven o'clock.

He must have passed the woman on the stairs. She wasn't expected. No one had told her. She walked into the mortuary chapel, which she filled immediately with the strong odour of cheap scent. Alain, who had never met her, with astonishment saw her dash at Edgar and kiss him.

Edgar, for his part did not know how to take it. She was his mother, Eugène Malou's first wife, who had travelled from the Midi and was now saying in a low voice:

"I must speak to you later on . . ."

Then, looking around her:

"Where are the women?"

She was vulgarly dressed with something violet about her neck, and the powder on her face was tinged with violet too.

Edgar was glad to take her into the dining-room, whose door closed to again.

The undertaker's men came upstairs to take up the coffin. The hearse had just arrived, heavy and luxurious; people began to group themselves into a procession.

Alain stared hard at the silver headed studs on the waxed oak bier and, while they busied themselves about him, he started to conjure up his father's face in his mind.

Would those about him have believed it if he had admitted to them that he couldn't manage it? Certainly, he could vaguely imagine the familiar forehead, cheeks, nose, chin, and he could recapture Eugène Malou's voice, a little raucous and perpetually husky.

He could also imagine his short, almost fat figure, always full of life. For Malou was one of those men eternally in a hurry, that you wanted to hold him back by grasping a button of his jacket.

But to recapture him alive, so to speak . . . To see that look again for example, to remember him as the man he was . . .

What sort of man had he been? His son, who had lived with him for so many years, could not say, and it was only now that he made the discovery.

That's why he was staring with so much real distress at the coffin as it was being carried from the top of the stairs, while, in the dining-room, the women could be heard sobbing.

Had Alain realized up till now what a strange family he was living in? He was so used to it that he took no notice.

To take only that woman who looked as though she had come from a house of ill repute and who had been his father's first wife, who was Edgar's mother . . .

There were so many things he didn't know, so many questions that he had never had the idea of asking! He could hardly remember the life they had led at Bordeaux, and yet that wasn't more than eight years ago, so he must have been a grown boy at that time. They had lived in a pretty large flat, then in an entire house to themselves. There too they had had servants, a car, two cars at one time. They spent their weekends and holidays in an old château where workmen were always busy. They invited a lot of people. His parents went out nearly every evening, his mother wearing all her jewels, his father in dinner jacket or tails.

They spoke a lot about money. They were often without, but Malou always found some at the last minute. They entertained members of Parliament, senators, important people.

Then, at one blow, had come disaster, and they had moved; there wasn't much to move as everything had been seized. They had lived for a fortnight in a little hotel at Nantes. Was it true that they had gone off without paying the bill? Edgar had said so one day when he was quarrelling with his brother about their father.

They had lived in Paris too, only for a few weeks, in a furnished flat in the Ternes district, then they had come to settle here in a new town. Not straight away in the impressive house, but in a middle-class dwelling of the same type as Edgar's.

Did he know any more? Hardly. Everybody in the house lived as they thought fit. When they expected to sit down to table as a family, Eugène Malou would arrive with five or six guests, and they would go down to the state dining-room.

Madame Malou had jewels. She loved jewels. They were often the subject of discussion, too often. Recently particularly, since things had been tight and it was beginning to look like Bordeaux again, with the bailiffs and talk in the newspapers.

Had she refused to sell them to help her husband hold out for a few weeks longer? Had Eugène Malou got hold of them? She claimed so, that she had nothing left. But, suddenly, Alain had doubts.

The master of ceremonies placed the family in a line behind

45

the hearse, and, after a moment's pause, they set off for the cemetery, for Eugène Malou, who had committed suicide, had no right to the church funeral service.

They walked slowly, they stopped for a tram, then the procession must have moved forward for a while at a quicker rate which separated the ranks and lengthened the column. Edgar had turned round.

"There are a lot of people anyway," he said with satisfaction. "A lot of people I didn't expect to see . . ."

The men first, then the women, and, at the end, people they didn't even know by sight. François Foucret had discreetly withdrawn from the family line and walked with the workmen and tradespeople, speaking to nobody.

And so they went along for half an hour, through streets less and less busy. As they passed quite near to Edgar's home, he twisted round to catch sight of his house, which he always looked at with satisfaction, then the signs of the tomb masons and florist shops, which announced the cemetery, appeared.

In the main pathways there was gravel, but even there they stumbled about in a wet clay, where their feet slipped. When a pool of water covered all the path, some of them took a running jump at it, others preferred to walk on the graves. Then finally there was the freshly dug hole, the people who pressed one up against the other, the coffin that was lowered, the rope which came up again.

Edgar was weeping. Jules Dorimont was blowing his nose. Alain kept his eyes dry, but he was paler than the others, and his gaze sought that of Foucret, who came up to him to shake his hand without appearing to do so.

"Be brave, Monsieur Alain . . ."

And, quieter, stealthily:

"You're not leaving, are you?"

He shook his head. He wanted to stay in the town. It seemed to him that to leave, like the others, would be a sort of treason. There were still so many details that he wanted to know!

Without anybody telling him to, he took the flowers within his reach and threw them into the grave, then, suddenly, he broke away from the crowd and left. Foucret caught him up. His brother looked at him in a dissatisfied way, for that was not the way things should be done.

"I don't know if you've thought about what I said to you, Monsieur Alain. . . ."

It was cold. Alain felt a tickling in his nostrils which promised a cold in the head.

"I've found out something else, by chance . . . For, a little while ago, I was speaking to Gabriel, the waiter at the Café de Paris. . . . Well! on that day, after having sent his car away, your father went into the café to telephone . . . Usually, it's Gabriel who gets the numbers for him, but, that time, your father didn't want him to . . . He left a few minutes after three, on foot, and it wasn't until after four o'clock that the accident happened . . ."

Then, at three o'clock, was the last time that Eugène Malou was to use the car, and he knew it, for it was to be driven the same day to the pound. It was seized like the rest, and Arsène, the chauffeur, had been dismissed.

They came out of the cemetery. They were followed by groups of people, who spoke in loud voices of their business. Some of them went into a little café with steamed-up windows, where it must have been warm and where the atmosphere probably smelt of old marc.

"Don't you want to take the tram, Monsieur Alain?"

They stood waiting for it, and, at that moment, Peters, the red-headed boy, came up to his classmate.

"The others asked me to bring their excuses. It was impossible for all of us to be absent from school together. We shall see you again, won't we? You're not going away?"

The rest of the family caught them up, and everybody took their places in the tram through which an icy draught was blowing. Alain stood on the platform with his two companions. He looked at his uncle, his brother, his cousin, whose heads were swaying curiously to the jolting of the tram.

They were his relations, and he examined them with interest, as though he had never seen them. Were they still his relations? Clearly there had been a connection between him and those people, but that connection no longer existed.

With Eugène Malou dead, each was going to go his own way. Who knows? Probably, that evening, the house would be empty. They had spoken about it for the last two days, and particularly on the evening before. They had talked it over until two in the morning, drinking a bottle of brandy discovered in a cupboard.

47

Corine and her mother had quarrelled again. Uncle Dorimont tried to calm them down and uttered soothing words. Aunt Jeanne cried.

Bertrand, who was not an orphan, gazed enviously at his cousin the whole time. The two boys had hardly uttered a word to each other, but Alain had constantly felt the stares of the other fixed on him.

"I must tell you, Monsieur Alain . . . If I had dared, I would have suggested taking you to my home . . . I spoke to my wife about it . . . Probably it's impossible, you must stay there . . . People are saying that everybody's clearing out . . ."

It was likely. When they had gone to bed at two in the morning, no decision had been arrived at. That was always the way when the family were together. They all talked, talked, and they never managed to reach an agreement.

"With your permission, Monsieur Alain, I shall come and see you later in the day...If you've got visitors, I shan't disturb you..."

"Thank you, Monsieur Foucret . . ."

"I'm getting off here . . ."

Only Alain and the red-headed boy were left on the platform.

"Are you going to work?" enquired Peters with, in his turn, a sort of envy. "What are you going to do?"

"I don't know."

"If I were in your place, I'd try to get on the newspaper."

And, remembering the attacks that the *Phare du Centre* had directed against Eugène Malou, he could have bitten his tongue off.

"It's possibly not as wonderful as all that . . ."

They got off. As though by chance, they took the little sloping street where the drama had taken place, and they passed the chemist's. Edgar must have been explaining to his uncle how it happened, for he was pointing out the dispensary, then the pavement, Estier's house.

"I'll leave you here, old chap . . . I must fly . . ."

All that was left was a gloomy group walking into the square with the fountain. It was again deserted. There was nothing left. Everything was finished.

"Has anybody got a key?" asked Edgar.

Nobody had and they were obliged to ring. It was Aunt Jeanne who came down and opened the door.

48

"Already . . ." she exclaimed, being used to funerals with mass and absolution. "That was quick! . . ."

There were flower petals lying about in the hall and on the stairs.

"Now, Jules, this is what my sister and I have decided . . ."

No one had thought of closing the door of the dead man's room, and Alain undertook it. For a moment, he was on the point of shutting himself up in his room to await the end of the palaver that was beginning again, but he decided to follow the others into the dining-room, where he stood with his elbow resting on the mantelpiece.

"You've made up your mind not to go?"

He nodded.

"You know that your mother has the right to make you. What exactly do you hope to gain by staying?"

"I don't know . . ."

"You'll have more difficulty in finding a job here than anywhere else. Today, people came to the funeral as though nothing had happened, but tomorrow, they'll be as they were before . . ."

"I don't mind."

"Let him do as he likes, Jeanne," sighed Madame Malou.

"Right! At any rate, we'll take your mother with us. She can stay with us as long as she wants. She must have time to get over it. It isn't as though we have got a lot of room, or that business is good, but it's our duty. There remains the question of your sister."

"There's absolutely no point in going over it again," cut in Corine, buried in the depths of an armchair, her legs crossed, a cigarette between her lips.

"You wouldn't have spoken like that when your father was alive."

"My father never bothered about my business."

And that was true. That fact struck Alain. It was a revelation to him. Had their father ever interested himself in them? To bring them presents, yes, the finest and the most expensive. No child, to their knowledge, had had such fine playthings as they. And, when the family was in funds, they had had as much pocket money as they had wanted.

But did he bother to find out if Alain studied or not? He, himself, used to put his father's signature on his school reports,

49

and his father knew it. As for Corine, she had always lived as she liked. Who hadn't lived as they liked in that house where the very servants, when there were any, did as they thought fit?

And now, for the first time in his life, Alain asked "Why?"

He wondered what sort of man his father had been. For example, he remembered the way the latter used, at certain times, to put his hand on his shoulder, saying: "Son . . ."

"Son . . ."

That was affection. It was much more than affection. He must really have loved his wife to put up with her tempers and whims as he had done.

What sort of man was he?

"Has my mother gone?" enquired Edgar after a good while.

He had hesitated over the word "Mother."

"Yes, she has gone and I hope I never see her again. She must be at the solicitor's office at the moment. She's made up her mind that there's a will and your father left her something. It seems that he promised her he would. There's no point in it anyway, since there's nothing to share. She was furious. She hurled a heap of insults at my head. Jeanne had to show her the door . . ."

"What's happened to the jewellery?" Edgar went on.

"You know they were sold a long while ago."

"All of them?"

"Yes, all of them. Do you want to search my things?"

"The pearl necklace as well?"

He had seen it a few days earlier and she knew it.

"They're false. The real necklace was pawned in Paris, and your father gave me the replica. If you really want to . . ."

He hesitated. Clearly he doubted Madame Malou's word, but he dare not demand a necklace which he was told was false.

"On the other hand, I think you inherit your father's signet ring. I'll bring it to you straight away. If you agree, Alain shall have the shirt studs and cuff links. As for the ruby tie pin, the one he always kept, I thought, that if you both agree, I would give it your uncle as a souvenir . . ."

Jules Dorimont made a show of protesting.

"There remains Bertrand. What can I give to Bertrand? There's the amber and silver cigarette holder. . . . Do you smoke, Bertrand?"

"A little, Aunt."

There was a feeling of constraint. She went and fetched some little boxes from her bedroom, spread their contents on the table.

"There was his gold cigarette case, but he sold it a fortnight ago. This silver one is at least twenty years old . . ."

"I'll take it," said Edgar.

"While I think of it, children, there are also his clothes which were not included in the seizure. Edgar is too tall. So is Alain. But Jules, if they were altered . . ."

"What about some food?" said Corine impatiently.

"There's nothing ready. Jeanne suggests, and she is right, that we should go and have a bite at a restaurant . . ."

"The train's at half past five."

"There's still the question of Corine . . ."

"Can't you bloody well leave me in peace?" She sighed.

"Mark you, I don't know what I should do with you in Paris. There's no room to put you up in the Boulevard Beaumarchais."

"You see!"

The Dorimonts' bookshop and flat was in the Boulevard Beaumarchais.

"Without mentioning," put in Jules, "that to find a job these days . . . By the way, what sort of work are you going to look for?"

"Don't you think it would be better to stop worrying about me? I'm old enough to look after myself."

"All the same, I don't like leaving you here. Unless you lived with your brother . . ."

Edgar thought that they were speaking of him and was just about to declare that his house was not big enough. But they meant Alain.

"You don't get on too badly together the pair of you. Alain will be at work all day and will probably take his meals in a restaurant."

"If you like . . . We shall see . . . In any case, someone has already found me a small furnished flat . . ."

They didn't ask her who. They avoided mentioning the name of Doctor Fabien, who, possibly to avoid appearing at the funeral, had gone off to a neighbouring town where he had to perform an operation, or so he claimed.

"Does that suit you, Alain?"

He shrugged his shoulders. He was in such a hurry to get them out of his sight, all of them, for what they were worth! And yet he didn't tire of watching them, scanning their features, listening to the sound of their voices. There was a number of questions he would have liked to ask them.

Did he know where his father came from? It was never mentioned at home. The little he knew about it he had learnt from the papers.

If they could be believed, particularly the *Phare du Centre*, the most spiteful one, he wasn't even a Frenchman, and their real name was Malow or Malowski. Furthermore, according to rumour, Alain's grandfather, his father's father, had appeared one day from nobody knew where, from the East at any rate, knowing neither how to read nor write, speaking some incomprehensible gabble, with no papers, with no certain identity.

Was it true that he had worked as a labourer on the construction of the St. Gothard tunnel?

They didn't possess a single photograph of him. Late in life, at the age of fifty or more, while he was working in the quarries in a little village in Cantal, he had had his son by a woman to whom he wasn't married. She was supposed to have been a drunkard, anybody's woman.

He must be dead. Of course he must be, because he was more than fifty when his son was born. But what about the woman? What was her name? Did Madame Malou know?

Again, the papers said that as young man Eugène Malou had had dealing with the Anarchists, first at Marseilles, then at Lyons and finally at Paris.

It was at Lyons that he must have married Edgar's mother, a factory girl so they said at home. A prostitute, so the newspapers insinuated.

And of all that, he, Malou's son, the grandson of Malow or Malowski, knew nothing.

And now his father had killed himself with a bullet in the head. Everybody was going off now, each his own way. Edgar was sorting out the shirts and vests that could still be used. He went through the shoes too, for he had small feet. As for the business, particularly the Malouville development, the solicitor had advised the widow to leave it well alone. It was in the hands of the official receivers and its liquidation would leave a heavy debt.

"Even if there is anything to inherit, it would be as well to refuse it to avoid an unpleasant surprise later."

"Are we going to eat or aren't we?"

They made up their minds. They looked for their hats and coats, the women planted themselves in front of mirrors.

"We mustn't forget the key."

The house was left empty, completely empty for the first time for a long while.

"Where are we going?"

"We had better find a quiet restaurant."

"So that it looks as though we are hiding?"

"Corine is probably right."

They went to the "Chapon Fin," but asked for one of the private rooms on the first floor. Alain reflected that he could have been lunching at that moment in the Foucrets' little house and he continued to hold his tongue, watching them, listening to them.

"Have you found a job?" his cousin asked him across the table.

"Not yet. I shall find one."

No matter what. He was ready to do any job, even an errand boy's. Anyway, from now on he would be like the rest of them! He hadn't protested when they had decided that he should live with his sister, but he had quite made up his mind to do nothing of the sort. For a few days at the most if it were unavoidable.

What was the use of telling them? It would only cause fresh scenes, and he was sick to death of them. He knew them well, he knew his family: they shouted at each other, swore at each other, issued contradictory orders, then, in the end, everybody just did what they wanted.

Let them go! That's all he wanted. And he began to count the minutes. From time to time he looked at the little electric clock set in the wall. He ate mechanically.

His mother, too, had been married before meeting Eugène Malou. She had been the wife of a member of Parliament for the Loire, who, quite recently, had been a minister for a few months.

She had left him for Malou. Once when mother and daughter were quarrelling as they used to do periodically, Corine, because her behaviour was being criticized, had flung out:

"What about you? Would you have ever become father's wife if you hadn't been caught in the act?"

Was it true?

What appalled Alain was that he had lived up to now without thinking about these things, without trying to find out the truth. Had he remained so much a child that at seventeen he still lived in a sort of lethargy?

He had been a child, then a schoolboy like the others. A little shyer than the others, precisely because things went on around him that he didn't understand or that he didn't want to understand.

Some pupils avoided playing with him. One of them said to him outright:

"My parents tell me not to."

And yet he had not turned in on himself. He had never had that crafty look about him, for example, that he saw on his cousin's face. His father was a father, his mother a mother, his sister a sister. Edgar a chap he didn't like very much, but whom he considered to be more weak than wicked.

Suddenly, for the last three days, he had a passionate desire to find out. Particularly a desire to know that man who had been his father and whom he had never worried about in his lifetime.

In a confused way, he felt he would never learn anything from the family.

Instinctively, his mind turned towards Foucret, he wanted to question him, he wanted to plumb the depths of so many mysteries.

When lunch was finished, Jules Dorimont made as though to take his wallet out of his pocket, but—as he quite expected—Madame Malou stopped him.

"No, Jules. This is my business. Because there was no ceremony at the church and we didn't have any cars, the funeral cost much less than I thought it would. I've got nearly thirty thousand francs left. I'm going to leave ten thousand to Corine and Alain. That's the best I can do for them because I don't want to be a burden on you, and I'm no longer their age. In Paris, I'll manage somehow . . ."

What a strange woman she was, thought Alain, who did not now look on her at all as his mother. He was convinced that she was deceitful, that she had always been deceitful. If Edgar, who was used to speaking to the point, had spoken of the jewels, it meant that he had more than suspicions.

Corine had had hers for a long while, possibly because she was a woman too. It was already more than two years ago when, one day, she had flung at her mother:

"I can see your game, don't worry. You cry poverty but it doesn't prevent you from building up your little pile."

Was she right? And then was it true that, if his wife had helped him in the last days, Eugène Malou would have had no need to disappear?

It was too hot in the room. The waiters were anxious to clear away, for it was late. Nevertheless they asked for liqueurs, and sipped them slowly.

"Is your luggage ready?"

"It'll take me half an hour. For, you can imagine, with what the bailiffs have left me!"

They walked out in Indian file, and everybody stared at them. Alain came last a little ashamed to be part of the group, and he was shocked to see his sister wave her hand to two people she knew.

Back to the house again, which they were only to occupy for a few more hours.

They searched in every place to which they still had access so as to leave nothing lying about.

"The papers! . . ." said Madame Malou, noticing a green suitcase full of letters and documents.

Edgar opened his mouth, but Alain spoke first and, for the first time, with a firmness that astonished him:

"I'll take care of it," he said.

"What do you want to do with them? It would be easier to burn them. They're business letters, bills. . . ."

He was so firm that his mother gave way:

"If you want to! . . ."

It wasn't long before Edgar disappeared on the pretext of a call that he had promised to make at the office.

"I'll say goodbye to you for Marthe and the children . . ."

And, as he went on speaking in a whisper, Alain gathered that Marthe was again pregnant, something which he had not known until then.

"You must excuse my in-laws for not coming. They were very delicately placed."

"Of course . . ."

He embraced Madame Malou contritely, shook everybody's hands lingeringly.

"I hope you'll get on well," he said to Alain. "But you would do better to try to get into the Civil Service. There are also some good jobs in the Colonies now, while here you will be always up against hostility. I know all about it, because I have a very hard time keeping going."

Let's get a move on, so that it will be all over and done with once and for all. Will the women never be finished with putting on lipstick and powder? Is Madame Malou at last sure of having in her handbag the key to her small case which she will let nobody carry?

"Are you coming to the station?"

Corine said yes. Alain had to say yes also.

"We'll have to have two taxis in that case. I suppose you'll come back here afterwards to get your things. You won't sleep the night in the house, will you?"

Alain would have done so willingly, but on his own. He wouldn't be frightened any more, once the others had gone.

"Hallo! Would you send two cars round to Monsieur Malou's straight away?"

Corine had made a mistake and had spoken of Monsieur Malou, of Monsieur Malou who was dead.

"They're coming at once."

They looked at their watches. The trunks and cases were taken downstairs.

"I'm counting on you, Corine, whatever happens, to avoid . . . Well, you understand . . ."

"Of course, Mother . . ."

"As for you, Alain . . ."

She wept a little embracing him and had to re-do her make-up. And all the time Bertrand Dorimont gazed at his cousin in the

56

same envious way, his cousin who was going to live alone, or practically.

"The taxis are here . . ."

They crowded in. The station wasn't far. Jules Dorimont went to get the tickets at the booking office. He didn't forget the platform tickets for the two who were not leaving.

"And so I've lived nine years in this town," murmured Madame Malou standing by the coach. "I hope I never set foot here again."

That was all. They kissed each other on the cheeks. They watched them through the window, settle themselves in the compartment as best they could, then the train moved off.

"And there we are!" said Corine.

She looked at her brother and raised her eyebrows at seeing him look so pale and serious. Then she shrugged her shoulders.

"What are you going to do now? Are you going back home?"

He didn't know.

"I've got something to see to in town; it will take me half an hour. Go and get your things together. Tonight, we'll sleep at the hotel. I'll book two rooms. Tomorrow morning, I hope, we can move into my furnished flat."

They walked through the booking hall.

"I'm counting on you not to make yourself disagreeable. I don't know what's been the matter with you these last few days, but you have a funny way of looking at people."

He contented himself with replying: "I'm going back home."

In the tram. Alone. Standing on the platform. He watched the pavements, the shops, the lamp-posts go by, and it all made up a world that he had never felt he was a part of.

It was a curious thing, when he reached the square and went to put his key in the lock, that he was seized with panic, he didn't dare go into the empty house, remained prowling about and finally waited, standing in an alcove, while a fine rain fell all about him.

An hour went by, and another hour. A car stopped, not a taxi, a long, beige-coloured car that he knew. Corine jumped out on to the pavement and the car moved off silently. She stretched out her hand to the bellpush.

Only then did he come forward out of the patch of shadow. She jumped as she saw him loom up behind her.

57

"Were you waiting there?"

He didn't explain to her that he had not dared go in alone. He said nothing to her. He turned the key in the lock and felt for the switch.

"You frightened me!"

It didn't matter. He followed her upstairs and mechanically turned his head away because he could see her thighs.

CHAPTER FOUR

AT first he had no idea of the time, nor where he was. Nor did he understand the nature of the thing that had awakened him. It was, in fact, a rhythmical measure which had reached him in the depths of sleep—a little like the way the music from a military band in an adjoining street will set you marching in step, despite yourself. Now, the rhythm was marked by a metallic squeaking and, at the end, right at the end, when he opened his eyes, Alain had been conscious of a human moaning, regular, rising and falling, a strange cry, a happy cry such as he had never heard in his life.

About him everything was in darkness. He was at the hotel, he remembered now, at the Hôtel du Commerce, opposite the station, where he and his sister had gone for one or two nights. They had dined together in the dining-room with its little white tables, where an enormous mahogany dresser stood with the solemnity of a mighty organ. He recalled the starched tablecloths, the waitresses in black and white, wearing bonnets, the bottles of red wine and the napkins spread fanwise in the glasses. He remembered the smell, the tick-tock of the clock with the wide black border, Corine's gesture as she powdered her face after the meal.

"I am going to bed straight away," he had stated.

It was only half past eight, but he had hardly slept at all on the preceding nights.

"So am I," his sister had replied.

Nevertheless, she had taken a newspaper with her in case she couldn't get to sleep. They had said goodnight in the corridor. He was already in bed when she tried to open his door.

"What do you want? I've put the bolt on and I'm in bed."

"Oh, very well, then. Goodnight, I was coming to see if you were all right."

He had fallen asleep and now he was staring at a crack of light on the same side as the noise was coming from. He remained in darkness. He didn't stretch out his hand to reach the light switch at the head of the bed. He began to remember. A wall separated him from his sister's room. She had number seven and he number nine. He hadn't seen any communicating door earlier, because it was masked by a wardrobe. But the body of the wardrobe did not reach right down to the floor. Between its legs, could be seen a gap under the door of nearly an inch.

It was the first time that this had been brought to his notice, but Alain understood the meaning of the rhythmical measure, of the moaning, and he blushed to think that it was his sister who moaned like that, with, now and again, a curious sort of sob. It was his sister who revealed to him—and on the night of his father's funeral—a thing which he was only vaguely aware of and for which he had always, instinctively, felt a sort of repugnance.

Probably because of his classmates when they spoke about it, at school, did so in a dirty way. Probably too because the women who brushed by him sometimes in the shadows in certain dark streets speaking to him as they did so—and who for him were the synthesis of all that whole business—used foul words, repellent gestures.

Alain would have liked to stop his ears, and he vainly thrust his head into the pillows; the rhythm went on. And now a man's voice joined in, the moaning increased until it became a cry, after which there was suddenly a silence.

Then in the heavy stillness of the silence, a laugh, a little laugh, young and fresh, Corine's laugh.

"I'm exhausted," she said. "And I didn't want to this evening ... Did I call out? . . ."

"A bit! . . ." replied Fabien with satisfaction.

Neither of them moved. If they had made the slightest movement, Alain would have heard them, so clearly could he distinguish the slightest sound. Despite himself, he began to imagine both of them, and the images conjured up were so painful to him that for a moment he wondered if he had the courage to dress himself and walk out, to go anywhere, never to return.

"Let's hope that Alain heard nothing!"

59

And the surgeon said jokingly:

"I suppose that at his age he knows what it is!"

"Give me a cigarette."

Only then did Fabien get up. He walked across the room, bare-footed. The characteristic noise of bare feet could be heard on the linoleum. Then the crackling of a match.

"Aren't you cold?"

"On the contrary, I feel too hot. I must turn the radiator off before going to sleep. Talking about Alain . . ."

"He's being a bit of a nuisance by insisting on staying here! Why couldn't he have gone to Paris with his mother? When everything was going so well for us, when we are at last left in peace."

"He won't hang on to us for long, you see. I know him. I'm sure that when he's found a job, he'll want to live on his own."

"In the meanwhile?"

"You can come and see me when he's out. We can get rid of him, in the evening, by sending him to the cinema. Is there a telephone in the flat?"

"I had it installed. I thought of that too."

Again silence.

"No, not straight away, Paul. I've had a hard day you know!"

"Did everything go off all right?"

"Just about."

"What about the jewels?"

"I'm sure that mother has them, but I couldn't get her to admit it."

"What a laugh. Didn't she ask you what you were going to do?"

"Hardly. She suspects, but she prefers not to hear it said in words."

Alain lay motionless. He stayed in bed, all tense, his nerves taut, hardly breathing. When they began again next door, he clenched his fists, but still did not move.

For a long while he had thought, or more precisely, he had sensed that Corine was like that. That's why he felt so ashamed when she appeared nearly naked, sometimes completely naked in front of him, with her too rich flesh, too much alive, which made him think of exactly what was going on in the next room.

Why did she have to be his sister? Were there many others like

60

her? He wondered. He tried not to think so. It shocked the idea that he had formed of life, of men and women, the relationships between human beings.

Was his mother like that too? He suddenly asked himself the question. He preferred to think not, he would have given anything to be able to answer no, but he remembered words he had heard, the story of her first husband, then her marriage.

If she had been caught in the act, as Corine claimed, it meant that she used to have secret meetings with Eugène Malou. In a hotel like this one?

He forced himself not to think about it and yet he thought about it despite himself. He began to classify the people he knew, those he was intimate with particularly, into "those-who-were-like-that" and the rest.

His father for instance? He hadn't the twinkling eyes, the rake's smile of Fabien the surgeon. He was a man who only worried about his work.

And yet, when Alain thought about his father's first wife, that creature who had suddenly emerged from the past, he saw that he was obliged to alter his opinion.

His father too? Then everybody was? That couldn't be possible. It was too filthy. It hurt him.

When his friends at school, with shining eyes, a curious smile on their lips—not an open smile—used to get together to tell each other stories of that type, he would move aside, disgusted. He hadn't been far from thinking that such things didn't exist, that they were inventing it, that things didn't happen like that.

Now he was finding out that they weren't lying, that it was true, that his sister was one of them, possibly his mother—and why not his aunt Jeanne too? who still made her face up at the age of fifty!

He wanted to run away, to be alone. Was François Foucret...? No, he was too decent, dependable. Alain would go and see him as soon as possible. Not before he had found a job, because Foucret would want to help him, and he was determined to manage, on his own.

It was essential to find a job as soon as possible. He wouldn't go and sleep at his sister's place, as she had invited him to.

"You must admit," she was saying next door, as she smoked

61

her second cigarette, "that everything has worked out marvellously for us . . ."

She probably meant their father's death. Alain didn't want to see Corine again. In a little while, when they had finished next door, when Fabien had gone, he would get up quietly and leave. Should he leave a note saying something like, "I have heard everything!"

What was the use? Corine wouldn't worry about him. So much the better if he didn't stay. They would be that much better off.

He wasn't crying. He didn't cry all night. He was terribly tired and, in the end, he didn't know whether he was dreaming or lying awake.

How did he employ the time? He was making classifications, putting some people in one group and people who to him seemed different in another. But that wasn't enough. It was more complicated than that. He was discovering many species.

Themselves, for instance, the Malous. They were obviously different from the others. His father was like nobody he knew, he was from a race apart. He had stamped himself on all the household. His mother, Corine, himself made up a world that was the Malou world.

To prove it, his mother's sister, Aunt Jeanne, who had the same blood as his mother, who had received an identical upbringing, was quite different and seemed to all of them like a stranger.

What about Bertrand her son? He and Alain had no point in common at all. That was so true that, for two days, Bertrand had been staring at him unceasingly with curiosity and envy.

But Alain, for his part, was clearly different from Corine.

It was very complicated. Possibly he was half asleep. He had the sensation of a long and painful road, of making an essential discovery, and he strove to penetrate ever more deeply into understanding.

"Are you going already?"

"It's one o'clock," answered the man.

It was thus that Alain found out that he had hardly slept at all, that Fabien had arrived just after he had gone to bed.

"Are you going to send your car for my luggage?"

"Aren't you afraid that your brother . . . ?"

"Don't worry about him. He can either get used to it or else . . ."

62

He was dressing. He could be heard dressing, the rustle of his clothes, the noise of his shoes. Then they kissed. Corine, in her turn, walked barefooted to the door to draw the bolt, while Fabien felt about for the switch for the landing light.

The light stayed on for more than half an hour. Was Corine reading a paper as she smoked a last cigarette?

"I'll go before she gets up . . ."

He had no money. His sister had the ten thousand francs his mother had left for both of them. He should have asked for his share earlier.

What would he do tomorrow, out in the street, with no money. He had nothing to sell, only a few worthless clothes. Had the other guests heard Corine's moaning, as he had? Would they perhaps meet him downstairs tomorrow and stare at him?

His mind was assailed by images which he strove to thrust aside, then the images dissolved into grotesque shapes, proof that he slept, and when someone knocked at his door it was broad daylight.

"Alain . . . Alain . . ."

He grunted.

"Open up . . . What are you doing?"

He opened the door mechanically before he remembered his resolutions of the evening before. She wasn't dressed. She was in her dressing-gown.

"You frightened me . . ." she said.

"Why?"

"I've been knocking for a good five minutes. I was wondering if you had already gone out."

"What's the time?"

"Nine o'clock."

And indeed noise could be heard coming from every floor of the hotel. There was the rattle of crockery from downstairs, a van in the yard, a maid with a vacuum cleaner on the corridor carpet.

Alain had dived back into bed so as not to show himself in his pyjamas, for he was extremly bashful. For a moment he wondered if his sister dare sit on his bed, after what had happened. She did so with all the calmness in the world. Why did he blush? What exactly was he thinking about as he turned his head away?

"A car is calling for us at ten o'clock."

63

"Not for me."

"What do you mean?"

"I shan't be going."

"Don't be silly! What do you want to do?"

"I want you to give me part of the money that mother left for us. Half or however much you want, it's all the same to me. I'll find a room in a small boarding-house and . . ."

"What's put those ideas in your head?"

She glanced mechanically at the dividing wall and must have suspected something, then decided to thrust unpleasant thoughts from her.

"Just as you like, Alain. We wouldn't have got on well together for long, would we? How much do you want?"

"I don't care!"

"Three thousand?"

She was swindling him. Why not share it out equally?

"A man hasn't got as many expenses as a girl. You'll get a job more easily than I shall . . ."

He stared sulkily at the bright crack between the curtains. It seemed at last that the sun was shining outside.

"I'll go and get them for you . . ."

To square accounts. And she came back with three notes which she laid on the dressing-table.

"I've written my address down for you. Come and see me when you want to. Let me know what happens. If you want any help, don't hesitate . . ."

She was standing looking at him and suddenly a certain degree of tenderness—due probably to remorse came into her gaze. She leaned over him, her soft breast rubbed against him, She kissed him on both cheeks, on his forehead.

"My poor old brother."

Probably, because she was very conscious of his not being like her, like them. She felt sorry for him.

"There'll always be a bed for you at my place . . ."

He still didn't move. He waited impatiently, his eyes closed, to be alone so that he could weep freely.

By midday he had already found a job where he would begin work on the following day. Wasn't that a miracle?

Another miracle, the first miracle, the cold but bright sunshine, which welcomed him in the street, and a miracle, too, was the lively, bustling, humming life which surrounded him, getting closer and closer to him as he approached the town centre. He hardly knew the town at ten o'clock in the morning, for, usually, at that time, he was in school. The coming and going of the lorries, of the delivery vans, the bustle of the housewives in the shops filled him unawares with a sort of delight which was very like a taste for life. Even the sight of a café waiter cleaning the windows of a brasserie with whiting was interesting enough to cause him to stand for a good while on the pavement.

He walked along aimlessly, with no particular goal; although he knew he was looking for a job, he had not the least idea which door to knock at. Two or three times he thought of François Foucret. He looked forward to going to see him, to having a long talk with him. But not before he was out of his difficulties.

A hundred yards from the Café de Paris, in the street with the trams, where the pavement is narrowest, some men who were hoisting a piano up to a window obliged him to stop for a moment. At that spot there was a dingy window surmounted by the words:

JAMINET BROTHERS, PRINTERS

Behind the dingy glass were notifications of funerals and weddings, pamphlets, visiting cards and, in one corner, a written card:

WANTED, YOUNG MAN TO START IN THE OFFICE.

He knew that there were two big printing concerns in the town. He had never been interested in them, but he knew it. The other, belonging to Monsieur Bidois, was the wrong one because it printed the *Phare du Centre*, which had so bitterly attacked his father recently. It was a place where they dabbled mainly in politics. Monsieur Bidois, a tall, ill-kempt man, was a town councillor, and had twice stood for Parliament.

Jaminet's printing works was that of right thinking people and particularly of the clergy.

It was strange, for Eugène Malou had been more left wing, an old anarchist, if rumour were to be believed; and it was the left wing people who had so persistently opposed him.

"May I speak to Monsieur Jaminet, please?"

The office was badly lit. There was hardly any sun except in the courtyard, where, under a shed, could be seen some hand-carts and bales of paper. A typist, working at her machine near the window, paid no attention to him. A thin man, whom he had already seen, but whom he hardly remembered, looked at him with some surprise. It was only later that Alain thought that he had evidently recognized him, that many people whom he himself did not know, knew that he was Eugène Malou's son.

"What's it about?"

"It's about the job . . ."

A flash of astonishment, a moment's hesitation.

"Will you excuse me? My brother's dealing with it. I'll go and see if he's in the works."

He was outside a long while. Probably—this too only occurred to Alain afterwards—they were discussing what they should do. There were two Jaminets, hardly distinguishable one from the other, although there was three years difference between them. Both of them were thin, with the yellow tinge of hepatics. Both were married, had children and lived in the same house, whose rooms they shared.

Jaminet the younger came in without his brother, whom Alain had first seen.

"Would you leave us a moment, Mademoiselle Germaine?"

He was clearly embarrassed.

"Sit down, Monsieur . . . Monsieur Malou, isn't it?"

"Alain Malou, yes."

"My brother tells me . . ."

"I saw you were looking for a clerk."

"Of course . . . of course . . ."

"Because I must leave school to earn my living . . ."

"I understand, Monsieur Malou, I understand."

"I am studying for my school certificate next summer. I don't know if that is sufficient for you . . ."

A gesture of his hand indicated that he wasn't worried about that.

A small glass window revealed quite a large workshop, with walls of staring white, where rows of machines stood out sharp and black, as though sketched in indian ink. And the majority

66

of these machines, with a silent attendant leaning over them, were working with the slight rumbling of well-oiled gears.

"I thought your family were leaving the town?"

"I decided to stay. As long as I find somewhere to work, of course."

"I understand."

Of the two, Jaminet was the more embarrassed, particularly when the other looked at him with his calm and candid eyes.

"You don't think that this new type of life will seem very hard to you?"

"I'm ready for it."

"Your father was one of our customers."

He didn't say if he had paid his bills. It was likely that he hadn't paid all of them.

"I should be very happy to be of service to you. Nevertheless, I won't hide from you that . . ."

He was worried. He pulled mechanically at his fingers.

"You see, Monsieur Malou; it's a beginner's post. I'll add that it's a post without much future. My brother and I suffice for all the important business. The office work is done by Mademoiselle Germaine, who has been with us for eight years. The position that we want a young man for . . ."

Was Alain listening? In the last few moments he had firmly made up his mind to get the job, whatever happened. He couldn't have said why. The dark offices, the walls hung with posters and calendars, the smell of ink and hot oil, of paper, of gum, the black machines in the whitewashed workshop, and even the handcarts in the yard, in his eyes together constituted a calm and reassuring world with which he felt an imperious need to associate himself.

"Let me tell you, first of all, in a few words, what the work consists of. I suppose you have no notions of the trade?"

He frankly admitted his ignorance. In his mind he already classified Jaminet, both Jaminets, with their shyness, their good will, their not very well cut clothes, the two families living in the same house—the children could be heard running about on the floor above—he classified them in quite a different category from those he had thought about last night as he stared at the shaft of light under his sister's door.

Certainly not these!

Their house reminded him of the peace in churches where he had only been for marriages and funerals.

"First of all there's the daily routine which will hardly concern you . . ."

Was it a manner of speaking or a promise? For Alain it was as though he were already one of them, and all his life he was to be grateful to the younger Jaminet for those words.

"I'm talking about the little printing jobs, visiting cards, announcements, handbills. It's local custom and Mademoiselle Germaine looks after it very well. There are also the playbills for travelling companies and the two cinemas. The most important jobs are our papers, our reports and our directories. We have two linotypes working all day long . . ."

Alain didn't know what linotypes were, but the word pleased him. Everything he was discovering here pleased him.

"Strange as it may seem to you, we work for customers a long way off. For example, each week we print a newspaper which is published at La Rochelle and has nearly three thousand subscribers. We do another paper for Orleans, without mentioning a certain number of diocesan and parochial reports. It is also we who print the *Bulletin Hebdomadaire de la Boucherie Française*, because our prices are much lower than those of Paris and the majority of large towns. About thirty publications in all, to which we must add the periodic directories, particularly for pilgrimages . . ."

He indicated some pigeon holes, containing boxes full of index cards.

"The publications for our subscribers are sent direct from here. So there are lists to be kept up to date, changes of address, notices for new subscriptions to be sent out at the end of the year—and that's the busy time. This indexing work is quite monotonous, I won't conceal from you, and yet it requires the most careful attention because the subscribers are touchy, and the slightest slip brings down complaints on us."

"I think I shall be able to manage," Alain said.

Jaminet still hesitated. Then Alain thought he understood that the other was wondering if he were like the other Malous. That, in short, was what was worrying him. Was this work the sort of work for someone who had spent all his life in the Malous' home, who was himself a Malou.

68

"You know, Monsieur, I am very painstaking. I can spend hours on the same job. If you were to ask my teachers they would tell you . . ."

He was so frightened of one word that would destroy his hopes! And so desirous of becoming part of Jaminet's business.

"As for the salary . . ."

"I was coming to that . . ."

"I am on my own now. I haven't many needs. I am hoping to settle in a boarding-house, and since I've got sufficient clothes, I only want to earn enough to pay for my food and lodging."

"Is your mother still here?"

"She left yesterday."

He blushed. He was frightened that his sister might be mentioned.

"And you preferred not to try your luck in Paris?"

It was funny. It seemed as though he understood. Yet he was a man who led a quiet and uncomplicated existence.

"Will you excuse me a second?"

He opened a little window and called:

"Emile . . ."

That was his brother, the one Alain had seen in the first place, and it wasn't long before he came into the room.

"Monsieur Malou has decided to give it a try. He is very willing. I have told him all about the work we shall expect from him . . ."

Alain sensed danger. The elder brother, behind his back, must be making signs of dissatisfaction to the other.

"Come here a moment," said the younger one. "Will you excuse us, Monsieur Malou?"

And they went into the works, where Alain saw them arguing, standing in front of a large metal table. After a few minutes, the younger one came back alone. He had won his point, but he didn't seem very proud of it.

"I hope you will understand our hesitation. Usually positions of this type are given to young people from families in very humble circumstances, who are used to a certain discipline and a hard life . . ."

"I assure you . . ."

"I believe you, Monsieur Malou . . . My brother and I have

69

decided to give you a try. It is you particularly who will have to judge if you can adapt yourself to this way of life. You will work with me, for my brother concerns himself more particularly with the machine shop. When will you be ready to begin?"

He nearly answered: "Straight away." For he was frightened to see them change their minds as soon as his back was turned.

"Tomorrow . . ." he stammered.

"Right, tomorrow. The office opens at nine o'clock. You will possibly be discouraged at first, because, on account of the new subscriptions, it is the hardest time of the year. Is your handwriting good?"

"Quite good."

"Do you know how to use a typewriter?"

"A little."

Because last Christmas, he had asked for and received a portable machine and, during the last few months, he had used it for typing his homework and compositions.

"Well then, we'll see you tomorrow, Monsieur Malou."

And there it was! It was all over! He was a man! He was earning his living! He hadn't yet begun to earn it, but he would be earning it tomorrow. There was a big triangle of sun in the yard as he crossed it. Half of the street where the trams ran was bathed in sunlight. He walked briskly and nearly directed his steps towards the school, where it wouldn't be long before his friends would be coming out, to tell them the news.

But it was likely that they wouldn't understand his delight, his deliverance. There would be too much to explain to them, including Corine, for them to understand.

He didn't quite know where to look to find board and lodging. It was a world he knew nothing about. Then suddenly, as he made his way through the crowd, memories of smells, sights, sounds came back to him in snatches. When he was going to school in the morning, he often used to go round by the old market place, particularly in the springtime.

It was an old square, with houses all awry. Nearly all of them were cafés, inns which, at eight o'clock, were packed with lorry drivers, with countrywomen surrounded by baskets of vegetables and fruit, cages full of cackling fowls.

The odour of coffee and white wine could be smelt from the middle of the pavement. The house on the corner, roofed with slates, was older than the others, with a vast courtyard always crowded with carts and wagons, stables where, in the gloom, could be heard the noise of horses' hooves.

"The Three Pigeons" said the sign.

There were two steps to go down. The floor was flagged. Buxom girls went from table to table. There they ate food brought from the country off the table tops, but, along a corridor which also smelt of the country, there was another room, white-washed, with curtains at the windows, a service table in the centre, little tables around.

Why had he always dreamed of eating in that room, of sleeping in one of those bedrooms where they put the sheets and bed-clothes on the window-ledges to air?

It was as though he were treating himself to a luxury. It gave him so much pleasure that he was a little ashamed, the day after his father's funeral, and he mentally asked the latter's forgiveness. There was less animation at the "Three Pigeons" at that time of day. The majority of the market gardeners and country people had left. Those who remained were already heavy with wine and brandy.

"I would like to speak to the landlady, please."

An open door revealed the kitchen on the right, with its sizzling and strong smells, girls bustling about, a fat woman with a protruding stomach under her apron who demanded in a sharp voice.

"What is it?"

"A young man who's asking to speak to you."

She had a frying-pan in her hand. She put it down, wiped her fingers on her apron, put her hair straight and came and planted herself behind the counter.

"What can I do for you, young man?"

She too wrinkled her eyebrows. She too must have been wondering where she had seen him.

"Excuse me, Madame. I would like to know if you could give me board and lodging."

"For how long?"

"I don't know. Probably for several months, for a very long while."

"Have you come from Paris?"

"No."

71

"Are you in the Civil Service? Or the lawcourts? We have one of the gentlemen from the courts who takes all his meals here . . ."

"I work for Jaminet, the printers."

She called:

"Désiré . . ."

And an already ageing man, very flabby, with his trousers hanging loosely round his hips, got up from a table where he was drinking with some customers.

"This young man wants board and lodging here. Do you know if number 13 will be vacant?"

"He hasn't written, has he?"

"No, but he said he was coming back."

"Well, if he hasn't written . . ."

With an offhand glance at Alain:

"Have you told him the price?"

"Not yet . . ."

"And have you told him we don't like people coming in late?"

Because they had to get up early in the morning, for the market. Alain found himself in the same state of mind as at the printing works. It seemed to him that come what may he must get room 13 and that he couldn't bear to live anywhere else but in that house.

"I never come home late . . ."

"It would be very sad at your age if you did! Have you been away from your family for long?"

"My father's dead."

"Oh, I understand. Well, you know, I warn you that here we don't stand on ceremony. There are no frills! I do the cooking myself and I answer for it. But for anybody that's difficult to please . . ."

The landlord had gone back to his table, where he poured himself some wine, picking up his conversation again with a couple of country folk.

"Have you any luggage?"

"I'll fetch it presently. In half an hour."

"Are your papers in order?"

"I'll show you them."

"The price is thirty francs a day, with a quarter of a litre of wine at each of the two main meals. You get hors-d'oeuvres,

72

entrée, meat, cheese, dessert or fruit. If you want to see your room..."

He said no. He was in too much of a hurry to move his things into the house. He didn't yet know if the price agreed with what he was going to earn. Monsieur Jaminet had forgotten to quote a figure.

"I'll be back straight away..." he said feverishly.

"Do you live here?"

"Yes. In half an hour's time..."

He ran rather than walked to the Hôtel du Commerce. He stopped a taxi in front of the station, put his cases in.

"The Three Pigeons..."

He hadn't seen Corine. He didn't want to worry about her. From henceforth he had his own life to live, and he was so anxious to enter in on that life that a traffic jam at the crossroads, which held them up for a little while, seemed to him a threat. Supposing, in his absence, they had let room 13? Those people didn't know his name. They might think he wasn't coming back.

He jumped out of the taxi.

"Here I am," he announced.

"Well, you have been quick! Do you want to eat straight away or take your things up first? The other gentlemen aren't here yet. You have a few minutes in front of you. Usually, they sit down to table at half past twelve. Julie! Come here... Take this young man up to number 13. Look first of all and see if the room's been done..."

It was all wonderful, the old staircase with its odours, the curious corridor, upstairs, with its unexpected windings, its even more unexpected steps, with the number on the doors painted in light green, and the light coming in through the ceiling by a lantern light.

The room was bigger than he thought, bigger than the Hôtel du Commerce, the floor made up of little red squares on to which two rugs had been thrown. There was an iron bedstead with a crucifix above it, a black fireplace, a wash-handstand without running water, and the window was so low, so near the floor, that he nearly had to kneel down to look out.

"Have you got everything you want?"

A round mahogany table, two odd chairs, one with a straw bottom, and a wing chair. As for the clothes, they were hung on

73

the wall, where they were hidden by curtains of flowered cretonne.

It was bright. It was cheerful. Too cheerful. He grudged himself for being so cheerful. He remembered the glances of Bertrand, his cousin, who seemed to be envying him so much, the glances of Peters, the red-headed boy, who also seemed to think him lucky.

He began to feel ashamed. He murmured to himself, as he unpacked his cases and threw the contents on the bed.

"Forgive me, Father . . ."

Tomorrow morning, he would be working with Mademoiselle Germaine, whom he had hardly seen, but whom he liked already, because she was part of the world he was entering, and on Sunday he would pay a visit to François Foucret.

Not for a moment did he think of his mother, nor of his sister. As he was going down the stairs, which he was not yet used to and which twisted strangely, he felt a hand on his shoulder.

"This way, young man! . . . Turn to the left in the corridor . . . The gentlemen have just sat down to table . . ."

He blushed as he crossed the threshold of the dining-room, because as he entered into life, he was conscious of all his mistakes, of all his ignorance. He felt that he came with such empty hands!

CHAPTER FIVE

ALAIN had taken the number three tram, a little after two o'clock, almost opposite the Café de Paris. It was Sunday. There was a brightish sun, but the wind, at some street corners, nipped your nose and your ears. That morning, from the window of his room, he had seen, for the first time that winter, a light vapour on the breath of the people hurrying to mass, and the paving stones rang sharply under their heels.

He hadn't realized that the number three tram went to the cemetery too and, for a moment, he knitted his eyebrows, when he saw two or three families carrying chrysanthemums.

He wasn't going to the cemetery. He was going further on. At one point, the street became wider, became the main road, although still cobbled and lined on both sides by single-storied houses, the majority of them grey, some in red brick. On the right, above the housetops, the hill could be seen with houses backing on to it, and smoke was coming out of all the chimneys, twisting in spirals and sometimes wreaths against the dark background of the slopes stripped of their greenery by winter.

As a contrast, on the left, the row of houses seemed to hang on the edge of the valley so that the sky appeared deeper there than elsewhere.

They passed the cemetery, where the majority of the families got out. The people who remained were carrying parcels, and Alain understood when he saw them get out at the hospital that it was visiting day. Opposite there was an inn, with green painted tables and chairs outside, and transparent advertisements on the windows.

The tram went on for another hundred yards, and there it turned back, the trolley was moved to the other side, the rails came to an end. The houses began to be more widely spaced. There were gaps between them, low walls, lengths of hedge with little gardens behind. Rabbit hutches made from old planks, hens closely penned behind wire netting and, on the black ground, a few dark green cabbages, a few leeks with yellowing leaves could be seen.

Alain walked along, his hands in his pockets, and the houses grew scarcer and scarcer. A few cars passed him. It was the first time that he had travelled this road on foot and he realized that the road was extremely long, that the town didn't seem to end, that the suburbs bit deep into the countryside.

After passing a petrol pump and at a spot where the road swept round in a curve, he saw a gigantic sign, five or six times bigger than those which advertise apéritifs or tyres along the main roads of France.

AT MALOUVILLE
YOU WILL FIND THE SITE AND THE HOUSE
OF YOUR DREAMS

An arrow several yards in length pointed in the direction he was going. The hill, on the right, was wooded. He passed a quarry, then a real farm. He reached a crossroads, and the road to Paris continued to the left, dropping gently down into the valley where a river flowed, while he slanted off to the right, along the side of the hill, and little by little the countryside was transformed.

There were woods now, alternating with meadows where white cows grazed. Far off, between the trees, two towers could be distinguished against the pale blue of the sky, those of the Château d'Estier, to which all this land once belonged.

MALOUVILLE: 1 KILOMETRE

And his heart was beating. It was a long while, several months, since he had been here. At a bend in the road, Malouville was revealed to his sight, and in the sun of that Sunday it was a dazzling, unexpected spectacle.

On the right side of the road, in a wide curve, the hill dropped a little and became no more than a few gentle slopes, and, viewed from afar, it was a bright jumble of white, pink and red houses springing out of the greenness.

It was not a village like the others. It was not a town. Wide avenues marked out by trees which, planted, only a few years ago, were still frail, and the avenues bore the name of these trees: Acacia Avenue, Lime Avenue, Pine Avenue, Oak Avenue . . .

On the left, before arriving there, the traveller passed a huge building crowned with the words: Eugène Malou & Company, in monumental letters. They were the offices, the workshops. For years, it had been the scene of busy activity, but, now, all the doors were bespangled with seals, a copy of the act of seizure was pasted on one of the windows.

He walked on with his long swinging stride, reached the first houses which in no way resembled those he had just seen in the main road. Rather they were villas, toys, so much so that it was to be wondered if they had been built to be lived in or to give pleasure to the eyes.

They were widely separated from one another by lawns, by gardens, and the brightest colours of the rainbow were to be found here, all the shapes, too, that a child might contrive to create with a box of bricks.

Smoke was coming out of some chimneys. Curtains moved as he passed by. About forty houses, at the least, were inhabited. Nearly as many remained empty, some uncompleted, without doors or windows, and everywhere, between them, land already staked out was awaiting purchasers.

The avenues, the streets were marked out, cemented over, with their pavements, the telegraph and electric light poles. Some of them did not have a single dwelling and yet had plates bearing their names.

He went out of his way to go through the central square which reminded one of a world exhibition, with its big mosaic pool, its lawns, its blocks of stone, its fountain which didn't work, its too new benches and its bandstand.

Alain had come here alone one day with his father. Eugène Malou had walked him along these avenues, had stopped by the pool where, at that time, goldfish were swimming.

"What are they going to put there?" he had asked.

Then his father had put his hand on his shoulder with a gesture that he knew well. He had said half seriously, half ironically—one never knew when he spoke in that way:

"One day, they'll probably put my statue there."

He set off walking again, reached the southern part of Malouville and knocked at the door of the only inhabited house in that part.

It was Madame Foucret who opened the door to him, in her apron, a soup bowl which she was in the act of wiping in her hand.

"Monsieur Alain! . . ." she cried. "What a surprise! My husband will be pleased. Can you imagine it, just as we were having lunch he told me he wouldn't be surprised if you came to see him today . . ."

"Is he out?"

"Of course not. He didn't go fishing for that reason. He's in there . . ."

She pointed to the next room, speaking in a low voice despite herself.

"Is he asleep?"

"Oh, that doesn't matter. He's having a siesta, as he does every Sunday. I always tease him about that. Now, he can have his siesta every day, can't he? But he doesn't have it during the week. Although he's got all his time free, it doesn't alter things. He wouldn't go to bed for all the money in the world. On Sunday, for instance . . ."

77

And opening the door, she called:

"Foucret! . . . Foucret! . . . It's Monsieur Alain . . . Take your overcoat off, Monsieur Alain, so that you don't catch cold when you go out . . . I'm a little bit behindhand with my washing up because we had a visitor all morning and we ate late . . ."

The wireless was playing quietly in one corner. The house inside had the same toylike appearance as outside, with its rooms designed to give the maximum of comfort and cheerfulness. The windows were wide, the kitchen all in white, its implements enamelled.

François Foucret showed himself in the doorway, his grey hair sticking up a little, one side of his moustache falling over his lips, and as he spoke, he felt for his braces behind his back, brought them down over his white shirt.

"I was just saying to my wife . . ."

"I've just told him about it . . ."

"Forgive my receiving you like this. On Sundays . . ."

"He knows. We've just had a little chat . . ."

"Will you have a drop of something to warm you up, Monsieur Alain?"

"No thank you, I never touch alcohol."

"Sit down. Make yourself comfortable. Take the armchair. The road wasn't too long for you?"

He lit a meerschaum pipe with a cherrywood stem.

"When you think that that was how they caught him! With their four blessed kilometres of road! At the beginning, when they were all for him, it was a question that didn't worry them, they considered it a detail.

"What could be easier than to extend the tram lines? Instead of stopping at Ganette, they could go on to Malouville.

"They promised him a bus route, anything he wanted.

"Ten, twenty times, the town council talked it over. And each time your father treated them handsomely. Some of those gentlemen had very sticky fingers, you can take my word for it.

"One fine day, they came to the conclusion that it wasn't a matter for them, that Malouville wasn't in the urban district and that application should be made to the County Council.

"More months, not to speak of years. Still there were palms to be greased, dinners, presents, little favours of every kind.

78

"'In a few weeks you'll have your bus route, Monsieur Malou, you can count on it.'

"And the building went on! And the road was finished at a cost of millions.

"Then all of a sudden it wasn't the County Council's business at all, but the Ministry of Transport, and that was in Paris . . .

"A fine bunch of rogues, they were! Your father started afresh in Paris, saw members of Parliament, ministers, who cost him a lot more and only gave him fine words in exchange for his money.

"Then, because people here were getting annoyed, which was understandable, since, for someone who goes to work, it's hard to go to town twice a day on foot and to come back at nightfall, so, as I was saying, your father wanted to clear the matter up and he bought a coach to work the run himself.

"I don't know if you remember the row that caused? They refused him the right to carry passengers. They refused him a licence. The Tram Company and the Bus Company began an action against him.

"You can believe me if you like, but he still didn't give up.

"'You deny my right to carry fare-paying passengers,' he came back at them. 'All right. I won't make them pay anything. I'll carry passengers free.'

"And yet they found I don't know what in the law to prevent him.

"I wondered if he weren't going to beat them in the end despite everything.

"'You don't want me to carry them in my coach? All right! I haven't got a coach any more. I've sold it to the inhabitants of Malouville, who have one share each. They've got the right to club together to buy a motor coach and to travel in a vehicle which belongs to them.'

"There was a case about it. In the end your father was defeated.

"Do you know that story?"

"I didn't know the details."

He didn't dare say that he knew almost nothing about his father's business, or about his father himself. That man before him, massive, placid, taking little puffs at his pipe, knew much more about Eugène Malou than his own son.

79

"It appears that you are all alone at the moment."

"Who told you so?"

"People talk a lot. And now there are even some, among the most ruthless, who are sorry . . . From what I've heard your mother's in Paris?"

"Yes, with Aunt Jeanne. I've been working since Friday."

"If it weren't so far, I had meant to invite you to come and live here, where there's room. Even with a bike, it's hard going in winter."

"I'm working for Jaminet, the printers, and I've taken a room at the 'Three Pigeons'."

Foucret and his wife looked at each other. Alain wondered what they were thinking. They both of them looked pityingly, and he couldn't understand why, since he had never been so happy in his life.

"Monsieur Jaminet is very kind, particularly the younger, Monsieur Albert. Their secretary too, Mademoiselle Germaine . . ."

He was full of it. He said the names like a child who has just started school recites the names of its teachers.

"Also Madame Poignard, the landlady of the 'Three Pigeons', is kind to me and looks after me very well."

"Mélanie . . ." specified Madame Foucret from her bedroom, where she was busy with her make-up, having left the room door open.

"Everybody calls her that. She told me to call her that too, but I don't dare."

"She's a good woman. If only her husband drank a little less . . . But it's the business that causes that . . ."

And Alain was happy to speak of old Poignard who was always a bit tipsy from the morning onwards. As the day wore on he became more flushed, more indolent, more pop-eyed, but nothing else, except a slight stutter, betrayed his drunkenness.

"You'll have a piece of cake with us, won't you? I'm going to make some coffee."

"You mustn't put yourself to any trouble for me, Madame Foucret."

"It's no trouble. You've seen how handy the kitchen is. It's the best part of . . ."

She stopped short, and Foucret hastened to speak of something else. Forgetting that she was speaking to Eugène Malou's son, she had nearly said: "It's the best part of the house . . ."

Alain understood. He understood all the more because of a certain sense of awkwardness which he had been feeling since his arrival; of course, the house was pretty, neat. He still realized that something was lacking. The armchair he was sitting in, for example, a wicker armchair with red cushions, didn't seem to fit in at all, as it would in the houses he had seen all along his way. It could have been put in any corner.

The Foucrets' old furniture, too, looked lost in these surroundings. Foucret himself, in his white shirt, with no collar, braces, slippers.

Alain remembered the little gardens behind the hedges, the cabbage plots, the rabbit hutches, the hens and the rubbish heaps. He remembered how, on summer evenings, he had seen the men digging or doing odd jobs, the women watering the plots where vegetables were beginning to show through.

Could such shacks be built around the houses of Malouville? Could they hang about outside, in clogs, in their shirt sleeves?

Here, in the square, instead of the dark shops of the suburbs, old women selling vegetables, grocers' shops smelling of cinnamon and paraffin, with jars of sticky sweets in the windows, there was a big bright co-operative store with the goods ranged on whitewood shelves.

"When I think of all the spokes they put in his wheel . . ."

"Do you think the people who live here are happy? . . ."

A little ill at ease, a little hesitantly, Foucret said:

"They're getting used to it. You see your father was far-sighted. For example, when they objected that the estate was five kilometres from the town, your father took paper and pencil. He quoted figures, the number of cars sold each year, and he proved that, in a little while, there would be many fewer households without cars than households with cars . . .

"So, when people have a car, they want to use it, don't they?

"They told him that people, particularly those with small fixed incomes—and it's those with small fixed incomes who've come to live here—like to have a garden with vegetables, animals . . .

"He answered that eggs were cheaper in the shops, that rabbits are a nuisance and don't bring in any money, that, in a few years'

81

time, nobody will take the trouble to grow vegetables. I can still hear him saying:

" 'What about the cinema? You're forgetting the cinema! You can't go to the pictures and water your garden. Now, the cinema...'

"He gave more figures. The number of cinemas, the number of people who go each evening. He wanted to build a picture palace at Malouville. He had already set up a bowling alley, skittles, two tennis courts...

" 'There'll be a swimming pool,' he said, 'and folk will prefer to go swimming than gathering grass for the rabbits.'

"He was ahead of his time, you understand."

But wasn't François Foucret rather putting a brave face on things? Wouldn't he too have preferred one of those houses lining the main road, not far from the trams and the town, with a dirty little garden and sheds made of planks of wood?

"They were all with him, at the beginning, all, you might as well say, without exception. You are too young to understand. Your father had more say than the mayor, than the member of Parliament, who were proud to be seen with him. I remember the great banquets, particularly when a minister came from Paris to award him the Légion d'Honneur. I was there, not at the top table, but I was there, because your father always insisted on his staff being present at all the junketings. They said then that Malouville would be a model city which all the others would want to copy..."

Madame Foucret spread a red checked cloth on the table, took some china from the sideboard.

"It was only two or three years later that the difficulties began, when they saw that it was going to be dearer than they had thought. It was the business of the modern sanitation which started the first attacks. It would take too long to explain it to you...

"Then there were some people, municipal councillors, among others, who had received sites for nothing and sold them at any old price to make money.

"Bigois joined them, I don't know why, because for a while he claimed to be your father's best friend, and it was at his place your father had his printing done before he went to Jaminet.

"There are some rotten people about, Monsieur Alain! I think my wife would like us to sit down to table...

82

"You don't find it too hard working at the printers?"

"At the moment I am enjoying it very much."

"Your father often spoke to me about you."

His wife looked at him as though to make him be quiet. What might he have said that he shouldn't?

"He was very fond of you, he was! You didn't perhaps realize it, because he was a rather shy man in those matters. For example: When he gave me this house . . . He said nothing to me about it. He just told me to supervise the work and added:

"'Make that one as you think, old chap.'

"For he used *tu* to practically everybody.

"'It's only fair that you should build one as you want. We'll see what it looks like.'

"When it was finished he came to see it.

"'You think it's all right?'

"I think so, Monsieur Malou.

"'You really like it?'

"If the chap who buys that house isn't happy in it, he'd be a hard one to please.

"'Well, you just move in, and I'll come for the house warming.'

"Then, when he came to break the bottle of champagne, he laid the deeds on the table, all in order.

"I was even more pleased when, on the days he used to look round the building sites, he would come in here and sit in that chair where you are now. He asked for a glass of ordinary red wine, because he wasn't very fond of all the proprietary wines they used to serve at the receptions.

"'A drop of the old red stuff, François.'

"They got him, Monsieur Alain, but it doesn't mean that all that's finished with . . ."

Another look from his wife.

"Try a bit of the old woman's cake. Your father ate a piece more than once. If you don't mind, I'm going to have a drop of red wine, because I don't fancy coffee at this time. If you feel like a drop . . ."

It was warm. He felt very cosy. Alain almost forgot that his father was dead. It seemed to him that he was going to see him, to speak to him; at the same time he was a bit jealous of the Foucrets, who had known him better than he had.

"How old are you, Monsieur Alain?"

"Seventeen in a month's time."

Another glance from Madame Foucret to her husband. A glance which meant: "You see!"

Were they hiding something from him? Couldn't they speak openly in front of him?

"Only," he added, "during the last few days, I feel much older."

"You must come and see us often. One Sunday, I'll show you round Malouville and tell you the story of every stone. I don't know what they are going to do now. It seems that the Count and Bigois hold the majority of the shares. People say that they'll get a bus service without any difficulty and that next year they'll build fifty houses. As they say where I come from, someone's got to do the dirty work first, if you see what I mean? It's a fact though that, if it hadn't been for your father, this would still be Monsieur d'Estier's grounds . . .

"There is something that perhaps you don't know and I must tell you. Do you know why he is a count? I found out from my nephew who is a clerk in a solicitor's office in town. Before the revolution his family was quite simply a family of horse copers. They called themselves Patard. They went from fair to fair. They used to fake the horses up for sale. When the revolution came, they bought national property including the château which had belonged to the Counts d'Estier. It's even said that it was the Patards who denounced the latter, who were hiding in a farm, and who had them guillotined.

"They took their place, then, forty years later, they found a way of changing their name and getting the title. Your father had a good laugh when I told him that. I'm sure I made him happy that day.

"Another piece of cake, Monsieur Alain?"

His mouth was full of crunchy cake, melting, sweet, scented, and his head was swimming a little in the cosy warmth of the house.

"Oh! I can tell you a lot more! I understand why your father, busy as he was, couldn't manage to tell you everything. There are some who, perhaps, one day, will offer you their hands to shake and who are swine. There are others . . ."

A glance from Madame Foucret. A shadow had just gone past

84

the window. A man, outside, was knocking his shoes before pushing the door open. He came in, a fishing rod in one hand, in the other a bag containing a few roach.

"I beg your pardon . . ." he said as he saw the guest.

And Foucret:

"Come in! I suppose you recognize him. It's Eugène's boy . . ." He bit his lip and added rapidly:

"Eugène Malou's. . . . It's Alain. . . ."

"Will you have a bite with us, Monsieur Joseph?"

Why was there a feeling of awkwardness? He sensed that the incident was unexpected. The man put his fish in the kitchen sink, wiped his hands on the red-bordered towel which was hanging up, held out his right hand to Alain.

"It's a pleasure, young . . ."

He also checked himself:

"It's a pleasure, Monsieur Malou. Excuse my being so dirty. I was in a muddy spot on the river bank, and I happened to slip."

"Go and get changed," Foucret said to him, for his corduroy trousers were muddy up to the knees.

"Hurry up and come and have something to eat with us."

So the new arrival had a room in the house, where he behaved exactly as if he were at home. Madame Foucret laid another place, cut another piece of cake.

In a low voice, Foucret was explaining:

"He's a good chap, Monsieur Alain, a man your father was also very fond of."

His wife was obviously the keeper of the household secrets, because once again she looked at him sternly. François Foucret wanted to come out with it all. His glances meant:

"Come, he's a big lad, he's a man, he's Eugène's son, and we can speak in front of him . . ."

She compressed her lips all the same as though to tell him to keep silent, and he didn't know what to do.

"And so your mother's gone away?" said the new arrival whom they had called Joseph, returning into the room wearing clean trousers.

He had a direct look which didn't waver, his voice was a little hard. The words that he had just uttered had fallen from his lips like an accusation.

"She's in Paris with my aunt Jeanne."

85

"And your sister Corine?"

Alain kept quiet, ashamed. Why did it suddenly seem to him that these people had as much right as he to concern themselves with his family? Despite the precautions they took, despite their reticence, they seemed to be as much the heirs of Eugène Malou as he.

"With Fabien, I suppose?"

He was watching the young man. There was something hard and yet kindly in his eyes.

"Why didn't you go with your mother to Paris?"

Alain almost felt like weeping. He would so much like to have said to them: "Because it's my duty to stay here, with my father. Because someone really had to stay to . . ."

He couldn't have explained further. He preferred to say with a touch of pride:

"I'm working."

"At Jaminet's," Foucret interrupted.

"Are you living with your sister?"

He tried to maintain his calm.

"I'm at the 'Three Pigeons'."

The two others, now, were taking it in turns to make little signs to the one named Joseph.

He was a rather small man, very thin, who, because of that, seemed young. When his face was studied closely it was seen to be lined with fine deep wrinkles that are more usually seen on some old women than men.

One could sense that his body was as hard as iron. He had brown eyes, also small, brilliant.

"Didn't your brother Edgar try to get you into local government?"

They knew it all, they guessed it all. And there was something in Joseph's voice that was aggressive and gentle at the same time. Alain felt chilled by him and also attracted. He felt as though he were only a child, as though, for the first time, he found himself with men, and he would have liked to prove to them that he was a man too, and that they could trust him.

They weren't enemies. Enemies wouldn't have known his father as they knew him.

"Did Eugène . . ."

He checked himself again. All three of them spent their time

86

checking themselves, which meant that when he wasn't there, they spoke a different language.

"Did your father keep his papers?"

"I've got them. There's a suitcase full. I took them to the hotel. I shall read them. I want to read them . . ."

He wanted to shout at them. "Why on earth don't you trust me? You know things that I don't know. I am young. My father didn't speak much at home about his business. He avoided speaking in front of me. Only from time to time, would he put his hand on my shoulder, and then it seemed that I felt his tenderness, I used to say to myself that he was counting on me one day to . . ."

François Foucret said slowly, filling a new pipe which he had taken from a rack:

"You see, Monsieur Alain, Joseph Bourgues is an old, a very old friend of your father's. Leave me alone, Marie. The boy's big enough to know more about it . . ."

Probably his wife had tried again to make him quiet:

"Joseph Bourgues knew your father better than anybody else. That's all I can tell you. He can do what he likes; for my part . . ."

He didn't finish and his sentence was followed by a long silence. Bourgues was eating a piece of cake which he washed down with red wine. He was watching the young man closely.

"How old are you?"

"Seventeen in one month."

Marie Foucret seemed to be saying to him: "He's young."

"And you are satisfied with working?"

"Even if someone offered to pay for my studies, I should refuse to return to school."

"Why?"

The question came out cleanly, cutting, like all the remarks of this little thin man.

"Just, because!"

He couldn't have explained himself. Because he had the impression at last of living like the others, of wandering no longer on the edge of the crowd, but of being in the crowd. Because, at the "Three Pigeons" . . . No! It was more complicated than that. He was powerless to explain what he felt and he wanted to cry, feeling his helplessness.

87

He would so much like to have been on an equal footing with them, to have their trust.

"You preferred to remain on your own, so to speak."

He stammered, without really understanding the meaning of the words he uttered:

"Yes, with my father . . ."

"Then you must come back and see me."

"I would like to."

"Because I shall have a lot of things to tell you . . ."

Alain believed him. He trusted him despite his cutting tone. The Foucrets, husband and wife, had now moved into the background. It seemed as though they were making way for the thin little man, as though the latter alone had the right to speak.

"Are you afraid?"

"Of what?"

"Of anything."

"I want to . . ."

The words wouldn't leave his throat from self-consciousness. He was going on to say: "I want to know my father. I want to do what he would have wanted me to do. As for the others, I hate them . . ."

His sister, yes! His brother, yes! His mother? He was tempted to say yes, he realized it for the first time. He blushed for it, but he couldn't do anything else. And his aunt Jeanne, and his uncle, and his cousin! He remembered that scuttling away, straight after the funeral, and he clung to him, the man, Eugène Malou, who was his father, whom he knew so little, whom he had hardly known at all, and against whom the whole world had been in arms.

He had tears in his eyes.

"I hate them . . ." he said, his fists clenched.

"You must come and see me. I can't go into town, so that you'll have to put yourself out. You had better not mention my name to anybody."

He hesitated and, looking the boy straight in the eye, he said:

"Remember this carefully: Joseph Bourgues. . . . Sentenced to ten years prison . . . Ten years forced residence . . . Escaped from Cayenne thanks to Eugène . . . I mean thanks to Eugène Malou . . . Ten years in Havana. . . . I'll tell you all about it another time . . . After that, Eugène found a way of bringing me here . . ."

His stare was heavy, heavy.

"That's not too much for you to bear?"

"I don't understand what you mean."

"You don't want to leave us?"

"No."

"You're not frightened?"

"No."

"Then we'll see each other again often, Alain."

His christian name, suddenly, his christian name, preceded by no Monsieur, seemed for Alain to be a sort of consecration which gave him unforgettable joy. His heart really leapt in his breast.

"If my father . . ."

"Don't speak about Eugène before you understand!" cut in Joseph Bourgues, getting up and lighting a cigarette.

It was getting dark. Madame Foucret was sitting at the table, her two hands folded on her stomach. She felt it was time to clear the table and sighed.

"Eugène was a great chap," Bourgues went on, as though he were looking for someone around him to contradict him, which would give him the chance to spring.

He repeated:

"A great chap, you will see!" And with a swift movement he pressed the electric light switch and dispelled the gloom.

CHAPTER SIX

IT was his favourite time. Not immediately after the lamps in the office and workshops were lit, because he did not like to see the day linger outside, particularly the steel-grey light in the courtyard, and often they had to put the lights on very early, sometimes they were on all day long. The beginning of his time, as he mentally called it, was when the children came home from school.

The electric lights had already been lit for some while. The iron stove was roaring. It was a stove of old-fashioned design, of a type he had seen nowhere else, and he would willingly have agreed that it had its own life, that it was a personality, and not the least important one in the office. He had got himself put in charge of it. Before him, Mademoiselle Germaine had replenished it from time to time and raked the cinders out with the end of the poker.

In the early days, he had watched her doing it enviously, like a child. He didn't yet dare offer himself. He felt too new. But, once when the coal scuttle was empty and he had been to fill it in the outhouse, he muttered as he opened the stove:

"May I?"

Next to the office was a staircase, which led up to the first floor where the two flats of the brothers were opposite each other. The corridor led directly into the courtyard, but the door leading from the office to the corridor was nearly always open, so that the household noises could be heard, the thousand familiar noises of the two families.

Why did Albert Jaminet, the younger, the one he liked, have a short, thin wife, dark and dried-up, always suffering from headaches, always complaining or in a bad temper, while Emile, the elder, had an agreeable wife, young-looking, pink and cheerful?

It shocked him. Ten times a day Albert's wife would lean over the banisters upstairs, and call her husband sharply, and the latter would dash out as though he were terrified of being caught in the act of doing something wrong. They could be heard whispering. She wanted him to give her a hand, or something was worrying her, or else she would send him on some errand in the neighbourhood; he never complained; he would come smiling back to his seat, satisfied with having done his duty.

A little after four o'clock, when Alain's favourite time of the day was beginning, the children would return from school; Albert's two boys were nine and ten, his daughter fifteen, and she always hung about for a moment in the corridor to glance at the new clerk. Emile had twin girls, twelve years old, and an older boy who was studying in Paris.

They could be heard walking about, scuffling their feet, the chairs on the floor; the smell of the cocoa for their meal wafted down to the office, then there was a long silence, the hour devoted to homework; and he imagined them all by the table lamp, sucking the ends of their pencils or pens, while the dinner simmered in both kitchens.

Mademoiselle Germaine typed. She typed quickly, without

looking at the keyboard, her fingers performing a sort of dance on the machine, and the clink of the roller at the end of its travel set the rhythm.

On the other side of the window hatch, in the staring white factory, the machines worked away with a noise of well oiled gears. Monsieur Emile corrected proofs or supervised the setting up of a page on the stone.

Monsieur Albert was more likely to be poring over his estimates and accounts, and Alain moved back and forth, sometimes climbing the steps to reach the highest row of shelves where the card indexes were stored.

He was already familiar with the cards and the names of the subscribers to the various papers, reports, directories, some funny names, some improbable ones. There were people who were always changing their address, others whose card had gone twenty years without a change.

His work did not prevent him from thinking, or from listening to the sounds from above, or from looking at the back of Mademoiselle Germaine's neck covered with a golden down.

That day, as Monsieur Emile was putting on his hat and coat to call on a customer in town, he almost said to the young girl: "I've got a new friend."

And probably, he would have gone on to add with pride: "A new friend who treats me like a man. . . . And, you know, he's not anybody . . . He's done two years in prison. . . . He escaped three times, the first two times into the forest, where, the second time, he was found nearly dead, the third time in a boat no bigger than a nutshell in which, nevertheless, he sailed from island to island in the Caribbean sea, alive with sharks . . ."

What a memory he had of the road he had trodden the evening before by the side of Joseph Bourgues! And how naturally it had happened! When it had got dark, when, little by little, they had fallen silent in Foucret's house, he had got up, out of politeness, so as not to impose on them too long; he had announced:

"It's time I was going home."

Then, while Madame Foucret helped him to slip on his overcoat, Bourgues had quite naturally got up and put on a short hunting jacket.

"I'll come part of the way with you," he had said.

The others must have understood that it was important, because Foucret had not suggested coming with them.

They had set off walking slowly, at a stroll, first of all across the building sites, then along the road, and the sky was clear, the trees stood out blackly, the ground rang under their feet.

"Your father and I were about your age when we met . . ."

Had he gone on using the formal *vous* after that? Not for long in any case. Almost from the start the old convict had used *tu* without apologies, and Alain, who had never liked people to be familiar with him, was grateful.

"It was at Marseilles . . . Your father sold newspapers . . . He waited in a dark little street behind the *Petit Provençal* printing works . . . Many of them waited in that day, to dash up to the hatch to collect their pile of papers with the ink still wet, and then it was a race to see who could get to the Canebière and the big cafés first . . . I was working for a carpenter, in the same street, on the ground floor . . . My father was a wheelwright in a village in Provence . . ."

Alain had passed through Marseilles several times, when he went with his parents to Cannes or Nice. Why had he never stopped there? If he had known the town better, he could have conjured up precise images in his mind as his companion spoke to him.

"We'd both of us done other jobs . . . Among other things, we had the idea of buying the sweepings of the drawers and stale lime leaves from chemists' and herbalists', and we used to mix them together, anyhow, put them in tins on which we stuck a label "Indian Tea" . . .

"We went from house to house, in the suburbs, in the villages: 'How pale the child is, lady . . . It's evident you've never heard of Indian Tea, the best remedy for anaemia . . . With three tins, you'll make a giant of him . . .'

"Indian Tea was good for everybody, for everything: for old people, women in childbirth, constipation, diabetics . . .

"We worked up to Lyons like that, but our great ambition was to reach Paris. It took us months to realize it. One fine day we landed at the Gare de Lyon and a few nights later, to earn a bit of money, we went and humped vegetables at the market with the tramps.

"At that time, not far from the markets, in Rue Montmartre,

92

there was a little narrow dark shop with only a few faded pamphlets in the window, and there we were to become regulars, because it was there the young Libertarians, whom some people classified with the Anarchists, used to meet.

"Both of us became Libertarians. We read all the pamphlets, all the books, all the tracts. We went to secret gatherings and political meetings. We demonstrated in the streets.

"You young people of today can't imagine it. We spoke of nothing but the welfare of humanity, and a general upheaval seemed to us to be the only way of bringing this about.

"Among our comrades of those days, there are some who have since become ministers, newspaper magnates, important dignitaries of the Légion d'Honneur; there is also a member of the Academy and others who have gone to the bad; during the 1914 war, some of them died in prison and two or three were shot in a ditch at Vincennes.

"But what I want you to understand, young fellow, is that they were very decent people, that the majority of them were decent people, that only a few of them, excluding the police spies, were rats.

"We talked a lot about bombs. We made I don't know how many of them, but we always finished up, terrified, by throwing them into the Seine to get rid of them.

"We threw one, however, which did damage and caused some deaths, in a big restaurant which still stands and where the members of parliament and of the senate used to gather.

"They were eating there, sumptuously, just at the time when the police and the military had received orders to fire on the strikers in the mines in the North.

"Your father wasn't in it, I tell you that straight away, not to whitewash him, but because it's the truth. As it happened, it was by chance. A day or two earlier he had gone into hospital.

"He knew what we were doing. I used to go and see him and keep him informed.

"'Are you sure it won't do more harm than good to the cause?' he used to ask me.

"I had been drawn with three others to go and place the bomb. It wasn't I who carried it, but I was caught and got ten years.

"It was at that time that your father set up house with a girl,

93

decent enough, but not very intelligent, who was a waitress in a restaurant. He hadn't a penny. Nevertheless, he told my lawyer to tell me not to worry.

"And he kept his word. For one year, two years, I had no news from him. I had two attempts at escaping on my own, and both times I was caught again, the second time, I nearly left my bones in the tropical jungle.

"I was still in the infirmary when a warder came looking for me and told me I'd do well to hurry up and get better. He was a Corsican, a blackguard, but your father had paid him the necessary and he behaved properly.

"Are you beginning to understand why I was pleased to see you? You'll understand better later on, because there are some things that you don't yet know, because, since that time, Eugène and I have often chatted together.

"If it pleased you, I can tell you now that it is with your father's full agreement that I am speaking to you as I do."

"Did he tell you to?" asked Alain, moved.

And they walked on with an even step, smoking their cigarettes. And for the first time in his life Alain felt he was really a man.

They reached the Genette district, the trams, the hospital, and there, quite naturally and as though by common consent, they turned back.

"I prefer not to walk that way," said Bourgues simply. "Mark you, I've got papers in the name of Joseph Brun, all in order. Don't forget the name if anybody asks you about me. Your father sent them to me.

"I landed at Havana, where there were fifteen other Frenchmen in my position. The Cuban government didn't worry us as long as we kept quiet. The French Minister left us alone too, and even, once, knowing who I was, he employed me as a head waiter in the Legation.

"I met a French woman, a fat placid girl, Adèle, who was doing what she could to make ends meet, but she didn't have much success, because she didn't know how to handle men.

"We became friends. She used to invite me to her room, where she cooked dishes from home. It was there that I realized that, if she was not much good as a prostitute, she was a cook of the first order.

94

"We set up in a little French restaurant together. There were only six tables, and they were always booked in advance. Adèle got enormous, so fat that at the end she could hardly sit down.

"That lasted for years. I daren't return to France. It wasn't until Adèle died that I felt homesick and I wrote to your father. You were living at Bordeaux. He was rich. I used to see his name in the papers. I used to think that he had probably forgotten me or that he preferred not to remember. Nonetheless, a few months later, I received identity papers and money that I didn't need, because I had had time to put some away.

"That's the story, my lad. Eugène came to meet me off the boat, and we embraced each other.

"I burst out laughing on seeing how little he had changed. Because, you see, and this doesn't make him any the worse, he always kept the tastes of his youth. I remember once when he had won a sum of money in a bowling competition—it was at Marseilles—he spent it all in half an hour on buying himself a check suit, a red silk tie, fine shoes with different kinds of leather let in.

"To impress people, and also possibly for the pleasure of giving pleasure, he would give as a tip twice what the meal had cost him.

" 'Keep the change . . .'

"That was his expression. He loved to act as a great lord, quite satisfied afterwards to live several days on bread and milk coffee.

"On my return I didn't want to tag on to him, without mentioning that I might be recognized and get him into trouble.

"I lived in Paris, where there is less danger of being caught than anywhere else. I worked. I had a little business in Montmartre.

"He used to come and see me from time to time. Both of us used to go and eat in little grubshops that we knew, and he took care not to bring his big car and chauffeur.

"He had his ups and downs, but they were all the same to him because he felt sure of coming out on top.

" 'I'll get 'em,' he often used to say. 'And it's nice to think that when you're the son of my poor devil of a father, who didn't even know his own name or the country he came from . . .' "

"Did he mention us to you?"

"Sometimes. Particularly you, towards the end. Because he

95

wanted to have me near him. He had just given Foucret a house and perhaps he had an idea in the back of his head when he did so. He asked me to go and live there, and we used to see each other several times a week.

"Those are a few of the things that I wanted to tell you about your father. The others, your mother, your sister, your idiot of a brother, wouldn't be interested in them."

"He told you so?"

"Never mind. Now, I'll add this: whatever you want, advice or anything else, come and see me. Do you understand? You'll see if you are going to like it at Jaminets'."

"I think I'll like it very much."

"Don't speak too quickly. Come and see me when you like, as often as possible. I've no reason to move. I've nobody in the world. The Foucrets are decent people."

"I like them very much too . . ."

He was on the point of becoming sentimental. They were back again at the tram terminus, and the full moon was rising behind the trees.

"There's a tram coming. Off you go! . . ."

He would have liked to stay longer, show his new friendship in some way, but he didn't know how to go about it, and it seemed as though Bourgues was becoming harsher, shorter, and his voice more impersonal.

"We'll meet again soon."

He held out his hand. His companion moved away without seeing it, and disappeared into the darkness of the road.

Why couldn't he tell all that to Mademoiselle Germaine? It would have given him so much pleasure to show her that his father was different from what they thought!

He had been feeling as though he were drunk since the evening before. He felt more cheerful than he could ever remember, and several times before going to bed he had murmured:

"Father . . ."

The father of Marseilles, Lyons, Rue Montmartre . . . The man who used to go and meet his boyhood friend in the grubshops . . . And who was determined to get them.

To get whom? He couldn't have said precisely, but right in his heart he understood, or thought he understood.

To get them! All of them! The Estiers, the Bigois. All those

96

whose palms he had greased, filled their bellies and who had turned against him. It was a breed he was after, a way of life.

Then, since morning, he had had other, more confused thoughts on which he didn't want to dwell.

Broadly speaking, hadn't that man whom he had hardly known, whom he hadn't bothered to know, because he couldn't imagine that a human being could be different from his appearance, that man who had died on the dirty floor of a local chemist's shop, hadn't that man been on his own all his life?

Alone, no, because there had been the Foucrets and the old convict. But apart from them?

His elder son, for example, the child of his first wife, who logically, according to Alain's way of thinking, ought to have been like the Malous of the old days, thought of nothing but earning promotion in the County Hall . . .

His wife, Alain's mother . . .

And Corine . . .

He didn't want to make himself unhappy. He was working in his overheated office where he already knew all the play of light and shade. He would go and see Joseph Bourgues often. He would have liked to see him straight away, but he didn't dare go to Malouville that evening. He was waiting until next Sunday. If Bourgues went fishing—he mustn't upset his habits—he would go with him and sit quietly beside him.

Upstairs, from time to time, one of the children would speak to his mother to ask her a question about his homework. The others went "Hush . . ." And he imagined them huddled over their books stopping their ears with their fingers.

The telephone rang. Mademoiselle Germaine always answered it, it was part of her prerogatives.

"It's for you, Monsieur Alain."

Who wanted him? He was suddenly worried, and it could be heard in his voice when he said "Hallo!"

He had already recognized the voice and he was upset.

"I must speak to you. I've got some important things to say to you. Will you come and see me after you've finished work? What time do you finish?"

"At six o'clock."

"It's only five minutes from your office."

"I don't want to go there."

"You're being silly. You needn't worry: he won't be here."

"I still don't want to go."

"Just as you like. You know I needn't bother to talk to you about it, but I think it's better that you should know."

She must have put her hand on the mouthpiece, turned round and said a few words to somebody, because he could hear a slight murmur. So Fabien was at her place.

He was on the point of hanging up.

"Listen, since you haven't any more sense than that, I'll see you at the Café de Paris at six o'clock. Don't keep me waiting because I haven't a lot of time!"

He said yes, because he couldn't do otherwise, but he was furious to see his family already invading his new life.

When he went back to his seat, Mademoiselle Germaine hesitated before speaking. She did so very gently, not without a certain diffidence.

"Monsieur Alain . . . Above all don't take this the wrong way . . . We're both employed here . . . So I'd like to warn you, so that you don't get told off . . . The directors, particularly Monsieur Emile, don't like people to have personal phone calls . . ."

He blushed.

"I hope I won't have any more . . ."

"Are you annoyed? . . . Not that it's any of my business . . ."

"I assure you, Mademoiselle, that I am not annoyed and that on the contrary I am grateful to you . . ."

"It's because of the works people, who sometimes take advantage of it. If everybody started having phone calls . . ."

His hour had been spoilt, he could not quite say why. He had lost his cheerfulness. He was worried about the meeting with his sister. What did she want? He would so much have liked her to be living in another town, or even—and it was for the first time that this kind of thought crossed his mind—that she were dead in their father's place.

At five to six, as usual, he put his boxes of files away, climbed the step ladder, which always gave him pleasure, tidied his drawers and went and washed his hands in the enamelled basin in the workshop. At the same time, Mademoiselle Germaine took off her jersey, which she put away in a cupboard, and, after having brushed up her blonde hair, put on her hat, coat and gloves.

They walked side by side out into the street, where she turned to the left while he went to the right; they shook hands, said goodnight; and in the shadows there was a little old woman who waited motionless, Mademoiselle Germaine's mother.

Opposite was a lighted cinema. Further down, the Café de Paris, with its big windows more discreetly lighted and the figures around the tables, the balding heads of the card and domino players, ringed with smoke.

From outside, he saw that his sister had not yet arrived and he nearly didn't wait, yet he went in, looked for a free table, and, without taking his overcoat off, ordered a glass of beer. Gabriel, the waiter, called him Monsieur Alain and carefully wiped the table in front of him.

A few minutes later a car pulled up. Corine in a fur coat, with light stockings, jumped out on to the pavement, which she crossed quickly, and came towards her brother.

"It's not very clever of you to make me waste my time."

"Is he waiting for you?"

"What's that to you? If you knew him better, if you weren't a stuck up little brat, you'd behave differently. A port, waiter."

She searched in her handbag for her cigarette case.

"It's thanks to him, so it happens, that I found out what I want to tell you. You can write and tell mother if you think it will serve any purpose. For my part, I don't want anything to do with it, because I intend to involve myself as little as possible in the family affairs."

He had the impression that the people at the next table were listening to them and he felt ashamed. Everybody knew them. Everybody was certainly looking at them.

"He went to play bridge yesterday at the home of one of his colleagues where there were several doctors, among them Doctor Lachaux, the throat and ear specialist. They chatted and, as doctors usually do among themselves, they spoke of their patients . . ."

She slowly blew the smoke of her cigarette out in front of her, looked at the time, glanced out of the window at the car waiting for her.

"It was in that way that he found out that father was very ill . . ."

So unexpected was this piece of information in the commonplace atmosphere of a café that Alain sat motionless, his chest constricted.

"This is what I know . . . You can do what you like with it. On the day he died, about three o'clock, father telephoned to Doctor Lachaux to ask him for a consultation . . . He insisted on seeing him straight away . . . He seemed very worried . . . Lachaux knew him, but had never examined him . . . He told father to come and see him at once, that he would find a moment to see him . . . Father went to see him . . . He was blunt . . . You know how he was sometimes.

" 'I want you to examine me and give me a straightforward yes or no . . . I don't want any encouragement . . . I don't want any more-or-less vague hopes . . . Yes or no, Doctor, nothing else . . .'

"And he opened his mouth.

"You know that he often used to suffer with his throat. He suffered from it all his life . . . We used to make fun of his hoarse voice.

"Lachaux didn't need to make a long examination.

" 'Yes or no, Doctor . . .' he repeated. 'There's too much at stake, you see, for me not to be certain now . . . Consider carefully your responsibility . . .'

"And Lachaux said yes.

"That meant that father had cancer of the throat and the beginnings of a cancer of the tongue.

"It seems that father took it very well. He chuckled. He asked how much he owed.

" 'Take advantage of it while there's some left,' he joked, opening his wallet.

"Lachaux started to speak of an operation, but father cut him short.

" 'I know! I know! I know nearly as much about it as you do. I've been expecting it for years.'

"And shaking hands with the doctor, he left.

"A few minutes later he was ringing Count d'Estier's bell.

"So I'm wondering now, if he did what he did afterwards because of his money troubles or because he knew that he was condemned to death.

"You remember how he hated illness. A cold, the 'flu made him furious. He considered the slightest illness as a weakness.

"That's all I wanted to tell you. It doesn't alter anything, because the harm's done, but it's perhaps just as well that you know.

"To end with, and while we're about it, let me add that you're behaving like a child and that you're making my position difficult. I can't see what's dishonourable in your sharing my flat, since you would never meet you know who.

"Instead you go and put yourself in a pub, and everybody in the town knows about it. You can imagine my feelings, but, I'll say again, I've never expected any good from the family.

"That's all! Goodbye! . . ."

Upon that, she swallowed the rest of her port, picked up her handbag and cigarette case, and walked towards the door which Gabriel opened for her with a bow. A few seconds later the door banged to, and the car moved off from the kerbside.

Alain had written to his mother on Sunday morning in his room at the "Three Pigeons", before going to Malouville. An undemonstrative letter, because there had never been much demonstration of affection between his mother and him. It was rather like schoolboy homework, and he took the chance to describe his room, the dining-room, the judge's clerk who ate opposite him, old Poignard always half tipsy and Mélanie's tasty cooking. He also spoke of his job with the Jaminets and the work he did, but not too much.

"It is miraculous," he concluded, "that I have found my feet so quickly and that overnight I have found a way of keeping myself. If you want any money, I can send you part of the three thousand francs that Corine gave me. I shall be paid in a fortnight's time, at the end of the month, and that will be enough for my bill at the inn.

"Give my love to Aunt Jeanne, her husband and Bertrand. I hope that your health is good. For my part the cold that I feared did not materialize . . ."

He was walking through the streets so automatically that he was surprised to find himself at the "Three Pigeons". The habit had been easily acquired. Mélanie, seeing him come in, cried:

"Is something wrong, Monsieur Alain?"

He could contain himself no more. He wanted to confide in somebody.

"My father was very ill," he murmured.

She didn't seem to understand. Perhaps, she was thinking, that since he was dead, it mattered little whether he had been ill or not.

"He had cancer in the throat. He found out half an hour before he killed himself."

"Do you think that that was the reason? Here, drink a drop of something. Yes, come on, it will do you good . . ."

She had poured him out a glass of rum.

"It's terrible how many sick people there are in the world. Particularly at our age. Luckily you've still a long way to go. Take my husband who looks as strong as an ox . . . A year ago he had to have an operation on his bladder, his prostate, as they called it . . . There are some days when he can't piss, if you'll excuse the expression, and he has to have a rubber tube fitted . . . He's frightened . . . He doesn't want to go to sleep because he maintains he won't wake up . . . It's since then that he's taken to drinking . . . You only see him downstairs, when he looks well enough, but at night, when he's suffering like a martyr with his pot, I promise you he behaves like a little boy . . . Drink it up, Monsieur Alain! . . . Of course cancer's serious . . . I had a cousin who had it in her breast and she died leaving little children . . . If he really had cancer perhaps it was just as well . . . But are they quite sure?"

"Certain."

"Go and sit down at the table . . . I'm going to make you a ham omelette to begin with . . . Don't think any more about it . . . If we're going to start worrying about who's dead and who's alive . . ."

He let himself be pushed into the dining-room, where there were only two commercial travellers at the round table, under the centre light. The red-headed judge's clerk had not yet arrived; a cat was curled up, on a chair, and a waitress in a white apron, the nicest of them, Olga, was standing at the dessert table.

"You must certainly have something to eat . . . I don't want it to be said that my boarders grow skinny . . . Give him good helpings, Olga . . . And give him half a bottle of a good wine . . ."

It was funny. All that chattering, of which he would have been incapable of repeating a single word, that he had hardly heard, seemed, in a manner of speaking, to have lulled him to sleep. He no longer felt any sharp sorrow, or had any clear conception. He only felt the aching of his heart.

"Poor father . . ."

And as he ate his soup with bread dipped in it, he imagined his father in Doctor Lachaux's consulting-room. His father who would have put a bold face on things, who would have said almost cheerfully:

"Is it yes or no?"

And then, since it was yes . . . If he had been all right, would he have gone on with the struggle? Would he have gone on fighting, for that enormous house which was a sort of chasm, for all those people who, for years and years, he had, in a manner of speaking, carried in his outstretched arms, for his wife, for Corine, for him, Alain, who had been quite satisfied to continue going to school and had never had the curiosity to find out what manner of man his father was?

It was yes! And there were seals on all the doors; and the building sites were closed, and the business was in the hands of the receiver. And all the vultures were gathering, each morning, the newspapers crushed him under the weight of treacherous rumours.

It was yes, and he didn't even have a few thousand francs of liquid money, of fresh money, as he used to call it in his better days, no money for medical care, for necessary operations. For operations which he knew would decide nothing, wouldn't cure him, would only serve each time to put off the day of reckoning for a few months.

He hadn't gone home after leaving the doctor's. Whom should he turn to? What should he do?

He had gone to Count d'Estier and possibly he had decided to play double or quits; possibly, since he was superstitious, he had said to himself as he raised the door knocker: "If this succeeds, I go on!"

It hadn't succeeded. Estier had proved to be intractable. Estier hadn't taken any notice of the revolver that his visitor was brandishing. Implacably he had thrust him out of the house.

Into the gutter! Into the gutter from which he had sprung! Into the gutter where Eugène Malou had decided to end it all, possibly because it was warmer, more friendly, more kindly than his house.

"Well, young sir?" asked Mélanie. "Let me know what you think of this omelette. It's all for you . . . You've got to eat it all, and, to follow, there's veal stew, the same as you ate on the day you arrived . . ."

He wanted to take her by the hand to thank her. The faces of the commercial travellers became misty before his eyes. Yet, he managed to eat all that she wanted him to, he even drank his wine, without realizing it, sniffing from time to time.

Was it in little eating houses like this that his father liked meeting his old friend Bourgues?

"You see you feel better . . . Now, if you take my advice, you'll go to bed with a good hot water bottle. Olga, put a hot water bottle in his bed . . . Tomorrow is another day . . . And there'll be others . . ."

He couldn't very well embrace her in front of everybody! He left the table embarrassed, said goodnight awkwardly to the two travellers and went slowly upstairs.

When Olga brought him the hot water bottle she said:

"You see, I know just what it's like, too. It's only four months ago that I lost my mother. Wouldn't you like some tea, something hot to make you sleep?"

He said no, thanked her, put the bolt on the door. He went to bed certain that he wouldn't be able to sleep. For a moment he moved his tongue about in his mouth wondering whether he too had got cancer.

In his imagination he saw Mademoiselle Germaine, on the dark pavement, taking the arm of her little old mother always with the same gesture. He saw the Foucrets, man and wife, him with his pipe, her with her little blue checkered apron, but he couldn't manage to conjure up the features of Joseph Bourgues he tried hard for a moment without success, then suddenly with no transition, he fell asleep.

When Mélanie came up to bed at ten o'clock and put her ear to the keyhole, nothing could be heard in the room but his regular breathing.

CHAPTER SEVEN

IT was on Wednesday morning that the incident of the door took place. It was very cold, a penetrating cold, and it would not be long before the low, grey, troubled sky dissolved into snow.

It still wasn't snowing by ten o'clock. Alain had heard the voices of the two sisters-in-law on the landing of the first floor. The little thin one, Albert's wife, was asking the other:

"Do you want anything from Lecoeur's?"

"No. In any case, I must go out this afternoon."

And Madame Jaminet came downstairs. Following the corridor, she passed the open door—Alain glimpsed her as she was putting on her gloves—and then, without apparent reason, she closed the door ostentatiously.

He was so surprised that he turned round to Mademoiselle Germaine. The secretary, for her part, was looking at Albert Jaminet, who was pretending to have seen or heard nothing.

Then, as soon as she was in the yard walking rapidly towards the gate, his wife realized that she had forgotten something and retraced her steps. She didn't make for the entrance but the office.

"Good morning, Mademoiselle Germaine," she said, passing near to the latter to go and speak to her husband.

Alain, not knowing what he should do in such circumstances, had stood up and bowed; she saw him; for a second her eyes were on him; yet she did not return his politeness, even by a nod of her head or a movement of her eyelids.

"Give me some money, two or three hundred francs . . ."

Albert Jaminet took them from his wallet. As she was going out, she turned to him.

"Don't forget what I told you about the door . . ."

Why was that sufficient to upset Alain for the whole day? He had wanted to close that communicating door, once, on his first day. It had been Mademoiselle Germaine who had shook her head at him, from her seat. He hadn't thought to ask why. He had understood that the door should remain open. It pleased him, because he wasn't sensitive to the cold, and the office was very small, the iron stove gave out heat like a locomotive and it wasn't long before the warmth was oppressive.

Perhaps he was mistaken, but he could have sworn that the incident of the door had been staged for his benefit. Why? He searched his mind. He knew that Madame Jaminet was not easy to get on with and he was beginning to suspect that Monsieur Albert was not as happy as he wanted to appear.

When he was called upstairs, it wasn't often with the intention of being agreeable to him. He always remained calm, serene. He never raised his voice. With his brother Emile, too, he had a certain air of humility, which didn't prevent him from sticking stubbornly to his point of view.

It was silly of course, but Alain would have liked to see Monsieur Albert with the pink and smiling wife of his brother, while Monsieur Emile got on as best he might with the little dark woman who was as snappish as he.

For a long while there was a feeling of awkwardness in the office. Then, a little before midday, the snow began to fall, the first of the year, lightly at first, then in big whirling flakes.

Mademoiselle Germaine did not go home to lunch, because she lived a good way from the centre of the town, and she brought her food to the office, warmed her coffee on the stove in a little blue enamelled coffee pot. Albert's wife had returned. No one had seen her, but she had been heard in the corridor; her husband went upstairs in his turn.

Alain hung about purposely for the opportunity to have a few words with the typist.

"Tell me, Mademoiselle Germaine, was the door of the corridor left open before I was here?"

She hesitated before answering, but, as she had blushed a little—she blushed easily—she could not withdraw:

"Yes," she said, "it was always open, because there's not much air in the office. We tried opening the skylight which gives on to the factory, but then a smell of hot oil and melted lead came in. Besides when it's very cold, it's thanks to that door that the stairway is not freezing. Several times, when it's been closed by mistake, Madame Jaminet has come and opened it . . ."

"So," he concluded, "it is thanks to me that she closed it today."

"Not necessarily. She's subject to moods. You have no need to worry."

There was another reason why that day was a bad one. It was a pity, because otherwise he would have been delighted by that first snow which was not yet lying on the pavements, but which was already whitening some roofs and the shoulders of passers by.

Returning to the "Three Pigeons" he saw, on a wall plastered with advertisements, a new poster, whose yellow ink had not yet lost its brilliance.

BANKRUPT SALE OF RICH FURNITURE

Then followed the list, the list of their furniture, because it was their property that was being put up for auction in this way. There was another poster for the house, a third for the work-shops, the material, the concrete mixers, the lorries.

He didn't think much about it while he ate, but he thought about it again in the street and he continued to be worried about that door which had been so spitefully closed. Why was he so sure that it had been done spitefully, a spite directly aimed at him?

He read the poster from one end to the other. It made him want to walk by the house where he had spent nearly eight years, in the little square, and the latter was miraculously covered with snow, there was snow too on the cupid so lightly perched on his base.

Some yellow posters, the same ones, were stuck on the gates, on the ground floor shutters. The sale would take place on the following Monday. They would open the doors wide. From Sunday onwards, the crowd would be admitted to admire the furniture, the knick-knacks, the pictures that Eugène Malou had collected and of which he was so proud.

Alain had liked practically nothing of what there had been in the house, but this hurt him nevertheless. He went on thinking about it all afternoon. Was his father's taste good? He couldn't say. When they were younger and still got on together, his sister and he lumped the whole lot together as horrors.

Their father had only liked two sorts of furniture and pieces: those of the time of Louis XIV and those of the Empire, which gave a rather surprising appearance to the house.

In the main drawing-room, for instance, he had installed a monumental fireplace for which he had paid a fortune in a château in Bourbonnais. It dated from the fifteenth century, and the grey stone was carved from top to bottom; it was a mass of different sized figures, knights in armour bearing standards, devils, beings with two horns and apocalyptic beasts.

Between the windows, on the faded carpets, there were chests of the same period, their woodwork so riddled by worm that it crumbled in the hand. There were also church pews, statues from monasteries and abbeys.

Other pieces, all mahogany and bronze, with gilded sphinxes, coverings sewn with bees, recalled the luxury of the Empire and Alain remembered a detail of which he, as a child, had been ashamed without knowing why: he had been laid in a cradle which was an approximate reproduction of that of the King of Rome.

Was his father an upstart, as certain of his schoolfellows used to hurl at his head, when they quarrelled? And why, in their mouths, did the expression have an unpleasant meaning?

Was there no merit for Eugène Malou in the effort that he had made? Was he ridiculous? Even Joseph Bourgues had smiled—affectionately it is true—speaking of his way of dressing, his over-ornate shoes, his too light suits, his loud ties.

Why had his father spent so much money in collecting furniture, objects which would have been better in a church or in a museum than in a house?

It troubled him. He would have liked to open his heart to someone about it. He vaguely felt that there were some things that he did not yet understand.

The bitterness of people against his father, for example. If he earned a lot of money, if he seemed rather too enthusiastic in doing so, it was not for love of money, to hoard it, like a miser, for he spent it with the same ardour, redistributed it about him immediately.

Was it the act of an upstart? He paid more than the price for things and people; that again was one of his manias. It would have needed little for him to say to a dealer—and had he not done so on occasion? "It's too cheap. I'll give you twice as much."

From vanity? Was Eugène Malou a boaster? He liked to mention the names of important people who were his friends, to let it be known that he was on friendly terms with this member of Parliament or that minister.

But was it possible to forget the young man he had been, who used to sell papers on the Canebière and who, in order to "get to" Paris, went from door to door selling the Indian Tea?

"I'll speak to Bourgues about it," he promised himself.

Would Bourgues be able to explain the whole mystery of his father to him? Wasn't he himself incapable of understanding all one side of the man who had been his friend?

The closed door, near him, gave him an uneasy feeling, despite himself. He felt it like an insult. It also seemed to him that Albert Jaminet did not behave quite the same towards him.

By the way, had Emile Jaminet, his brother, ever spoken to him directly? Yet he often came into the office. He had sometimes wanted to consult the cards in the files. Without a word to Alain, as though he hadn't seen him. In the morning, when he came in, he simply greeted him with a wave of his hand.

Did he begrudge his being there against his wish, in some measure under the protection of his brother?

It so happened that it was he who actually opened the celebrated door. It must have been cold in the workshop, because he had come and installed himself in the office about half past three, to correct proofs. He wiped his forehead two or three times, got up once to close the shutter of the stove, then, a quarter of an hour later, unable to stand it any more, he went and opened the door.

Mademoiselle Germaine and Alain exchanged glances. Albert Jaminet, whose back was turned towards the door, noticed nothing. The lights had been on for a long while. The snow was still falling, but by now the flakes were less consistent and on the pavements turned into a sticky mud. That was important as well.

Because, when the children returned from school, the eldest, Yvonne, Albert's daughter, was wearing galoshes over her shoes. She stopped in the corridor to take them off so as not to dirty the stairs. The galoshes were tight, and she stood for some while, first on one foot, then on the other, looking into the office.

Then, without a door being opened on the first floor, a voice came down from the landing saying sharply:

"Now then! Yvonne."

"I'm coming, Mummy."

"Straight away."

Alain's ears turned purple. He suddenly thought he understood. He remembered the glances that the young girl used to throw him as she went by in the corridor. So her mother had noticed it. But how could she attach any importance to it, how could she find any reason for fear in that childlike curiosity?

It humiliated him. It seemed to him that it classified him unfairly among "the others", people like his sister Corine, like Fabien, like some of his schoolmates who sniggeringly told dirty stories.

Madame Jaminet came downstairs. Not to go out. Not to come into the office. The only reason why she went out of her way was to shut that cursed door.

As she did it, she glanced into the room and said sharply to her husband:

"As soon as you've got a moment, oblige me by coming upstairs."

He didn't answer, remained hunched over his work, as though he expected it. It seemed to Alain that she exchanged a brief glance with her brother-in-law. Why wasn't it those two who made up a pair?

There was still only a vague threat, a general uneasiness in the house, and it affected Alain as though he sensed a catastrophe coming.

He thought of his father, of the house in the little square, of the furniture that was to be dispersed; at the same time he looked round at his peaceful surroundings, as one looks at things about to be lost.

A good ten minutes went by before Monsieur Albert got up and, with a sigh, went towards the door. He almost left it open from habit, had to come back to shut it and then went slowly upstairs.

And he stayed upstairs a long while, almost half an hour which was not his custom. The wife and husband were not in the room where the children were doing their homework, but in the drawing-room which was seldom used, just over the office, so that they could hear a murmur of voices.

When he came down again, he tried to act naturally, but he seemed anxious, ill at ease, so much so that his brother looked at him curiously.

Albert went back to his seat, opened a file containing some estimates, tried to work for a while, gave it up and opened the door leading to the workshop saying:

"Can you come for a moment, Emile?"

Alain knew he was the cause of all that. He wondered in what way he had been lacking towards Madame Jaminet. He had always been very polite to her. He would willingly have gone shopping for her, so much did he like the firm and wanted to stay there.

The two men stood in a corner of the workshop, as far as possible from the workmen, and spoke in undertones. Mademoiselle Germaine must have guessed what was happening, because she seemed embarrassed and typed violently, as though she feared that her companion might question her. Probably she knew things that he didn't know.

It was nearly six o'clock. Only a few more minutes, and Alain would put his files away, and slip on his overcoat after having tidied up his drawers. Why did he have a presentiment that today would not go off like other days?

He could only see Albert Jaminet's back, but, from the way his shoulders were hunched, he guessed that he wasn't feeling very pleased with himself and that, if he was still holding out, it was to satisfy his conscience.

Already Mademoiselle Germaine was taking off her jersey and putting it away in the cupboard. Alain was thinking about getting himself ready, when Albert returned alone from the workshop, where his brother was pretending to be interested in the working of a machine.

"Will you stay for a moment, Monsieur Alain?"

The young man's legs weakened under him. To have done with it, he nearly said:

"I understand ... I'm going. ..."

Hadn't he felt that it was something of a miracle to find this position straight away, to slip so easily into the cosy life in the office? He was already attached to his files. The evening before it was he who had taken down a last minute article dictated by telephone from Paris.

"Good night, Monsieur Albert. Good night, Monsieur Alain."

She held out her hand before putting her glove on and turned her head away at the sight of the tears in his eyes.

There were now only the two men in the room, or rather a man and an adolescent. Was Alain mistaken? He could have sworn that he sensed someone outside the door leading to the corridor, that Madame Jaminet was there listening, spying.

Monsieur Albert must have been thinking the same thing, because he looked at the door two or three times coughing before beginning to speak.

Alain felt a bit sorry for him. He would have liked to help him. Looking at his employer he tried hard to smile bravely.

"Listen, Monsieur Malou . . ."

It was the first time he called him that.

"When you came here last week, I was certainly a bit surprised but with things being what they are, I considered that there was no reason why you shouldn't earn your living. Despite certain objections . . ."

Those of Monsieur Emile, of course!

"I wanted to give you a chance and I must admit that I have no criticism to make of your work . . ."

Now, of the two, he was the most disturbed. Alain knew it. He was going to leave. Everything had to begin again.

"At that time, I was unaware of certain things which it is difficult for me to talk about and I think you will realize what I mean. Unhappily you are not the only member of your family here. Don't think I'm blaming you, because it's obviously not your fault. But we are in business, Monsieur Malou. We must be all the more circumspect because we have some rather special customers. You know that we do most of our work for the Bishop's palace and for a certain number of religious orders. . . ."

"I understand."

The other gestured to indicate that he had something more to say.

"Even today, there was an unfortunate scene of which you are as yet unaware. It happened this afternoon, and my wife learned the details of it by telephone . . ."

Alain remembered having heard the telephone ring on the first floor, a little before or a little after four o'clock.

"I would rather that you excuse me from telling you about it. Anyway, it is no business of mine, and there are others who will undertake to inform you . . ."

"My sister?"

Monsieur Albert nodded.

"I shall only add that Madame Fabien is a school friend of my wife, her best friend. And now I'm sure you will agree with me when I say that it is better, for you and for us . . ."

"Thank you."

"Just a moment . . ."

For Alain was already walking towards the coat stand.

"Obviously, since I have nothing to blame you for, I owe you a month's salary . . ."

He wanted to add something else, but he looked at the door, and the presence that he sensed behind that door prevented him from speaking. He had taken out some bank-notes, not from his wallet but from the till, because it was office expenses.

"I'm very sorry," he admitted in a low voice.

"Thank you, Monsieur Albert. I understand perfectly. I realize that the wrong's on my side."

He didn't want to cry in front of him and he felt the tears welling up in his eyes. In the workshop, Monsieur Emile had his back to him.

"You will find all the cards up to date. In the left hand drawer I have put all the current changes of address. The list is complete."

That was all. If it weren't for the door, they would probably have said more, but they contented themselves with shaking hands.

"Good-bye, Monsieur Albert. And thank you!"

Yes, thank you. He owed it to him. He went out clumsily, bumping into the doorpost, and, once in the yard, he turned up the collar of his overcoat, sniffed, thrust his hands into his pocket.

The melting snow was still falling, and he didn't feel like hanging about in the street. He wanted to lie down on his bed, to go to bed without eating.

But did he still live at the "Three Pigeons"? In his mind the printing works and the inn were united, the one being as it were an extension of the other.

Was he going to tell Mélanie straight away that he had lost his job? Would she understand that it was not his fault? That he had done all he could?

It seemed as though they had purposely chosen the road he followed to stick up the greatest number of yellow posters. Never before had he noticed so many fences, so many hoardings. On all of them the poster stood out, newer than the others. He saw an old gentleman who, despite the weather, was taking notes in a diary, under an umbrella.

He almost went in through the yard and directly up to his room, but he was frightened of annoying Mélanie, because he had never acted in that way. He usually walked through the bar, where she never failed to speak to him, to tell him what was on the menu. This was the slack time, almost empty, for the inn was busiest in the morning at market time. There were only two or three old men playing cards with the sleepy proprietor.

The door bell sounded. He walked down the steps, saw the fat woman come out of her kitchen and straight away, by her expression, he knew that here too something had happened.

"Is it you already, young sir?" she said, throwing her dishcloth on the sink.

She often called him that, very affectionately, with a touch of condescension.

"Come through here for a moment . . ."

She led the way into the dining-room where there was only Olga finishing laying the tables.

"Leave us alone, Olga, my dear."

Mélanie did what he had never seen her do: she sat down in a room reserved for her boarders. She sat down as though for a long conversation and signed to him to sit down opposite her. The napkins, with their numbered rings, were in their places on the table, and the bottles of wine with the names of their owners.

"No one's said anything to you yet, I suppose?"

He could think of nothing to say immediately and putting her finger to her lips, she said:

"Hush! Don't speak too loud. She's upstairs . . ."

She moved her chair forward, her knees touching Alain's.

"When she arrived here an hour ago, I didn't then know what had happened. To tell the truth, I didn't know her. I had already seen her go by, but I wouldn't have recognized her.

" 'What time does my brother come home?' she asked me without even a good afternoon.

"She came in a taxi. She had kept it waiting. I guessed who she was by a certain likeness in the expression.

"Then she asked me if I could give her a room near yours and, when I wanted to know for how long, she replied that she didn't know.

"She looked rather queer, her face all smeary. She had been

crying, for the black on her eyelashes had run and her lipstick had spread.

" 'To tell the truth, I haven't many rooms . . .'

" 'In that case, will you perhaps put a bed up for me in my brother's.'

"I wasn't going to do that, you understand. I thought about the taxi which was still waiting, and, despite myself, it upsets me to see a meter turning for nothing.

"Then I said to her:

" 'I'll give you a room for the moment and, for the rest, we'll see when Monsieur Alain gets home.'

"She had two big, very heavy cases taken up. I think she threw herself on her bed fully dressed. A little while after she rang, and she asked Olga to take her up something strong.

"Wait! Don't go up to her now. She didn't ask for a glassful but the bottle. So that, by now, I'll bet anything she's asleep . . ."

He listened as though in a dream, with no response. She had laid her hand on his knee, and he felt its warmth through the material.

"There's one who would have done better to go to Paris with her mother! In that way, at any rate, she wouldn't have caused you to worry. I learned the story hardly a quarter of an hour ago, from someone who saw it all happen—he's just gone out—because he's the boy in the grocer's shop just opposite the house where this . . . happened.

"You know Doctor Fabien's house, don't you?"

He had passed it quite a time ago now. It was a big square building, of the XVIIth century, with three tall windows and a porch with several steps. It stood in the Rue du Palais, and its garden, at the bottom of which Fabien had had his clinic built, gave directly on to the park.

Opposite, in the street itself, there was a grocer's shop with two windows where piles of lemons, oranges and bananas could always be seen, for it was kept by some Spaniards.

"I don't know why they were so rash, or what happened before. According to what they say, Madame Fabien has been fed up with it for a long while. I am sorry to tell you all this, but it's known by everybody in town and it's just as well that you are aware of it.

"Fabien has always been a philanderer. I imagine that his wife,

115

who doesn't go in for that sort of thing, had resigned herself to it. But on condition that it didn't become a threat to her, you understand.

"One day with one, one week with another, it wasn't very important provided she felt sure of her position.

"And as long as your father was there—don't take what I say the wrong way—it was a sort of guarantee for her.

"Anyway, this afternoon, when it was already dark and there were only the windows of the grocer's shop lighting a bit of the pavement, the doctor returned home in his car. Instead of stopping it just in front of the steps, he left it two houses farther off in the darkness.

"He went indoors, perhaps to get something, perhaps to say that he wouldn't be back for dinner.

"Hector, the boy from the grocer's claims that Madame Fabien was watching for him from behind the curtains. And, just then, his daughters came home from school. They recognized their father's car and they went up to it.

"Your sister was inside waiting for him. It seems that the doctor had got into the habit of taking her everywhere with him.

"It's impossible to know if the little girls talked indoors. It's quite likely.

"And then a big scene started. Hector claims that their shadows could be seen coming and going like marionettes on the curtains.

"What is important and what not everybody knows, young sir —let me finish and above all don't start crying—is that Madame Fabien, whose name was Hantot before she married, has a lot more money than her husband and it was with her dowry that he had the clinic built.

"She seems soft and insipid when you see her ordinarily, but I know by experience that they are the worst of all when they let themselves go.

"He's one of those men who can't deny themselves their pleasure; but who, afterwards, begin to be frightened of the consequences.

"The car was still beside the pavement with your sister in it. When the door of the house opened it wasn't Fabien who came out, but his wife, and she strode towards the car.

"She must have been in quite a state to make a scandal like that in the street, because she's been well brought up. She opened the car door. She began to talk. Hector, from his doorway, couldn't yet see your sister hidden in the darkness. Then, suddenly, Madame Fabien leaned over, seized her arm, and pulled her out of the car by force.

"She went on speaking, in a voice that was becoming more and more a shout. The other began to shout in her turn, while passers-by stopped and curtains could be seen moving at the windows.

"They are still talking about it in the town now, you can bet! And they'll talk about it still for a long while to come!

"All this time, Fabien stayed prudently at home, and the two women went on squabbling away, cursing each other like market women.

"Finally, Madame Fabien tore the fur coat off your sister—it seems that it was her husband who bought it for her—and threw it on the ground, in the mud, then began to stamp on it.

"People didn't dare go too near, because they were embarrassed, and Hector, who supplies the Fabiens, didn't leave his doorway.

"They probably scratched each other a bit, he told me, but I'm not sure, because it all happened in the dark.

"Anyway your sister ended up by going off without her coat, slipping along against the houses, while the other one went back into her house and slammed the door.

"I know Fabien's reputation, and I'm sure he'll drop your sister. She has already done him a lot of harm professionally.

"What I wanted to say to you, before you go upstairs, is don't let yourself be drawn into anything. She shouldn't have come here immediately afterwards, and I feel that she's hoping to hook on to you.

"It's none of your business, my young sir. You are a decent young chap, full of pluck, I'm beginning to know you. You've had your share of misfortune, and nobody holds anything against you, personally.

"But if you start worrying about that girl . . . I don't want to make you unhappy, but I feel very much obliged to tell you that I won't keep her in this house. She's not the type for the 'Three Pigeons'. Women like that, you see, cause trouble wherever they go.

"Come on, you've been very brave. You haven't even cried. Olga must get on with laying the table, because it won't be long before the gentlemen arrive.

"If I can give you a bit of advice, don't go upstairs now. You're going to come into the bar and have a small glass of something and afterwards you'll have your dinner quietly as though nothing had happened. They won't dare say anything to you, even if they know about it yet. And, if someone starts on you, it's I who'll answer him.

"As for your sister, when you see her, you can tell her that she is big enough to make her own way and that she would do well to take a change of air. The air here is no good for her. Everybody will be on Madame Fabien's side, and I can't blame them. Come on! Come with me. There's another day tomorrow . . ."

Awkwardly he tried to smile to thank her. It had only needed a few hours! And there was a door closed on him by some ill-disposed hand who, that morning, had given him an intuition of the catastrophe.

If only he had realized that there was a whole town around him, a town which now, in his eyes, took on the aspect of a character as mysterious as it was threatening.

Not only did he not know the town, but he did not know his father. He had innocently believed that he was going to settle himself cosily into the community and mingle in the everyday round.

He could still hear the voice of Bourgues, on Sunday night, repeating his father's words: "I'll get them."

The words were beginning to have a meaning for him. Whom? he had asked. Get whom? Now, he understood that it probably meant "All of them".

Not Mademoiselle Germaine, nevertheless. Not Mélanie. Not even poor Albert Jaminet. He made exceptions. He realized that he had a vast sorting out to do and in the meanwhile he allowed himself to be led like a child into the low bar where old Poignard, who suffered with his bladder, was playing dominoes while drinking some vin rosé.

"You're going to have a little glass of something, only one, and you will stay here while I go and look after my cooking."

He was beginning to doubt Bourgues himself. The idea of

going upstairs, presently, to find himself face to face with his sister revolted him.

Had she really emptied the bottle? Would she be drunk? He had seen her like that once when she had come home very late: she had walked backwards and forwards through the rooms throwing her clothes on the carpets, becoming more and more naked, white and blonde, so immodest, so shameless, that several days had gone by before he dared look at her.

She had hurled coarse language at him, that night. She had jeered at him, then, suddenly, right in the middle of the room, she had been sick, and he had had to take care of her, after having thrown a dressing-gown on her body which she had spitefully pushed away.

That was possibly the worst memory of his life. Who can say? Worse than the sight of his father dead in a chemist's shop.

Lunel, a young man of about twenty, who worked in a laboratory and had board and lodgings at the "Three Pigeons", arrived first, then, immediately after, the red-headed clerk of the court.

The lodgers never shook hands. It was a sort of agreement. They said good morning and good evening, and each one took his place at the round table; they passed round the soup tureen, then the dishes: Lunel, more often than not, read as he ate.

Soon, Alain would be obliged to go upstairs. Suddenly, with the cheese, a desire to run away from it all came over him. He would leave without even going to his room, without saying a word. He would rush to the station and catch the first train to arrive, not for Paris, where there were Malous, but for any provincial town.

"Everything all right, young sir?"

Mélanie put her hand on his shoulder, and he blushed as though she had guessed.

She said to him in an undertone:

"Above all don't let yourself be trampled on!"

His retreat was cut off. He was being watched. They watched him into the corridor, then on to the stairs. He turned the switch. He was going to push open the door of number 13 when a voice from the neighbouring room asked:

"Is that you, Alain?"

He gave himself a last moment of freedom. He stood still and didn't answer. But Corine had recognized his step: the springs of a bed squeaked. There were footsteps, a door which opened.

She was wearing a black silk dress, all creased, of which she had unhooked the bodice, and her features were puffed up, her eyes red, her mouth bad, her hair in disorder.

"What are you waiting for? . . . Come in . . ."

He was sure that Mélanie was listening at the bottom of the stairs.

CHAPTER EIGHT

THEY would probably have stayed talking all night if they hadn't been interrupted. And of that long conversation which was often nothing more than a monologue on his sister's part, but which at one time seemed to be developing into a sordid scene like the one that had taken place in the street, outside Fabien's house, of those hours during which his blood was constantly in his head, his memory was afterwards to be clear and incoherent both at once.

Even the next morning, he could only remember snatches, like tunes and rhythms in music, and they remained confused in his memory; among those snatches, some constantly came back to him despite himself in a tiresome repetition that he had all the trouble in the world to get rid of.

The first thing he saw as he went in was a tin tray on the floor with a bottle and a glass. He noticed immediately that the bottle of brandy was still half full, and he sensed that the glass hadn't been used and that the brandy had been drunk from the neck of the bottle. On the same tray, were stubbed-out cigarette ends, with traces of lipstick on the paper, and smoke was wreathed around the electric light bulb hanging by its flex.

Why did it seem to him that the room was more wretched, less friendly than his? There were the same little dark red squares on the floor, the same whitewashed walls, an identical window in its embrasure with its too short flowered cretonne curtains.

The iron bedstead was black with a white counterpane, Corine's two cases, placed in a corner, had not been opened. She had thrown her wet hat in another corner; she had possibly stamped on it in her temper.

He saw all that with one glance, and the little crucifix above

the bed, a coloured print of Millet's *Angelus* on the other wall.
It was warmer here than in his room, and it wasn't just an
impression, he understood why later; a stove pipe, coming from
the ground floor, and running right through the room from
bottom to top, was burning hot.

"Is that all you have to say to me?" asked Corine peevishly,
when she had closed the door and saw him standing in the middle
of the room.

She walked over to one of her cases and tried to open it but she
first had to find her keys in her handbag.

"I suppose they've told you everything?"

From her case, overflowing with a disordered jumble of under-
wear and clothes, she drew out a nightdress, a dressing-gown, a
pair of blue heelless slippers, then, as she spoke, she slipped her
dress over her head, displaying a pink petticoat.

"What did they say to you? They told you downstairs, didn't
they?"

He knew that she would undress completely before putting on
her nightdress, and he turned his head away.

"Anyway, I gave that Madeleine her money's worth, I can tell
you! Her name's Madeleine . . . and do you know what that fat
slug's family used to call her, what she wanted her husband to go
on calling her? . . . Chouchou, if you please . . . You can bet your
life I called her Chouchou, and I also told her that she stank so
much that Fabien couldn't sleep in the same bed with her and
that, every morning, her maid had to hold her nose when she
brought her breakfast to her in her room . . ."

He turned round too quickly. She was still in the process of
pulling down her nightdress which had caught on her wide hips,
and that put her in a bad temper.

"You can sit down. It's exasperating to see you standing there
in the middle of the room . . ."

There was an armchair covered in red rep and he placed
himself there, opposite the bed into which she finally slipped,
arranging the pillow behind her back and lighting a fresh
cigarette.

There was a pause. He could remember a wait which seemed
very long to him, during which both of them watched each other,
not on the sly, but almost coldly. It was then that he saw that his
sister's eyebrows, if she did not pluck them, would have been

very wide and would almost have met on the bridge of her nose, where the skin could be seen swelling and slightly smoother.

Because the wait was getting unbearable, he murmured:

"What are you going to do?"

"You don't imagine I'm going to give up my place to her, do you?"

"Talking about places, I've lost mine."

"Because of me?"

He nodded and she scowled:

"The bitch!"

"Listen, Corine . . ."

"Listen, Alain, if you've come here to read me a lesson, I'll tell you straight away you're wasting your time . . . I know you've always been a bit naïve but now's not the time to be blue eyed . . . I hate that bitch, do you understand . . . And because one of us must give up her place to the other, it'll be she . . . You must have thought that you were going to be rid of me, that I would go to mother in Paris . . . Admit it, that's what you were thinking, weren't you? . . . Well then! I'm not! Even if I didn't love Paul —and I do—I would stay if only to annoy her, only to show her who I am . . . If only you could have seen that so-called well-brought-up woman hurl herself on me, spitting out all the bad language she could lay her tongue to . . .

"I'm a whore, perhaps . . . All right . . . But I love Paul, I do! . . . I don't hold him with my money . . . I love Paul, and he loves me, do you understand that, you little idiot who never understands anything?

"For you've never understood, and now less than ever . . . If you could see your face, if you could see your eyes . . .

"That reminds me—let me tell you straight away, because I'm frightened of forgetting—that mother wrote to me about you . . . You haven't written to her, have you?"

"On Sunday . . ."

"She hadn't received your letter then . . . She hadn't got your address . . . She reminded me that you were still only a minor . . . You need a guardian and a deputy guardian . . . You must go and see Maître Desbois who will tell you what to do . . . Mother will be your guardian and probably your uncle Jules your deputy guardian . . . Now, tell me exactly what they told you, what they're saying in the town."

"I don't know . . . Downstairs, I learnt that there had been a scene between you and . . ."

"Between me and Chouchou . . . What next?"

"Nothing . . . They told me you were upstairs . . ."

"And you took care not to come up straight away . . . Admit you were ashamed . . . Go on, admit it, you fool! . . . Your employers certainly told you something too . . ."

"Very vaguely . . . Madame Jaminet is Madame Fabien's friend . . . I think they telephoned each other . . ."

"Pack of blackguards . . . But I shall have the last word, you see! You needn't worry . . . It's my turn now to ask you what you are going to do . . ."

"I don't know . . ."

"You would do best to go to mother . . ."

He heard himself say—and it astonished him as well—with a firmness that was quite unpremeditated:

"No."

"I was forgetting that you hate mother too . . ."

"I don't hate her."

"You hate her . . . You hate me . . . There's only your father who . . ."

Yes, that was how it must have started. He didn't remember the exact sequence. Neither did he remember what Corine had said at first about their father. Moreover, she didn't say "our father" but "your father" as though they weren't brother and sister.

About the same time, she drank a large mouthful of brandy, lit a fresh cigarette. She was sitting up in bed, her expression hard, and although she was looking at him in the face, she seemed to be speaking for herself alone.

"He wouldn't have been upset by what's happened, don't you worry, because he was used to it . . ."

"Used to what?"

"Used to what, you ask . . . To all that sort of muck, my poor idiot brother . . . If you think he didn't spend his life in muck! . . . You think that I ought to spend my time other than I do, don't you? . . . Oh! I don't forget that I've been beautifully brought up . . . In the best convents and in the most expensive schools. . . . Except that I was moved from one to the other from time to time because they made life unbearable there for me . . .

Not because of me, either . . . Because of your father . . . And also because there were times when there was no more money . . .

"I still wonder how you managed to live for so long in the house without noticing anything . . . You're young, I know, but that's not a reason . . . At your age, I knew more than you, I assure you . . . And I realized it, too . . . It's true I didn't go about with my eyes and ears stopped up . . .

"Admit it, that's what you used to do . . . so that you should be left in peace! . . . Because you didn't want to know! . . . If you think I didn't understand you . . . It needed father's death and all that followed to make you look facts in the face . . . And not even then! . . . What did you find to do? . . . You went begging for a place as the meanest clerk in a little printing works . . . And you probably said thank you when they chucked you out . . .

"They won't chuck me out, my lad, do you hear? . . . They all think I'm going to leave . . . They think they've got rid of me. Well, I'm going to stay . . . And tomorrow or the day after, Fabien will come and ask my pardon . . . He'll beg for it. . . . He'll crawl at my feet . . . It's not worth while telling you why because you would blush again like a girl. He needs me. . . . He won't have a good night's sleep, he won't! It'll take weeks, perhaps months, but it's Chouchou who'll go . . . Despite the children! . . . Despite everything. . . . Despite the clinic . . .

"And if your father were still alive, he'd say I was right . . . Do you imagine that he never got kicks in the backside? That he wasn't chucked out more than a hundred times?"

"Listen, Corine . . ."

But she was listening to nothing. It was she who was speaking and her voice was becoming harder and more excited. Several times, during the evening, the neighbours tapped on the walls or on the ceiling to ask them to be quiet, but she didn't care.

"So! I'm a whore . . . And what did our father marry? . . . Yes, I'm speaking of mother . . . You don't want to know anything about all that . . . But you'll know it, all the same, because you've got to, because, otherwise, people will go on laughing at you . . . He wasn't very rich at that time . . . He was just beginning to grow his claws . . . He was working for a little newspaper where the articles cost more if they didn't appear than if they did . . . You don't understand that either? . . . A blackmailing paper if you prefer it . . . And Dorchain, the member of Parliament, was his boss . . . And your father was very proud of sleeping with a member of parliament's wife . . .

"They were caught, both of them . . . You are wondering, perhaps, how I found out all the details? . . . You are forgetting that when you were still a kid, about five or six years ago, there was a quarrel between us and the Dorimonts . . . There were some pretty scenes there, too . . . Although it doesn't stop mother from accepting aunt Jeanne's hospitality now . . .

"Well, it was aunt Jeanne who told me . . . She detested our mother then, and she used any means . . .

"Do you know that after getting his divorce, Dorchain said to your father, 'Now, my poor chap, you're landed with her!'

"And father had her for twenty-two years . . . For twenty-two years she kept her hold on him, because, in spite of her dreamy appearance, she's a woman who knows what she wants . . . And she got the jewellery that she was after . . . And she gave the receptions that she had dreamed of giving . . . And she had her personal chauffeur, her lady's maid, her butler . . .

"And we lived through all that, my poor frightened Alain!

"They dressed me like an expensive doll, I had the finest toys in the world, for Christmas they didn't think twice about buying me a horse and giving me a riding master.

"But when, a little later, I went to boarding-school, my fellow pupils avoided speaking to me after a while . . . Their parents told them not to . . . Because I was Malou's daughter! . . .

"So you think, as Chouchou does, that I'm a whore . . .

"I could tell you stories all the night . . . The most extraordinary thing is that you are the only one who doesn't know them . . . People tell them to each other, here as everywhere else . . . And they've been strewn over little newspapers of the type your father started in . . .

"Ready money! . . . That's what he used to say . . . We were always short of ready money, and you don't know, do you, how it was obtained at the last minute? . . .

"By the way, what have you done with the case of papers?"

"It's in my room."

"You must give it to me . . . You're too silly to know how to use them . . . You wouldn't even understand . . . While I'll probably find something with which to rub their noses in their own shit . . .

125

"Are you shocked? Did you think they spoke any other way in the family when one of those fine scenes developed, at the end of which mother would sometimes go and stay at a hotel for a few days?

"You didn't know that either, did you, you idiot?

"And there you are, as stiff as a poker, looking at me with horror . . . And it wouldn't take much for you to go and join the others' side, would it? . . .

"The others . . . All of them such as they are . . ."

Words that Alain had already heard uttered by Joseph Bourgues. But the old convict hadn't that excited voice, nor a face contorted with hatred.

He would like to have told himself that his sister was drunk. He could easily see that although she had been drinking, she nevertheless kept full possession of her wits.

She was, in a way, pouring out her heart, getting rid of all she had never said, except in snatches, during her quarrels with her mother, except too, possibly, in private conversation with Fabien.

He was appalled. Memories came back to him, images: for example his sister when she came back, in breeches and boots, from riding, her whip in her hand, her features still indeterminate and with blonde curls escaping from under her jockey's cap.

He remembered magnificent teas to which she invited her friends, while he was still too young, all those little girls being served by serious faced waiters in white gloves.

"You must remember one thing, you see, Alain, that we are not, and we have never been, people like the others, and that the others hate us and despise us.

"Even those who came to eat at our table! Even those who had need of father!

"They used to say with a little understanding smile: 'I've been invited to dinner with the Malous! . . .' or again: 'I'm going to spend the weekend at the Malous' country house. . . .'

"And those words were always accompanied by a wink. They came to our place as they went to the theatre. They came to see, from close up, in his own house, the man who thought he was the king of the building trade, his wife who imagined she was a society woman . . .

"Don't think I'm exaggerating. Father allowed the expression to be printed in a newspaper: *The King of Building* . . . He pretended to laugh at it, but he believed it . . .

"I remember a sort of prospectus he had printed on very expensive paper to send to all the officials and to all the town halls . . .

"Malouville—doesn't that word make you laugh?—Malouville was only to be an experiment, a sample of what could be done . . . Your father dreamed of getting a law passed that all the towns of at least fifty thousand inhabitants should be obliged to build a model city like Malouville in their neighbourhood . . .

"You'll find the prospectus in the case . . . It speaks of hovels, of filthy suburbs, of the necessity of sowing the seed of the towns of tomorrow throughout all France . . .

"Malou was supposed to create all that . . . He was to be allowed to float a huge loan, a national loan . . . And he, with all these millions, these hundreds of millions . . .

"Don't you laugh? Don't you even smile? There were people who came to our house and who also pretended to take all that seriously . . .

"Then, after having flashed these hundreds of millions before them, they were tapped for a few thousand franc notes, sufficient to pay the butler who had just served them and who sometimes went months without receiving a centime of his wages . . .

"What about my marriages, Alain? . . . You remember my marriages, don't you?

"You used to go to school, to college . . . You came home and you shut yourself up in your room to study or to read and I bet you used to stick your fingers in your ears. . . .

"At table, you looked so absent minded, you were so little with the family, that I've often seen father look at you with astonishment, then shake his head and sigh.

"After all, perhaps it suited him since you were his favourite. Perhaps he thought that you would become a real man of the world.

"Ten times at least they tried to marry me off. The age didn't count, I swear to you! . . . As long as it was a brilliant match . . . Either money, a lot of money, or else a title . . . Or else a leading position in politics.

"And dinner followed dinner . . . And the gentleman was nursed along. . . . And it always ended in the same way . . . One fine day he would disappear never to return . . .

"What could I have brought to them, eh?

"I would have brought them a father-in-law, Eugène Malou, and a mother-in-law who thought she was a great lady because she had jewels and sat twenty or thirty people down to her dinner table . . .

"You've never seen them squabbling, have you, over putting the cards with the guests' names in their places? . . . What was the rank of this one in the Légion d'honneur? . . . did a minister take precedence over an academician? . . . Monseignors were the only ones we have never entertained, because bishops and archbishops are cautious . . .

"What do you expect to come out of such a muckheap, eh? Look at me as though I were a monster as much as you like, but get it firmly fixed in your head that none of us is any better . . .

"I've had lovers, and it all began with a friend of father's . . ."

"Be quiet, will you?"

"All the same, you must get used to it . . . I've slept with Count d'Estier, for example . . ."

He rose, red with anger:

"Corine . . ."

"So what? . . . Sit down . . . Be quiet! . . . Do you think your father had any scruples? He slept with the majority of his typists and sometimes things were made a bit difficult for him. . . . He tried to sleep with one of my friends who was my age . . ."

"You're lying!"

"Just as you like . . . Ask mother or Aunt Jeanne . . . Ask anyone . . . It's obviously not what's taught in schools, and you still see life and people through your school . . ."

He was aghast. He stared hard at her and he would have given anything to make her keep quiet . . . Yet, he listened . . . Something kept him in this bedroom, in front of this girl who was his sister and who, to keep herself at a certain pitch of excitement, put her lips from time to time to the neck of the brandy bottle.

"We are not even upstarts, because real upstarts have money,

128

and we have only ever had debts, in a manner of speaking we have lived off our debts . . .

"And it is precisely for that that a dazzling display was necessary . . . Your father thought it was necessary to dazzle people and he didn't know what to think up next . . .

"Has our house ever seemed like a real home to you, eh? Have you ever felt comfortable there anywhere but in your room? Or even there? They thrust a sort of catafalque on you for a bed because it had coats of arms above it . . .

"I often wondered why father put up with mother's temper; why he didn't divorce her in his turn, and I think that finally I discovered the reason: first of all it was because she had been the wife of a member of parliament, a man who had been a minister and who might become so again . . . Next—and it's probably the most important—because he needed her. He knew little about polite society while, for several years before him, she had led a life of receptions and she was acquainted with the elementary rules . . .

"We are nonetheless the grandchildren of our grandfather, Alain. And we have nothing in common with all these people around us; we can expect nothing from them, remember that. . . . They hate us and despise us . . . That's why I'll not let myself be pushed about by a Chouchou . . .

"I'm lucky in having something that she hasn't got . . ."

She nearly made an obscene gesture but it was only sketched. "I'll use it and I'll win the fight. I'll be Madame Fabien, you see. They'll receive me in their homes, and what does it matter if they whisper in corners . . .

"Do you know what the Countess d'Estier did before she was countess?"

"She was at the Casino de Paris, not even as a dancer but as a nude. Moreover, that's probably the reason why Estier put money in father's business, to avoid father starting a campaign of rumours in the papers.

"It didn't stop her being Countess . . .

"Are you beginning to understand?"

He didn't answer. His head was spinning. The air smelt of tobacco and the brandy, and sometimes it seemed to him that it was he who was drunk. Sometimes his gaze lighted on Millet's *Angelus*, and those people, standing in a field with their hands joined in prayer, appeared to him to belong to a dream world.

It seemed to him that everything about him was dark, that outside the white cube of the bedroom there was nothing but blackness, cold, melted snow.

He was annoyed with himself for not standing up, for not defending his father against this girl, who from the depths of her bed, searched for the crudest and most spiteful words, the most revolting image.

"Be quiet, Corine," he begged.

"You'll come back and talk to me when you've read the papers in the case."

"How were you able to read them?"

"Because I opened it one day when father wasn't there."

"You went through his things?"

"Why not?"

He gazed at her bewildered. He couldn't conceive how he could have lived beside her without guessing at her character.

"I could also tell you that mother lied, that, if she went off to Paris so lightheartedly, it's because she had the major part of the jewels with her. She would never have allowed them to be sold, you can bet. I know her too well. She used to fight bitterly for them. Sometimes, I've heard your father beg her to allow him to pawn at least some of them to help him out of a nasty hole . . .

"'And what should I do if anything were to happen to you?' she replied. 'What would happen to the children?'

"She abandoned us nevertheless . . .

"Both of them cheated, that's something else you don't know. Each one was trying to hoard money . . .

"It's not worth crying about . . ."

"I'm not crying."

It was the beginning of a cold which made his eyes so red and prickled his nostrils.

The bottle was empty, and Corine was on the point of asking her brother to go downstairs and fetch her another. But there was not a sound in the house. It was very late. Long intervals elapsed without their hearing footsteps in the street.

"You do what you like, become a clerk like your brother

if you think fit . . . Only, I warn you, you won't prevent me from doing what I please . . .

"Possibly it is I who take most after father . . . He fought against them all his life . . . I bet that if he hadn't been ill, if he hadn't found out that he was condemned to death, he would have gone on . . .

"Do you know what I think he went to ask d'Estier for? Just enough to end his life peacefully in a clinic . . ."

"That's not true . . ."

"As you like . . . That's still my idea . . . So, when he saw that even that was impossible . . ."

"Be quiet, Corine! . . ."

He wanted to strike her. In a few hours she had just trampled on everything that he had known up to then. He thought of Joseph Bourgues who had spoken such a different language.

He had come back stronger from their night walk along the road beyond Genette, with the feeling that from henceforth he was a man.

Yet hadn't Bourgues and Corine said roughly the same thing? Differently, in a different way.

Corine was full of hatred. She had spat out her hatred and it had splashed him; he felt physically sick.

Neither of them took any notice of the time.

"Even his illness . . ."

He nearly used force to make her be silent, he was so frightened of what was to follow.

"You won't believe me, but I know what I'm saying. I've spoken a lot to Paul about it. His cancer . . ."

He opened his mouth to say no, for he guessed.

"It's the result of an old attack of syphilis . . ."

He closed his eyes and sat motionless. That word, for him, was the most atrocious of all.

"Don't be frightened for yourself . . . I've found out about it . . . I've done better . . . I had a Wassermann test and the result was negative . . . It happened a long time ago, you see, at the time of his first wife . . . And, since you were born after me . . ."

Now, he was crying. One word was sufficient, a word which henceforth would haunt him all his life. He had fallen over the arm of his chair, with his face hidden in the crook of his arm, sobbing.

131

"You're as stupid as they are! . . . You listened to all the rest, which was much more serious . . . And then, a little word like that . . ."

"Be quiet!"

He had shouted with all his might. He was standing up, with tears running down his cheeks, his mouth twisted. He clenched his fists. If he had had some object in his hand he would probably have struck the girl with all his force, possibly he might have killed her!

"Be quiet, do you hear? . . . If you don't, I don't know what I shall do . . ."

And with his face thrust up against hers, his fists still clenched, he panted, without managing to catch his breath:

"You're a . . . you're a . . . you're a . . ."

She exhaled her breath ladened with alcohol and nicotine into his face. She was beautiful, she knew it. But not for him. He hated her face with its sensuous lips, quivering nostrils, eyes full of sparkle.

"A whore! . . ." she completed, laughing. "Oh yes, that's the word . . . Chouchou shouted it at me a little while ago . . . You shout it too, young Malou, son of Malou . . ."

Then she burst out laughing, a laugh that swelled her throat and that she couldn't stop.

He was threatening:

"Be quiet!"

She went on laughing with that laugh that was making him mad. She wasn't his sister, she wasn't a woman laughing, she was a female, a disgusting female, who, for fun, from hatred, from spite, had just dirtied all that remained to him in the world.

"Be quiet!"

He wanted to be calm. He was almost in supplication before that eternal laugh which was becoming hysterical, before that swelling throat, that milky skin of her neck, those breasts that were protruding from her nightdress.

"Be quiet!"

Then someone knocked at the door and he froze. The laugh froze too, so suddenly, that the room seemed quite empty. He had to swallow. He could not speak at once in his natural voice. The knock came again, little taps both discreet and commanding at the same time.

"Who is it?" he managed to get out, running his hand through his hair.

"Open the door . . . It's me, Mélanie . . ."

He hesitated a moment. It seemed to him that his sister was signalling to him not to open, but the landlady's voice carried such conviction that he obeyed mechanically. He drew the little bolt, painted in the same green as the door. It was Mélanie who pushed it open.

She said:

"It stinks in here . . ."

She only glanced at the bed, very quickly.

"Don't you realize that it's gone two o'clock in the morning and that you're preventing the whole house from sleeping?"

"I'm sorry . . ." he stammered.

"Right, come on . . ."

Afterwards, he was astonished at the docility with which he obeyed. He didn't look at his sister. He forgot to take his overcoat and hat. He followed the fat woman into the corridor and didn't think it strange that she should be fully dressed.

Had she dressed herself again purposely, because she wasn't the type of woman to show herself in her night attire? Had she been sitting up until now? Had she listened to their conversation?

She opened the door of number 13, after having closed Corine's room, and it was she who switched the light on.

"You're going to get into bed straight away . . ."

There was sternness in her voice, a sternness without animosity. She spoke to him as though to a child . . .

"And you will do me the pleasure of going to sleep, my young sir . . . As for her, whether you like it or not, tomorrow morning, she's clearing out . . ."

She glanced around her to make sure that he wanted nothing.

"Would you like me to bring you up something to drink?"

"No, thank you."

He had no more energy, no more strength. His head, his limbs were drained. He remained standing in the middle of the room without realizing where he was or what he should do.

He wasn't crying, but he still had a salt taste on his lips, his forehead was hot, his hands burning . . .

"You're going to put the bolt on as soon as I've closed the

133

door, and if she tries to come and start on you again, I forbid you to open it . . ."

He promised with a nod.

"Sleep well . . . Sleep as long as you can . . . Unfortunately I've no medicine to make you sleep . . ."

She still hesitated to go. Possibly she wanted to put her hands on his shoulders in an encouraging gesture or even, she who had never had any children, to hug this tall, awkward boy to her soft bosom.

She repeated as she went out:

"Sleep well . . ."

Through the intervening wall he heard his sister get up, then get back again into bed. He heard the click of the light switch.

As he was stretching out, he caught sight of the celebrated suitcase and nearly went and opened it. He was too tired. His head was spinning. It seemed to him that he was beginning a serious illness, and he felt a sense of relief. Because then he needn't worry. The others would accept the responsibility in his place.

He would have liked to be ill for a long time, in a bright room, with a nurse who would prevent him from speaking and bring him soup and remedies from time to time.

His lips pouted. He felt himself a little child, and unknowingly he hugged his pillow in the crook of his arm as he would have done with a human being, a grown up who had taken up the burden of his life for him.

Only when she heard him breathing regularly did Mélanie tiptoe away down the corridor. As she passed the neighbouring door she could not refrain from putting her tongue out.

CHAPTER NINE

ALAIN hadn't realized that it was Saturday. He found the door wide open and Madame Foucret, with clogs on her feet, an apron of coarse blue linen over her pink petticoat, in the process of cleaning the house. She got up, surprised and embarrassed. She immediately put her hands to her hair done up in curlers.

"You must excuse me, Monsieur Alain . . ."

The weather had changed again. That morning the sun was shining, during the night there had been a frost, the ground was hard, the earth crumbly. Why did the woman stare at him like that? Was it because his long figure seemed out of proportion, against the light? She opened her mouth and nearly said something to him, nearly told him that he'd changed; he guessed it. He knew very well that there had been a change in him, he could feel it himself, even in the way he walked, his gestures, but he didn't know that it could be seen at first glance.

"Do come in. I'll clean a spot for you."

She wrung out her cloth over her bucket as she explained:

"Foucret has gone off on his bike to Jamilly, three kilometres from here, where he has a pair of rubber boots to get repaired . . . They're beating for rabbits, tomorrow morning, in the Ormeaux woods."

Did she guess that this time he hadn't come for her husband?

"Come in and have something to drink first of all . . . Monsieur Joseph has gone fishing . . . If you want to see him, you'll find him under the bank, not far from the Three Oaks . . . He always settles himself there . . ."

"I'll go and find him," he said.

"Wouldn't you like a glass of wine? Something hot? You can have some coffee in a few minutes . . ."

The Sunday before, he would have given way, to please her, because he wouldn't have dared refuse. Today he said calmly, quietly, firmly, but very gently:

"No thank you. I shall probably see your husband on my way back."

He couldn't have got thinner because he had just spent two days in bed. He had always been thin. He hadn't even been ill. Only a slight cold which left him with a red running nose and stinging eyelids.

It was as though they had agreed, he and Mélanie together, to pretend that he was ill. When he had woken up about midday, she must have been straining her ears from downstairs, because she had come up straight away.

"Don't worry, young sir," she had announced, "she's gone . . . Let me see your tongue . . . Good Lord, how hot you've been! . . ."

The sheets were soaked, and both the pillow and his pyjamas.

135

"I jolly well thought you were in for something . . . But we'll take care of you, and it will soon be over . . . Olga, bring some sheets and a pillow slip. . . ."

As if mainly to distract his thoughts. She had nursed him, made a fuss of him. First it was a bowl of soup, then a cake, then some hot lemonade. But she knew as well as he did that he wasn't ill, that it was all to take his mind off things.

Nevertheless, that morning, he still felt a bit weak. In the tram to Genette he had come over hot once or twice and he had walked along the road which seemed to him to be longer than last Sunday, with a rather shaky step.

He passed through the avenues on the building sites, noticing, a long way off, the pedestal in the middle of the stretch of water that was waiting for, that would go on waiting for, his father's bust.

He had no trouble in finding the Three Oaks; at the foot of the hill, he took the footpath that zigzagged down to the river's edge. Once he was there, he was a little surprised, and a bit put out, not to see Joseph Bourgues. He moved a few paces to the left, from where he could see quite a long stretch of the bank, but there was no fisherman.

He turned round and it was only then that he saw the man he was looking for, sitting on a flat stone, near a willow, his rod in his hand, his gaze fixed on a tiny red float sticking out of the sparkling water.

Bourgues hadn't heard him, didn't know he was there. He was so motionless, so silent, everything was so still and silent around him, that Alain was impressed.

A little smoke was rising, in the still air, from a cigarette that the old convict had between his lips and which nearly drooped down to his chin. Now and then, he inclined his head slightly, probably to get a better view of his float, to be ready to strike.

He only moved from his fixed position when Alain was standing a few yards from him and he didn't get up, only moved his head, murmuring:

"Is that you?"

"Don't you say *tu* to me any more?"

"Of course . . . I'm sorry, Alain . . . Sit down . . . There's a stone a little further up . . ."

136

Something had changed between them too. Six days earlier, there had been a mature man, nearly an old man, walking along the road with a child.

Today there was no longer a child. Alain was in no hurry to speak, to ask the questions that he had promised himself to ask. He, too, sat motionless on his stone, holding his long legs folded under him with both hands, looking at the surface of the water, with, now and then, a brief glance at his companion.

"I've read my father's papers," he said at last.

"Oh!"

Joseph Bourgues sat waiting, avoiding looking at him, as he pulled gently in his line and changed the bait with meticulous care.

"I found an old photograph of my grandfather."

In an old wallet which only contained some photographs, some yellowing papers, cracked along the folds. The photograph was a zinc plate which must have been made at a fair. The features were half rubbed out. It was of a man with tousled hair, white hair so thick that it was like a mane, bushy eyebrows, tiny eyes, almost hooded, a strong nose and a drooping moustache which hid his lips.

The most striking thing was the untamed expression, untroubled yet distrusting both at once, with which he was gazing at the lens. How had they managed to drag him in front of a camera and hold him still there? He wasn't very happy. He was there to please somebody, but he stared peevishly at the black cloth under which the photographer must have disappeared.

There were other photographs in the wallet, particularly one of Eugène Malou, at sixteen or seventeen, in the company of a young girl with flat bands around her forehead held in place by a ribbon.

"There's an aeroplane painted on the backcloth, isn't there?" asked Joseph Bourgues. "Then I know it. We were together. It was at a fair at Aubagne. I had a girl friend with me too, but I don't remember the name of either of them."

A photograph of Eugène Malou as a conscript, with a whole group.

"I wasn't there then, because I was a year older than your father."

Then a dapper young man, better dressed, looking proud of himself: Malou in Paris.

A roach wriggled at the end of the line and splashed the water a little in the green can into which the fisherman dropped it.

"Was my father dishonest?"

The question had come at last, asked quietly in a neutral voice. The calm of a winter's morning in the woods was still all about them, with, now and then, a rotten acorn falling from a tree, sometimes, as well, the rustle of a bed of dead leaves at the passage of a rabbit.

"Listen carefully to what I'm going to tell you, Alain . . ."

He took his time to give more weight to what was to follow.

"Your father was a man. And that, believe me, as you will find out for yourself one day, is a rarer thing than being respectable."

It was vague, and yet Alain had the impression he understood.

"A man, you see . . . Unfortunately you can't explain it, it's something you feel . . ."

"Yes . . ." said the young man with conviction.

"Anybody can be respectable, sometimes without wanting to. There are lots who are law abiding simply because they are frightened, or because they're tired, or not very well. There are others who were born like that, into respectable families, and it's never occurred to them to change. Am I respectable?"

"I think so."

"Well, your father was worth a hundred times more than I."

"You've seen his father's photograph, but you haven't seen his mother's. It was his mother that brought him up. She was known as the mad woman in the village. Have you noticed that, in nearly every village, there is a simple-minded soul or a mad woman? She never knew what a bed was; she slept on the ground on a heap of rags, which didn't stop men coming after her when they had drunk a drop too much. Sometimes a group of them together! It was more fun, you understand.

"And do you know what made your grandfather famous in the district? It was because he ate crows, weasels and all kinds of revolting animals.

"He refused to believe that the mad woman's child was his. It

138

was much later when he had proof of it, once when he looked more closely, when Eugène was twelve. The old man saw a little spot, like a pin head on his left iris, and he had exactly the same thing himself, in the same place.

"It was then that he took the lad into his own home.

"And that lad, all by himself, became your father, with his house, his servants, his cars, his workmen and heaps of people in high places who came to eat at his table."

He looked stealthily at the young man, but it would have been impossible to guess what Alain was thinking. In fact, the words of the old convict were superimposing themselves on his sister's. It was like a duet for two voices whose double melodic line he followed consideringly, without haste.

He was pleased he had found Joseph at the water's edge, because that interview would have been impossible in the house. And he was also grateful to his companion for going on fishing. Bourgues was wearing a leather coat and a cap with a patent leather peak, as the men on the railways do. A big scarf was wrapped round his throat. From time to time he leaned forward and threw a small ball of earth into which he had mixed some hemp paste into the water, near his line.

The questions were all laid out, neatly in order, in Alain's mind.

"Is it true he began by blackmailing?"

The other started, but remained still, avoiding looking at him.

"You see, Alain, I'm now fifty-eight. I spent a year of my life in prison, two years in a penal settlement. I lived in Havana in exile, and I've known all sorts of men. So it's difficult for us to judge men and things in the same way."

"I think I shall understand . . ."

"There are honest and dishonest people. But what there's most of, at a certain level particularly, when one rises however little in what they call the social scale, are fakes or, if you prefer, respectable people who commit dirty tricks on the sly. Your father, when he earned his living writing in small newspapers, got to know people of that sort. His employer, his fellow workers, knew how to take advantage of them. Instead of being indignant or shutting their eyes, they made them buy their silence."

139

A veil had fallen over Alain's face, he had closed his eyes for a moment.

"Don't forget what Eugène started from. You haven't yet been hungry. You haven't yet found yourself at night, in a town, without a halfpenny in your pocket, without a place to sleep, except the pavement. You'll hear heartrending stories about that. But they weren't written by people who went through it. Because then you've only one idea, one only, do you hear—his voice became hard—never more to sink as low again.

"For when you're down to a certain level, there's nobody to hold out his hand to you. People go by, well fed, well dressed, their pockets full of money, and not one thinks of stopping. . . ."

He fell silent. Alain was silent too. Then he blew his nose. Then finally, after several minutes, Joseph went on in his normal voice.

"At that time in Paris there were people making a lot of money, so much money that they didn't know what to do with it and they prided themselves on going and losing millions in a single evening at Deauville."

"The Société d'Urbanisme?" asked Alain who had read the papers in the green case.

"By giving bribes to municipal councillors, to people still higher up, by falsifying the awards, they had managed to get the contracts for building not just a few blocks, but whole districts on behalf of the Paris County Council.

"I was in Guyene. I don't know how your father got his hands on certain documents.

"A press campaign would have done no good, or rather no newspaper would have agreed to undertake it, no member of Parliament would have dared to take the scandal up before the house. Because there were dozens of them receiving money . . .

"Quietly, with his paper in his pocket, your father went and asked the company for the job of advertising manager.

"They would have laughed in his face if he hadn't had his paper with him. But he had it. He had off-handedly put a copy on the desk.

"They understood, and he got the job.

"That was the way he earned his first money which allowed him to start in business in Bordeaux."

"I understand."

"Others who started like him, have climbed much higher. Your mother's first husband became minister and will probably be so again."

"Weren't you in the Libertarians?"

"What I'm going to tell you is true, however strange it may appear to you: I am still a libertarian and your father was always one. Only, it's something I can't explain to you.

"It's something that you have inside you and can't be changed. It's easy to laugh at us and say:

" 'As soon as their bellies are full and they've money in the bank they become worse than the middle class.'

"It's not true, Alain . . .

"And the proof that it's not true, is that your father is dead and that on Monday they are going to auction his house and furniture, while Count d'Estier continues to get rich . . ."

Still the two voices . . . Corine's, shrill, with great outbursts of temper and flashes of hatred; Bourgues' monotonous and calm, flowing along like the water in the river.

Moreover, there were some letters, one, among others, from the Société d'Urbanisme, which Alain knew by heart and which still made him blush.

"My dear Friend,
          I have received your recent letters and telegrams safely. I have not replied sooner because I have been away on holiday. I quite understand that you are in difficulties at the moment and I am sorry that, once again, I am not in a position to help you out.

As for the matter you mention, may I remind you that it is now several years old and could not be brought up without appearing ridiculous. General B . . ., the chairman of our board, has even decided that in future he will lay before the courts any matter arising from business transacted by a former board of directors.

I hope that you will find a way of overcoming your difficulties elsewhere and believe me, dear friend . . ."

Was that the one that had administered the kick in the backside that Corine had spoken of?

"There are people who love money for itself and people who don't," went on Bourgues slowly. "Eugène loved it so little that he threw it out of the doors and windows, gave it away to the first comer in a way that was sometimes ridiculous. Ask François Foucret. Ask the daughter of the postmistress, whom he sent to Switzerland for four years ..."

Because of Corine, Alain nearly asked: "Was she his mistress?" That would have been out of place between them. It seemed that here, on the river's bank, where the little red float quivered, the same words, so disgusting and humiliating in Corine's mouth, became pure.

"There are a hundred others who owe to him what they are today because he couldn't reject anybody of good will. He would have liked everybody to be happy, except the blackguards, the cowards, the ..."

The others, in other words! Yes, Alain was beginning to understand, to distinguish "the others" more precisely.

"He didn't want to be poor. He wouldn't accept vegetating in mediocrity either, because he had risen from too far down for that. That's probably the truth of the matter: the lower you come from, the higher you must rise. Cost what it may. I think, for example, he would have preferred his father's life, the hut on the edge of the quarry and roasted crows to the existence of your brother Edgar.

"He had to have everything or nothing, precisely because he was Eugène Malou.

"He had to have Malouville and his statue.

"He had to have, at his table, waited on by his footmen, those people who could never imagine that a man of their type could be the son of a madwoman.

"He had to give of himself to the uttermost to keep going up.

"In the end he wanted the struggle for its own sake.

"It's for that that I told you Eugène was a man. Even if someone had told him that he would end wretchedly, he would have put up the same fight, because he had to. No matter how hard, do you understand?

"He was on his own, the only one who believed in him, without ever anyone to lean on, without anybody, except little people, except a few—not all—of those who received his generosity—to admire him or trust him.

"He carried all your household on his back. Each morning he had to find so much money, for your mother, for your sister, for the servants. . . .

"He found that money, year in year out, he found it, little Malou, who hadn't even a legal identity . . .

"He didn't get it for nothing, did he? It's hard to get money out of pockets, harder still to get it out of the safes of those who've got a lot.

"To those, you must promise more each time. And Eugène knew how to promise. Out of the two of us, it was he who sold the most Indian tea, and I've seen him sell ten packets to an old priest suffering with piles, which didn't prevent him selling some to his servant with hay fever."

Did Alain smile? His face had relaxed. He had stretched his legs out for a moment. He wanted to say like a child who is being told a nice story: "Go on!"

They were far from everything but not, as with Corine, shut in by four walls surrounded by darkness. They were there at the river with its reeds, with the bare trees made solemn by winter, with a few birds hopping on the frozen leaves which lay ruddy on the ground.

"I read the prospectus . . ."

Bourgues turned to the hill behind them and beyond which Malouville with its bright houses lay invisible.

"There were some who laughed and who still laugh. They called Eugène a charlatan. Yet, I bet, that in a few years' time, Malouville will be at the height of prosperity.

"Probably a son of Count d'Estier will be its mayor then, or another of those who, today, demand its legal liquidation.

"Because it needs men like your father, who see big, to get people like that moving . . . They are so frightened for their pence, that if you didn't promise them ten times as much, they would never risk them.

"It took even me some time to understand and it was Eugène who helped me.

"You see, it needs people like Eugène, who have madness in their blood, to get anything done.

"The others let them get on with it for a while. If necessary they give them a hand. Right up to the time when they think they can get on without them and without having to share the cake.

"Weren't you asking me if your father was a respectable man?"

And he threw a fresh pellet of hemp paste near his line on which a gudgeon hooked itself immediately.

Some expressions fixed themselves in his head as though underlined in red ink: "Your father was always alone . . ."

All alone to carry them on his outstretched arms. And that was true. He could bear witness. He could remember his father's return home, on certain evenings, his shoulders bowed, his voice hoarser from having argued all day. He could see him collapsing into an armchair.

And Alain suddenly understood that at those times, Eugène Malou would have liked to have them all around him, affectionate and considerate. If only for example Corine had knelt down to take off his shoes and put on his slippers . . . If only his wife had said to him as she slipped her arm about his shoulders: "Not too tired, I hope?"

Alain was ashamed of himself and the rest of the family. He, for most of the time, without cause, possibly from shyness, possibly from bashfulness, or because he didn't think, because he took his schooling seriously, hastened to shut himself in his room with a book or writing.

Yet how many times had his father's gaze followed him as he left him like that?

"Are you off?"

"I'm going to do my homework."

A kiss on his forehead, quite short, because you didn't dare appear too demonstrative with a man like him.

"Off you go, son . . ."

And Corine needed money to go out. And their mother needed some for the house, for the dressmaker, for her sister Jeanne, for God knows what.

Money! Always money!

And Eugène took out his fat wallet from which he drew the notes. He would promise:

"You'll have the rest tomorrow . . ."

For tomorrow was another day, another struggle, and, in the meanwhile, he sometimes fell asleep, exhausted with fatigue, his mouth half open, in his armchair.

There would be no one with him when he woke up and made up his mind to go to bed.

Money . . .

They would have it, they had to have it. It was up to him to produce it. It was up to him to know where to get it. It was up

144

to him to find a new way of making it fall into his pocket, into their pockets.

"Do you understand, Alain?"

And Joseph Bourgues had considerately asked him:

"You won't catch a cold, will you?"

Not once had he asked him what he meant to do. Yet, he must know. They knew everything in Malouville. He certainly knew all about Corine.

"Someone came to see me about you . . ."

It was right at the end of their conversation, a little before the old convict packed up his rods, while the sun was high in the sky.

"Perhaps you don't know him, but you must have seen him. It was Rendon, the accountant."

"I've heard my father speak of him."

"Rendon worked for him for fifteen years. He's got a twisted face, shifty eyes and a thin drooping moustache. You would think he squints but it's because his head is always twisted to the side. Rendon, who knows me, who knows everything, came to ask me if you were a chap with whom one could talk business.

"He's got some money saved up. He's got two or three houses, here, which belong to him and he must own others in the town. He's artful. Your father needed him, because he understands the law better than anyone, particularly company law.

"Among the papers your father left, there are some that he would like to have. He would take them over, you understand.

"In his hands, it's likely they would cause trouble. He travelled to Paris on purpose to meet your mother, and your mother told him that you had the green case.

"He knows that with young people it's all or nothing and, because he hardly knows you, he came here to get information before tackling you.

"I let him have his say. You'll see what you think. He suggests two solutions. Either he'll buy all the papers from you in one lot, and I think he would pay a good price, or you would draw up an agreement. He would undertake the work and would share the profits . . ."

"What did my father think of him?" asked Alain not without a certain anxiety.   .

"He looked on him as the lowest of creeping things."

"So do I."

Bourgues repeated:

"So do I."

They looked at each other and suddenly they were almost happy.

"Before going back to the Foucrets', there's something else I must say to you. I think that now's the time, although your father didn't precisely say in what circumstances I was to tell you."

It was proof of trust on Bourgues' part, a bit as though Alain had passed his final examination with success.

"The evening before the day they put the seals on the house, your father took down three little paintings.

"He possibly wasn't a connoisseur of art. He bought to please the artists and to decorate the walls. For his own part, he would probably have preferred coloured prints. One day, when he was getting an expert's opinion on his paintings, because he wanted to borrow money on them, he found out that there were only three that had any real value.

"He took them down last week. He rolled them up and brought them to me. They are under my bed.

"'I don't know what might happen,' he said to me. 'The others will always get by. Some have even taken due precautions.'"

"My mother . . ." thought Alain.

"'Alain is young. I suspect that he has more ideas in his head than he likes to show. It is possible that a certain amount of money will help him get on his feet. You know what I mean. He mustn't start too low down. By selling the canvases in Paris, he should get several hundred thousand francs . . .'"

Alain had made no answer. Bourgues hadn't asked any direct questions.

"At any rate, they are there for you," he concluded. "Now we had better go back, because mother Foucret is a decent woman, but she doesn't like people to be late at table."

How many things was Alain beginning to understand, even that feeling of relief that he'd had the previous Sunday when Bourgues had spoken to him going along the main road!

It wasn't only on his own account that the ex-convict spoke.

146

He was a messenger, whom his father had carefully left for his son against the time when he should be no more.

Hadn't Bourgues said to him, during their conversation that morning: "He was as bashful as a child"?

In speaking of his father, of Eugène Malou, whom Corine and so many others had called an adventurer and a master blackmailer.

Wasn't bashfulness the reason why his father had never taken him by the shoulders, to speak to him alone, to open his heart to him?

A hundred times he had hovered around his son, as the latter now realized, with the hope of finding out what the big lad about whom he knew practically nothing was thinking.

And he entrusted another, after his death, with the task of studying the young man and helping him if necessary.

The bearded grandfather who ate crows, looked like a caveman, and lived on the edge of the village in his hut by the quarry.

Eugène Malou, short and thickset, with irregular features, bulging eyes, a harsh voice, was always a being who defied classification, who made people look round at him, even when, dressed by the best tailors, he got out of his limousine.

Alain, the third of the line, could attend the most expensive school in the town without attracting attention. Even in company with Estier's son for example, it was he who, with his long face and quiet eyes, appeared the aristocrat.

And even his father had not dared speak to him.

For fear of questions probably, of a whole series of questions; for fear of one of those smiles that Corine was so generous with, that put Malou back in the old man's hut; for fear of being judged too harshly, by a look.

He made fun of Edgar, the elder son, openly, sometimes aggressively, as of someone who was not of his race, who was a traitor—a stupid baaing sheep accidentally born among wolves.

Alain was the mystery. Alain was the third link, the future of which his father knew nothing, the unknown at whom he sometimes darted anxious stealthy glances.

Alain was the continuation of the story of which Eugène had written the first chapters and whose end he would not know.

They walked side by side, the messenger and the young man.

Alain had offered to carry the fish kettle and the other had not prevented him—the young man was grateful to him.

The weather was very bright. The sun was cheerful. Little drops were forming on the crumbling crust of ice which covered the earth and the faded grass.

"Always remember he was a man . . ."

Bourgues nearly added something else but he was too shy. He kept it back but not without his companion completing it mentally:

"He was a man and he loved you very much . . ."

After all, he loved only him because he was the only one who had never betrayed him.

Wasn't it really that which he was meant to understand?

And he, for years, had not realized it, had lived isolated in a house whose mysteries he preferred not to know. He had lived like a stranger with that man who had watched him anxiously.

"I don't want to trouble the Foucrets . . ."

"They would be upset if you didn't come and have lunch with them. Your father was very fond of them too."

Yet Corine had not lied: all that she had said was true, was true in a certain manner. The two voices still intermingled, but it hardly worried Alain any more.

Outside, François Foucret was trying on his rubber boots which had been patched that morning and which came half-way up his thighs.

"This is a pleasure, Monsieur Alain . . . I was sure that you would come and lunch with us . . . The old lady will be pleased . . ."

The smell of good cooking, the warmth of a house that had just been cleaned thoroughly throughout, a few blazing logs to give life and cheerfulness.

The two men, Bourgues and Foucret, questioned each other with a look.

Bourgues seemed to say by his peaceful demeanour:

"Yes, of course! He's all right . . ."

And southerner that he was, he would probably have added, if he had found himself alone with the old foreman: "He's a fine chap . . ."

And to be a fine chap, or to be a man, in his language . . .

CHAPTER TEN

IT was as though he were convalescing during those two days.
His movements were slow and careful, and he smiled only the
barest smile, a smile which seemed to ask things to be gentle, or
to thank them for not being hostile.

He was attentive to everything, a smell which came up from
the kitchen, the comings and goings of Olga as she did the
rooms, a sunbeam distorted by a windowpane. He enjoyed
everything and gave thanks to everything, with that rather
pale smile which worried Mélanie.

The bells, for instance. Never had he heard so many bells as
on that Sunday, while he was sitting alone in the cellar, the
green case beside him, the open boiler within arm's reach,
licked by the flames, the big pipes bandaged like sick limbs.

He was burning the papers handful by handful, and, at one
time, all the bells of the town began ringing together. The
parishes answered one another across the roof tops. Had the air
a particular resonance, because the frost made it purer? The
sounds of some bells came from very far off, in a wide circle,
from the suburbs, perhaps from the country.

He could see the pavement lights gilded by the sun. People
went by, of whom he could only see the lower part of their
bodies, but he felt they were in their Sunday best, their step
was brisker than on weekdays, he imagined them coming from
Mass, the women pinched in by their corsets, the girls all
scented; then the pastrycooks' shops from which they came out
holding white packets by a loop of red string.

The world of those Sundays was still unknown to him, with
the crowds, after lunch, making for the cycle racing track, the
football pitches, the cinemas filling little by little, the stuffy
cafés which smelt of apéritifs.

"The Three Pigeons" was nearly empty. On that day he was
the only lodger in the house. For the first time he saw Mélanie
with her spectacles on her nose, reading the paper in the bar at
the counter, while old Poignard must have missed his companion to help him drink his red wine.

"You'll have a glass of wine with me, Monsieur Alain, won't
you?"

He had drunk it, out of good will for Poignard. He would

have liked to please everybody. He savoured all the odours of the house and possibly he was already feeling regret. Couldn't he have stopped there indefinitely? Why couldn't he have chosen the humblest possible walk in life? There was a stable boy who was entrusted with drawing wine in the cellar. He lived in the family with the proprietors and the maids. He had found his niche. Couldn't Alain have become a stable boy, or anything else, under the protection of the kind-hearted Mélanie?

He had lunched with them. He looked almost gay. Then for the last time he had taken the tram to Genette, he had gone to Malouville, where his friends had welcomed him; there had been sweet cake at four o'clock, long intervals of peaceful silence around the table where the wine trembled in the glasses.

With Bourgues and Foucret, walking between them both, he had gone round the estate, stopped before the base on which there would possibly never be a statue, had revisited the spot, at the waterside, where, the day before, Joseph had been fishing.

It was all on a different plane from the other days. There was as much difference between those two days and ordinary life as between low mass at six o'clock in the morning and a *Te Deum*. It was as though invisible organs gave breadth and majesty to the surroundings, and accompanied their step and gestures with ecclesiastical rhythm.

Nothing was lost. Each detail was engraved for always.

The return to Genette, with the two men, the platform of the tram which was packed, the Café de Paris, where he went in and drank a glass of beer, not because he was thirsty, but because he wanted to sit down in there just once more.

As he still had a trace of his cold, Mélanie took him a glass of grog in bed, and the night was scented with rum, and in his dreams was a slight perfume of rum which he recognized in his room, on his sheets when he awoke in the morning.

Even the meeting with Corine had that soft gentleness. He did not think he would see her again. When he went out about eleven o'clock, when the inn was at its busiest, she was waiting outside, at the corner of the street. She must have been watching for him for a long while, because her face was blue with the cold. She hadn't dared go in. She was frightened of Mélanie.

"I'd like to have a few words with you, Alain."

He agreed. He set off walking and she fell in step beside him.

"I'm told that you're leaving."

He showed no surprise and went on listening to her with a sort of distant forbearance. For he was very far away, in the clouds. So far away and so high in the clouds that it seemed to him that he could have spoken with his father. Didn't he feel his presence about him? Wasn't it to him that he addressed that pale smile?

"I know father left you some paintings . . ."

She had probably found that out from Rendon, who must have gone to see her and who wouldn't rest content until he had got the last possible advantage from the heirs of Malou.

"Do you intend to use that money?"

"No."

"You know what my position is here. It's not an easy one. Fabien will come round, but it might take weeks. But that's by the way . . . You don't like me speaking to you about that . . ."

"It's all the same to me."

Her brother's attitude disturbed her, worried her; and she hastened to finish.

"I think you could leave me some of it. It's essential that I keep going, and that it doesn't look as though I'm begging."

"You can take them."

She didn't dare believe him. She was frightened in case he should change his mind.

"Where are they?"

"Give me your address and they'll be brought to you."

She scribbled it for him on a scrap of paper, half an envelope which she took out of her handbag. It was in a furnished house, overlooking the park, which didn't have a very good reputation, but which was the most luxurious the town offered.

"Will you see mother?"

"I don't know."

He hadn't paid attention to the direction they were taking and there before them was the little square where they had lived, with its fountain in the middle and its patrician houses.

Before theirs, the one that had been theirs, there was a crowd and all heads were raised towards a man perched on an improvised stage.

The sale had begun.

151

"It's horrible," said Corine. "I can't watch that. Are you coming?"

He shook his head.

"Shall I see you again?"

"I don't know."

"You won't forget the paintings?"

Another shake of his head. He didn't kiss her. He didn't shake her hand. Yet at the time he didn't bear her any illwill. It wasn't her fault.

"Goodbye, Alain."

"Goodbye."

He stayed there, standing behind the others, watching a procession of worthless objects, because they usually begin with those kitchen utensils, glass jars, assorted objects which were grouped into lots and the sight of which provoked laughs.

Why should he be unhappy?

He still had something to do before lunch. At midday exactly he waited on the corner by Jaminet's yard, for on Mondays and only Mondays, Mademoiselle Germaine lunched in town with a woman friend. He saw her coming, wearing a little red hat and a navy blue coat. He also saw the office door and thought of the other door, the one that had been shut with so much hatred.

"I wanted to say goodbye to you . . ."

"Are you leaving? Are you going to your mother?"

He said no and, as he gave no other explanations, she didn't dare question him.

"I would just like you to know that I shall remember you with pleasure."

He would have liked to shake Monsieur Albert's hand. There, too, he could have lived. There, too, was a niche in which he had been tempted to hide himself.

He lunched quickly and got to his brother's house before two o'clock. They had just got up from the table. The children were being dressed for school.

"It's you?"

"I've come to say goodbye to you."

"Are you going to your mother?"

Why did they all ask him the same question? And why did nobody think of his father, who was much more alive?

"You'll have a glass of something? Of course you will . . ."

Edgar took the tray out of the sideboard, with the tiny glasses, rimmed with gold, the decanter containing a drop of marc.

"I wish you good luck. You're right to leave, because, here, you would have too many people against you. Even my position's difficult, and, without my father-in-law's influence, I should probably be obliged to ask for a posting . . ."

It was Edgar who was embarrassed, who kept glancing at the time by the Westminster chiming clock. Alain still had that ghost of a smile on his lips, his bearing was quiet and gentle.

"Goodbye, Edgar."

He kissed his sister-in-law. Never had he seen the town so clean, so bright, so cheerful, thanks to the frost and the winter sun. Behind the school wall he could hear the noise of playtime and he stopped thinking of all the playtimes he had known.

He wasn't unhappy. He would never again be unhappy. He had understood what Joseph Bourgues had meant when he uttered the words: "Your father was a man."

A man, that was the expression. A man who was the son of a man who himself was descended from a man.

He nearly went back to watch the sale, but he decided to wait for Peters, the red-headed boy who had been his best friend at school and who had taken the trouble to come to the funeral.

"Is it true you're working?"

"I have been working . . . I shall work again."

"Are you changing your job?"

"I'm leaving."

"Are you going to your mother?"

It wasn't possible to explain to them something which nevertheless was so simple. Of course he wasn't going to his mother, he was going to nobody.

"I wanted to say goodbye to you, and tell you what a decent chap you've been . . ."

There! Now, his pilgrimage was over, now, he'd only to return to the "Three Pigeons" to pack his bags. They told him that a certain Rendon, a fellow with a drooping moustache, had come to see him and had been asked to return the next day.

The good-hearted Mélanie laughed:

"That way he'll leave you in peace, young sir."

And he had to pass the time away, quite quietly, eating,

drinking a last glass with everybody, embracing Mélanie who nearly smothered him hugging him against her ample bosom.

It was she whom he asked, after having looked long in the mirror, to examine his left eye.

"Have I got a little blemish on the iris?"

"What idea have you got in your head now? Of course not. There's nothing there."

"Look carefully . . ."

She fetched her glasses.

"Does it hurt you?"

"Can you see anything?"

"Only just! You don't want to worry about that. It must be a birthmark."

So it was! The mark of the Malous! He had it, like his father, like his grandfather, and he felt a solemn joy.

It was eleven o'clock when a taxi stopped in front of the door. François Foucret got out in company with Bourgues.

They loaded the luggage into the car. They passed through the streets where the gas lamps made garlands of light and they saw the big clocktower of the station.

He felt tired, but he wasn't sad. He only wanted to stop for a moment, to stop the course of time for a moment. He felt a vague pang in the pit of his stomach, as at the moment of plunging into cold water.

But there was a whole lot of things to do, book his ticket, register his trunk, look for a compartment, then go to the refreshment-room and buy mineral water and sandwiches. The two men followed him, and he spoke to them naturally saying:

"The train gets in at half past six, doesn't it? It won't be quite light. I like the Gare de Lyon. It's my favourite."

He asked Joseph to send the three paintings to his sister, whose address he gave him without thinking of copying it himself. What was the use?

He was cutting the threads. All the threads. Mélanie was on the other side of the wall, and Mademoiselle Germaine and Monsieur Albert. In a few minutes the old convict and the worthy Foucret would be swallowed up in their turn in the past.

As he watched them on the station platform, they already no

longer had the same solidity as at Malouville. It's true they were no longer at home, that they felt awkward, that Joseph felt a bit anxious.

The hands of the clock moved on by jerks and the train exhausted the steam from its brakes. Railwaymen were tapping among the wheels of the coaches.

"Take your seats . . ."

Only handshakes? Foucret's palms were so calloused that they left an impression of a rasp. Bourgues' eyes bored deep into Alain's.

Only then, when he looked down on them, leaning out of the door, he nearly cried. He searched for something to say to them. He found nothing. He contented himself with stammering, just as the train moved off.

"He will be pleased!"

The compartment was empty. He hadn't wanted to travel first class, as before, but neither had he wanted to travel third class. He was in the second class and it seemed to him it was better thus.

Formerly, his father had landed in Paris by third class. But he was the son of old Malow, or Malowski, and the mad woman.

Then he had travelled first class, and possibly his only mistake had been not to get there via the seconds.

Alain had lowered the blue shade on the lamp. He had stretched his full length on the seat, his head on his travelling bag. He didn't close his eyes. Lights went by on the blinds. People were still going by in the corridor.

"Won't I, Father?"

He knew very well what he meant. Nobody else, not even Joseph Bourgues, could understand.

There was something to be settled between him and his father. They hadn't known each other in his lifetime, but he wasn't too late.

Above all he must be a man, and he had decided he would be one. It seemed to him that he had begun.

That was why he had left, to escape the temptation of sink-into the "Three Pigeons" or into the warm friendship of Foucret and Bourgues.

He must also avoid the temptation of hating, and he didn't

155

even hate his sister, he had been kind to Corine, the evening before, although he hadn't kissed her.

One day, he would go and see his mother as he had gone to see Edgar and his wife; but later on when he was settled. He would go and visit them at the Boulevard Beaumarchais, in Aunt Jeanne's house.

He hated nobody. That was too easy.

All alone, he had chosen his path. Perhaps not quite alone, because he thought of his grandfather, of the mad woman, of his father.

He had to find his proper place and he thought he had found it. In any case, he would try honestly, with all his might. The rocking of the train lulled him, and little by little he slipped into a doze without losing consciousness; he knew that it was Alain Malou who was there, stretching his length in a second class compartment, and that Alain Malou was going to Paris to meet his destiny.

He would work at anything, usher in a cinema, waiter in a café, anything they wanted. He would take his examinations one after the other, not so much because he wanted to be educated, but because it was the most difficult way. Didn't thousands of young men study at Paris while they earned their living?

Why shouldn't he become a doctor?

That would put him neither too high nor too low.

And the Malous had always been either too high or too low, because they had had to work so quickly.

Now he had time. He had the time to sleep.

The train whistled as it sped through the countryside white with frost. One by one, little remote stations were swallowed up in the past, the house in the little square with the fountain was completely swallowed up too, and so many things, so many people with it.

There was only left a sleeping Malou, who would soon wake up to a new life and who, in his sleep, occasionally moved his lips.

A Malou who would do his uttermost, all a man can.

"Won't I, Father?"

Coral Sands, Bradenson Beach, Florida.
February 22, 1947.

156

ACCOUNT UNSETTLED

translated from the French by

TONY WHITE

Part One

ELIE'S CORNER

CHAPTER ONE

THE LODGER IN THE GREEN ROOM
AND THE NEW LODGER IN THE
GARNET ROOM

CHILDREN'S shouts rang out in the yard of the school across the way and Elie knew it was a quarter to ten. At times, he would wait impatiently, almost anxiously, for this violent rending of the air by the voices of two hundred small boys bursting out of their class-rooms for recreation. It really seemed as if, each morning, a few minutes before this explosion of sound, silence hung more completely over the area, as though the whole place was on the wait.

For the last ten minutes at least, that day, Elie recalled only the scratching of his pen on paper. He hadn't heard the tram go by at the corner of the street. There must have been at least one, because they went by every five minutes. He had heard nothing, not even the landlady coming and going, and he began to listen carefully.

He had no watch. He had only owned one in his life, his father's silver watch, which the latter had solemnly handed him when he left Vilna. He had sold it ages before and there was no alarm clock in his room.

When Madame Lange came up, earlier, to the first floor with her bucket and brushes, it meant it was about nine o'clock. She used to come up as soon as the vegetable-man had gone by.

As usual, she had begun by doing out the pink room, Mademoiselle Lola's, with its two windows looking out on the street. Then she must have moved on to the yellow room, occupied by Stan Malevitz, where the first thing she always did was to light a coal-fire in the stove. To make it catch quicker, she used to pour on some paraffin, and the smell mixed with that of burnt kindling, would find its way to Elie.

She was late. She must have already knocked on his door. His room, the green room, as it was called, was halfway between the ground and first floors, and had been constructed over the kitchen, with a zinc roof which made it suffocating in summer and freezing in winter.

It was November and it was cold; Elie, to write at his table in front of the window, had slipped on his overcoat, and had got up after a few minutes to put on his cap.

She would be sure to ask him:

"What are you doing in there, Monsieur Elie? Why don't you go down and work in the kitchen?"

And he would answer:

"You didn't ask me."

"I don't have to tell you every morning, do I? Won't you ever get used to making yourself at home?"

Sometimes, on her way up, she would remember to stop at his door and call to him:

"Are you there, Monsieur Elie? Would you mind going downstairs and keeping an eye on my soup?"

At other times, she forgot. She thought a lot. Often, while she was doing out a room, she would talk to herself, frowning. Twice a week, Elie had a morning class at the University. They weren't necessarily on the same days, and she couldn't get used to it. To her, the University was like the school across the way, and he should have gone there every morning at the same time.

He had a cold. Every winter, he had a cold which dragged on for months, with ups and downs. Although the bit of sky, framed by the chimneys of the nearby houses, was bright blue, the air was cold, especially in his room, and he sighed with relief when a door opened on the landing and he heard Madame Lange's footsteps on the stairs.

"Are you there, Monsieur Elie?"

Getting up, he answered in his strong Polish accent:

"Yes, Madame."

Just as he'd expected, she grumbled, as if she was annoyed:

"Why can't you go down instead of shivering there in your overcoat? How many more times have I got to tell you? Hurry up! You go and sit in the kitchen and put some coal on the fire."

She was thin, with drab fair hair, white skin, grey eyes and always looked tired.

"There's no need to take your overcoat."

He knew she would immediately open his window, because she couldn't stand his smell. She had never admitted it to him. But she had remarked:

"It's funny how everyone has a different smell. Every room, too, for that matter. Perhaps people don't attach sufficient importance to it before getting married. For instance, I could never get used to my husband's smell."

The latter had died ten years earlier, during the Great War and since then she took in students as lodgers.

"I still prefer a man's smell to a woman's. Mademoiselle Lola's make me feel sick and, every time I go in her room, I fling the windows wide open."

It was also the first thing she did when she went into Elie's.

He picked up his books and his work, and went down into the kitchen, with its steamy glass door. In the large brown enamel casserole, the soup was bubbling gently and, in the middle of the black, iron stove, between the two ovens, the oval hole for poking the fire was glowing red-hot.

When he had shut the door and put a shovelful of coal on the fire, he could at last sit down at the oil-cloth table and breathe a sigh of relief. The warmth began to steal through him, bringing a flush to his cheeks, making his skin tingle, the smell which lingered was a wholesome smell of onions and leeks, and the sounds were unobtrusive, familiar ones, the quiet roar of the fire and, from time to time, red cinders falling through the grate or the lid of the saucepan rattling.

All these wrapped him round far better than his overcoat which dated back to Vilna, and it was as comforting as snuggling down in bed and touching a hot-water bottle with your foot.

In twenty minutes or half an hour, Madame Lange would come down again and put something on to cook, then go up again and do out the attic rooms on the second floor which she and her daughter occupied.

In Vilna, too, everyday life had a regular rhythm which kept time to the noise of a saw or a plane in his father's work-shop, but he had always loathed that rhythm and, throughout his childhood and adolescence, had dreamt only of escape.

A voice came from the top of the stairs:

"Is anything burning, Monsieur Elie?"

He went over to the glass door, opened it and answered:

"No, Madame."

Ever since Monsieur Lenizewski had passed his finals and gone back to his own country, Elie was the oldest lodger in the house, where he had come three years earlier, not speaking a word of French. He had seen the arrival of Stan Malevitz, who gave gym lessons to pay for part of his education, then, a year later, in 1925, Lola Resnick, who was born in the Caucasus and whose parents had taken her to Istanbul at the time of the Revolution. They still lived there. She had been to spend her last holidays with them. Stan, too, had gone back to Poland for the holidays. Only Elie was too poor to afford the journey. If he had had enough money, he would have had to make it.

Leah, his elder sister, wrote to him:

Father would like you to tell him if Liége looks like Vilna, what the houses are like, how they eat there and if there is a synagogue.

Back there, they lived in Oszmianski Street, two hundred yards from the Tagorah synagogue which played an important part both in their family and local life. There was a synagogue in Liége, too, which he had come across accidentally, but in which he had never set foot.

He heard the bucket, the landlady's footsteps as she went and put her utensils out in the yard and came back into the kitchen, wiping her hands on her apron.

"Have you put some more coal on?"

She put some on, too. The house, like the one in Vilna, had its rituals. For instance, the stove was flanked by two buckets of coal, and you didn't use the same sort for cooking as for a slow-burning fire. You also had to know what angle to turn the key to regulate the draught.

"Are you staying here? Can I go up to my room?"

Deep down, she was glad that at least one of her lodgers was worse off than she was.

"You can help yourself to a plate of soup. It hasn't been strained, but if you take it from the top . . ."

162

"No thank you, Madame."

He knew it annoyed her when he invariably refused anything she offered him, but he couldn't do otherwise. She knew that, too. Sometimes they quarrelled. Once, she had cried.

"I'll be down again in a quarter of an hour."

He had never been up to the second floor, which belonged to the two women. There was no heating up there, because no one ever took up any coal, and the light came through skylights in the roof. Naturally, the best furniture had been put in the lodgers' rooms.

Immediately after making her daughter's bed and her own, Madame Lange changed, did her hair and put on a clean apron.

She had been up there ten minutes and she was no doubt undressed, when somebody rang the front doorbell, someone who didn't know the house because he pulled too hard, almost tearing off the chain.

Elie waited a moment, listening to the noises from upstairs.

"Would you mind going and opening it?"

"Right away, Madame."

As he went along the passage with its imitation marble painted walls, he saw the shadows of two legs in the strip of light which filtered under the door. He opened it, found himself looking at a man of his own age and, as if he felt some presentiment, his face clouded.

If he had followed his instincts, he would have shut the door and told Madame Lange, when she asked him, that it was a beggar who had rung. Some came by almost every day.

The school yard, across the way, was empty. There was no one in the street, except the young man who was standing in the doorway, looking at Elie, intrigued and surprised.

Instead of immediately saying what he wanted, he stopped to think. His eyes wandered from Elie's reddish, almost frizzy hair to his popping eyes, his thick lips and finally to his clothes which, like the overcoat, also dated back to Vilna and, when he spoke, he said with a slight smile:

"I take it you're Polish?"

He spoke in Polish, in an accent Elie recognized.

"Yes. What is it you want?"

"I've come for the room to let."

He jerked his head at the notice which, stuck in one of the ground floor windows, announced that there was a furnished room vacant.

"I take it you're a student, too?" he went on.

He seemed amazed that Elie didn't return his smile and left him out in the street, not asking him in. Madame Lange called out from high above the well of the stairs.

"What is it, Monsieur Elie?"

"Someone for the room."

"Will you ask him to step in? I'll be down in a minute."

The newcomer had heard, but he didn't seem to have understood and still looked puzzled. He wasn't a Pole, he was a Rumanian.

"Come in. The landlady's coming down."

Elie stood back a little in the passage to make room for the stranger, and was about to return to the kitchen and leave him there. He could have opened the door of the front room, which was, in fact, the one to let.

It was the best room in the house and, formerly, it had been used as a drawing-room. The wall-paper was garnet-coloured. Besides the bed, it had a chaise-longue, which Elie had always gazed on with envy.

"Do you speak French?" the Rumanian asked him before he had time to go away.

He nodded.

"I don't. I've only just come. I should have been here last month, when term began. At the last moment, I had to have an operation for appendicitis."

He spoke simply and quite cheerfully, happy to find someone who understood him, and, as Madame Lange came downstairs, he added:

"Do you mind staying to translate?"

Even before she was down, Madame Lange, smelling of soap, protested:

"Didn't you show him the room? Since when have we received people out in the passage?"

She could tell Elie was jealous. He knew she could tell. Both knew each other well and there was often a sort of little war between them. For instance, it annoyed him to see her putting on that sugary look to welcome the prospective lodger.

164

"I'm sorry, Monsieur. Monsieur Elie's always so vague, he forgets his manners."

She pushed open the door of the garnet room as Elie said with satisfaction:

"He doesn't understand French."

"Is it true you don't speak French?"

The young Rumanian shook his head with a smile, and asked Elie:

"What did she say?"

"She asked if you spoke French."

He was a Jew, too, but a different kind from Elie. He had sleek brown hair, jet-black eyes, a dry skin and he was dressed more smartly than most students. Among the thousands of foreigners studying at the University, there were only two or three dozen like him, whose parents were rich and who were more often seen in cafés than lecture-rooms.

"Tell him, Monsieur Elie, that it's the best room in the house. It's a little dearer than the others but . . ."

Elie translated in a flat voice:

"What did he say?"

"He wants to know if you do full board."

"I serve breakfast and you know what we do for supper. As for the midday meal . . ."

He translated again and the Rumanian answered.

"What did he say?"

"He'd rather have full board."

The room had been empty for three months and, as term had begun, there was little hope of letting it till the following year.

"Tell him it depends. Usually, I don't do it. We might be able to arrange something."

Had she noticed the newcomer smelt of perfume? Elie had noticed it all right, with a glow of satisfaction, knowing that Madame Lange had nothing but contempt for men who used perfume.

"He says he's not hard to please. He wants to live with a family, so as to learn French quicker. The first year, he'll hardly go to any classes."

It took another ten minutes.

"What's his name?"

"Mickaïl Zograffi. He'd rather you called him Michel."

165

"As he's happy about the price, ask him when he wants to come."

Elie went on translating, sometimes turning to one, sometimes to the other.

"As soon as you'll let him. Straight after lunch if possible. His things are at the Hôtel de la Gare."

As he left, Michel Zograffi stooped and, to Madame Lange's surprise, took her hand and kissed it, and she blushed, either perhaps with embarrassment or with pleasure.

When the door was shut, she murmured:

"He's a very well-brought up young man."

Finally she gave vent to her delight.

"The room's let, Monsieur Elie! How about that? And I was afraid I'd have it empty all winter! How is it, since you tell me he's Rumanian, that he speaks Polish like you?"

"Perhaps he comes from near the frontier. Or perhaps his mother's Polish. It's possible, too, that his father's of Polish origin."

"He didn't haggle over the price. I should have asked more."

She looked on Elie more as one of the family than as a lodger.

"Do you think he's rich? Did you see the signet-ring on his finger?"

Both of them were back in the kitchen. She took a piece of meat from the cupboard, put some butter to melt in a saucepan and peeled an onion.

"You've no need to go up to your room. I'll let you work in peace."

He was in a bad mood and pretended to be wrapped up in his work.

"I'll have a bit more to do getting his meals, but it's worth it. Do you think Rumanians eat the same as us?"

No one ever worried about what he liked or didn't like. It was true he didn't have full board and that he bought his own food. There had never been any real boarders in the house, for the simple reason that, up till then, none of the lodgers had been well enough off.

Whether it was Mademoiselle Lola, Stan Malevitz or Elie, each one had his little tea-pot or coffee-pot and his tin with his bread, butter, cold meat or eggs.

To prevent them dirtying the rooms with paraffin stoves and

166

above all, through fear of fire, Madame Lange let them wander about the kitchen and, afterwards, sit down together at the big table.

Mademoiselle Lola and Stan had their midday meal out. Only Elie stayed in the house and, each day, cooked himself an egg.

"You'd do better to eat some meat, Monsieur Elie. At your age, you need your strength."

He would shake his head and answer:

"I don't eat the flesh of animals."

Once, he'd added:

"It's disgusting."

And it was true that for a while, at the beginning, he had been a vegetarian on principle. Since then, his nostrils twitched at the smell of grilled steak, but he had arranged his budget once and for all, and his menus never changed: in the morning, a bottle of yoghourt, a roll and a cup of tea; at midday, an egg and bread and margarine; at night, bread and an egg.

"Do you think he'll get used to the house?"

"Why shouldn't he get used to it?"

"He must be used to a more luxurious life."

Madame Lange always made out she didn't care for the rich, that they were all selfish, but she couldn't help treating them with respect.

"Is Rumania beautiful?"

"The same as anywhere else."

"Am I disturbing your work?"

He answered coldly:

"Yes."

She was annoyed with him, and came and went round him without saying a word.

Half an hour later, a key turned in the front door. It was Louise, Madame Lange's daughter, who came back to lunch, which meant it was twenty-past twelve, because it took her about twenty minutes to come from the telephone exchange where she worked.

She took off her coat and hat in the passage, tidied her hair, and glanced in the mirror at her face, which, like her mother's was always tired.

Madame Lange had opened the kitchen door.

"Good news!" she called out.

167

"What?" asked the young girl apathetically.

"I've let it!"

"The garnet room?"

There was no other room vacant, so the question was redundant.

"Yes. You'll never guess how much. Mind you, I shall have to provide full board."

"Oh."

Louise came in, didn't address Elie, whom she'd seen that morning and was used to finding there, lifted the lid of a saucepan and asked:

"Where will you give him his meals?"

"In the dining-room, of course."

"What about us?"

"We'll go on eating in the kitchen."

She looked at Elie, who had raised his head, and they seemed to understand each other. All their habits were going to be disturbed by the new lodger.

"Please yourself. It doesn't worry me. Except that you'll complain even more about being tired."

"If he pays as much as the other three put together, it's worth it, isn't it?"

It was forming a kind of mist round them. Nothing in the house had changed, objects and smells were still in the same place, and there was a patch of sun, as there always was about that time, on the white wall in the yard. Elie picked up his text-books and his exercise-books so they could lay the table, but their manner and voices were already no longer the same.

"Where are you going, Monsieur Elie?"

"To take my things upstairs."

In the passage, he thought he heard Madame Lange whispering to her daughter:

"He's jealous."

When he came down, the oil-cloth had been covered with a red check table-cloth, and Louise was laying the knives and forks on the table. Would she be like her mother one day? She was slightly taller than her, just as thin, and she had the same fair hair and the same pale grey eyes.

Unlike Madame Lange's determined features, hers were sad and dull and, even when she smiled, she only half-smiled, and that was rare enough, as though she was afraid of tempting fate.

On two occasions, before she grew up, she had been confined to bed for several months with a disease of the bones and, for years, she had worn a steel-ribbed corset.

The doctors made out she was cured and that a relapse was highly unlikely. Maybe she didn't believe them?

Elie found her beautiful. He had never seen anyone with such soft, delicate skin, or who seemed so fragile. He had never flirted with her. The idea had never occurred to him. But, since he was indifferent to his sisters, the idea that Louise was like a sister was a satisfying, if disturbing one.

At midday, Mademoiselle Lola and Stan not being there, they ate in the kitchen, which saved lighting a fire in the dining-room and fetching and carrying plates and dishes. It was the time Elie liked best. They each had their own place at the table, Louise facing him, Madame Lange with her back to the stove. He took his tin out of the cupboard, unhooked his little stove, fried his egg and laid his bread and margarine on the table.

"Don't you eat meat in your country?"

"Other people do."

"How old were you when you stopped eating it?"

"Sixteen."

It was true. He had been through a mystical phase when he felt pity for every living creature.

"I only hope he's not hard to please."

She was thinking of the new lodger, rather anxiously, because she hadn't resisted the temptation of some extra income, and it worried her, made her feel that the others might regard her decision as a betrayal.

"He must come from a good family. Won't you really have a plate of soup, Monsieur Elie?"

"No thank you, Madame."

"How many more times are you going to ask him, mother?"

"I can't think why he has to be so proud."

She was spoiling for a row, merely because her conscience was uneasy. Now and again, she had a row with Elie who, on such occasions, left the kitchen, slamming the door, and went and shut himself up in his room. Once he had smashed a pane of glass.

Madame Lange took an hour or two to cool off and feel remorse.

That same afternoon, they were once again alone in the house. Eventually, she tiptoed up to the entresol and listened, her head bent.

"Monsieur Elie!" she called softly.

He pretended not to hear, so she had to knock on the door. Without getting up, he asked:

"What is it?"

"Can I come in?"

On such days, he locked his door. He would sulk.

"I'm working. You can say it through the door."

She didn't realize he sometimes had childish fits of rage. He would throw himself on his bed and bite his pillow, not crying, but saying words which sounded like threats. When he eventually came down, his face would be swollen, and his eyes, bigger than ever, would look as though they were going to pop out of his head.

When he first came to the house, three years before, she had said to her daughter:

"Mind you don't stare at him. He's so ugly! He might guess what you're thinking."

They stopped noticing it. It never again occurred to her to compare him to a toad.

"Do you know, Louise, the new lodger doesn't speak a word of French? He must have arrived yesterday or the day before, and someone must have told him about this place."

She kept harking back to him, more worked up than she was willing to admit.

"It's always the same. At first, you imagine things, because you don't know people. When Monsieur Lenizewski came, I thought I'd never stand him a week. I remember the second day, I pointed out to him how he banged the doors and might break them. He answered: *'What I break, I'll pay for!'* He had me in tears. Even so, he stayed four years and his mother came all the way here to thank me."

She kept getting up to take things off the stove and help her daughter and herself.

"Have you got a cold?"

Louise made out she hadn't. She had a cold every winter, too, but it was on her chest and lasted several weeks.

"You're breathing badly."

170

"Perhaps it's because I'm too warm."

It was always too warm in the kitchen, and its windows were permanently steamed up, but that was just what Elie liked about it. Sometimes, in the afternoon, when Madame Lange was going round the local shops, he would be alone in the house, and he would settle himself in a chair in front of the stove, and put his feet in the oven.

"When is he coming?"

"This afternoon."

Louise left at ten past one, because she started work again at half-past. Elie put his things back in his tin, washed his plate and his knife and fork, while the landlady cleared the table.

That was a bone of contention, too.

"It's more trouble you getting in my way than washing your knife and fork for you."

He didn't answer, but put on his stubborn look.

"Won't you tell me why you must insist? One plate more or less . . ."

It was his own idea. He accepted nothing for nothing. Besides, he could have answered that one day she'd end up reproaching him for what she'd done for him. It had happened to a lodger who had stayed there only three months. Madame Lange had offered him to the others as an example.

"He's so easy!"

He had been foolish enough to accept a plate of soup at eleven o'clock every morning and, once, when he was ill, a bucket of coal, which hadn't been charged up to him.

One day, he announced that he was leaving and they found out it was to move into another lodging-house in the same street, where the lodgers were allowed to entertain women.

Madame Lange had gone on about it for a week; she still brought it up over a year later.

"When I think what I did for him! He was always going round with holes in his socks, and I used to go and take them from his room and darn them on the quiet. Do you suppose he gave me so much as a word of thanks? He carried on as if he hadn't noticed. Once when he had just received a letter from home and he looked worried, I asked him: *'Anything wrong, Monsieur Sacha? I hope no one in your family's ill?'* He merely answered: *'That's my business.'"*

171

The kitchen was tidy again.

"Go and fetch your books, Monsieur Elie, and come and settle down again."

He shook his head.

"What's the matter?"

"Nothing. I have to go out."

It wasn't true. She sensed it. It was another way of sulking. He hadn't any friends. He had nothing to do at the University at that hour. He wasn't the sort who enjoyed wandering the streets, especially in cold weather.

If he was going out, it was so as not to be in the house when the new lodger arrived.

"Please yourself."

She saw him come downstairs a little later, a knitted woollen scarf round his neck, his hands in the pockets of the overcoat which was too long for him and whose greenish colour marked him as a foreigner.

He slammed the door as he went out, and that was a sign, too.

CHAPTER TWO

LETTERS FROM BUCHAREST AND THE LACE CURTAINS

ALL day, the sky had kept its cold dawn brightness and now, at three o'clock, a few snow-flakes were falling, so lightly that they melted without trace. Across the way, the lights were on in the class-rooms of the school.

As on every Thursday, Madame Lange, wearing her best clothes, had gone shopping in the town centre and wouldn't be back till five; at half-past five, she might go and pick up Louise at the telephone exchange which was on her way.

Elie had already been alone in the house for an hour, sitting with his work in the over-heated kitchen, his cheeks flushed and his eyes bright from his cold. When he wasn't going out, he didn't wear a tie and often kept his pyjama jacket on under his coat all morning. He only shaved two or three times a week, and today the stubble on his cheeks was nearly a quarter of an inch long.

From the very beginning of his stay, Madame Lange had said to him:

"I can't understand why, at your age, you aren't smarter."

She had hesitated imperceptibly before saying the last word. What she was thinking was: cleaner.

She had added:

"I sometimes wonder if you do it on purpose."

She hadn't gone into details, but her eyes had wandered on to Elie's nails, which were always ringed with black.

The Rumanian could have been at the University, where he had joined the Mining Engineering Faculty. It was possible, too, that he was in a café in the centre with some of his compatriots, because he had come across one or two.

He hadn't yet quite become part of the lodging-house, and yet, in the week since he crossed its threshold for the first time, he had become its leading character. Even when he wasn't there, he was, most of the time, the person in question.

In the mornings, for instance, the landlady avoided making a noise because he stayed late in bed, and she could be heard telling Mademoiselle Lola and Stan as they went out:

"Tiptoe down the passage. Close the door quietly."

Before going up to do the rooms, she would turn to Elie:

"There we are! That's his place laid. Tell him the butter's in the larder. Will you keep an eye on my fire?"

In contrast to Elie, the new lodger was scrupulously clean and spent a lot of time washing himself. As there was no bath in the house, he used to go every other day to the local public baths, and he had even asked Elie if there was a Turkish baths in the town.

His father and mother were the same. They were people who belonged to a world Elie had seen only from a distance. One morning when Michel had gone out, Madame Lange, who was dusting his room, had brought two photographs into the kitchen where Elie was working. Each of them was framed in solid silver.

"Look at his mother. She looks almost as young as him, and yet it's a recent picture, I can tell by her dress."

She had that particular kind of beauty which is usually found only among actresses or, more precisely, because of the way she held herself, rather proudly, she made you think of a singer.

173

The father was handsome in his own way, too, rather small and dry, with a thin, determined face.

On the second evening, Elie had already had to act as an interpreter, translating Madame Lange's questions.

"Ask him if his father's in business."

He repeated the words in Polish and Michel answered obligingly.

"My father's in tobacco. He travels a lot. In fact, he's nearly always travelling, because he has branches in Bulgaria, Turkey and Egypt."

"Does his wife accompany him?" asked the landlady.

Michel answered, with a ghost of a smile:

"Rarely. She stays at home."

"Has she any other children?"

"Only a daughter, aged fifteen."

Every other day, Madame Zograffi wrote her son a long letter, and the first thing he did when he got up, still wearing pyjamas, his hair tousled, was to go and open the letter-box.

"Have they many servants?"

Michel answered, awkwardly:

"Only three besides the chauffeur."

Meanwhile, Louise sewed away in her corner, not even looking up. She never asked any questions, didn't seem to be listening and, when she saw the Rumanian, merely nodded her head and moved her lips slightly by way of greeting. It was as though she avoided looking at him.

At midday, a certain feeling of unease persisted, after a few days. Elie and the two women went on eating in the kitchen while Michel had his meal, all alone, in the dining-room. Each day, he had a special dish to himself, and he was allowed a sweet which consisted either of fruit or pastry.

In the evening, as before his arrival, everyone had dinner in the dining-room. The old lodgers brought in their tins, and ate their own food, while only the new lodger was served a hot dish.

He never remarked on it. Except when he was asked questions, he avoided talking and observing his companions too closely. Besides, in the evening, it was nearly always Mademoiselle Lola who would tell some story, in a mixture of French, Russian and Turkish, laughing easily and shaking her ample breasts.

She was a handsome-looking girl in her way, fat but radiant,

174

always cheerful, and she ate sweets from morning till night. She made out she was a student; in fact, she never went near the University, she couldn't have passed the entrance exam, but took classes at a private commercial school which she preferred not to talk about.

The meal over, each one went up to his or her own room while Madame Lange did the washing-up and, tactfully, Elie was usually the first to leave, even though he was the only one who had no fire in his room.

Stan worked late, he knew, because he could see his light across the yard. Mademoiselle Lola must be reading or idling, probably lying on her bed, staring at the ceiling, dreaming and eating sweets.

Michel Zograffi had been out twice and, the first time, Madame Lange must have got up to go and open the door to him because he had forgotten his key.

One evening, leaving the table, he had asked Elie:

"Would you like to come and have a drink with me in town?"

He had blushed imperceptibly when the Pole answered:

"I never drink."

Besides, it was true.

"We could drink tea."

"I don't like cafés."

He didn't know enough about them to say that, he had only glanced furtively into them as he passed by, though some of them looked as peaceful and reassuring as Madame Lange's kitchen, and students spent hours there, some chatting away over their drinks and others happily playing billiards in the back room.

He preferred not to be in anyone's debt, even for a glass of beer or a cup of tea. Had Michel understood? Was he annoyed at his refusal? There was no way of telling.

That Thursday, all morning, Elie had been wondering what he would do once the landlady had gone out, and he had been hesitating for an hour now, trying to work, ashamed of the temptation to which he would finally succumb.

When he got up to put some more coal on the fire and saw snow-flakes floating down through the still air of the yard, he decided to stop resisting and went out of the kitchen, along the passage and, opening the front door, glanced into the cold, empty street.

In a whole week, Michel hadn't once come back before five in the afternoon, and it was often nearly six before he put his key in the door.

For the first time since the new lodger had become part of the house, Elie went into the garnet room where the heat was even more pleasant and enveloping than in the kitchen, and it was different, too, because there was a stove kept permanently lit and you could see the flames dancing through the mica.

It wasn't dark yet but, because of the curtains which veiled the windows, it was almost in semi-darkness, and the outlines of objects in the corners of the room were beginning to blur.

Because it used to be the drawing-room, the windows were better decorated than in the other rooms, first with lace curtains which entirely covered the panes of glass, then with heavy, draped, velvet curtains, gathered like old-fashioned dresses, which were drawn at night. On the sills of both windows were ornamental copper pots containing green plants.

The two silver-framed photographs, of Michel's father and mother, stood on the mantelpiece and, between them, were boxes of Turkish cigarettes. The dark oak table, an old dining-room table, was piled with papers and books, among which was a French-Rumanian dictionary, and the new lodger used to pace up and down for hours repeating words from it to himself.

Elie tiptoed towards the chest of drawers, as though it was important not to make any noise, as if he wasn't alone in the house, and his movements were furtive and, now and again, he would turn quickly towards the window through which the street looked as if it were covered in mist.

The first object he found was a gaily-coloured box which Michel had received three days earlier and which contained Turkish Delight. There were only five or six pieces missing. At first, Elie closed the box without touching the sweets, then picked up one of a pile of letters in the same drawer.

Was it because of those letters he was there, like a thief, an agonizing feeling in the pit of his stomach and in his legs, as they began to tremble uncontrollably? Perhaps he couldn't have said himself. He was fulfilling a need. And he felt a need, too, to perform a ridiculous childish action, to open the box again, take out a piece of Turkish Delight and stuff it whole into his mouth.

He knew from Michel that Madame Zograffi originally came from Warsaw and that she wrote to her son in Polish.

Mickaïl darling,

If your father knew I wrote to you every other day he would scold me and make out I go on treating you like a child. He arrived in Istanbul yesterday. I received a telegram from him this morning. The house, in spite of your sister being here— she is just now at the piano, playing Chopin—seems emptier than ever.

I wonder if I shall ever get used to living such a long way from you . . .

Elie didn't need to look up at the photograph on the mantelpiece to picture the woman who wrote so passionately to her son that he might have been her lover.

He skipped whole passages, anxiously looking for the most emotional and personal phrases, which brought a flush to his cheeks, and, when he had thumbed through the pages of the first letter, he picked up another, and had to go over to the window to have enough light.

My one and only Mickaïl,
You've been gone twelve days now and . . .

His mother couldn't write to him, because she had died two years earlier. He hadn't gone back to Poland for the funeral. The journey would have cost too much. Besides, he hadn't wanted to.

Mothers, in his district of Vilna, weren't like Michel's. His own had had fourteen children and, especially during the last few years, hardly seemed able to tell them apart. She brought them into the world, in the room next to the work-shop, while the boys played outside and the girls stayed indoors, still and pale. The little creatures swarmed round her, and the elder ones looked after the younger ones. When they were three years old, she sent them out into the street, and only stood in the doorway, hands on hips, when she called them for meals.

All the women in the district, after several births, were fat, shapeless, with breasts that hung down over their bellies, old before their time, with swollen ankles that prevented them from walking.

Perhaps they loved their children, too, in their own way. They washed them, put them to bed, dished them out their soup as though that was all they had been born to do and, at night, going to sleep, Elie used to hear his mother walking to and fro in the kitchen while his father read the paper.

His father didn't write to him, either, probably because he was ashamed of his hand-writing, but his sister Leah's letters invariably began:

Father asked me to tell you that . . .

Nearly all his sister's letters, usually monthly ones, were written in his father's name, after which Leah would add, from herself:

I am keeping well. I have so much work to do for the family that I don't think I shall ever get married. Look after yourself. Don't get too tired. Don't forget you never had a strong chest.
Your sister.

It wasn't from them he received the money which enabled him to study, it was from a Jewish organization which, after he had completed his secondary education, had offered him a scholarship. Later, when he had his degree, he would have to pay back part of the sum given him.

His mathematics professor, at Vilna, considered he was the most talented pupil ever to have passed through his hands. At Bonn, too, in Germany, where he had spent a year, he was considered an exceptional student, and he enjoyed a similar reputation here. If he rarely set foot in the University, it was because he was preparing his thesis and because in two years, possibly in only one, he would have obtained his doctorate.

Then he would become a professor, too. He wouldn't go back to Vilna, or even to Poland. He would almost certainly spend the rest of his life here, where he had, in a sense, carved a niche for himself and, if possible, he would never leave Madame Lange's house.

My great big baby, how I'd love to be holding you in my arms . . .

He wanted to read everything, and at the same time he was ashamed of being there, for fear of being caught.

Just as the thought crossed his mind, he looked up, hearing

steps on the pavement, and recognized the figure of Michel making for the door.

It was so sudden and he was so paralysed, that he couldn't tell if the Rumanian had looked at the windows as he went by. It struck him that it was a natural, almost automatic thing to do, but he hadn't time to think. He was helped by the fact that it was darker in the room than outside. The curtains were less transparent that way than the other, but the paleness of his face might have been visible from outside.

With a trembling hand, he pushed the letters back in the drawer and shut it, trying not to make any noise.

Michel was standing in the doorway, invisible, searching his pocket for his key.

Elie hadn't time to reach the kitchen; he left the room, shut the door behind him, and stretched out his hand towards the front door, which he opened just as the other was holding out his key.

Michel was obviously surprised and Elie stammered:

"Did you rap on the letter-box?"

There was only an old lady in black on the pavement opposite.

"No."

"I thought I heard . . ."

Perhaps Michel's surprise was because he saw the Pole looking so worried. Elie had never been able to conceal his emotions. What really gave him away was the blood rushing to his cheeks and making his ears read. He then began to stammer.

"I'm all alone in the house . . ." he murmured, turning his back and going towards the kitchen.

He heard the student going into his room, and it sounded as if he hadn't shut the door behind him. Back in the kitchen, he sat down again on his chair, took a pencil and tried to look as if he were working, though his hand was still shaking and he could feel the blood throbbing away in his temples. He had no idea how many minutes went by. He didn't even hear the glass door open, and he gave a jump when Michel's voice, very close to him, said:

"Am I disturbing you?"

He shot him a furtive glance. The Rumanian didn't seem annoyed. On the contrary, he was the one who seemed worried. Perhaps he hadn't opened the drawer, or the box of Turkish Delight.

179

"Do you mind if I stay with you a few minutes? I know you're working, but . . ."

It wasn't impossible that he had come back early on purpose, knowing that Madame Lange would be going out that afternoon. Rather awkwardly, he went and sat down, at the far end of the table, in Louise's place.

"You've been here a long time . . ."

Bit by bit, Elie was getting a grip on himself and his eyes were already less bright.

"Will you promise to answer my questions frankly?"

He nodded.

"Since I've been here, I've felt out of things. It was so unpleasant that, after the second day, I felt like looking for other lodgings."

Elie didn't dare ask him why he hadn't. He hadn't recovered his composure enough for that.

The light was turning grey and it would soon be time to light the lamp. The Rumanian's angular features were lit by the window near which he was sitting, and Elie noticed he bore an uncanny resemblance to his mother, to the point of looking slightly effeminate. Or was it slightly childish? His dark, bright eyes fixed his companion with a look of frankness and sincerity. He seemed to be saying:

"Here we both are and I'd so much like to tell you what's on my mind, and ask you to help me! You're three years older than me. You know this place, the people here . . ."

But those weren't the words he spoke. He said, in his rather sing-song Polish:

"Everyone's so nice to me, maybe too nice. I'm spoiled as though I were different from the rest. They don't realize it makes me feel embarrassed. For instance, at midday, I have my meal alone in the dining-room, and it's as though I were in disgrace."

"If you have your meal alone, it's because you don't eat the same as the others."

"But I'd like to eat the same as the others! And have my tin of food in the evenings, too."

"You asked for full board."

"Because I didn't know. I thought that was what always happened. I don't want to be different, don't you understand? I daren't tell Madame Lange, she's so obliging."

Elie suddenly felt malicious, he couldn't help it.

"It's because you bring her in more money than the rest of us put together."

It wasn't even true. To be precise, it was both true and untrue. She was interested in money, definitely. At the same time, she felt a need to give pleasure, to make people happy and make little sacrifices for them.

"Is that true?" murmured Michel, his face clouding.

"Till now, her lodgers have been badly off, on the whole. Stan gives gym lessons to pay for his education. Mademoiselle Lola's the richest, but she couldn't afford full board. There are other lodgings for people like you."

"I'm happy here. I like my room and the atmosphere here. I don't want to change."

Would he have spoken so sincerely if he had discovered Elie's indiscretion?

"I came to ask your advice. Would Madame Lange be offended if I didn't have special meals and if I did the same as the others?"

"She would be disappointed."

"Because of the money?"

"Yes. And also, perhaps, because she's proud of having a real boarder at last. I heard her saying so to a neighbour."

"What did she say?"

"That you were very rich and that your mother almost certainly used to be an actress."

"She's never been in the theatre. So you don't advise me to . . ."

"No. You mustn't change anything."

"I can't even have lunch in the kitchen with the three of you?"

It would have been easy to fix it all up, but Elie didn't want it fixed up, on the contrary, he wanted the Rumanian to remain a stranger in the house.

"You could ask her. If I were you, I wouldn't."

For the first time, Elie realized he was jealous. He couldn't have said what of. He wasn't proud of the feeling, but it was stronger than him. He added:

"Madame Lange and her daughter need the money you give them. They are very sensitive. If they feel . . ."

He was surprised to see his companion so affected. It seemed to be a great disappointment to Michel not to be able to become more involved in the lives of the other three.

His question took Elie off his guard:

"You don't like me, do you?"

And, when the latter couldn't think of an immediate answer, he went on:

"I feel you don't want to be my friend."

It was almost dark and the oval hole of the stove was glowing more brightly.

"I realized it the other day when you refused to come into town with me."

"I never go to town, except to work with my professor."

"Why?"

"Because I'm poor."

It was his turn to talk, but he couldn't help his voice faltering.

"And also because I prefer to remain alone here, in my corner. I don't need anyone."

It annoyed him that the other was studying him curiously, as if he didn't believe him.

"I've never needed anyone, not even my parents."

He said this with a certain malice, because of the letters.

There's no point in having illusions, and then one day finding out that, whatever you may think, that man is alone in the world.

"Are you unhappy?"

"No."

"Don't you love other people?"

"No more than they love me."

"Haven't you ever loved anyone?"

"No."

"No woman?"

He gave barely a flicker of hesitation.

"No."

Louise's image had just entered his mind, but, in all honesty, he didn't feel he loved anyone. Near her, he felt contented, but he never felt the need to talk to her. It was her presence that was gentle and soothing. She was part of the house. To Elie, she personified the house, and they could have lived there together, spent their entire existence there, safe from the hurly-burly outside.

In Vilna, he'd never had that feeling of peace and security. The swarms of people in his district, in his section of society, had a harsher and more violent character; at every step you could sense the struggle for life, children in the streets had the faces of old people, and, at five, little girls stopped playing with their dolls. In the winter, long winters which lasted more than six months, you could see them trudging, barefoot, through the snow and at home he and his brothers used to fight over a pair of boots.

From a distance, it seemed to him like some inexorable process of fermentation; people were like insects, being forced to devour each other in order to survive.

It was because of those months of snow and blizzard that he was sensitive to the cold, and spent hours with his feet in the kitchen stove.

It was because of that fermentation that he shut himself up in Madame Lange's house, as though he had at last found shelter.

Louise had soft, white skin, and a peaceful, resigned look. She came and went noiselessly, seeming hardly aware of what was going on around her.

One day, when he had had a temperature, she had laid her hand on his forehead and he had never known such a peaceful feeling.

Perhaps it was like some child's dream: he could see himself, once he had become a professor, still living in the same house, and Louise looking after him. He didn't think of her in terms of a wife, only as a companion. He could go on working in the same place, by the saucepans with their rattling lids, and the red cinders falling, now and then, through the grate of the stove.

Stan Malevitz and Mademoiselle Lola had never given him offence. They were rather like furniture round the house, into which the alien presence of Michel had suddenly entered. At times, he would have liked to force him to go yet, at others, he felt he had become necessary to him, too.

"What kind of life would you like to live?" the Rumanian asked him thoughtfully.

He answered proudly:

"My own."

"I don't know about myself. I'd like to do something on my own, not depend on my father. It's funny you don't want to be my friend."

"I didn't say I don't want to."

183

"Let's say you can't."

Elie was about to get up and switch on the light, because they could hardly see each other and, if he had done so, both their futures would almost certainly have been different.

It was the half-light which gave their words another implication, a sort of hidden meaning; it was the half-light, too, which made Michel's dry face as eloquent as an old painting, which gave him the courage, after a long silence during which he was struggling with himself, to stammer, looking away:

"You were in my room, weren't you?"

"Did you see me?"

Without realizing it, Elie adopted an aggressive tone.

"I wasn't sure. I thought I saw someone moving behind the curtains. While I was looking for my key, I peered through the key-hole and there wasn't anyone in the passage."

Elie stared at him without saying a word and it was the Rumanian who, embarrassed, hesitated and stumbled over his words:

"What were you doing?"

It was as if he were afraid of the answer.

"I stole a piece of Turkish Delight," Elie flung at him, as he got up; he couldn't remain seated any longer.

He hadn't yet switched on the light.

"That's not all."

The other was now waiting for him to admit that he was looking for money. The idea made him boil inside and, his voice still resonant, he went on:

"I read your letters. Your mother's letters! That was why I sneaked into your room like a thief. I took a piece of Turkish Delight out of sheer defiance. I read your letters. Do you want me to tell you what they said?"

Almost in a whisper, his eyes riveted to the figure moving about in the half-light, Michel muttered, terrified:

"No."

He hadn't expected such an outburst or what he sensed lurking behind the Polish boy's voice and words.

"That's what I stole from you. Because I did steal something. You don't understand. It doesn't matter. Immediately afterwards, you came and offered to be my friend. You knew. Not about the letters. You thought I'd gone into your room to steal your money.

184

Because I'm poor and I might be hungry. Because I still wear the old clothes I had in Vilna. Then you wanted to shake my hand. You felt sorry for me."

Michel, his eyes bulging, didn't move, his fingers tensed on the table.

"I don't need money and still less do I need pity. I don't need anyone, neither you, nor Madame Lange, nor . . ."

He almost, just as when you lose control you swear so as to comfort yourself, said Louise's name.

He didn't need Louise either. He had never needed a woman.

"You were asking my advice in that soupy voice and yet you knew! I'm sure you went and looked in your drawers when you came back and . . ."

"I didn't look in my drawers."

"I read the letters."

"There was nothing secret in them."

"I stole from you."

With an abrupt movement, needing to escape from the tunnel in which he was struggling, he switched on the electric light, and they blinked in its harsh glare and stared at each other, both equally ashamed, looking away as though by mutual consent.

It wasn't merely that the half-light had vanished. There was a sort of exaltation which came for a second and went, leaving them empty, with nothing further to say, no gesture to make so that, for a while, they remained motionless.

When Elie moved, it was to lift the top off the stove and put some coal on the fire. Then he stooped and gave it a poke, and looked at the time on the clock, its copper pendulum beating out the rhythm of the house.

Michel hadn't stirred, hadn't moved an inch and yet he was the first to speak.

"I should like to be your friend," he said, emphasising every syllable.

"In spite of what I admitted to you?"

"Because of what you admitted to me."

"I wish I'd never said anything."

"I don't. I know you better now. Perhaps I shall know you really well one day."

"What do you want from me?"

185

"Nothing. You to help me to get used to things."

Elie almost asked:

"What things?"

But he knew the answer. Michel obviously needed to get used to the place. In particular, he needed to get used to the life. One of the letters contained a revealing phrase:

. . . If your father knew I wrote to you every other day, . . .
and make out I go on treating you like a child . . .

Two large dark eyes, sad and worried, like the eyes of a dog looking for a master, were trained on him, and perhaps it was now his turn to feel sorry. Or was it inspired by his urge to be the stronger?

"We could try," he murmured, looking away.

Then, so as to rid them of their embarrassment, the Rumanian made a joke, like a small boy.

"Who knows? Perhaps I'll have my tin, too, one day."

Voices, at the front door, restored a familiar atmosphere. They recognized Mademoiselle Lola's piercing tones.

"After you, Mademoiselle," said Madame Lange.

The Caucasian girl switched on the light, and the lamp hanging over the staircase came on.

It had coloured glass, red, yellow and green, which reminded you of a church.

Madame Lange, as always, when she came back from town, was laden with parcels which she dropped on the kitchen table with a sigh of relief.

"Back already, Monsieur Michel?" she exclaimed with surprise, forgetting the latter couldn't understand.

She glanced at them in turn. Nothing, outwardly, revealed what had been going on, and yet she frowned and studied Elie closely.

"You have got a long face," she said. "Anyway, I hope you haven't been quarrelling."

"No."

"Did anyone call?"

"No."

She made sure there was some coal on the fire and, before taking off her coat and hat, put a saucepan of water on to boil.

186

"Now, off you go, the pair of you, while I get my supper ready."

Mademoiselle Lola had gone upstairs. Elie murmured in Polish:

"We'd better leave the room."

At the foot of the stairs, they parted without exchanging a word, Michel to the garnet room where a gentle warmth pervaded, and where there were letters and sweets in the drawers, Elie up to the green room, where he put on his overcoat and his cap so as not to feel cold.

CHAPTER THREE

THE COUPLE IN THE CORNER

ONE morning, the postman, instead of slipping the letters through the box into which you could hear them falling if you were in the kitchen, rang the bell, which he only did when there was a registered letter or a parcel.

It was twenty past eight. Louise, who began work at half-past eight, had been gone a few minutes, huddled in her dark coat with its squirrel collar and trimmings, and wearing her squirrel hat. Mademoiselle Lola, with the excuse of an icy wind, had decided not to go to her classes, which wasn't unusual and could hardly have made much difference. She had come down in her pink dressing-gown, looking like a huge doll, and each time she moved, showed a little more of her bosom, which revealed itself as remarkably firm.

Madame Lange had made various signs to her while she was eating: but the Caucasian girl never understood her signs, or pretended not to.

"Mademoiselle Lola!" she had finally whispered. "Be careful. You're showing."

"Who's showing?"

"You are."

She went off into her throaty laugh.

"Is it wrong?"

"There are gentlemen present."

Stan Malevitz didn't seem to have heard, and ate away without

187

a word, as usual, looking at a book which lay open beside his plate.

"Does it worry them?" asked the fat girl.

"If I were you, I'd be the one who was worried."

"On the beaches of the Black Sea, boys and girls bathe in the nude and nobody minds."

"That's disgusting."

Mademoiselle Lola was suddenly furious, as sometimes happened. She got up and, turning to the door, flung back:

"It's your mind that's disgusting."

When the bell rang, she had just got back to her room. Michel hadn't yet left his, and there had been no sound from it, which meant he was still asleep. Elie, standing in front of the stove, was making his tea and watching his egg. At that hour, the smell of paraffin which Madame Lange used to light the fire still hung about the air.

"I'll go," announced the landlady, as Elie made a move towards the door.

He was the only one of the lodgers who answered the bell, made up the stove and knew in which corner of the sideboard to find change to give to beggars. It was nearly always Elie who opened the door to the milkman and handed him the white enamel dipper, saying:

"Four pints."

Through the glass door he saw Madame Lange taking a parcel from the postman and signing the book. When the postman had gone, she remained still a moment, looking at the address with surprise, then came back towards the kitchen without knocking at the Rumanian's door.

Stan got up, stopped in the doorway and, clicking his heels, made a bow. It was probably tact that made him withdraw, because Madame Lange was about to undo her parcel.

His manners involved some complex subtleties.

He never talked about himself or his family. He had merely indicated that his father was a teacher in a Warsaw school and, bit by bit, Elie had discovered that he was in fact only a supervisor, maybe a caretaker.

Stan had fair hair, dressed with great neatness, not a wrinkle in his clothes, and every night he laid his trousers under the mattress. He held himself and walked like an officer. On the walls of his room hung foils and a fencing-mask.

"You can stay, Monsieur Stan. You know quite well there are no secrets in this house."

"I'll be late for my class, Madame Lange."

In the early days, he used to bend double to kiss the landlady's hand while she was busy cleaning the shoes.

"Now, this is no place for that sort of thing, Monsieur Stan! You can say good morning like everyone else."

He never mentioned money, either. No one knew how much he received each month, because his letters and cheques were sent poste restante, and there were no photographs in his room, except one of a school group in his last year, in which he was wearing a cap.

Whenever she was intrigued or moved, Madame Lange used to laugh; it was a form of modesty and, undoing the parcel, she murmured:

"I wonder what I can have been sent from Rumania. Unless it's some Turkish Delight, like Monsieur Michel gets every week!"

She gave a cry of surprise.

"Look, Monsieur Elie! My goodness! Isn't it lovely!"

She held out a blouse of some fine material, embroidered in many colours, the kind that women wear in the Balkans, and immediately broke into nervous laughter.

"Can you see me doing my shopping in that?"

She was delighted and disappointed at the same time.

"It's far too beautiful for me!"

Elie looked on, not saying a word, but carried his tea and his egg over to the table and sat down.

"There's a letter, too. It must be Monsieur Michel who had it sent."

She read it and then handed it to the lodger.

"Read that! It's in French. I wonder what he must have said about me to make her write like that."

It was in an educated woman's handwriting.

Chère madame,

Allow me to say how happy and relieved I am that my son has found a place like yours. In every letter, he tells me about you and the good care you take of him. I must admit I was dreadfully worried when his father decided to send him abroad. I feel less so now I know he is with you.

189

*In some ways, Michel is still a child, as you must have
noticed. Also, don't hesitate to tell him off if necessary.*

*I enclose a little something from my country. My French
has become so bad with the years that I have asked a friend to
write these few lines for me.*

My very best wishes and sincere gratitude,

Votre.

The signature was in a different ink and handwriting.

"Don't you think it's charming of her? I'll never be able to
wear the blouse, nor will Louise, but it's given me more pleasure
than if it was something useful."

She looked at Elie who handed back the letter with a frown.

"Are you still jealous?"

"I'm not jealous of anyone."

"That's because you don't love anyone. I don't believe you. I
can hear Monsieur Michel getting up. I must go and show him
his mother's present. It's my turn today to have a letter and a
parcel. It doesn't often happen."

She was already calling down the passage.

"Monsieur Michel! Monsieur Michel! Can I come in?"

She had the blouse with her.

Elie swallowed his breakfast hurriedly so as to avoid seeing
him, and went up to his room. Ever since the Turkish Delight
and letters incident, the day the first snow fell, things in the house
had gone on as usual, and relations between Elie and the
Rumanian hadn't changed superficially. It was true they seldom
found themselves together in the same room, though.

Elie had gone on translating Madame Lange's questions and
Michel's answers. Once, at midday, when it was sunny, the landlady had called to him in his room.

"Monsieur Elie! Would you come down a minute?"

Michel was out in the street, making the final adjustments to
his camera which was pointing at the house.

"He wants to take a picture of me at the front door, but I'd
like him with me. It's for his mother, you see, so she knows what
kind of house he's living in."

She was wearing a clean apron and had been to tidy her hair.
All Elie had to do was click the switch and that was the photo
Michel sent to Rumania.

190

"Take one of Monsieur Elie, too," the landlady had suggested.
He had replied sharply:

"I never let myself be photographed."

Michel had looked at him unsurprised, as though he understood him and bore him no grudge, merely seeming a little sad. Elie had often felt that look on him and it seemed to say:

"Well? Still not friends?"

The Rumanian seemed sure of himself, sure that one day he would manage to win round the Vilna student. Used to being loved, it clearly surprised him that anyone should, without good reason, persist in remaining hostile to him.

He patiently avoided reacting whenever Elie was cold to him; of the two, it was Elie who became embarrassed first and, unable to recover his composure, went and took refuge in his room.

He was no longer able to work there. Today, for instance, because of the icy blast, it was as cold in there as outside on the pavement, and Elie had to slip into bed fully dressed and wait for the other to leave for the University.

He had hardly heard the front door shut and his footsteps die away into the distance before he picked up his books and went downstairs, with that aggressive look he wore whenever he was annoyed with others or with himself.

In the kitchen, Madame Lange greeted him with:

"Where's the sense in going and sulking upstairs in the cold? You're blue in the face. Hurry up and warm yourself!"

He spread his hands out above the stove, and shivered unexpectedly.

"You just wait and see. One day, because you're stubborn, it won't be a cold you'll catch, it'll be pneumonia. And then where will you be? I've already told you that Monsieur Michel would be only too glad to let you work in his room when he's not there, and I can't understand why you won't let me have a word with him."

"I don't accept favours from anyone."

She longed to answer:

"You accept plenty from me."

Because he used to come down and work in the kitchen so as to benefit from the fire. It was true that he did something in return for her by stoking the stove, keeping an eye on the soup and answering the bell when she was upstairs.

"It's not worth arguing about all over again. I must have a word with you about something that's really worrying me. I didn't want to mention it but, ever since I had that letter from his mother, so full of trust, I've had no idea what to do. I've been thinking about it all morning. I was going to give him a lecture during breakfast, but I didn't dare."

"It's hard for a woman. With you, it's different. Do you know what's going on, Monsieur Elie? I found out only three days ago, when I was dusting his room.

"Monsieur Michel has been going around with bad women! You'll see for yourself . . ."

And, without waiting for any reaction, she hurried into the garnet room and came out holding some photographs. These ones weren't framed. They had been taken with the same camera as the photos of the house.

"I'd never have thought anyone could let themselves be photographed like that!"

There were six in all, four of one woman and two of another. The women were naked, sometimes on a bed, sometimes standing by a window.

They had been taken in two different rooms, rooms furnished very ordinarily, the sort you can rent by the hour, with no personal possessions in them.

The light was poor and the prints lacked clarity.

One of the women, the younger and prettier, looked awkward, embarrassed at being naked, while the other, whose breasts were as large as Mademoiselle Lola's, had taken up cynically obscene poses.

"Would you have believed it of him? I wonder how he came to meet girls like that, seeing he's only just arrived here and only knows a couple of dozen words of French. What really worries me is that he'll come back one of these days with some horrible disease."

The words, in her mouth, were somehow as crude and worrying as the black triangle on both women in the photos.

"Perhaps I ought to write to his mother, she's been so kind and trusting, but I'm afraid of worrying her."

"You mustn't," he said regretfully.

"Do you think I'd do better to speak to him? I'm sure he hasn't the faintest idea what he's risking. I suppose you wouldn't like to do it, would you?"

"It's nothing to do with me."

"He's younger than you."

"Only two years."

"He's mentally much younger. You can see he has no experience of life. That sort of woman's only out for his money. They'll ruin his health. Ever since he told me he'd met some Rumanian friends, I've been worried, because, if they were decent young people, there'd be no reason why he shouldn't ask them here."

She was really tormenting herself.

"Think about it, Monsieur Elie. Do it for me. I'm sure he'd listen to you. He respects you. I must go up and do the rooms. You'll take in four pints of milk as usual, won't you?"

She had left the photos on the table and, when she came back to fetch them and return them to their place, Elie who was looking at them, stepped back sharply. Had she noticed? Looking at them, earlier, he had felt the blood rise to his cheeks and, when the landlady had mentioned horrible diseases, he had turned away so she shouldn't notice his embarrassment.

He had had a disease like that, here, two years earlier, and he had had difficulty looking after himself without Madame Lange noticing. Now, the girl who had given it to him was so remarkably like the one in the photograph with the big breasts that he wondered if she wasn't the same. There was no reason why not. Both had adopted clumsy, exaggerated, erotic poses.

In his district of Vilna, where the boys and girls began their sex lives early, he had never had any dealings with a woman. He'd never thought about it at Bonn, either.

It was in Liége that it had happened to him for the first and only time in his life. Because, one evening when he'd lost his way, he'd come to a street where, in every window, there was a woman in various states of undress, making signs to the passers-by. There were some in the doorways, too, stepping out in front of the men and saying dirty words.

He had been afraid, at first, and had passed by very quickly trying not to look at them, pulling away violently each time one of them caught him by the arm. Arriving in a quieter street, he'd stopped to recover his breath, amazed to find his heart thumping against his chest.

One day, in Vilna, when he was eight or nine, and his parents had sent him one evening to do some shopping some distance from the house, he had heard footsteps hurrying along behind him in the crisp snow. He hadn't dared look round, convinced that someone was chasing him, probably so as to kill him, and he had started to run as, behind him, the footsteps had quickened, too.

He had run for at least five minutes before reaching a well-lit traffic crossing where he'd stopped, hot and out of breath, near a coach-driver dozing on the seat of his sledge.

His heart was beating the same way as it had, later on, in Liége, in the street with the women. No one had caught up with him. He hadn't heard the footsteps again and they had presumably gone off in another direction.

That evening, he had forced himself to go back the same way and, arriving home, hadn't breathed a word about what had happened.

Here, he'd been round the mass of houses and, controlling the panic which was making his legs tremble, he had gone down the street again, more slowly, now and then glancing furtively at the lighted windows. After two years, he still remembered the nagging tune of a pianola in one of the houses with its doors open, and a ghastly woman who'd tried to grab his hand and whom he'd angrily shoved away.

Once again, he'd reached the end of the street and circled round so as to enter it at the same point.

He had just decided that it must happen that evening and he was waiting till he felt calm again: this time he was able to look at their faces and figures; in one window, he noticed a girl sewing, her head bent over her work and, when she looked up and saw him passing, she gave him a reassuring smile.

She was dark, younger than the others. She couldn't have been more than twenty, and she had the same sad, resigned look as Madame Lange's daughter when she was sewing and seemed not to hear what was being said round her.

He didn't turn back. He decided to go round a final time and stop on his next walk through. Other men were passing along the street and, when he returned a few minutes later, the blinds were down and the door shut.

He only went on another twenty yards. A large, fair-haired woman, leaning against a door-post and busily knitting some pale wool, said something to him in a husky voice. He went in without looking at her, and she shut the door behind him, pulled down the blind and took the counterpane off the bed.

When she closed the door again and said good-bye to him in the dark, she added:

"Don't worry. It's just one of those things."

Three days later, he realized he was ill. So as not to have to pay a doctor, and to avoid asking some student who might have helped him, he had consulted some books in the University library and treated himself.

Even now, he wasn't sure he was completely cured. He'd never had any further dealings with a woman. He hadn't felt the urge.

The soup began to bubble in the saucepan. The first red cinders fell through the grate. The wind was whistling in the chimney, and Madame Lange went down to the cellar to fetch a bucket of coal for Mademoiselle Lola.

It was a grey day. The following day, ice covered the roads like black varnish, Stan put on his galoshes, and an old woman fell down at the end of the street and two men helped her to her feet.

He hadn't spoken to Michel, as Madame Lange had asked him. When the Rumanian, that evening, was getting ready to go out, she looked at Elie as if to say:

"Go on! Now's the time."

He didn't move, his face expressionless.

"You shouldn't go out in weather like this, Monsieur Michel. You'll freeze to death."

"I'm just going to have a drink with my friends and I'll be back."

He had brought with him from Rumania an overcoat with an astrakhan collar which, in a town where only a few old men wore them, made him cut a strange figure. By contrast, he seemed even younger. The cold made his skin drier and put roses in his cheeks.

"Any woman would be glad to have eye-lashes like his!" Madame Lange remarked, after he had shut the door.

Elie spent the evening downstairs, alone with the two women. Louise had spread out some material on the table, covered it with a brown paper pattern and, holding some large scissors, her mouth full of pins, snipped away carefully.

Not far away, Madame Lange had placed a bucket on the ground between her legs, and was peeling potatoes and dropping them one by one into the cold water, her apron full of peel.

Elie didn't speak. It was only on rare occasions that he conversed with them. He was absorbed in his work and sometimes stared at them in turn, as though he was looking through them.

"Apparently we're going to have as cold a winter as in 1916."

Madame Lange was talking, but she didn't need an answer. From time to time, she made a remark, which she sometimes left unfinished, and that was enough for her.

"That was the winter we suffered most from lack of food. I remember having to walk twelve miles to go and fetch potatoes from a farm, and having to hide every time I saw a patrol. That was the same winter my husband was killed in Flanders."

Monsieur Lange had been an N.C.O. in the regular army. Two blocks away, there had been a barracks where, in his time, he had spent his days drilling recruits. There was a photograph of him on the wall, in uniform, with the medal he had won attached to the gold frame.

Without Michel, life would have gone on the same every evening and Elie would have remained happy. Madame Lange didn't understand him, and thought he was jealous of the Rumanian.

The photographs to which she attached so much importance were just another example of her lack of perception. He knew, as he had known from the very first, that an alien presence had entered the house and that no good would come of it.

"Are you sure you've cut the arm-holes large enough?"

"Yes, *maman*."

"That's what you said last time and then, afterwards, you had to unpick the dress."

Even trivial remarks like that gave Elie a feeling of security which he had never known elsewhere. Contrary to what Madame Lange imagined, he felt not the slightest envy of Michel. Nor did he suffer from being poor. He wasn't tempted to go and meet friends in a café and talk a lot of rubbish. Nor was he interested in photographing naked girls in their rooms.

Only a few weeks earlier, he would have asked nothing more than to go on living as he was and, at the time, it seemed easy.

"Is your thesis going all right, Monsieur Elie?"

"Yes, Madame. Not fast, because I've come to the hardest bit. tomorrow, I'll have to go and work in the library."

Now and again, he had to go and work in the University library, so as to look up things he couldn't find elsewhere. It was an atmosphere he liked, too, with green lampshades that threw pools of light on the tables and bent heads.

"I wonder if Monsieur Michel will come back late."

"Don't worry so much about him, *maman*," said Louise in a tone which shocked Elie.

"His mother would be the first to ask me to keep an eye on him."

"He's twenty-two."

"Even so, he's only a child."

"For some time now, you'd think he was the only person who mattered."

Was she jealous, too? She had spoken more nervously than usual, and Elie didn't know whether to be pleased or worried.

"You'll understand one day," sighed her mother.

The subject was closed there, because Madame Lange finished the potatoes and went and rinsed them under the tap, before putting them in the soup-pot.

For ten minutes or so Louise and Elie remained alone together in the dining-room, and the young girl was now pinning her dress together. He didn't say a word. Nor did she.

When she looked up, he could see her rather pale face, the delicate curve of her neck, the slight arch of her back, and he felt happy. He had never wondered what her body was like under her wool dress. It had never occurred to him that a man could want to hold her in his arms.

"Have you much more to do, Louise?"

"Less than a quarter of an hour, *maman*."

"I'm off upstairs. I've had a heavy day. Will you put the lights out?"

Madame Lange wasn't afraid of leaving her daughter alone with Elie.

"Good night."

Stan had gone out, too, to give a gym lesson. In the evenings, the trams in the next street only went by every quarter of an hour, and you could hear the sound of their brakes when they pulled up, you could picture them, with their yellow head-lamps and the odd silhouette of a passenger, plunging into the streets lit only by occasional street-lamps. It was ten o'clock when Louise rolled up her pieces of material and slipped them under the cover of the sewing-machine. Quite naturally, as though talking to a brother, she asked him:

"Are you going up?"

"Yes."

It was rare that they switched off the lights and left the room together. She went and switched off the light in the kitchen, too, also making sure that the key of the stove was correctly adjusted, and he waited for her, holding his books, in the passage, lit by the lantern in yellow, green and blue, with patches of red towards the ceiling.

He let her go upstairs first. When they reached the entresol, she stopped to say good night, after which all he had to do was go into his freezing room and slip as quickly as possible into bed.

When Michel got back, it was past midnight and Elie still hadn't gone to sleep.

Next day there was rain, and more rain the day after, seemingly endless rain, and in the main streets some of the shop windows kept their lights on all day.

That afternoon, Elie crossed the river to go and work at the University. He had a long talk with his professor, a world-famous mathematician, and they discussed an important point in his thesis.

"Aren't you going home this Christmas?"

Elie said no. The professor stared at him curiously through his thick glasses. He sometimes used to look at him like that, after they'd been working together, as though he were studying some strange freak.

It was the fifth day, after a dull and empty Sunday, that Elie made his discovery.

He had spent the morning in Madame Lange's kitchen. Immediately after lunch, he had gone to the University, hurriedly leaving the house so as to avoid Michel's suggesting they went along together. It was still raining, a few greyish flakes mingling with the sheets of rain, and he walked along with his hands in the pockets of his old overcoat, his scarf powerless to stop the water dripping down his neck.

In the library, damp footprints led to every occupied chair, and the water streamed down the window-panes, distorting the black branches against the sky.

At half-past five, he got up and put on his overcoat without having spoken to anyone, merely touching his cap as he passed the supervisor.

The bridge wasn't far away, with the dull murmur of the river flowing beneath and the lights flickering here and there on the moving surface. Instead of taking the busy street to the right, where the trams skirted the pavements and where, almost every week, there was an accident, he cut through down an empty street with only the sound of the rain and his own footsteps for company.

Every fifty yards, the street-lamps threw a pool of light, and between the pools there was almost complete darkness.

There was a patch of waste land, a little farther on, and, set back slightly from the houses, a fence which denied access to it. It lay just between a patch of darkness and a pool of light.

Elie stared straight in front of him. He was probably looking down on the ground so as to avoid the puddles. An automatic reflex. He wasn't aware of what he was doing. He couldn't have said what he was thinking about or why, when suddenly he looked up and turned to his right, aware that he was passing a motionless figure. Because of the rain he was skirting the houses, and it was as if he had almost knocked into someone huddled in a recess.

It wasn't one person, but two, and the man had his back against the fence round the patch of waste land, and the woman had her back to Elie and was clasping her companion and looking up at him, her lips pressed to his.

He hadn't looked on purpose. In fact, he was so embarrassed that he almost stammered an apology and, just then, he recognized Louise's squirrel toque and collar, and her sad profile which he knew so well.

He had recognized Michel, too, not only by his coat, but by his shape and his black hair, which he had let the rain get at, because he had taken off his hat.

It only lasted a few seconds. He stopped himself from turning round. He was sure his senses hadn't deceived him. What he wasn't sure was if they'd recognized him. The pale, blurred image of their two faces, of their two mouths pressed together, haunted him.

He still had over five minutes in which to compose himself, but when he got back to Madame Lange's he was still red in the face, and she grumbled:

"You're going to have a temperature all right. I bet your shoes leak."

He realized his eyes were bright, slightly moist, and his face a bit swollen. There was nothing he could do about it. He had always been like that. When he was little, his mother only had to look at him to say without fear of correction:

"You've done something you shouldn't."

Perhaps that was why he had virtually loathed her.

"Go and put on your slippers before supper. I'll give you a couple of aspirins tonight."

He caught a glimpse of himself in the mirror, as he went by, but preferred not to look. The front door was already open. Louise came in and stopped in front of the hat-rack to hang up her things and take off her galoshes.

"Is it time to eat?" he heard her ask in her normal voice, pushing open the glass door of the kitchen.

"We're waiting for Monsieur Michel. He won't be long."

Elie was on the stairs and hesitated before coming down, tempted to make out he was ill, and go to bed. He would probably have gone through with it, if it hadn't been for the dampness and cold that hung about his room.

When he heard a key turn in the door, he quickly made his way to the dining-room where Mademoiselle Lola was already in her place, getting her food out of her tin.

He nodded to her without speaking, went to fetch his tin and passed close to Louise without looking at her.

"Now, children, seat yourselves. I can hear Monsieur Michel coming."

She was busy preparing some fried potatoes for the Rumanian, and the fat was spluttering over the fire and blue smoke filled the kitchen.

"What are you waiting for, Louise?"

"Nothing."

She followed Elie, sat down at the table and, when he risked looking up at her, he was surprised and disappointed to find her the same as any other evening.

200

She didn't take any notice of him. Presumably she didn't know he'd seen them.

All he noticed was that her lips were a lot redder than usual, and her face seemed more animated. Only he could have noticed the difference, it was so slight, and it could have been put down to the rain and the cold.

"Hasn't Monsieur Stan come down?"

"Just coming, Madame!" said the latter on the stairs.

It always took a while before everyone was in his place with his meal in front of him. Michel was the last to sit down and Elie had the impression that, unlike Louise, he was trying to look at her, while a barely perceptible smile, sign of his light-hearted mood, played on this thick, womanish lips.

As Madame Lange served him, she remarked:

"I hope you're not going out tonight in this weather?"

He looked at Elie, waiting, as usual, for the translation, but Elie, forgetting his part, stared out vaguely in front of him.

"Sorry!" he murmured, when he saw everyone looking at him. "What did you say, Madame Lange?"

"I said I hoped he wasn't going out tonight. I don't want to spend Christmas nursing colds."

He translated and caught a delighted twinkle in the Rumanian's dark eyes.

"I shan't be going out," declared the latter cheerfully.

He didn't need to translate, Madame Lange had guessed from his tone of voice and his expression. It seemed to Elie that Louise was trying to repress a smile, too.

He was the only one who, during the course of the meal, knew what they were up to. They avoided talking to each other. In fact, it was Mademoiselle Lola who chattered away, because Christmas had been mentioned, describing Christmas in the mountains where she lived.

Sometimes, as if carelessly, Michel's and Louise's looks met. They warned each other not to stay too long. In fact, their eyes touched, as lightly as birds, while an expression of almost childish contentment spread across the Rumanian's face as he hurriedly bent over his plate.

The change on the young girl's face was subtler, almost invisible; it wasn't joy, there was no sparkle in it, it was more like a look of serenity and satisfaction.

It was as though she had matured, as though she suddenly felt a great potential richness inside her.

"And what do you eat when you get back from Midnight Mass?" asked Madame Lange.

Mademoiselle Lola began to list her country's traditional dishes, as Elie drank his tea and Michel, it seemed to him, shot him a glance of reproach.

SIX O'CLOCK MASS AND BENEDICTION

THE house, like nature, had its seasons, which Elie had come to know. Each year, for instance, first when it drew near to Christmas and you could hear the children in the school singing Advent carols, then a second time at the beginning of Lent, Madame Lange went through a period of devotion.

Instead of being satisfied, as she was during the rest of the year, with Low Mass on Sundays, she made a point of going to six o'clock Mass every morning and returning to church at the end of each afternoon for Benediction.

Now and then, Elie, who was a light sleeper, would hear her alarm go off on the second floor at twenty to six. It was about the time when the bells of the church, whose roof could be seen just above that of the school across the way, were beginning to toll; shortly afterwards, the landlady would go downstairs, carrying her shoes, though it didn't prevent her always making the same step creak.

Elie would lie there with his eyes open in the dark, listening to the pulse-beat of the house and, after remaining still for a while, he would imagine he could hear the sleepers breathing in their rooms, or the shuddering of their springs as one of them turned over.

Madame Lange didn't go into the kitchen before Mass, but sat on the bottom stair and put on her shoes, and, when she had shut the door and plunged into the cold and empty street, the bells would ring the second time.

Mass was short. There were only a few people there, old spinsters and widows, dressed in black like herself, scattered about the vast nave, staring at the candles on the altar. At half-past six, she was already back and the first thing she did, before taking off her coat and hat, was to light the stove.

Little by little, the house would start its morning routine, first with the smell of burning wood and paraffin, then with noisy footsteps to and fro in the yellow room on the first floor, where Stan Malevitz did his limbering-up exercises before getting washed.

Later came the smell of coffee and, later still, Louise's footsteps on the stairs.

The following week, Louise didn't come down as early as usual. As in previous winters, she had 'flu, complicated by bronchitis and a sore throat. Since it wasn't possible to heat the attic which had no fireplace, she didn't stay in bed, but spent her days in an armchair, by the dining-room stove.

As a rule, a fire was only lit there for Monsieur Michel's lunch and the evening meal.

"You ought to go and sit in there, Monsieur Elie. You'll be better off in there than in the kitchen and my daughter won't disturb you."

Louise didn't complain and wasn't a difficult patient. Her mother used to go and fetch her a few books from the local library and she would read nearly all day, only breaking off to gaze at the grey sky above the white walls of the yard.

Ever since Elie had stumbled on the two of them in the corner, Michel hadn't said a thing, hadn't mentioned the incident, but Elie wasn't convinced that he hadn't recognized him. The Rumanian would look at him conspiratorially, some-times, with a kind of childish glee, as if to say:

"Life's good, isn't it?"

He was playing with it, relishing it, smiling his disarming smile and showing his clean, white teeth.

He knew a little Russian and, sometimes, at table, teased Mademoiselle Lola, who never got annoyed with him, but laughed till she was gasping for breath, with her curious throaty laugh, taking every opportunity of resting her hand on the young man's shoulder or arm.

"You great fool!" she would exclaim. "He's a great fool, Madame Lange! It makes me wish I had a brother, provided he was like him."

And the landlady would answer:

"Are you sure it's a brother you want?"

Louise would seem not to hear, but carry on, absorbed in her own personal life, which was like a long interior dream, so that Elie sometimes doubted his senses, wondering if it really was she he'd seen, her lips pressed to the Rumanian's, up against the fence.

He wanted to hate the new lodger. He tried to. It was his fault that things in the house were no longer the same, that Elie had lost his peace of mind and that he wandered round like a cat that had lost its old place.

Was Michel aware of this? He lived his own life too intensively to bother about others and, because he was happy, everyone around him ought to be, too.

Elie now spent nearly all day, alone in the dining-room, with Louise. From time to time, he would go up to the entresol to fetch a text-book or exercise-book. Often, when he came down, she hadn't heard him and would give a start when she saw him close by.

"Did I frighten you?"

"No. You're the only one in the house who goes round without making a noise."

"Because I wear slippers."

He wore slippers with felt soles.

"When you're wearing shoes, too. I wonder how you manage."

He didn't do it on purpose. It dated back to his childhood. God knows their house in Vilna was noisy enough! He remembered having frequently scared his mother, who had said to him one day:

"You make about as much noise as a ghost."

It had made him feel sad, at the time, because he felt that there was more to the remark than the words conveyed. Here, too, in the street, once, when he'd stopped to watch some children playing marbles, they'd suddenly turned round and, seeing him standing where they didn't expect anyone to be, they had taken fright and started to run away.

If he hadn't seen Louise in Michel's arms, he might have put off the work he did each afternoon in the library till later, so as to stay with her all the time her 'flu kept her in the house.

Now, it no longer had any meaning or any attraction. Michel

didn't stay in, either. He continued to go out in the evenings to see his friends and, perhaps, the girls he photographed, naked in their rooms. Only occasionally, Elie thought he caught a brief exchange of glances between him and Madame Lange's daughter, but he wasn't sure, and he wondered if that embrace in the rain hadn't been a chance one.

He was seldom in the house at five. Even so, he knew that the landlady, after stoking and regulating the stove, put on her coat and hat and hurried off to church, skirting the houses as she went.

Benediction lasted longer than Mass, because there were a great number of prayers recited, and you could hear them being murmured from outside. She normally got back about twenty past six, when the lodgers came back in turn, and their communal life began again. More often than not, Michel arrived back last and sometimes his breath smelt slightly of drink.

On Monday, about half-past four, as he was working under one of the green lamp-shades in the library, Elie suddenly had a violent headache which took away his zest for research that day. It was getting near the holidays and the streets were black with people, flowing in a continuous stream past the lighted shop-windows, crammed with goods.

As he passed the wall of the church, he heard the booming voice of the priest reciting prayers and the answering murmur of the congregation. For a moment, he was tempted to climb the steps and push open one of the baize doors which he had never been through, but whose creak he knew so well. Partly through laziness, and partly through tact, too, he didn't do it. He had never been in a Catholic church. Scores of times, Madame Lange had urged him to come, saying:

"Wait till you see how beautiful it is! And you'll hear the great organ."

He had heard it, from the street, passing by on Sundays, particularly after High Mass, when the doors were opened wide and all the faithful tramped dully out.

As he approached the house, the streets became darker, emptier and, as he turned the final corner, he was the only person on the pavement.

It was only when he was a few steps from the door that he noticed a thin strip of light filtering between the curtains of the garnet room. It was barely five o'clock. He was amazed that Michel was back. He didn't however, open the door silently on purpose, in fact he didn't realize he hadn't made a sound, and he made his way normally towards the end of the passage where the dining-room door was open.

He immediately noticed that Louise's armchair was empty. Nor was Madame Lange's daughter in the kitchen. The door which led from the dining-room to Michel's room was closed.

What surprised him most, what made him draw in his breath, was that he could hear no noise. Even when he went up to the door and put his ear to it, he couldn't hear the slightest murmur, not even a whisper, and he remained for some while, his ears cocked, a look of physical pain on his face.

Against his will, he finally succumbed to the temptation of stooping and looking through the keyhole, and he almost knelt down, supporting himself on the door-post.

When he could see, he didn't move and it seemed to him that, all the while he was looking, he wasn't breathing. All he could feel was the blood throbbing in his wrists and neck.

The light in the room was reddish, like the silk lampshade. The bed was on the right, a very high bed, and Louise was on the edge of it, her legs apart in the same attitude as the girls who made Elie feel so embarrassed, while Michel, standing up, was thrusting at her with great rhythmic movements.

He could only see their profiles. The young girl, possibly because of the lighting, seemed very pale, her lips the colour of her skin, her nostrils pinched, her eyes closed. Her face was expressionless, and so still you might have thought she was dead.

Michel didn't speak, didn't smile and, from where he was, Elie could hear his breath coming and going in time with his movements.

When it was all over, Louise gave two or three twitches, her face screwed up, so that you couldn't tell whether it was from pleasure or pain, the man remained still a moment, stepped back a pace, gave a short, sharp laugh, and stretched out his hand to help her to her feet.

Elie stood up, too, left the dining-room and stopped in the passage to hang his overcoat on the coat-rack. He could hear them talking in the room.

He went up to his own room and, without switching on the

light, flung himself on his bed. He clenched his fists and forcibly gritted his teeth. Incredible ideas flashed chaotically through his mind with volcanic force, and from time to time a word recurred to him which didn't necessarily mean anything, yet was nonetheless an expression of what he was feeling.

"I'll kill him!"

Kill! With the incoherence of a child who has just suffered some cruel deception, he repeated the same phrase in a whisper, through clenched teeth:

"I'll kill him!"

It wasn't a plan, still less a decision. He didn't want to do it, but saying it comforted him. He couldn't cry. He had never cried in his life. When his mother beat him, she ended up by seeing red, because of what she called his indifference, and shouted at him:

"Cry! Go on, cry! Aren't you made of the same stuff as other people? You're too proud, aren't you?"

It wasn't true. He wasn't proud. He wasn't doing it on purpose. It wasn't his fault if his face went red, if his eyes became bright, yet remained cold, and if he couldn't show his feelings more.

He had forgotten his headache. He felt pain everywhere, as though his entire self were one great wound. He had at last come to hate Michel. He hated him. Till the day he died, he would see Louise as he had just seen her, so close that he hadn't missed a flicker of her face.

Was it the first time they had done it? They weren't clasping each other. There was no love, no affection, in their attitude, in the way they moved. Almost immediately afterwards, when Elie was out in the passage, they had begun talking in their normal voices.

Now, Louise must have gone and sat down again in her armchair. Several voices were audible, he could hear the poker in the kitchen stove, the door opening to admit Stan Malevitz. Only Mademoiselle Lola still had to come back.

He wondered if he should go downstairs. He would have liked to do something extraordinary, it didn't matter what, something as dramatic as his discovery, but he couldn't think of anything.

"Monsieur Elie!" The landlady was calling him from the foot of the stairs and, to his surprise, added:

"Mademoiselle Lola! Supper-time!"

And Mademoiselle Lola came out of her room, where she must have been before Elie got back. She couldn't have gone out. Louise knew. The two of them weren't worried. Who knows? Perhaps they had heard Elie come in, too, and that hadn't stopped them, either.

Someone was coming upstairs. Footsteps approached his door. He jumped to the foot of his bed as Madame Lange murmured:

"What are you doing there in the dark?"

"I'm resting."

Clumsily, he added:

"I've a very bad headache."

"Come down quickly or you'll catch cold."

He obeyed. She always grumbled at him, but he felt sure she liked him, really. She was the only person in the world who showed him any interest, if not affection.

"Have you been back long?"

Both of them were on the stairs. The doors were open. They could be heard from down below. He ought to have answered that he had been there nearly an hour, so as to worry them, but he didn't dare.

"Shortly before you."

The others, including Louise, were at table. The door of the garnet room, through which Michel had entered, was still open and, throughout the meal, it worried Elie. Although he could see nothing inside, because the light was out, he couldn't help remembering the bed.

For a long time, he didn't dare look at Louise and she, when he finally gave her a disapproving look, was wearing her normal expression, though she was less pale than earlier. Two or three times, she answered her mother's questions calmly.

"It's starting to freeze again," announced the latter, "and I wouldn't be surprised if tomorrow we get some real snow, the kind that settles."

Then, turning to Elie, she said:

"Ask him if they have snow in his country."

He was about to refuse. It all struck him as ridiculous, almost revolting. For a moment, the setting, the faces round the table, the clatter of knives and forks, the house itself and the alien town around them ceased to be real.

What was he doing here, so far from his place of birth, among people he didn't know, who didn't speak his language and who had nothing in common with him?

"Aren't you going to translate?"

"Yes. Sorry."

Even his own voice rang strangely in his ears. Why translate a question to which he knew the answer?

Michel had barely answered when Madame Lange asked:

"What did he say?"

"That, some winters, they have more than three feet of snow."

"Even so, it's warmer down there than here."

"It's very hot in summer, very cold in winter."

"I don't think I'd like that climate."

Louise didn't seem to be taking any more notice than usual. Mademoiselle Lola began, as she always did whenever someone gave her a lead:

"In the Caucasus, in my country . . ."

And why didn't he ever talk about his? Madame Lange sometimes remarked:

"Anyone would think you were ashamed ot it."

He wasn't ashamed, but he didn't want to go back there, either, because he had no happy memories to lure him.

"You never seem to want to talk about your parents and, when your mother died, you didn't cry. Weren't you fond of your mother?"

He had merely answered:

"No."

She had been cold with him for several weeks because of that answer. Was Louise fond of her mother? Was she fond of Michel? Did he have the slightest affection for her? Was there anyone in the whole world who was capable of really loving another?

He ate mechanically, because he wasn't hungry. He felt he was blushing and that the landlady would eventually ask him what the matter was. She never missed that sort of thing. But she never, for instance, asked her daughter what she was thinking about, when she went off in a dream.

It came immediately after a pompous remark by Stan Malevitz about skating-rinks in Warsaw.

"Is anything wrong, Monsieur Elie? I hope you haven't had bad news?"

"No, Madame," he said, as Louise turned towards him and eyed him closely.

He was thrown and, gulping his tea down the wrong way, choked and held his napkin to his face.

"You're not yourself. For some days now, you've not been at your best."

"I never feel very well in the winter."

"If only you'd build up your strength! You can't stay healthy working like you do and eating practically nothing."

That was what worried him most here. She knew he hadn't enough money to buy more food. She repeated:

"If I were you, I'd do anything, even sweep the streets. You could give lessons to students less advanced than yourself."

A week earlier, she had suggested:

"Why not give French lessons to Monsieur Michel. He's looking for someone. He'd pay whatever you asked, he doesn't know what to do with his money. It'd mean an hour or two a day and you could eat properly."

"No, Madame."

"You're too proud, that's the trouble with you. It'll be all very well when your pride lands you in the grave!"

He had no need to turn to Louise because, if he did, he was sure she would understand. Perhaps she already had. She went on watching him closely and he lost his composure, wishing someone would speak and distract their attention from him.

He didn't want to look at Michel, either, whose rather mawkish perfume had reached him across the table.

"I've often noticed that, as the holidays draw near, foreigners often feel unhappy. It's understandable. They see other people getting ready to enjoy themselves with their families. Ask him, Monsieur Elie, what they eat at home on Christmas night."

She went on again almost immediately:

"I'm sorry. It never occurred to me he was a Jew, too."

That produced a silence.

He didn't get to sleep that night till about three or four in the morning, when there hadn't been the faintest sound for ages either in the house or from the town. He heard the last tram go by, then, much later, the voice of some drunk, and after that, the church bells rang out the hours and half-hours. He tried not to move, because it was warm only where his body lay and, if he stretched out his arm, his hand touched the ice-cold sheet.

Several times, he thought he had a temperature and was going to be ill. He knew it wasn't true. It wasn't true, either, that he was keeping his eyes open and that his thoughts were getting muddled, distorted, sinking into the unreality which was gradually becoming more important than the reality.

For instance, at times, it was as if he had two identities. His body lay huddled up in the sheets, the blankets pulled up to his nose, and his thoughts were whirling round in his large head of red hair. At the same time, he was watching that body, examining it with a certain disgust, coldly studying those remarkable thoughts, strung out like beads on a rosary. They were no pleasanter than his puffy face and his frog or fish eyes. Perhaps his mother hadn't loved him because she found he was as ugly inside as outside, and that was why he had never had any friends, and why no woman had ever looked at him as women look at other men.

What was he jealous of? He was only a lodger like the rest of them in the house, he wasn't even like the rest, because he was the poorest and Madame Lange shouldn't have done him any favours. He took advantage of the warmth of the kitchen and dining-room. He took advantage of their company and the sound of their voices. He was the one who cunningly hung on to them because, deep down, something he would never have admitted to anyone, which he loathed to admit, he was afraid of being alone.

He was robbing them, Louise even more than the rest. Not having the courage to make advances to her and risk being repulsed, he rubbed himself against her, contenting himself with her company, the rhythm of her breathing and the sight of her pale face.

Now, because she was making love with a man, a natural thing for a male and a female, he was jealous. He already had been, before then. He would have been, even if nothing had happened between her and Michel.

Because, in short, he was bound up in the lives of others, and because he wouldn't allow their lives to change.

What had he hoped, without ever being able to formulate it clearly? He hadn't planned to go back home when his studies were over. He didn't want to go anywhere else, either.

Like a child who imagines it will never leave its parents, he would have found it natural to stay there for the rest of his life, with Madame Lange carrying on her daily routine and Louise keeping him company.

It was absurd. Michel was right. And it was precisely because Elie felt this that he grudged him his presence and even his existence.

He was accused of being proud. Everyone, beginning with his mother, had been wrong. Including those who, like his professor, thought him self-sufficient and viewed him with a mixture of admiration and apprehension.

He wasn't proud. He wasn't self-sufficient. Only, what he needed from others, he took without their realizing it. Deep down, he was a thief. And a coward.

As for Louise, he had laid claim to her just as Michel had. Not in the same way. He hadn't thrown her down on a bed. He hadn't wanted to. The idea frightened him.

He was no less involved with her, unknown to himself, more intimately even, than the Rumanian, so much so that he suddenly felt as though he had been cut off from his roots.

It was inevitable that he would come to hate Michel. It was indispensable. It would comfort him not to have only himself to hate.

He dreamt that he couldn't sleep, that he was examining his conscience with icy detachment. The bells rang. It hadn't crossed Michel's mind that he might have done something wrong. He was innocent and, when Elie tried to condemn him, every voice round the table reiterated:

"Innocent!"

An alarm went off, bare feet touched a cold floor and he went off into a deep sleep, until there was a knock on the door and Madame Lange's voice saying:

"Are you ill, Monsieur Elie?"

He was forced to answer no in a sleepy voice.

"I've been calling you for at least ten minutes. It's eight o'clock. Monsieur Stan has already left."

His mind was a blank, his body slack. Downstairs, he forced himself to look straight at Louise who merely asked him:

"I hope you haven't caught my 'flu?"

When he had finished eating, Michel came down to breakfast,

smelling of eau de Cologne and a little powder near the lobe of his ear. He said a vague good morning to the young girl, not giving her any special look and, half-an-hour later, he could be heard hurrying off down the street.

A dozen times, that morning, as he was working barely a few yards from the young girl, the thought occurred to him:

"I'll kill him."

He didn't believe it. It was rather like Madame Lange always coming out with:

"Jesus, Mary and Joseph!"

And she almost certainly wasn't thinking about Christ, the Holy Virgin and his foster-father.

A voice called from upstairs:

"Will you take in four pounds of potatoes and a bunch of carrots, Monsieur Elie?"

He went through the routine mechanically, as though he no longer believed in it.

"Are you annoyed with me?"

He gaped at Louise, not knowing what to answer, and not realizing he hadn't said good morning.

"No."

"I was just wondering."

Once again he'd blushed and his ears were burning. The real reason for his confusion was that, at that precise moment, as he looked at her pale, composed face, he wondered if the same thing would happen that afternoon as on the previous day.

Could she guess what he was thinking? Was she like her mother, who had a flair for sniffing out the shameful thoughts people keep to themselves?

He went to the library after lunch. The snow began to stick to the soles of people's shoes and the tram-rails were inky black against the white of the street.

At half-past four he got up, returned his books to the librarian, and made his way to the river which he crossed at the same time as on the previous day.

As he passed in front of the church, he heard the same voices. Approaching the house, he walked more quietly than ever, carefully inserting his key in the lock.

He had seen the reddish strip of light between the curtains. Looking up, he had seen Mademoiselle Lola's darkened windows.

He stopped a moment in the passage to take off his coat and cap which were damp and, a few moments later, he felt some relief as he went into the dining-room, not because Louise was there, but because she wasn't.

He must have looked exactly like a burglar. He was one, because he was aware of what he was doing. It did not prevent him from going up close to the door and, without stopping to listen first, stooped down and put his eye to the keyhole.

Probably because it was a little earlier than on the previous day, he saw them doing other things, and their actions were as clear, the details as sharply defined as if he had been looking through a magnifying-glass.

The following day, and the day after, too, he was back in the same place, at the same time and, when they were all gathered together at table, he looked ill at ease, realizing that his voice wasn't normal, and that his eyes were flickering nervously over their faces and that everyone was noticing.

He didn't dare turn towards Michel, because of the latter's smile. Then Louise was acting naturally, so that no one could have guessed anything from her expression, her eyes didn't blink when they met Elie's, and there was a smile of subtle irony on the Rumanian's lips.

After the third day, Elie was so convinced that Michel knew he had his eye to the keyhole that he wondered if he wasn't forcing the girl to do certain things out of sheer defiance.

"I'm beginning to think you're really ill, Monsieur Eli. If I were you, I'd go and see a doctor."

"No, Madame."

"You've no idea what you look like. Take your temperature tonight before you go up."

It was a mania of hers. She had a thermometer in the soup-tureen belonging to the service she never used, her wedding present, in which she put small objects, buttons, screws and electricity bills.

Every morning, the first thing she did when Louise came down, was to stick the thermometer in her mouth, and she would watch her daughter out of the corner of her eye, for-bidding her to talk.

"A hundred and one point five."

The doctor hadn't been called to see the young girl, because it was the same every year. Her mother served her light meals, with the accent on custard and, all day, there was a jug of lemonade by the armchair.

Twice a day, she painted Louise's throat with iodine.

"I'm convinced you've a higher temperature than she has. Only you're too proud to . . ."

That word again, it was so stupid it made him clench his fists! "If I was your mother . . ."

She wasn't. She was Louise's mother and she hadn't noticed Michel's smile which, from morning till night, expressed his contentedness. Elie couldn't manage to define that smile. There was nothing he could compare it to, except the smile of a conjurer who has just brought off an astounding trick with the audience watching delightedly.

If he directed it at Elie more than at the others, it was because Michel knew that Elie was the only one who was in a position to appreciate it.

He was juggling, tossing balls up in the air, and they were returning obediently to his hand. Everyone was completely baffled. It was amusing.

Life was a funny thing. There they all were, all sitting round the table, under the lamp which threw an even light on all their faces, talking about totally unimportant things; each one of them, except Michel, was eating food from his tin; Madame Lange, who was forty-five, a widow and a know-all, was treating them like children and handing out advice to them, little suspecting that an hour earlier, behind the now-open door, on the bed you could see if you lowered your head, her daughter was adopting the same positions, making the same gestures as those creatures who appalled her so much!

The meal over, Michel once again felt the urge to go out. He came back at midnight. He must have been drinking, because he had difficulty finding the keyhole.

He slept on, next morning, lazing in bed, enjoying his half-sleep, while the landlady revived his fire.

"There's a letter from your mother, Monsieur Michel."

He read it without stirring from his sheets, smoking his first American cigarettes of the day. They were sent him from home. He was sent all kinds of luxuries. Everyone conspired to make his life a pleasurable game.

215

He didn't look round for Louise when he came into the dining-room, knowing that she was there and that she was his. All he had to do was open the door, later on, and beckon to her. She would come to him, obediently and contentedly, ready to do whatever he asked of her.

"Do you feel all right?" asked the professor with whom Elie had gone to work that day.

Him too! The same question! The same worried look, possibly not so much because of his physical condition as because of something else which they all sensed, but couldn't find words to express.

"I'm not ill."

"You haven't a temperature?"

The words recurred to him.

"I'll kill him."

And now, he began to wonder if it mightn't happen one day. For no special reason. For nothing at all. Because. . . .

He had to leave at half-past four.

CHAPTER FIVE

SUNDAY AFTERNOON AND MONDAY EVENING

IT was after what happened on the Sunday afternoon that the idea of punishment first entered Elie's head, immediately took root and replaced the other ideas which had been circulating there during the previous few days. With that last idea everything became clear and simple, nothing else remained, somehow, except a question of justice.

After the midday meal, Madame Lange had gone up to her attic room and spent an hour washing herself, as she always did when she went and spent the afternoon at her sister's, who had a cake-shop the other side of the town in the street which led to the cemetery. When she came down, she was wearing her best dress, her shoes which pinched, and she had put on a dab of scent.

"You're not going out then, Monsieur Elie?"

"You know quite well I only go out when I have to."

"Is Monsieur Michel in his room."

"I haven't heard him leave."

"You don't mind putting the soup on to heat up about half-past five?"

Louise wasn't well yet. Even when she was all right, she only grudgingly accompanied her mother to her aunt's, where the two sisters never stopped grumbling to each other.

The weather was dull and depressing, the town silent, the slightest noises coming over louder than during the week, and Madame Lange's footsteps could be heard until she turned the corner by the tram-stop.

Mademoiselle Lola had gone to the cinema. Stan Malevitz must have gone, as he did every Sunday, to the Polish Students' Club which was situated over a restaurant in the town's centre, where he played chess. Elie, sitting with his work in the dining-room, knew Michel hadn't gone out. Louise, too, her head buried in a book, not turning the pages, sat there motionless, patiently, while the minutes ebbed slowly away and the kitchen clock could be heard ticking through the door.

However, sometimes, without moving, she looked thoughtfully at the Polish boy, as though trying to understand, to solve some problem, and her look, which he was aware of, made him feel uncomfortable.

He had decided to stay, and he stuck it out for half an hour, unable to concentrate on his work. The atmosphere was stifling, so calm, people and things so still, that they oppressed him like some nightmare; on the other side of the door, Michel had stopped moving about, and it was Elie who was wondering, almost in desperation, what to do.

There was no sound of life anywhere, either in the street, or in the house and, if it hadn't been for the tram which, on Sundays, passed by only occasionally, it would have seemed like some dead world.

He was the first to move and it must have resembled a flight. Jumping up, he stared at his papers a moment, hesitating to take them upstairs, reached the door without saying a word and went up to his room, where there was nothing for him to do, and stood there staring through the window at the yard and the backs of the houses.

A week had passed, during which he had been living without any kind of support, without anything solid under him or around him. Even words lost their meaning when they were repeated all day, and especially at night in bed:

"I'll kill him!"

He had his ears cocked. He'd only been in his room five minutes, when he heard a creak downstairs, then some sounds too slight to be identified.

He did everything in his power to stop himself going down. The previous day, too, he had tried, almost regretfully, to stay under the library lamp until half-past five, but even so he had come away.

This time he hung on for a few minutes, maybe ten, he couldn't be sure, not having a watch or clock and, as he began to move again, he gave a sigh which sounded like a moan.

They couldn't have failed to hear him going down the stairs, at least one step of which creaked. He did nothing to avoid being heard, went back into the dining-room which was empty, Louise's chair unoccupied. Elie's being in the house had made no difference.

He had wanted to stop himself but, as before, he finally went over to the door. He stooped, knelt on one knee, his eye found the keyhole and peered into the room which, with the curtains apart, looked different.

He didn't see Michel straight away, he was out of his field of vision, but Louise was right in front of him, standing between the two windows, already practically naked, slipping a piece of white material off her body, then picking it up and putting it on a chair.

He hadn't seen her completely naked before, with her bony shoulders, her protruding spine and a hollow between her thighs, like a little girl's. She was embarrassed by her breasts, which she held for a while in her hands, the Rumanian remaining invisible.

Elie couldn't understand what he was doing until he heard the click of the camera.

So it had been planned beforehand. When Louise went into the room, the camera was already on its tripod. Now, Michel was moving it, placing the young girl near one of the windows so as to catch the light from the street. He was wearing flannel trousers and the top part of his body was bare, his chest covered with black, curly hair.

Before taking another photo, he held out a lighted cigarette to

Louise which she smoked awkwardly, and said something to her which Elie couldn't catch and which made her smile.

In the space of half an hour, he used two rolls of film while she obediently took up the poses he asked her. Now and then, he offered her a piece of Turkish Delight. When he photographed her on the bed, he went up to her twice to open her right leg wider, smiling with pleasure.

The last time he entered Elie's field of vision, he was naked, too, and without pausing, stretched himself on top of her.

It was then that he turned towards the door with an ironic expression, and whispered a few words in Louise's ear.

She, too, automatically looked round, immediately turned her head away and, from then on, avoided looking at the door.

Both of them knew he was there. Elie was now sure that Michel had known from the first day and, either through bravado or for a joke, he was deliberately making Madame Lange's daughter adopt certain poses.

Today, because the window was in line with the door, Elie's face must have cast a shadow behind the keyhole which, if he hadn't been there, would have let the light through.

It made the Rumanian laugh. He went on laughing and working away at Louise's body, while she kept her head turned away.

It was then, as he was watching the pair of them, that Elie decided, as if making a discovery:

"He must be punished."

It was becoming a question of justice. He wasn't yet capable of expressing himself clearly, but there was a revolt brewing inside him, one which had been nagging at him for days but which he hadn't succeeded in analysing.

It's like having a boil, for instance. First, your skin becomes tender in a certain place, till it really starts to throb and a small, hard head appears.

"He must be punished."

Punish was a precise word. Michel mustn't be allowed to carry on, indefinitely, with impunity. There was something monstrous, insolent in the happiness he was flaunting, and which he genuinely felt in every nerve of his body.

Elie had never seen a man before who was completely happy, happy in every way, the whole time, every minute of the day, and who innocently made use of everything round him, to add to his enjoyment.

It was not only Louise whom Michel was using today and the previous days, but Elie, too. It was Elie he was whispering about, as he stood by the bed, naked and unashamed, playing casually with the young girl's little breasts.

Two or three times he chanced to turn towards the door, and it was as if he wanted to speak to Elie, even call to him. He was on the verge, at one point, of going and opening the door. He took a step forward, still smiling, and Louise's voice begged him:

"No, Michel! Not that!"

What exactly would he have done if Louise hadn't stopped him? He didn't consider himself beaten and said one of the few French words he had learnt:

"Why?"

She went on, almost in tears:

"Please don't!"

She was in a hurry to get dressed. Without turning towards the dining-room, she made for the chair with her clothes on. Michel caught hold of her. She struggled, not very hard, and what happened then was entirely due to Elie's presence. Louise kept shaking her head, frightened of what was being asked of her, but her companion took no notice, and kept on smiling and whispering in her ear.

What would he have said to Elie if she hadn't stopped him opening the door?

Elie didn't dare wait, afraid he might have the same idea again. He felt convinced he had just plumbed the depths and that, from now on, the decision was made.

His preserve had been trespassed on. He had nothing, and yet they had managed to steal something from him. It was no longer possible to live in the house. And because, perhaps, of that laugh, earlier, it would no longer be possible for him to live with himself.

Such a crime could not go unpunished. The day before, when he had had thoughts of killing, without being really serious, Elie didn't know why it was, and thought it must have been because of Louise.

It was because of the other. He knew, now. He didn't need hate, only a sense of justice. If he didn't do something about it,

Michel would go on being happy and then, the moment such a thing was possible, the world was void of meaning and a life like Elie's became a sort of monstrosity.

Yet he wasn't the monster, it was the other one, who was stealing from them all and, on top of that, was stealing their sympathy.

From now on, Elie could calmly repeat to himself:

"I'll kill him."

Because he would kill him. He made his decision, as he was on the stairs, half-way to the entresol, and the door of the garnet room opened behind him. He didn't turn round. He knew that Michel, completely naked, was insolently watching him beat his retreat.

"I'll kill him."

And back in his room again, he added:

"Tomorrow."

After which he might recover some of his self-respect, but if he didn't, at least he would be revenged.

One person, one person in the world would know what he had done: Louise. Would she understand?

It was unimportant. Nothing had any importance now, because the decision was made. He was already feeling less wretched.

Instead of thinking of good and evil, of those who have nothing and those who have everything, he had to think in precise terms, of what he would have to do when the time came, not that evening, because it was Sunday, and Michel seldom went out on a Sunday evening, but the next day, almost for certain.

They must have been surprised in the garnet room to hear him come downstairs again, stop in front of the bamboo coat-rack and close the front door behind him. He didn't glance at the windows to see if they were behind the curtains watching him go.

Perhaps Louise was afraid he would speak to her mother? She surely didn't realize that it wasn't her that mattered, that her little story was overshadowed, and that the account Elie had to settle had nothing to do with her.

What he had to find out was, who would carry the day Michel or him?

And as Elie walked along streets where passers-by were rare and dusk was falling, Michel himself gradually began to lose his personality.

What really mattered was Elie and the rest. Elie and the world, Elie and fate. On the one side, there was himself, with his red hair and frog face, his two eggs a day, his blue enamel tea-pot and his overcoat which caught the attention of small boys in the street, Elie who had been wondering for years if there was a place for him anywhere and who, when he at last believed he had found one, saw himself being pushed out. On the other side were the rest, and that was the part Michel was playing.

Elie didn't hate him. He no longer needed to hate him. Perhaps it wasn't the Rumanian's fault. It certainly wasn't his fault, but it wasn't Elie's fault, either.

He had to save himself. It was essential to see justice done.

When he got back to the house it had been dark for some time and he was surprised to see Madame Lange, in her outdoor clothes, wearing a hat, and feverishly lighting the kitchen stove.

"Where have you been, Monsieur Elie?"

She spoke reproachfully, as though he owed her something.

"For a walk."

She was so surprised to hear him say the word, it was so unlike him to brave the cold outside unless he had to, that she stared at him, at a loss for an answer.

"You let the fire go out," she murmured gently, "and you didn't remember my soup. As for that daughter of mine, it never occurred to her to glance in the kitchen. When she's wrapped up in a novel . . ."

Elie's text-books and exercise-books were still spread on the dining-room table and Louise, who was once again installed in her armchair, avoided his eyes not knowing if he was trying to avoid hers.

He felt sorry for her, now, and, thinking over what Michel had done to her pallid body, he even felt a certain disgust.

Was it possible that, a few days earlier, her presence in the same room was enough to give him a feeling of peace and well-being, and that he had thought it perfectly natural to spend the rest of his life with her?

The warmth and light in the dining-room were no longer the same and, during supper, Madame Lange seemed like a stranger who, for some unaccountable reason was treating him with familiarity.

"Tell us what you've been up to, Monsieur Elie."

222

They were all there, except Stan, who must have been eating at his club. Michel was less confident than that afternoon, and after smiling several times at Elie without any response, he began to eye him rather anxiously. More with annoyance or perplexity. Elie wasn't reacting as he would have liked. Instead of playing up, blushing and appearing awkward as he did the previous evening, not knowing where to look, he suddenly seemed full of confidence and his eyes were cold and determined.

"As I said before, Madame, I went for a walk."

"All on your own?"

"Yes, Madame."

"Are you sure?"

"It doesn't matter whether you believe me or not."

"It must be the first time in your life that you went out when you didn't have to. You wouldn't be in love, by any chance?"

"No, Madame."

"Do you believe that, Mademoiselle Lola?"

"It doesn't concern me what others do. It's enough trouble having to worry about myself."

For three years, he had taken part in similar conversations, every evening, and he hadn't tired of them. Now, it was all over. He was no longer part of the house. It was as if it didn't exist. The house in Vilna, too, had lost its reality when he had left it, and he could hardly believe that the hotel room in Bonn, where he had spent a year of his life, hadn't crumbled into dust.

Round the table, no one suspected. When, now and again, Louise frowned, it was through fear of being pregnant, or it might simply have been the painfulness of her bruised flesh.

As for Michel, he thought he was alive and he was already nearly dead. Anything he thought no longer mattered. The wheel was running free. It no longer mattered what became of Elie and the rest.

"Don't you agree, Monsieur Elie?"

"What, Madame?"

"Didn't you hear what I said? I was talking about health. I was saying that I doubt if Monsieur Michel has a weak chest."

She turned towards the Rumanian, unconcernedly.

"I bet you've never had bronchitis, or even a cold in your head. Isn't that right?" She went on:

"Translate."

223

He did so, word for word, in clipped tones like a judge reading his verdict to a prisoner.

"What did he say?"

"That he's never been ill."

"Just as I thought. Some people have all the luck."

Precisely! That was what Elie was going to put a stop to, he knew how, he was working out a plan, which he was perfecting, in their very midst, yet he was still listening to what they were say-and and answering when he had to.

The gun was in the room, in the left-hand drawer of the dresser where Madame Lange kept her husband's belongings: a penknife, broken pipes, a pair of spurs, a service revolver and a box of cartridges. Like all the other cupboards in the house, the drawer didn't lock, and while the meal was going on round him, Elie began to stare at it with a feeling of contentment.

It wouldn't be long now. He wondered how he could have waited so long, how he could have been so blind as not to see such an obvious truth.

The great mistake was to permit impunity, because, then, everything is falsified, and the innocent believe they are guilty and in fact, become guilty through sheer weakness.

For a week, he had acted like a thief, every time he knelt down at the door to watch Michel cynically enjoying himself and, all the time, defying him.

"What are you thinking about, Monsieur Elie?"

"Me?"

Everyone burst out laughing, he had been so many miles away.

"You were looking positively ferocious. You looked as if you were getting ready to fight someone."

That made them laugh, too.

"Don't be cross. I was only teasing. I didn't mean to hurt you."

Then, feeling he was saying something positive he announced: "No one can hurt me."

Who knows? If he had been capable of crying he might have burst into tears at that precise moment and, from then on, everything would have been different.

He couldn't cry. It was Louise who cried, suddenly, through sheer nerves, left the room, burying her face in her hands and went and took refuge in the kitchen.

*   *   *

Next morning, in the dim light of his room, things seemed less cut and dried than the previous day, but as it was all decided, he didn't worry.

He had heard Madame Lange getting up and going to six o'clock Mass. A few minutes later, he had got up, as he'd planned because it was the only time of day when he could be sure there was no one in the dining-room.

He left off his slippers, but put his overcoat on top of his pyjamas. He had never had a dressing-gown. He didn't need to switch on the light, but groped his way, without going wrong; then, noiselessly, he opened the drawer, took out the revolver and cartridges and went up to his room again.

Because of the cold, he went back to bed but kept his eyes open. Though there were details he still had to attend to, there was no question of re-examining the main idea.

Thinking about the details helped him. It stopped him being depressed by the world which, that morning, struck him as a great void in which he would have been the only one who was struggling and not knowing why he was struggling.

While Madame Lange, back from Mass, was lighting the fire, for instance, and the familiar smell of burning wood and paraffin filtered under his door, he would sometimes wonder:

"What's the point of it?"

Was he in danger of questioning the whole thing? Tomorrow, the next day or the following year, it would all blow up again.

That was why he tried to concentrate on the details of his plan. His first idea was to pretend to go out that morning. He could make his departure convincing. While Madame Lange was doing the rooms, for instance, he would go and open the front door and stand for a moment on the step. It would be while she was doing Stan's room at the back of the house.

He would rush upstairs and say:

"I must leave at once. I've just had a telegram to say my father's dying."

He wouldn't be holding a telegram. All he would have to do is mime having stuffed it in his pocket. When you mention some-one's dying or dead, people never like to ask questions, still less appear suspicious. He would be in a strong position.

He would pack his case. She would help him. She'd have no reason to touch his overcoat, with the revolver in its pocket.

225

He would take the tram to the station, leave his things in the left luggage office, and he would wait till night, no matter where, some place where there was no danger of meeting anyone he knew.

As for his real departure, that would be on the night train which stopped at Liége at 11.45. He would take a ticket to Berlin, get off at Cologne and find a connection to Hamburg. He had often dreamed about Hamburg, because it was a large port and he had never seen a port. He had never even seen the sea.

He ate his egg, as he did every morning, forgot to take any notice of Louise and it didn't cross his mind that Michel was, as usual, asleep in the next room.

The idea wasn't a good one, he realized later on, as he was working in the dining-room. It would be better if the telegram business happened after instead of before. Firstly, because it would be easier at night. Also, because it wasn't certain that Michel would go out that evening. He thought of lots of other things. In the afternoon, he went to the library, keeping his coat on, because the revolver was in the pocket, and he didn't dare leave it in the cloakroom.

Even with night falling, the time passing and the warmth surrounding him, he didn't become excited again, and he felt he'd never been so calm in his life.

Glancing at the library clock, half-past four, he went through a bad patch. It was the time when on the other days, he went off, whatever happened, and glued his eye to the keyhole, and he was tempted to do it a final time. Oddly enough, it hurt him to think that they were together in the room and that he wasn't there to watch them.

It wasn't jealousy. He didn't want to be jealous. Since the previous day, all was clear and he didn't let himself question anything.

It was a difficult moment to pass through, that was all. He watched the hands going round on the clock-face, imagined Madam Lange stoking her stove and regulating the key before she went, then jogging along the row of houses, and going into the church, echoing with prayers.

He could see Louise getting up, as it at some signal; going towards the door and unthinkingly taking her place on the edge of the bed.

At half-past five, the bad patch was over, because that was the end of it, Madame Lange was back and it was his turn to hurry out into the street. He found the spot he had chosen, the fence round the piece of waste land, not because of the memories the place evoked, or through sentimentality, which would have wrecked everything, but because it was, in fact, a kind of strategic point.

First, it was a corner that was nearly always deserted. Then, less than twenty yards away, began a network of narrow alleys, into which it would be easy to dive without fear of being followed.

His first idea had been to wait for Michel half-way across the bridge which all the lodgers used to come and go into town and which, after a certain hour, no one crossed. Then it had occurred to him that water was a good conductor of sound. The explosion would make more noise there than elsewhere and there was a risk of its being heard at both ends of the bridge.

It was a pity. There was some mist. He had to avoid all romantics. It mustn't look like a drama of passion.

During supper, he murmured:

"I have to go out and see my professor."

As Madame Lange didn't say anything, he'd wondered if she'd heard and he had to repeat the remark. It would have been better not to. Besides, three or four minutes later, she showed she had heard.

"When will your thesis be ready?"

"I don't know. Maybe in a year."

He felt he had the need to add:

"Maybe never."

"You know quite well you'll get through. The way you've worked, you've deserved it. And you need it."

Whereas Michel didn't!

Why bother about what was said at table? Why bother to look at each of them in turn, as though they still had anything in common?

He had already left. He was going. He had to leave before Michel, in case the latter decided to go out. Nothing, up to now, suggested that he intended to stay in.

Madame Lange called him back just as he reached the end of the passage.

"Monsieur Elie!"

"Yes, Madame."

"Would you post a letter for me? You'll be passing the post office."

Should he have seen a sign there? Without knowing it, she was supplying him with a convincing explanation for the telegram which, until then, had been the weakest link. The main post office was just past the bridge and stayed open all night. It would be bad luck if he couldn't find a crumpled telegram in one of the litter baskets. People receive them poste restante every day and don't always take them away.

He had to act quickly, so as to be back in time at the spot where the fence lay back from the houses.

He didn't have to think any more, just act like a machine.

That was the easiest part. The painful period of gestation was over, so was the moment of decision.

He crossed the bridge, only had to glance into two litter baskets, as if he had chucked something away by accident, and found a telegram which said:

Arriving tomorrow eight o'clock. Kisses. Lucile.

He didn't smile, though he almost did. And, as he came out of the post office, he saw Michel making his way towards the town centre.

Now he would have to wait till he came back. All the streets around were lit, and there were a good many passers-by. Michel didn't see him and he was able to follow him at a distance.

In the main street most of the houses were cafés or restaurants, and Michel went into a very brightly lit place, with marble-top tables, where students were drinking beer under a cloud of cigarette smoke.

The hardest thing for Elie, now, was to have to wait for an hour in the cold, possibly two or more hours, without losing heart. The mist helped him, by distorting the lights and passers-by and giving the town a ghostly look.

From time to time, he went up close to the big glass windows in front, where he could see Michel sitting at a table with two young men. All three were chatting and smoking cigarettes. Michel wasn't drinking beer, but a small glass of some yellowish liquid.

On several occasions, he laughed. Perhaps he was telling them what had happened the previous day, and was referring to Elie

228

and the face he must have been pulling the other side of the door?

In a doorway, a little further off, two lovers were huddled together in the shadows and remained motionless for nearly an hour, before going off without a word towards a tram which only the woman got on to, while the man, standing on the pavement, watched her go.

It was cold and damp. Elie's throat began to feel sore, and it worried him because, when he had a sore throat, it took him weeks to get better.

At a quarter past ten, the three young men at last got up. It was Michel who paid. And it was he who walked between the two others along the pavement. They had been storing up their warmth and didn't hurry, impervious to the cold, one of the three even having his coat unbuttoned.

Elie took a short cut to the right to reach the bridge quicker and, when he crossed it, the mist was so thick on the river that the gas-lights were like yellow discs, not projecting any light.

He walked hurriedly, anxious to reach the fence, anxious for it all to be over.

He huddled in the corner, at the spot where Michel had been leaning, the night he held Louise in his arms. You couldn't see him as you approach. You could only see him from about two yards, and only if you turned your head in his direction.

Away at the crossing, where Michel was leaving his friends, they must have chatted some while as they shook hands. It took a long time. A quarter of an hour went by.

Then, suddenly, Michel's steps came echoing along the pavement. Elie drew the revolver from his pocket, making sure the safety-catch was off. There was nothing he could do about it. He had to punish him. It was no longer an affair between himself and Michel. It was a question of justice. The footsteps approached rapidly, rather jauntily. He felt the young man was humming, he wasn't sure, because his ears were beginning to buzz.

He had decided to wait till the last second, and only to fire at point-blank range so as not to miss.

He saw a body materialise, then a face, took a step forward, found himself close to Michel, so close that he could hardly stretch out his arm.

He fired immediately, but he didn't fire at his face on purpose. In fact, he didn't aim. It was as though the gun exploded at the

229

end of his arm, jarring it. At the same time, Michel's mouth and chin disappeared, leaving only a kind of red and black gap. The Rumanian didn't fall down straightaway, but looked at him, both surprised and imploring, as though there were still time to do something to help him.

Finally, he crumpled up, twisting round, and his skull rang against the flagstones on the pavement.

Elie hadn't moved. He forgot to run away. He almost forgot an essential part of his plan, too.

To pay his train fare, he needed more money than he had, and he would find some in Michel's wallet. Besides, by removing his identity papers, he would delay the police calling on Madame Lange. It was the worst part. He leant over, almost kneeling down, as he did behind the door, heard a curious noise, like a gurgling sound, in Michel's throat, thought he saw his eyes flicker, then, wallet in hand, began to run.

He lost himself in the maze of alleys, came out at a place he didn't recognize and had to make a wide sweep, before he found himself back at the house where all the lights were out.

He went straight up to the second floor, to the wrong door. Louise's voice called out in the dark:

"What is it?"

Madame Lange was in bed, too. She didn't switch on her light straightaway. Before she did, he had time to tell her what he had planned to say.

"What time can you get a train?"

"In thirty-five minutes."

"I'll help you pack your case."

She appeared in her nightdress, her hair in curlers, and he heard Louise's voice again:

"What is it, mother?"

"Monsieur Elie has to go. His father's dying."

A few minutes later, holding his case, he strode off towards the station and, crossing the bridge, hurled the revolver into the river as he had planned.

He had forgotten Michel, thinking only of his train which, at all costs he had to catch.

Part Two

THE OWNER OF CARLSON CITY

CHAPTER ONE

APARTMENT 66

THE phone ringing broke the silence so violently that even those outside heard it; some of them slowly turned their heads and pressed their noses against the windows to peer into the shadowy hall. Elie, busily working out his figures, glanced mechanically at the switch-board, swapped over a plug and unhooked the receiver.

"Carlson Hotel here," he said, as though he had been repeating the same words for years.

"Craig here."

There was a pause and Elie knew exactly what was coming.

"She hasn't come?"

"No one has, Mr. Craig."

"No message?"

"I should have told you."

For three days, Harry Craig, the director of the mine, had telephoned every three or four hours, and he wasn't the only one in Carlson City who was impatient.

Gonzales, who now combined the functions of hall-porter, luggage-porter and page, got up from his seat by the lift where he was reading a picture magazine, and crossed the empty, resonant hall, his footsteps echoing as if in a church. To see Elie, he had to go right up to the main reception-desk, behind which the latter was sitting at a table, with the telephone switch-board in front of him, and the pigeon-holes with the keys and guests' mail to his right.

With slow movements, his body heavy, Gonzales leant on both elbows and spoke so lazily he was almost inaudible.

"What did he say?"

231

"Who?"

"Craig."

"He didn't say anything. He's waiting."

"Do you really think so?"

Elie, once more absorbed in his figures, stopped listening, and Gonzales watched him carry on for a while, sighed, scratched his nose and went back to his seat where he resignedly took up his picture magazine again.

The clock over reception showed ten past ten and Manuel Chavez, the manager, still hadn't come down from his apartment. He had merely telephoned at about half-past eight, shortly after the post had arrived. Elie guessed from his voice that he was still in bed.

"Anything new?"

"Nothing, Mr. Chavez."

Half and hour later, his wife had asked to be put through to the kitchens to order breakfast.

The young married couple from Vermont, who had arrived the previous evening, had gone down to the dining-room where they found themselves on their own and, ill at ease and oppressed by the silence and emptiness of the hotel, had paid their bill and gone on towards Mexico, after filling up with petrol.

Only five rooms out of forty were occupied, all five by people working for the company. They were waiting, too. Two of them had announced that they would be leaving at the end of the week if there was nothing new. Everyone said the same, including Chavez, who was as fed up as the rest, and Harry Craig, in the offices down the street, who no longer tried to hang on to anyone who wanted to go.

Three months earlier, no reflection on the hotel, half the rooms had been taken, sometimes they all were, and the hall staff consisted of five or six, most of the black leather armchairs at the feet of the pillars were occupied from morning till night and, at drinks time, it was almost impossible to get near the bar.

Now, it was as if the town was dying. Sirens no longer rent the air announcing the changes of shift, the little wagons, suspended from cables which, at some points, ran above the streets, were standing still near the pylons, and the four huge chimneys of the kilns at the end of the valley were no longer capped with greenish smoke.

It happened all of a sudden when the machines, which for twenty years had been excavating the red earth from the mountain, eventually hollowing out a gigantic crater, had revealed a subterranean lake whose existence had never been suspected. Harry Craig, who was both chief engineer and director of the mine, had immediately phoned the big boss, Lester Carlson, in New York. The latter, unperturbed, had simply answered, as if his mind were on other things:

"I'll see about it. Meantime, do the best you can."

Craig was gasping and trying to explain to the man sitting in his Park Avenue apartment that it was impossible to go on with the development in the present circumstances, that there were important decisions to be made and that the eventual drying up of the lake created problems which. . . .

"We'll see to it, Harry. I'll call you in a few days' time."

Craig couldn't understand his lack of interest and, failing to understand it himself, how could he explain it to his subordinates? The foremen were beginning to think he knew more and was hiding the truth from them.

"Do we give up?"

The same had happened elsewhere, here in Arizona, and New Mexico, and also in Mexico, beyond the chain of mountains that spanned the horizon. All over the place there were deserted mines, and whether they were silver mines or copper mines, like this one, nature had regained control of what had once been streets, houses remained standing, empty and useless, and direction signs still stood by the sides of roads that led nowhere.

Usually, it was because the mineral yield wasn't great enough to pay the development costs. Sometimes, it was because a vein had been exhausted.

The Mexican workers, who went back each Saturday to their own country, had been the first not to return, because there was no work for them, so they wandered the valleys, looking for jobs on ranches. Others, Americans, usually technicians, had gone off to try their luck elsewhere.

Those who owned houses in the residential area, on the far side of the arroyo, and who were mostly married with families, spent a large part of their time round the offices, in silent groups.

"What's been decided?"

"We don't know. We don't even know where he is. He's left New York."

Lester Carlson must have been fifty-five. He had inherited the mine from his father at the same time as several others in the United States and Canada. He also owned a six thousand acre ranch about fifteen miles from Carlson City and, before his marriage, he used to spend a month or two there now and then, with about thirty or forty guests, for whom he chartered a special plane.

There were still about five thousand people living round about the hotel, all of whom depended on him and, every day, asked for news.

Unable to reach the big boss again by phone, Craig had sent him wire after wire. The second week, he had decided to make the trip to New York, but he found the Park Avenue apartment closed up.

It was only when he got back and was thumbing through the daily gossip columns, that he stumbled on the explanation.

Dolly Carlson, former cabaret dancer, who married Lester Carlson, copper-mine magnate, is in Reno to obtain a divorce. Lawyers on both sides are trying to conclude a financial settlement. The marriage took place in California, eight years ago, under the joint estate system.

After long negotiations with the bank, Craig had obtained the necessary funds to pay those technicians he was anxious to keep, and to support those workers who were burdened with families and couldn't go off and chance their luck.

Chavez, too, the manager of the hotel, had been left to his own initiative and had sacked more than half his staff.

Just as the Carlson divorce decree was about to be signed, fresh demands by Dolly Carlson have jeopardized the settlement and the lawyers are at their wits' ends.

It had taken them two and a half months to come to terms, during which time Carlson City grew a little emptier each day. It was May. The thermometer at the hotel door fluctuated according to the hour, between 90° and 100°. The huge ventilators in the ceiling turned noiselessly, day and night.

In the mornings, the hall was almost fresh, because the sun shone on the other side of the street, just opposite, where old Hugo rocked gently in his rocking-chair, between his cigarette-

234

counter and magazine-stall. Except when he lowed the shutters at night, nothing divided the shop from the pavement. It was more like a sort of porch, without a front or display-window, where everyone in town stopped for a moment or two during the course of the day.

Hugo, who weighed more than nineteen stone, never got up to serve his customers. They would take whatever they needed themselves, then go over to him, and he would stuff notes and change into the pockets of his vast yellowish trousers.

He accepted racing bets and would occasionally grab at a telephone, within arm's reach, so as to place them. God knows where, some bookmaker he had an arrangement with. In the entrance, there was a coloured boy who cleaned shoes, and Hugo would send him from time to time to the hotel for news.

"Hasn't she come? Hasn't she called or wired?"

Ten to fifteen men, according to what time it was, would be leaning up against the hall windows outside, just smoking and spitting on the ground, all wearing more or less the same clothes, blue trousers and white shirts, the Mexicans wearing straw hats and the Americans cowboy ones.

Mac, the barman, had suspended all credit, and spent most of the time alone in his bar listening to a small radio.

Elie took over at eight in the morning, only finishing at eight at night, when the night receptionist relieved him. The following week, it would be his turn to do nights. Before, three of them took it in turns, but the third man had got a job in a hotel in Tucson.

Chavez at last came down not by lift but by the stairs, because his apartment was on the first floor. Every morning he wore a freshly pressed white suit, his face was closely shaved, and his thin moustache looked as if it had been inked in.

He came and leant on the reception-desk, too, and watched Elie, vaguely as he was working.

"I don't suppose there's any news?"

"No, Mr. Chavez."

"I wonder if it's worth while putting fresh flowers in the apartment."

Whereas the houses in the town only had one or two floors, often only a ground floor, the hotel, built forty years earlier by Carlson senior, who founded the mine, was a six-storey brick

235

building. The sixth floor, set back, was surrounded by a terrace, and it was there that old Carlson had his apartment when he came to Carlson City. It was only much later, a few years before his death, that he bought the ranch by which he had in a sense, never profited.

His son, too, had often occupied the apartment, which was marked No. 66.

Now, three days previously, a wire had arrived, not from Reno, but from New York, saying:

Prepare apartment 66.

It was signed: *Dolly Carlson.*

Craig had had no warning at all. At first they hadn't understood. They had advanced theories till Mac, the barman, hit on the key to the mystery.

"Get this! The divorce is fixed and it seems they've signed the papers. It's just come over the radio."

"Who owns the mine?"

"All it said was they've split the property."

After Craig had called Park Avenue again, an unknown voice had answered:

"Mr. Lester Carlson caught the plane yesterday for Europe."

Out in the street, the sun was gradually driving back the shadows and soon, in the early afternoon, the venetian blinds had to be lowered and the ventilators were blowing in only warm air.

Like most of the inhabitants of Carlson City, except Chavez, the only person who wore immaculate white suits, Elie worked with his jacket off and his shirt-sleeves rolled up over fore-arms which were covered with red patches and fair hair though, when he was on reception, he always wore a tie.

"Maybe I'd do better to put fresh flowers all the same."

No one here had ever seen Dolly Carlson on whom, it seemed, the future of Carlson City would depend. If she hadn't received the mine in her share, why should she have wired for No. 66 to be got ready?

Chavez had barely moved off towards the florists, two doors away from the hotel, when the phone rang:

"Carlson Hotel here."

"Craig here."

His voice sounded more excited than earlier.

"Is Manuel there?"

236

"He just gone out. He's gone to the flower-shop. He won't be long."

"Is that you, Elie? Ask him to call me as soon as he gets back."

"Anything new?"

"Maybe."

Elie was dependent on a woman, too, about whom he knew nothing even though, ten years earlier, she had been the talk of New York society. Like so many others, longer than most, for seventeen years, he had had his own house here, a white house built of wood, surrounded by a large verandah, on the coolest side of the hill, across the arroyo.

The business and residential areas faced each other, both on a slope, and from the front entrance of the hotel Elie could see his own roof.

When the phone rang, it was for him, a woman's voice, his wife, Carlotta, who asked him in a strong Mexican accent:

"Has she come?"

"Not yet."

"She hasn't sent any news?"

"We still don't know a thing."

Gonzales left his seat by the lift to go and repeat to the men leaning against the front outside:

"Still nothing."

However, someone knew something. When Chavez got back, Elie said to him:

"Craig asked you to call him."

"Is there any news?"

They'd heard those words till they were sick of them, for three months, and they were almost ashamed to repeat them. Some of them touched wood or kept their fingers crossed when they did.

"He didn't say so."

"Put me through."

There was a phone on the desk. Elie dialled the number, then stuck his plug in one of the holes on the switch-board.

"He's on the other end."

"Hallo, Harry? Manuel here. . . . What? . . . Yes. . . . Yes. . . . I can hear you all right. . . . Who? . . . The agent? . . . And he doesn't know if she's coming here . . . I don't understand, no. . . . When? . . . Tonight? . . . I'll call him. . . . It's the only thing to do. . . . I don't see why he can't be asked for instructions. . . .

No! I shan't tell him how I found out. . . . Someone must have spotted her and mentioned it in town. . . . Yes. . . . Right away."

He hung up, frowning, looking rather impressed, and said to Elie:

"She's here."

"Where?"

"At the ranch. She came last night by car with her chauffeur, her private maid and her secretary. Craig just heard from the agent. No one was expecting her. They only knew who she was from the photos in the papers."

"Does she intend to call by here?"

"That's what I want to find out. I'll call him. Get me the ranch."

Chavez picked up the receiver.

"Hallo! . . . Hallo! . . ."

Someone had unhooked the receiver, but suddenly it was as if there was no one at the other end. After a while, however, he heard a woman's voice.

"Mrs. Carlson? . . . I can't hear you very well. . . . Her secretary? Would it be possible to speak to Mrs. Carlson? . . . Yes. . . . I understand. . . . I'm sorry I had to go on about it. In an hour or two from now? . . . It's about the apartment I was told to reserve. . . . At the Carlson Hotel. . . . No. . . . No one has turned up. . . ."

He was listening, surprised, toying with some matches, with Elie never taking his eyes off him and Gonzales watching him from a distance.

"I'm sorry. . . . I didn't realize. . . . No! . . . I've had no other instructions. . . . I'll wait. . . . Right. . . . Yes. . . . Thank you, miss. . . ."

He mopped his brow, confused, and gave Elie no explanation, merely ordering him:

"Get Craig for me. Quickly."

He lit a cigarette nervously.

"Harry? I've just called the ranch. . . . No! I didn't manage to talk to her personally, because she went out riding with the agent half an hour ago. . . . I got her secretary on the phone. . . . She asked me if the new owner had arrived, said some name I didn't catch, and which I didn't dare make her repeat. . . . The new owner, yes. . . . Those were her own words. . . . She didn't

238

give me any details but, from what I could gather, the mine is sold. . . . That's all I know. . . . She was surprised he wasn't here yet. . . ."

He turned towards the street, Elie got up and peered across the desk, to have a look, too, and Gonzales, with new-found agility, made for the door. The men outside had just turned, as one man, towards the end of the street and they seemed excited, there was something in the air, like an electric charge, as a large car, smothered in dust, finally appeared, gliding noiselessly along and coming to rest alongside the kerb.

Everyone had already noticed that it had a New York State registration number.

Before Gonzales could move in, a chauffeur in a black uniform had leapt from his seat and opened the door. A tall, well-built man of about forty, bare-headed, with fair hair and a pink complexion, got out first, and behind him followed a thin, dry man, smaller, who gazed round him without a word, crossed the pavement hurriedly and entered the hall of the hotel.

"I think it's him, Harry," said Chavez into the phone as the newcomers entered. "I'll call you back."

The chauffeur was outside, getting the luggage out of the boot. The manager hurried over to the two men.

"I take it Mrs. Carlson reserved No. 66 for you, gentlemen?"

The bigger of the two answered:

"Correct."

"If you'd be good enough to fill in your forms, I'll show you to your apartment."

Elie, unconscious of what he was doing, pushed the block of forms over to the visitor, forgetting to hand him a pen, and the man had to pick it up for himself.

For years, Elie had worn thick glasses, without which he was unable to read. But at a distance, instead of helping, the glasses distorted his vision.

Fixing his eyes on the smaller of the two men, he took off his glasses, and the lines on his face deepened, the blood rose to his cheeks and his huge eyes seemed to pop out of his head. He didn't move or say a word. The rest of the world ceased to exist. He wasn't even aware of the corner of the globe where he himself lived. Time and space no longer had any meaning.

Twenty-six years rolled back as, his eyes bulging and ear

humming, he stared at Michel and Michel stared back at him.

Elie had grown larger with the years. He had got fat. The hair on the crown of his head had become fairer, especially at the temples, and was even curlier, its colour somewhere approximately between red and grey.

Even so, Michel had recognized him, he was sure, just as he had recognized Michel. And Michel hadn't flinched. He had momentarily knitted his dark eyebrows. His face had registered mild astonishment and a slight smile, perhaps a grimace, too, had formed on his lips.

It was impossible to tell, because a large portion of his face had altered. Only his forehead and eyes remained unaffected; all the lower part, nose, mouth and chin, seemed to be of some other substance, waxy, less malleable, lacking muscular control, on which there were half-effaced scars.

Without his glasses, Elie could only make out vague lines on the first visitor's form; and then Michel walked up, quite naturally, took the pen and wrote, in his turn, without saying a word.

"Are there only the two of you?" asked Chavez obsequiously. "I expect you're hungry."

The taller man glanced at Michel, who shook his head, and the former answered:

"Not just now."

"Would you like something to drink?"

The procedure was repeated. After which, Michel glanced quickly again at Elie, and made for the lift. Chavez went up with them, and so did Gonzales, with the luggage, leaving Elie alone for a moment in the hall, swaying like a ship in a high sea, after which the door opened, three or four men entered, then a few more, slapping each others' backs.

"Is it him?"

He didn't hear them and didn't think of answering. Mac shot out of his bar.

"Is it the new boss? Which one? The small one, I'll bet!"

Elie blinked, his eyelids were still slightly red, put on his glasses mechanically and bent over the forms.

Mickaïl Zograffi, Hotel St. Regis, Fifth Avenue, New York.

He wasn't surprised. At the time, he had received a shock which, for a few seconds, had stopped his blood flowing.

For twenty-six years, he had known that one day that moment would come. Already, that December evening, as he walked away from the foot of a fence where a body lay, in an odd crumpled heap, he had had a presentiment, a half-certainty that the man would live.

He kept seeing, he had never stopped seeing the top part of his face, especially his eyes, which seemed to be both surprised and pleading, while the rest, from the nose down, was nothing but a dark hole, with teeth sticking out.

Did Michel, at that moment, ask him, in mercy, to finish him off? He had meant, and he should have done it, to fire a second shot, into his chest, for instance, at his heart, not to protect himself, because Michel knew, but through pity, so as to spare him further suffering.

He hadn't been able to. And, as he took the wallet from his jacket pocket, he hadn't been able to look, so he had turned away his face, convinced that if he stayed any longer he would faint.

He had never known what happened afterwards. In Hamburg, where he arrived next day, and where blocks of ice floated down the river, there were no Belgian papers and the German papers didn't mention the drama which had unfolded in Liége.

For three years, he had lived in daily expectation of arrest, and it was only much later, six years after leaving Liége, that he had sent a type-written letter from New York, enclosing a dollar-bill for a reply, asking a Liége newspaper to send him a copy for the 5th December 1926.

He had never received anything. For several weeks, he had called by in vain every day at the poste restante counter.

Even so, he was convinced that Michel was not dead. Years and years later a world war had broken out, tens of thousands of Jews had been massacred and, like Rumania, Poland had been cut off from the world by the Iron Curtain.

He had heard nothing from his relations, his father, his brothers and sisters, and they were doubtless all dead, though some of them might have been deported to Siberia.

The Zograffis might have met the same fate.

He knew nothing, except that Michel was living in some corner of the world, and that one day they would come face to face.

His own life had been no more than a kind of reprieve. One day, he would have to settle up. One day, Michel would turn up, as he just had, would look at him, without a word, and wait for him to speak.

"What are you doing, Elie?"

He stared blankly at Chavez, who had just come down again and chased out the busy-bodies, and answered without thinking:
"Nothing."

"Get me Craig right away."

He tried to dial the number; but because he had forgotten to put his glasses back on, after having just taken them off again to wipe his eyes, the figures were blurred.

"Craig?"

His voice sounded normal, but it didn't surprise him.

"Chavez wants to talk to you."

"Craig? Harry here. They've arrived. I said 'they' because there are two of them. At first I wondered which was the boss, but I guessed right away it was the one who didn't speak. In fact, he hasn't said a word yet. The other one does the talking. What? ... Just a moment...."

Then turning to Elie:

"The other form...."

Elie handed it to him:

"Eric Jensen.... Both give the same address. Hotel St. Regis, New York.... They came by car, with a chauffeur.... You know him? He came here a month ago? ... Jensen? ... No wonder I thought I'd seen him somewhere.... Tall and fair, yes, a kind of giant.... They're in the apartment upstairs.... The chauffeur stayed with them.... I asked them if they wanted something to eat and they said they'd call if they wanted anything.... I may be wrong, but Zograffi looks as if he might be a bit difficult.... What's that? ... If you like.... I'll have someone ask them.... Hang on...."

Chavez walked round the desk and stood by the switchboard.

"Ask No. 66," he said to Elie, "if they want to speak to Craig. If they do, put them through, but keep that phone connected."

Elie stuck in a plug.

"No. 66?"

"Eric Jensen speaking."

"Mr. Harry Craig wants to know if he can speak to you."

"Put him through."

Chavez listened to their conversation, and Elie could hear both voices on the phone.

"Jensen?"

"Yes."

"Craig here."

There was an awkward silence, at least for Craig.

"I hear you've just arrived."

"Yes."

"Is it true the mine has been sold?"

"More or less."

"Who to?"

"To my boss."

"Is he here?"

"Yes."

"When shall I see him?"

"He'll let you know."

"You realize as well as I do there are some urgent decisions to be made, don't you?"

"Yes."

"At this rate, in a few days, I shan't have a single technician left."

"I'll call you before then."

"Thank you."

"Don't mention it."

Chavez waited until the upstairs receiver had been hung up.

"Craig? I took the liberty of listening in. This guy sounds pretty cold, doesn't he?"

"All we can do is wait. How old is he?"

"Zograffi? About fifty. He must have had a bad accident, because the lower half of his face is rigid, sort of artificial. I wonder he can still speak."

Harry Craig hung up without comment. Someone brought the flowers Chavez had ordered a little earlier.

"Shall I take them up to No. 66?"

"Gonzales can take them."

The latter detached himself from his seat, took the two bouquets and closed the door of the lift. The manager, looking worried and anxious, remained leaning on the desk, not moving.

"It always works out different from what you imagine," he murmured to himself.

Needing an audience, he turned to Elie.

"Jensen came here a month ago, spent two days with Craig whom he used to know at college, and they had lunch and dinner at the hotel. I thought I'd seen his face before. He was on some mission, apparently, and was studying the situation so that his boss would know the set-up when he bought Mrs. Carlson's mine."

Elie didn't move. It was impossible to tell if he'd heard.

"What's the matter?"

"Nothing. I guess it's the heat."

The lift door opened and out came a worried Gonzales, holding the two bouquets.

"What did they say?"

"To take them back."

"Which one spoke?"

"The smaller one. He spoke kind of strange, in a whistling voice, like water boiling."

"Did you tell him they were from the management?"

"Yes. He waved me out and shut the door behind me."

Gonzales stood there dumbfounded, still holding the flowers.

"What shall I do with them?"

"Put them in the blue vase."

It was a huge china vase on the table in the middle of the hall where the week's magazines were arranged.

It was midday. Formerly, at that time, sirens went off all over the town.

The man who, shortly before, had been leaning up against the front of the hotel, had finished up in the bar, deciding to have a drink now that work might be starting up again.

The little shoe-black crossed the street.

"Was that the new boss?" he came and asked on behalf of Hugo.

"Looks like it," answered Chavez impatiently.

"Which one?"

"The smaller one."

"What's his name?"

"Zograffi."

The boy went running off, and through the windows they could see Hugo listening to his report and picking up the phone. He would probably be the first to have any news, because he had contacts everywhere.

The bell rang. Elie unhooked the receiver, listened and said:
"One moment. . . ."
Then to Chavez:
"Your wife."
"Hallo, Celia? I'm sorry. I haven't had a second. He's arrived.
. . . A man, yes. . . . No, it's not her. She's at the ranch. . . . Order
your lunch upstairs. . . . I'd rather not come up now. . . . I don't
know. . . . I don't know anything yet. . . ."

A waiter brought a tray with a cheese sandwich and a fish-and-
tomato sandwich, and put them down on Elie's desk with a cup
of coffee.

"What will you have for sweet? There's apple pie or fruit."

Elie stared at him uncomprehendingly, and the waiter shrugged
behind his back and signed to Chavez, as if to imply that the
receptionist must have got sunstroke.

CHAPTER TWO

THE HUT ON THE BANKS OF THE
ELBE, AND THE CHOCOLATES
IN THE DRAWER

WHEN the chauffeur came down, Gonzales showed him where
the restaurant was, though he didn't go in straightaway, but first
entered the bar where the others made room for him along the
copper rail.

"Rye!" he ordered, staring round curiously.

Then he said to the fair-haired barman who was filling his
glass:

"My name's Dick."

"Mine's Mac."

It was as though they were exchanging pass-words or recog-
nizing each other as long-lost brothers.

"New York?"

"Queens."

"Brooklyn."

Being so far away from home, the chauffeur purposely exaggerated his Brooklyn drawl and cool manner and studied the
huge men surrounding him with an amused look; some of them

245

were well over six foot, lounging around in tight-fitting blue trousers, wide-brimmed hats and multi-coloured leather boots.

"Like the movies!" he remarked out of the side of his mouth.

"Never come west before?"

"Never further than St. Louis."

"Stopping long?"

"You never know with him. Maybe a day, maybe a year."

He was aware that some of the prestige of the new boss, whom they'd only glimpsed, reflected on him, so he acted up to it.

"Have one on me, Mac. On the boss."

When he sat down in the restaurant, Chavez, who had been keeping an eye on him, went over to his table and stood there, hoping to find out a bit more about the new owner and, later on, went so far as to walk along the pavement with the chauffeur, and show him the track he had to drive the saloon down into the yard behind the hotel, where the garages and petrol pump were.

The manager's wife seldom came down before evening, and spent the rest of the time lazing around the apartment in her négligé. Chavez was very much in love with her, very jealous, and kept going up to see her the whole time.

That afternoon, he had scarcely left the hall and had only a sandwich for lunch. The two men in No. 66 had the menu brought up by the head-waiter. Once again it was Jensen who spoke over the phone.

"What have they ordered?"

"Steaks and a bottle of red Bordeaux."

A little further down the street, in the company block, Craig didn't dare leave his office, expecting to be summoned at any moment. Twice in less than an hour, he had phoned Chavez, and Elie didn't have far to go to fetch him.

"What are they doing?"

"They're finishing lunch. The chauffeur's busy washing the car."

"Haven't they asked for me?"

"Not so far."

The second time, there was some more news, but it wasn't likely to calm the chief engineer's apprehensions.

"Bill Hogan has just arrived."

"The professor?"

246

"Yes."

Hogan, who taught geology to Tucson University, was a tall, lean young man, with a boyish face, who was often to be seen wandering, on horse-back or by jeep, round the district, in the summer, sometimes going as far as Mexico, not hesitating to sleep out in the desert. He couldn't have been more than thirty-two and, while still a student, had won several prizes at rodeos.

"Did he have an appointment?" Craig inquired.

"He asked me to say he was here. They answered would I show him up. He was carrying a leather brief-case."

Gonzales had lowered the venetian blinds, so that it was no longer possible to see what was going on in the street. From time to time, Chavez mopped his brow. Elie, still sitting at his desk, had patches of sweat under his arms.

The thermometer must have been registering about 107° in the shade. There was no breeze and not a cloud in the sky, and for weeks it had remained the same uniform blue. The rainy season wouldn't be there for about two or three months, perhaps longer, it could happen; it could happen that it wouldn't rain more than three days in the year and, till then, there'd be sunshine every day, dazzling light and the line of shadows outside, withdrawing steadily from Hugo's shop towards the broad bay-windows of the hotel.

"Hot enough for you?"

It was the traditional joke, because Elie never complained about the heat, and the hotter it got, the happier he seemed. He seemed quite happy to perspire, and he gave off a strong reek of sweat; sometimes, when Chavez went into the reception cubby-hole, especially about four or five in the afternoon, he was almost knocked over by the stench.

Elie had noticed it. It didn't matter to him. He relished his own smell. Each year, he grew fatter and his flesh was acquiring an unhealthy consistency. He took no exercise, but merely walked twice a day, without hurrying, the quarter of a mile to his house. He ate too much, especially in the evening, was always hungry, and kept crystallized fruits and chocolates in one of his drawers.

Was it because, for so many years, ever since the time at Madame Lange's when he made do with two eggs and a few slices of bread a day, he had been hungry?

During those three years in Hamburg, it wasn't hunger which

247

affected his life so much as the cold and, when he thought about it, he found it hard to believe that there had every really been any summers. They had been short and rainy. The sun only featured very rarely in his memories, though he could clearly recall those misty mornings on the Elbe, could imagine he was still hearing the sirens of the damp, black ships anxiously seeking their courses and, most painful of all, the days when the snow melted and seeped its way into one's clothes and shoes.

In the early days, he was so sure they were looking for him that he didn't dare to try and find work, but changed his furnished room in the dock area every night. During the day, he walked the streets endlessly and, to avoid being recognized, had grown a beard which, badly sown, left gaps between the tufts of red hair.

The crowds were getting ready for Christmas, which he had spent shivering under a single blanket, and, a few days later, Michel's money exhausted, he had joined a group of men who wandered the streets carrying sandwich-boards.

The cold was sometimes so intense that he felt as if he were burning, and he had to stop himself crying out loud.

He had no idea what had happened in Liége after he left, except that Michel was not dead. He could still see his eyes fixed pleadingly on him. Even if he had only lived a few minutes, his friend must have given his name to the neighbours who had eventually come and bent over him. Or perhaps some passer-by or policeman doing his round had found him. Elie refused to believe he had lain all night on the pavement, groaning, and pleading with his eyes to be finished off.

Elie had paid. He had felt he was paying, but he didn't complain, never spoke to anyone, either, and one day made up his mind to cross to the Altona dockyards.

He had spent three whole years there, in a world of cranes and girders, workshops and docks, where there was nothing but metal and stone, a black and white universe edged with the still more implacable grey of the river beyond which, at night, the lights of Hamburg twinkled.

At first, he had been taken on at a dockyard where two of them lugged around metal sheets from morning till night. His physique wasn't strong enough to stand up to it. In vain did he clench his teeth and sweat till he ached in every bone of his body, the foreman spotted him and struck him off his list.

Then, for some weeks, he had done the workers' errands for a few *pfennigs,* fetching tobacco or hot coffee from the canteen where, afterwards, for some time, he had the job of cleaning the tables and floor, until at last, because the old man who held the post had been found dead one morning, he had been taken on as night watchman.

He worked at night, going his rounds regularly, a lamp dangling from his hand, and having to negotiate a narrow plank over a sewer, which made him feel giddy. By way of compensation, he enjoyed his hut and a small lead stove, which he stoked till the metal became red-hot and his flesh was roasting. He hoped that, by storing up heat, he would be able to stop himself shivering on his rounds, but he found he only achieved the opposite, yet he couldn't stop himself doing the same thing the following night.

His sister, not having his new address, which he had been careful not to give her, no longer wrote to him, and he had no news of his family, and no idea who was alive and who was dead; his one aim was to amass enough money to pay his passage on one of the boats he saw leaving almost every day for America.

Once he was there, he reckoned it would all be over. He wondered neither what nor why. It was a line he had traced in his future's unknown, a frontier beyond which life would be different.

That day had come after three years, six months of which he spent in hospital with an attack of pleurisy which wouldn't clear up.

When he landed in New York, he was wasting away, and he was afraid that the Immigration Authorities might refuse him entry on health grounds. He had given his real name, Elie Waskow, because it was the only way he could obtain a passport; the authorities hadn't asked him any questions about what happened in Liége; apparently no one was interested in catching up with him.

The first night, not knowing where to go, he had slept in the Y.M.C.A. on 14th or 15th Street, down town, swarming with Jews and foreigners like himself, where he was constantly surprised to hear Yiddish spoken. He didn't feel an outcast, less so than in Hamburg. He didn't feel curious enough to go and see the rest of the town, but found work straightaway, washing dishes in a restaurant and, for six months, he never ventured beyond the district.

He hardly ever left his little circle in Liége at Madame Lange's, either. He felt there was some danger lying in wait for him, if he was foolish enough to stray far from the house, and even the house itself was too big for him, so he shut himself up in the kitchen, huddled by the stove, and spent most of his time there in the fug.

It was the same here, where he never went to see anyone and never even made any plans. All he knew was that, one day, if he was lucky, he would live in a place where there was no winter, where he could enjoy the sun the whole year round.

It would take time. First of all he had to learn the language because America didn't consist exclusively of people who spoke Yiddish and Polish. He had bought a dictionary and a grammar. Working at his sink, his hands in greasy but warm water, he listened to the conversations around him, and more and more words became lodged in his memory.

One day, as he was thumbing curiously through a telephone directory, he had made a discovery which worried him. He didn't know any other families by the name of Waskow, only that his father had some cousins in Lithuania. Now, here it cropped up several times in the directory, and it was the same with most of the names he had known during his childhood.

He had a room in a cheap hotel with, as in every hotel in town, a reception-desk. The hall was dark and the lights were kept on all day. One evening, the manager, who was German and was called Goldberg, seemed to be watching him as he went by.

"What would you say to working here as night receptionist?"

Though it was much dirtier and smaller, he had sat in the same kind of cubby-hole as here in Carlson City, with a telephone switch-board, and a key-rack with pigeon-holes for the guests' mail.

The winters in New York were as cold as in Hamburg. The central heating worked erratically, no one could do anything about it, and the air was sometimes stuffy, sometimes freezing.

He was patient, and put up with poor quality food, though there was more of it than he had known up till then, but he began dreaming of doing the same job, much later on, in Miami. In Florida, he would at last be warm the whole year round, and would never again need to go any further.

He was warm, and could eat freely, eat till his belly was full and his head heavy! He watched people drinking and growing pinker, their eyes bright and their bodies sluggish. Eating gave him the same sense of well-being, the same feeling of plenty and security, especially when he could envelop himself in warmth at the same time.

Not once, since he had left Liége, had he felt the urge to open a book about mathematics, and he couldn't understand how, over so many years, he had devoted his time and energy to studying.

"So you're educated?"

When the manager put the question to him, he hadn't known what to reply.

"If you know a bit about accounts, you could keep the books at night, and I'd give you an extra ten dollars."

To earn more money, and so get nearer to Florida, he had bought a second-hand text-book on accountancy. It had only taken him a week to pick up enough, and he had been entrusted with the hotel's books. A year later, the hotel was sold to be knocked down and make way for a big block. The manager had found a post in Chicago. Elie had followed him there and, after a few days, was working in a new hotel.

In the telephone directory here, too, there were Waskows, Malevitzes and Resnicks, like Mademoiselle Lola.

He'd looked anxiously at the letter Z and found Zograffis, too, but none of them had the Christian name Michel or Mickaïl.

He had failed to notice the phone ringing, and what roused him from his torpor was seeing Chavez rush over to the desk.

"Reception here."

It was Jensen's voice from apartment 66.

"Would you ask the manager to come up?"

Elie turned to the latter, who was waiting.

"They want you to go up to No. 66."

As he passed the mirror, Manuel adjusted his tie, ran a comb through his hair and went into the lift, Gonzales closing the door behind him. At the same moment, the phone rang and a woman's voice said:

"Get me Mr. Zograffi, please."

"Who is it speaking?"

"Mrs. Carlson."

"Just a moment. I'll see if he's in his apartment."

He stuck in his plug.

"Mrs. Carlson want to speak to Mr. Zograffi."

Elie was relieved to hear Jensen's voice answer:

"Put me through."

He had been afraid that it would be Michel himself who spoke to him. What worried him most, ever since midday, was hearing the voice which had been described to him, the voice which whistled and sounded like the hiss of boiling water.

Michel had scarcely glanced at him and hadn't been tempted to speak to him, but it wasn't possible, even though Elie had grown so fat, that he hadn't recognized him. Besides, his eyes had registered something. Elie would have sworn that it wasn't really through surprise at running into him, and that Michel, too, had expected to meet him somewhere, someday. What must have surprised him was to see him so pink and fleshy, with a double chin and a fat, shiny face, behind a hotel reception-desk in Arizona.

What had Michel thought? He must have had some reaction. Elie, at the time, had been too overcome to judge, hypnotized by the lower half of that face which, one evening, twenty years earlier, had been only a bloodstained gap.

He didn't think he'd detected any hate in Zograffi's eyes. Of the two, it was the latter who had changed most, especially his expression, which had once been that of a carefree child, and which now focused itself on people and things with powerful intensity. . . .

Madame Lange had frequently said:

"Isn't it a shame, a man having eyes like that!"

What had Zograffi felt when he recognized Elie? He hadn't looked away or said anything. He had gone straight up to his apartment and, since then, seemed only concerned with business matters. Was it he now who was talking to Mrs. Carlson?

Elie could have found out, by listening in to their conversation. He didn't and, after a few moments, the indicator over the plug changed from black to white, which meant the call was over.

When Chavez came down again, he first finished the conversation he had begun in the lift with Gonzales, then Elie had the feeling he was eyeing him from a distance in a special sort of way.

Then he leant on the desk and said:

"They need a long table to spread their plans on. Gonzales

has gone down to the basement to fetch one of the collapsible tables we use for banquets."

Apartment 66 consisted of two bedrooms, each with its own bathroom, a large sitting-room, and a smaller one which could be used as an office.

"What are they doing?" Elie asked.

"When I arrived, he was on the phone."

"Which one?"

"Jensen. If I'm not mistaken, they've been invited to dinner at the ranch."

Chavez still seemed preoccupied, and Elie was convinced it was because of him.

"Do you know him?" Chavez eventually remarked.

"Who?"

"Zograffi."

"Why do you ask me that?"

"Because, while the other one was phoning, he asked me two questions about you."

"Did he mention my name?"

"I don't think so. No. He referred to the man on reception."

"What did he want to know?"

"First, how much you earn. I told him. I couldn't do otherwise because, as far as we know, the hotel belongs to him from now on. Then he wanted to know how long you'd been here and, when I said seventeen years, it seemed to make him smile. It's hard to be sure, because his face is so stiff. When he speaks, you can tell his jaw's been broken. There's some metal inside his mouth and he's lost half his tongue."

Elie didn't move but stared at the big book on his desk.

"Do you know him?" Chavez again asked him, not quite sure how to treat him now.

"I think so."

"Why didn't you say so earlier?"

"I wasn't sure."

"Are you sure now?"

"Maybe. Yes."

"Is it a long time since you last saw him?"

"A very long time."

"In the States?"

"In Europe."

253

The manager would know if he lied. Besides, Michel might have said more. He might even mention Elie again tonight, tomorrow, any time. Anything might happen, from now on, and it wouldn't help Elie to go away, either.

He had toyed with the idea, earlier, and he had been tempted to go and get his old car and dash off to Mexico, without telling Carlotta. But from the moment Michel had come across him again, it was pointless; all he'd have to do would be lift up the phone, and give instructions for him to be picked up and arrested, one or other side of the frontier.

Not once, in twenty-six years, had he bothered to study the criminal code, knowing that the day Michel caught up with him, he would have the right to decide his fate. Even without the law or the police, it was useless running away.

Anyway, whatever happened, Elie wouldn't protest. He was resigned. He was waiting.

"Were you at college together?"

"At the University."

Chavez wasn't surprised that his receptionist had been to a university. It was Zograffi who interested him.

"What was he studying?"

"Mining engineering."

"I begin to understand."

The phone was ringing. Elie picked it up.

"It's for you. It's Craig."

The manager spoke into the mouthpiece, without waiting for the other's question:

"They're working upstairs, with plans and blue-prints spread out on the carpet all over the room. They've asked me to send up a large table."

"Is Hogan still with them?"

"Yes."

"Didn't they mention me?"

"Not so far. I gather Mrs. Carlson has invited them to dinner tonight at the ranch."

Craig put down the receiver, angry and disappointed, not knowing what to tell the members of his staff who, ever since the new boss arrived, had stayed in the offices, waiting for news.

Everyone was waiting. Elie was, too, and because he felt slightly uneasy was absent-mindedly eating chocolates, and

254

Chavez was disgustedly watching him stuff them in his mouth.

He didn't smoke and he had never drunk. While others felt the need of a glass of spirits or a cigarette, he filled his belly. Mademoiselle Lola used to eat all day, too, ignoring Madame Lange's repeated warnings:

"You just wait and see! When you're thirty, you'll be so fat, you can't walk!"

The funny thing was, Carlotta was like that, too. When he first met her, she wasn't as fat as most Mexican women of her age and only ate at meals.

They were three sisters: Carlotta, Dolores and Eugenia, and the last two worked as maids for Craig. The father, who was very Indian-looking and made pottery, had built with his own hands the house they lived in on the edge of the village, and it was there that Elie, when he arrived, had rented a room.

He didn't eat with them, because he got his meals at the hotel. He only went back there to sleep, in the day when he was working nights, at night when he was on days. There were always hens clucking and pecking at the red soil in the yard. At the far end of the yard was a workshop, in which a potter's wheel hummed, like some giant insect, from morning till night. Sirens marked the passing of time, but what dwarfed all other sounds was Carlotta and her mother cackling on the verandah, as they washed and ironed the neighbours' laundry, every five minutes bursting into laughter.

Carlotta had very nearly the same laugh as Mademoiselle Lola, a deep, sensual, throaty laugh.

Her mother was enormous, with swollen legs, and she would probably become the same one day.

He hadn't married her for her looks. When he had thought about finding a place to live, he had had to find someone to keep house for him.

The parents had suggested Carlotta. For a long while, she had returned home every night, and it was unpleasant when he had come back from work at midnight to find no one there.

In New York, he hadn't been alone, he had heard people moving about and breathing, through all four walls of his room, and he could even smell them. He hadn't decided to marry Carlotta so as to avoid being alone. She had been rapidly transformed. The eve of their marriage, she was still a lively young girl who came and went all day long, and would burst out laughing, for no special reason, displaying her white teeth.

After a month, she could hardly stir herself from her armchair or her bed, and spent her time eating sweets or listening to the radio. Sometimes, when he got back, there were five or six women in the house, talking away, and in the evenings they sat in the shadows of the verandah.

Carlotta's mother and sisters used to come and visit her. Cousins would turn up from Mexico and spend a week or a month in the house, and there was always food on the table.

He was used to it. There were hens round the house now, too, and at least half a dozen ginger cats under his feet, and he had to take care not to tread on them.

Both were getting fatter, Carlotta even more than him and, almost in her forties, she was nearly as vast as her mother and had to walk with her legs apart.

The phone rang again. It was Jensen.

"Get me 242."

"Carlson City?"

"Yes."

He knew whose number it was, an Irish property-dealer called Murphy, because Elie had bought his house from him.

"Murphy?"

"Yes."

"Hang on. Someone to speak to you."

They only had time to exchange a dozen words and the call was over. Murphy lived six houses away. A few minutes later, he came running in, very excited.

"Mr. Zograffi," he said, with an air of importance.

"In No. 66. Have you an appointment?"

"He's expecting me."

Elie confirmed it.

"Send him up."

Chavez, who hadn't left the reception-desk, was chain-smoking and trying to work out what was going on.

"I wonder how he knew about that old crook, Murphy. He knew his phone number, so they must have already been in touch."

The phone rang again.

"Would you send up a bottle of Scotch and some glasses? Don't forget the ice."

256

"Soda?"

"No."

Time passed slowly. All day, there had been a group, across the way, round old Hugo, who was observing the hotel through his small, malicious eyes.

Most upset and wretched of the lot was Craig, who had taken such trouble to hang on to his best workers in Carlson City and who'd been given no word.

Someone else turned up, about half-past four, a stock-breeder, who had a ranch about a dozen miles downstream from the town.

"Mr. Zograffi!"

"Is he expecting you?"

"I imagine so. He wired me to come this afternoon."

It was true. Jensen gave the word for him to come up. Half an hour later, he asked for another phone number, Delao's, the lawyer, who was a personal friend of Craig's. Delao merely shook Chavez's hand as he passed, he knew Chavez, too, but didn't speak to him or mention the object of his visit to No. 66.

It was Delao, eventually, who phoned a quarter of an hour later, and called his own office, from which came his secretary with a portable typewriter.

"They've bought the ranch," Chavez murmured, trying to piece together the bits of the puzzle. Delao had obviously sent for his secretary to type a legal document.

He called up Craig and repeated :

"I think they're buying Ted Bryan's ranch."

"Is Ted with them?"

"Yes. So is Delao, who sent for his secretary. And that old swine Murphy, they called him first, and he seems to be in on it all."

"I'll be over."

Craig couldn't bear to wait around, fidgeting, in his office. He was a tall, thick-set brusque young man, and he drew Chavez over to the bar.

"I need a drink."

He had had more than one, that was obvious from the shine on his face. No doubt someone at the office had brought a bottle so as to help kill time.

He leant on the bar, while the manager, close by him, didn't have a drink but continued to watch the hall and hurry over to Elie every time the phone rang.

Craig drank two double ryes, looking more and more depressed, and finally gave the counter a violent bang with his fist.

"We'll soon see what he's up to!" he announced in his loud voice, making for the reception-desk.

He told Elie:

"Get me No. 66."

Then, receiver in hand, he said:

"Jensen? I've got to speak to the boss. . . ."

From where he was, Elie could hear Jensen's calm voice over the phone.

"I get the impression you've forgotten that, until the take-over, I'm still director of the company. . . . What? What's that. . . ?"

He was raging mad. He looked as though he was going to provoke a row, then he gradually calmed down, his voice grew quieter and he shook his head, murmuring:

"Yes. . . . Yes. . . . I understand. . . . Yes. . . ."

Then, finally, he said:

"Very good. Tomorrow at ten. I'll be there."

He repeated, as though the others hadn't heard:

"I'm seeing them tomorrow morning at ten."

He was making out he was in on things, but it was obvious he knew no more than Elie or Chavez.

Cunning so-and-so!

He returned to the bar. This time, the manager didn't go with him. Ted Bryan was first to come out, with Delao and the secretary.

"Shall we have a drink?" he suggested, half-way across the hall.

Delao answered:

"Not here."

"Did I do right?"

"We'll discuss that later."

Murphy came out of the lift shortly afterwards, with a delighted and mysterious look on his face, and shook Chavez warmly by the hand.

"What a guy!" he confided admiringly.

At six o'clock that evening, Craig, who was drunk, phoned

258

his wife to tell her he wouldn't be back for dinner. She was worried about his condition, so he repeated:

"Don't worry! I know what I'm doing! I'll have the last word, you'll see."

He walked hesitantly back to the bar and glared at the chauffeur, who was having a drink. He said nothing to him, merely examined him from head to foot, while Mac, the barman, motioned to him to take it easy.

At a quarter past six, the saloon drew up in front of the entrance. A few minutes later, the lift was called from the sixth floor and Gonzales hurried up in it.

Zograffi came out first, cold and impeccable, in black trousers and a creamy-white dinner-jacket. As Jensen, also in evening dress, went over with the key to the reception-desk, he stood there, in the middle of the hall, not looking at anyone, smoking a flat cigarette which had a smell Elie was sure he recognized.

Gonzales gave the revolving doors a push. Dick, the chauffeur, who was waiting on the pavement, opened and closed the car door.

The lights had just been lit. On the horizon, the sky was still a reddish-purple, and the mountains lavender-colour.

The car slid noiselessly down the gradient of the street, everyone watching it as it went.

Elie was the only one who hadn't left his seat to see it go. He was flushed. The sweat was collecting on his brow.

Michel hadn't even bothered to glance at him.

CHAPTER THREE

ELIE'S DEFENCE

At seven o'clock, Celia, Chavez's wife, came out of the lift and stood there for a moment gazing into the more or less empty hall, blinking, as though she had stopped in the entrance to some reception-room and everyone had turned to stare at her.

Everyone agreed she was the most attractive woman in Carlson City and she was aware of it. She also knew that one of her most effective charms was her childlike expression and, as soon as someone spoke to her, she would open her eyes with calculated innocence.

Her husband hurried along and took her off by the arm into the restaurant, where they had a table to the right of the door.

Every day she spent hours getting ready, never tired of seeing to her face, her hair, her hands, every part of her body, to which she had ended up sharing her husband's devotion, and the rest of the time, she lay around on a sofa, reading novels. Because she could never get used not to going round the apartment half-naked, Chavez insisted on her locking the door, and would often creep up stealthily to make sure she had done so.

At other times, a dressing-gown wrapped round her, she would lean out of the window and watch the slowly-moving passers-by in the street.

Her husband would sometimes catch her going to Hugo's to fetch some papers or cigarettes, and would be seen gesturing her to go back in and close the blinds, because he was jealous even of the looks men might give her.

A year earlier, when they had been making a film in the mountains, and the leading actor had spent two weeks in the hotel, Chavez had forbidden Celia to come downstairs, even for dinner, which they ate together in their apartment, and the maids claimed that, all that time, he had kept the key in his pocket.

Elie's dinner was served to him on a tray, behind the reception-desk. When he had eaten it, he phoned Emilio who should have been coming to take over for the night at eight o'clock and who lived at the far end of the town, and spoke to him almost in a whisper.

"There's no point in relieving me this evening, Emilio. I'll spend the night here."

"You can't stay twenty-four hours running on reception."

"I don't even intend to sleep."

"Is it true the new boss has arrived?"

"What's he like?"

"I don't know."

"All right. I'll do the day tomorrow. Thanks."

"It probably won't be necessary."

He didn't want to go away from the hotel. It seemed impossible that Michel hadn't something to say to him, no matter what, some message to pass on to him. Elie realized that, until then, his time had been completely absorbed by business yet, even so, he had managed to ask two questions about him. Just two, and it was the first which worried him most. Why had Zograffi, who was almost certainly the new owner of the hotel and the mine, asked how much he earned? Even Chavez, who knew nothing about either of their pasts, had been intrigued. And why hadn't Michel spoken to him, why had he barely glanced at him?

Perhaps, that night, when he came back from the ranch, things would work out differently, especially if, as was possible, Elie was the only person in the hall.

Michel must have asked himself at least one question:

"*Why?*"

Elie was sure he didn't know, he could remember the amaze-he saw in the man's eyes when he fired the shot.

Elie would explain to him. Because he did know. He had had twenty-six years in which to think up what to say, the day he found himself face to face with Michel, and now that day had arrived. He was in a hurry to get it over. Zograffi couldn't have been aware of his cruelty in passing the reception-desk without speaking. He must have got it all wrong. As soon as he gave Elie a chance to explain, he would understand.

What did it matter if he was the new owner of Carlson City? It could have been anyone, a beggar in the street, the situation would have been the same.

He almost forgot to phone Carlotta.

"Hullo, is that you?" he said in the same voice which he used to Emilio.

He could hear music the other end. She was listening to the radio or playing records.

"What is it? Aren't you coming back?"

"No. I'm spending the night at the hotel."

"I understand. The new owner has arrived."

The whole town knew. His wife, too, asked him:

"What's he like?"

She added:

"Is it true he's bought Bryan's ranch?"

"I think so."

"Will you be able to sleep a bit?"

"No doubt."

There were whole hours, at night, when the receptionist had nothing to do, and whoever was on duty would put the chain on

261

the door and have a doze in one of the leather armchairs. Emilio always took off his shoes.

When he came out of the dining-room, Chavez was surprised to find that Elie wasn't getting ready to leave.

"Is Emilio sick?"

"I phoned him not to come. I'd rather stay the night."

Celia remained behind her husband, and he looked at Elie anxiously.

"Did you get on all right, in the old days, at the University?"

"Why?"

"I don't know. I just wondered."

The former relationship between the new boss and the receptionist had him worried. He had a confused feeling that something was being hidden from him. However, he shrugged.

"Please yourself. I'm going with my wife to the cinema. I don't suppose they'll be back from the ranch before eleven."

He noticed Craig alone at the bar, went and took him by the arm, and sat him down in his car so as to drop him off at his home as he passed, while Celia followed them out without a word. Not having any customers, the barman shut his door and went off. Two of the guests went up to their rooms. There were two others still out and, in the hall, Gonzales and Elie kept a good ten yards apart.

The books were up to date. All he had to do was stay there for hours, all through the night. Elie, slumped in his chair, his eyes half-closed, began to rehearse the things he'd say when he was at last allowed to speak.

He had no idea what had become of Louise, and worked out that she would now be forty-five or forty-six, older than Carlotta. She was a mature woman. Perhaps she was married, with children? Perhaps she had had a relapse and had been sent to a sanatorium? In spite of Madame Lange's fierce denials, he was convinced she had tuberculosis of the bone.

Madame Lange would be an old lady. He wouldn't have been surprised, though, to hear that the house had remained the same, with different lodgers in the pink room, the yellow room, the green room and, who knows, a boarder, richer than the others, in the old drawing-room turned garnet room, with green plants in copper pots on the window-sills.

It was the only bit of his past which still lived on at all in his memories and, sometimes, watching Carlotta, he felt she was a mixture of Louise and Mademoiselle Lola.

He suddenly became terrified at the thought that Michel, who had brought an end to his life in Liége, might now bring an end to his life in Carlson City, and once again force him to leave. The thought caused him more intense physical agony than the cold in Hamburg and Altona, or the blackest nights in the dockyard. At the prospect of going away again, he was gripped with panic, and began protesting, alone in his corner, struggling, his brow covered in greasy sweat.

They had no right to demand it of him. He had paid for his place as dearly as a man can.

Michel would understand. He must understand. Elie would tell him everything, and reveal his thoughts, feelings and what he meant, in all their nakedness, a nakedness even more pathetic than Louise's, the Sunday of the photographs.

What Zograffi had to realize was that he had gone as far as he could, and that there was nothing more. Nothing. A void.

Let them do what they liked to him. Let them inflict some punishment on him. But don't let them make him go away. He couldn't do that. He would rather sit down on the pavement and let himself die in the sun.

He was tired. Did that word have as terrible a meaning for other people or for Zograffi as it did for him?

The phone rang, someone was calling from New York, a woman's voice.

"Carlson Hotel? I should like to speak to Mr. Zograffi."

"He is not here at the moment."

"Hasn't he arrived?"

"Yes. But he's gone out."

"He didn't say when he'd be back?"

"He's not expected till late tonight. Can I give him some message?"

"Don't bother. I'll call back."

It was a young voice, without a trace of foreign accent. He wondered if Michel was married, and that led him to wonder other things about him. It was odd how he sometimes thought of him as "Michel" and sometimes as "Mr. Zograffi," Zograffi more often than Michel, probably because of his expression which had changed so much.

"It's ten o'clock," said Gonzales, coming over and planting himself in front of the reception-desk.

"You can go."

Since they had stopped working the mine, they hadn't kept on any staff in the hall at nights and, if a guest came in late, it was the receptionist who worked the lift.

"You don't think I ought to stay?"

"Why?"

"Because of the big boss."

"It's not worth it."

"Did Mr. Chavez say so?"

"I'll take the responsibility."

Gonzales went into the cloak-room to change. When he crossed the hall, he looked shabby in his worn-out trousers and battered straw-hat.

"Good night."

"Good night."

He was almost sure, now, to show Zograffi and his companion to the sixth floor and, for a few moments at least, they would stand face to face in the lift.

He was annoyed when Chavez and his wife came in early. When they went up together, he hoped that the manager would go to bed. As he passed, he glanced at the clock and asked:

"Anything?"

"No. All the others are back in."

Half an hour passed and Chavez came down again, lipstick on his face. He noticed it as he passed the mirror in which he always glanced, wiped it off with his handkerchief and came over and leant on the desk as if he meant to stay there. At first, neither spoke a word.

"You don't know if he's married?" the manager finally asked.

"He wasn't when I knew him."

Then remembering the call from New York, he said:

"A woman asked for him about an hour ago."

"Didn't she give her name?"

"She said she'd call back."

"There's a photograph up there on the mantelpiece of a dark, very attractive woman, foreign-looking. It looks like a very old photo, so it can't be his wife."

"In a silver frame?"

264

"Yes."

"There isn't a portrait of a man, too?"

Chavez was surprised, and looked at him suspiciously.

"Yes. A man who looks remarkably like him. I suppose it must be his father and mother."

"Yes."

"Were they rich?"

"His father was in the tobacco business and had branches all over the Balkans and Europe."

"I wonder if they were able to get away in time?"

Why was Elie convinced that Michel was not married? If he had been, wouldn't there have been a third photograph on the mantelpiece, and maybe portraits of his children, too?

The woman from New York didn't sound like a wife. The idea of Zograffi being a bachelor appalled Elie, because it reminded him of the artificial jaw, the tongue which was only half there, the voice which was little more than a hiss, and suddenly, Elie, who had known so much loneliness, came to know a different sort of loneliness.

"Why do you want to wait for him?"

"No special reason."

He was frightened, now, really frightened of the conversation for which he had been waiting so anxiously ever since morning. Chavez still hadn't gone up to his wife. It became obvious that he had decided to be around when Zograffi and his companion returned from the ranch.

He began to pace the hall, smoking cigarettes and stubbing out the ends in the sand of the spittoons, and, every time he came face to face with the reception-desk, he stared at Elie as curiously as ever.

"Did you finish your studies?"

"No."

"Why not?"

"For personal reasons."

"Were you poor?"

If Chavez hadn't been there, Elie would have made himself some tea, because he was beginning to feel drowsy and his eyelids were smarting. Only half of the lights were on, part of the hall remaining in darkness.

"Here they are!"

265

They heard a car turning the corner of the street and, in fact, finally stopping in front of the hotel. A door slammed then another. Elie got up, so as to be clearly visible, and the manager hurried towards the door.

Zograffi came in first and it was true that, from a distance, he bore an almost uncanny resemblance to his father's photograph. Half-way to the lift, he stopped and Jensen came over to the desk to collect the key. His throat dry, Elie decided to say at least the words "good night". He did so, facing the two men, after a great effort.

Michel looked at him, surprised, frowning, as though he were trying to understand, then finally, with an imperceptible shrug of his shoulders, gestured to him as presumably he did to all his employees. From where he stood, Elie thought he heard him say:

"Good night."

He wasn't sure. There had been only an indistinct sound, a sort of gurgle, and the three men disappeared into the lift, Chavez closing the metal door.

Ten minutes later, the manager phoned from his own apartment.

"They don't want anything and they don't want to be disturbed. If anyone calls from New York, tell them to call back tomorrow after ten."

Did Michel still get up as late as he used to in the old days, and had he kept his habit of wandering about in his dressing-gown and slippers? As he wondered, Elie recollected the characteristic smell that hung about the garnet room, a mixture of Turkish cigarettes and eau de Cologne.

He still hoped there would be some sign. It was possible that Zograffi hadn't wanted to say anything in front of Chavez and that, in a few minutes, he would be on the phone to Elie and ask him to come up. Or perhaps, so as to avoid Jensen being there, he might come down?

Nervously, Elie left his cubby-hole and began walking up and down the hall.

Everyone was back in. There was nothing to stop him slipping on the chain and stretching out on one of the leather settees.

After about ten minutes, he went out into the street, crossed it and, from the opposite pavement, looked up to the top of the block where there were lights in only two of the windows. The sky was full of stars. Far away, crickets were chirping in the mountains. Across the other side of the arroyo, in the residential area, an occasional window was picked out in yellow, two or three of them, but not in his house. Carlotta would be asleep, as usual, with two or three cats on her bed.

If the phone had rung in the hall, he would have heard it from the street, and he stayed there a long time, his eyes fixed on the sixth floor windows until they suddenly turned black like the rest.

Then, the blood rose to his cheeks and his eyes smarted, which was his way of crying. He pushed open the door and slipped on the chain, not knowing where to walk in the hall, which seemed larger than usual.

Finally, he went into the cloak-room, climbed down the iron staircase leading to the kitchens and switched on the light. He sometimes had the urge, nearly always when he was on nights, and each time he felt like a criminal. He opened each refrigerator in turn, ate any old thing, a leg of chicken, some cheese, some sardines, there was always a large tin of them open and, before going up again, stuffed his pockets with fruit.

He could have had a cold meal prepared for him at night, like Emilio. He had the right to one, but it never occurred to him and when, next morning, he heard the chef complaining because some food had disappeared, he was careful not to let on that it was him.

As on other nights, he didn't sit down: as on other nights, he kept his ears open, afraid of being caught.

He was still eating as he was climbing the stairs, and was swallowing down the last mouthful without chewing, when it occurred to him he might find himself face to face with Michel.

But there was no one in the hall and he went round it suspiciously, as though he expected to find someone skulking behind one of the arm-chairs.

He would have to get his chance sooner or later. He was too tired to go on standing up, and he didn't feel safe away from his cubby-hole, preferring to spend the rest of the night inside on an uncomfortable hard chair than outside on an easy one.

It was one of those things that had to be explained, if you didn't know that there were others like him: he needed his corner.

Perhaps, ridiculous as it might seem, that was the cause of all

267

that had happened? But that wasn't where he'd begin. The first thing to say, because it was the essential point, was:

"*Whatever you may think, Michel, I never hated you.*"

It was odd how he began to think his speech in Polish.

"*I have tried. I have done everything to try and hate you, it would have been easy. I couldn't. It wasn't a question of hatred. It wasn't a personal question, either. I knew you couldn't do anything about it, but even so you took away everything I had.*"

He closed his eyes, trying to recapture the atmosphere of the dining-room in Liége, where he knelt in front of the keyhole.

He couldn't manage it. He saw himself sitting at the table, with his text-books and exercise-books in front of him, heard the murmur of the stove, saw the distracted figure of Louise sitting in her armchair but, when it came to the sight which had then haunted him so much, to the point of making him cry, alone in his room, he was no longer able to imagine her on the bed, the lower half of her body naked and pale.

It didn't matter, he had discovered afterwards. Louise was quite unimportant. What did matter was. . . .

Michel had become an important person, sparing, no doubt, with his time.

It would be foolish to try his patience. Elie had to find the exact words; if not, Michel might perhaps look at him again, as he had earlier, as if to ask him what he was doing there in his way.

Is that what he had in mind? Did Michel despise him so much, he wouldn't give him a chance of explaining?

He hadn't denounced him at the time, otherwise the police would have found a means of arresting him. They have lists which they keep for years and years and send to every country. In order to come to America, Elie had had to go and get a certificate from the Altona police, and no one had batted an eyelid, anywhere, when they saw him and heard his name.

So Michel had kept quiet. Was it because he had understood and had felt sorry for him?

But then, why wouldn't he spare him a minute's conversation? He had been busy all afternoon, of course. When he came back that night, he hadn't been, but it hadn't prevented him from going to bed without being curious enough to ask Elie any questions.

Why had he looked at him with an air of surprise? Because he had got fat and his red hair was thinning, or because he spent his time in the reception cubby-hole of a small hotel?

It was because of him, Elie, that the lower half of Michel's face was rigid, deformed, that he could only express himself by ridiculous noises, and that everyone who looked at him felt embarrassed. Could he expect him not to mind?

"My life has changed, too," pleaded Elie, *"because of you, I resented you, too, I tried to hate you, I decided to punish you."*

Let Michel punish him, if it made him happy. It was his right. Let him say what punishment he wanted and Elie would accept it in advance.

"Only please don't make me leave!" He couldn't do that again.

At least leave him his corner, this time. Or else kill him. Death frightened him. The idea of lying, still, on the ground, his eyes open, and people walking around him and eventually carrying him off before he rotted away, was even more terrifying than the idea of being cold. Kill him, if he must. And get it over quickly.

Michel couldn't be so cruel as to make him wait like that, on purpose. He was a busy man, with tremendous responsibilities.

"I know you've got a lot on your mind, decisions to make, people waiting, but it would only take you a few minutes to settle my case."

It was quite simple. All it meant was his being allowed to explain.

He had found the word to define the way Michel used to smile, his easy manner, and his gaiety which prevented people from taking offence. He was *playing* and he didn't realize it. He crushed people under his heel as you crush insects when you walk, and felt no remorse because he didn't know what wrong was.

"Do you understand what I mean? You were innocent and you had no idea what it is to suffer, to be cold, to be hungry, to be frightened, to know you're ugly and dirty and be ashamed of it. You had to have everything because you wanted everything and, from me, who had only my corner in Madame Lange's kitchen, and meant to spend the rest of my life there, you took. . . ."

269

That wasn't it. He couldn't recapture that clear and so very simple idea which he had hit on during those nights in Altona. Wasn't it fantastic that he had forgotten something so important? Then everything became clear, and he was sure that, if he had had Michel with him, he would have convinced him.

It was connected with the idea of innocence, but it wasn't expressed in the same way. It was vital for him to find it again and that the explanation should be a fair one, because he had no wish to deceive Michel, and he wasn't intending to appeal to his pity.

It was to his judgment. What he wanted was to talk to him, man to man, sincerely, more sincerely even than one talks to oneself.

"We're two men, just men, that's all, and suddenly I felt unhappy, I saw all my illusions crumble to dust. . . ."

How could he explain to him that it all began from what he saw through the keyhole, from the things Michel did with a sickly young girl?

For a long time, he hadn't given Louise a thought. No doubt it would be Michel who would remember, and ask:

"Why?"

It wasn't possible to answer. The truth was simpler. He'd say, without embroidering:

"I tried to kill you. I only succeeded in wounding you and I hadn't the courage to finish you off. You'd be right to avenge yourself."

The word "avenge" would shock Michel. That wasn't what Elie was thinking, either.

"Punish me."

As he had punished him, at the time. It was all cut and dried. It was obvious. If Michel wanted any further explanations, he would try and provide them. Too bad if he couldn't succeed.

He was asleep upstairs. Perhaps, when he breathed out, he made the same whistling noise as when he spoke?

The Chavez's were asleep, too. Everyone was asleep, Carlotta, too, in their house, with the cats.

Elie asked nothing of anyone, only to be left in his corner. He had asked nothing of Louise, either, or Madame Lange, content with the warmth they brought into the house. Carlotta hadn't understood, at first, that he wasn't annoyed when he came back and found the housework undone, because her sisters and neighbours had been there.

She was used to watching him sweep up, tidy up, often get the meals ready. She couldn't have thought him normal and probably wondered why he wanted to live with her.

What was the use of trying to explain?

"Judge me. Be quick about it!"

If only it were over! If only he were at peace, at last!

He ate, as though he were protesting against something, he didn't know what. And when there was no more fruit in his pockets, he went down to the kitchen a second time.

It comforted him to have a full belly. It was a proof that he existed.

He gradually dozed off, not sleeping, but losing consciousness sufficiently to come to with a start when dawn began to break and the town began to stir.

He felt as if he had just spent the worst night in his life, physically and morally cramped. Seeing his large green eyes in the mirror, he looked away, and went and rinsed his face and hands.

At six o'clock, two women, poor, thin Mexican women, started cleaning the hall, then the shoe-black opened Hugo's steel shutters and, shortly afterwards, a cyclist hurled in a bundle of newspapers which had just arrived at the station.

When Elie heard sounds in the kitchen, he went and shouted through the open door for some strong coffee to be sent up to him.

He realized, daylight having come, that it might be a long time yet, and lost hope that Zograffi would attend to his case straightaway. He was a business man, now. It didn't strike him as odd.

Emilio phoned.

"Don't you want me to come and take over?"

He hesitated. He had promised himself he wouldn't leave the hotel till he had had things out with Michel. Now, he wondered if he had the strength.

Quite soon, they would be having their breakfast sent up and would start making phone calls. Craig would be sent for, and others, no doubt, while Chavez, ever anxious, would spend the morning leaning on the reception-desk.

271

What hope was there that any notice was taken of him?

"All right, then, come on."

He wasn't giving up. He was merely going through that early morning feeling. The sun was already bright, it was warming up. He felt like stretching out, closing his eyes and sleeping. Really sleeping, not thinking about anything, or even dreaming. Sleeping at home, on his bed, still damp from Carlotta's body, with the golden light filtering in through the venetian blinds, the windows open and, all round him, familiar noises outside, the hens clucking, a dog barking and the strident voices of women calling to each other in Spanish, and talking so quickly, you'd swear they'd end up gasping for breath.

It was his corner. He would sweat, smell his gross flesh, and feel fat, dirty and cowardly.

He would plunge himself into sleep as though he'd never wake up and, when he opened his eyes, he would feel the same self-loathing as if he'd drunk too much the previous night. He didn't need spirits, though, to get drunk and have a hang-over. Even his eyes, that morning, were like the eyes of a drunken man, and the two women who were cleaning the hall looked askance at him.

It would come to an end. He had always known it would come to an end one day. He was still struggling, because he didn't have the courage to accept.

Was Michel, up in No. 66, aware of all this? Wouldn't he feel some pity? Wouldn't someone, some day, it didn't matter who, feel sorry for him?

Emilio arrived by bicycle, and went and left his straw-hat in the cloak-room. He was thin, with a small brown moustache, and a crooked face which made him look like a film villain.

Elie made room for him in the cubby-hole. Emilio leant on the desk and looked at the forms.

"Are they upstairs?"

"Yes."

"Any orders?"

"Not to disturb them before ten, even if there's a call from New York."

He was still hesitating to go, annoyed with himself for having given in to that early morning feeling. He no longer felt like sleeping or going far away from the hotel. He felt that by losing contact he was putting himself in danger.

"You don't look well. You're not sick?"

"No."

"I heard that he's buying up the ranches in the valley in the hopes of irrigating them with water from the lake. Do you understand? He'll pump out the water and start the mine going again. That'll take at least a year. The water will flow down into the valley and the soil, which was worth practically nothing, will produce crops of alfalfa, ground-nuts and even cotton. They reckon that Ted Bryan's been won over and that some of the others have sold, too."

Elie looked at him so blankly that Emilio broke off.

"Aren't you interested?"

What did it matter to Elie? Maybe Michel Zograffi had come to Carlson City to do business. But that business had already taken second place.

It wasn't possible that the same wasn't true for Michel as it was for him.

"See you tonight. Sleep well."

He saw that old Hugo had already moved into his armchair, and was beckoning to him to come and have a talk. He pretended not to notice, made for the foot of the town, crossed the arroyo which was as dry as it always was nine-tenths of the year round, and walked slowly up the slope on the other side.

The door was open; so were all the windows. There was a hint of a breeze. Carlotta was asleep and he had time to get undressed before she realized he was there. Together, they generally spoke Spanish. Or else he spoke English and she answered in her own language.

"Is that you?"

She moved over to make room for him. The bed was warm and damp. She pushed off one of the cats and it rolled on to the rug, miaowing.

"You're not too tired?"

He looked at her with the same indifference as he looked at his own body.

"You'll sleep better if I get up."

He didn't object and she sat on the edge of the bed, scratched herself under her breasts, finally got up, grabbed her dressing-gown and went into the kitchen.

He'd say to Michel:

273

"You see . . ."

The last thing he remembered was Carlotta throwing grain to the hens as they rushed towards her, cackling.

ZOGRAFFI'S CHANCE

WHEN Elie woke up, he heard Carlotta talking on the verandah to one of her sisters, Eugenia, who had married a Mexican foreman from the mine and had six children. Only the two eldest went to school; the others trailed at her skirts without seeming to worry her. Carlotta and she could gossip for days on end without getting tired, talking about nothing in particular, yet finding something to laugh about, hastily breaking off only when Elie appeared.

He had often wondered if Carlotta and her family weren't a bit scared of him. In any case, women, in his company, stopped being gay and natural, not only as though he were some stranger, but as though he were a creature of some other species which they couldn't understand. The other sister, Dolores, had four children; she would have had five if one hadn't died, and more if she hadn't miscarried almost every year.

The married men laughed at him behind his back, he knew they did, using a special word to imply that he wasn't a man, because Carlotta had no children.

Two boys and a little girl of Eugenia's were playing in front of the window, all three stooping to perform some mysterious rite with rainbow-coloured stones.

When he appeared on the terrace, after pulling on his trousers and thrusting his bare feet into his slippers, the two women, as he expected, stopped talking half-way through a sentence, as if they had been caught doing something wrong. Lying back in a rocking-chair, Eugenia had one breast out of her red bodice and her last-born, who was feeding at it, stared at Elie with his big, black eyes, just as baby animals at a zoo stare at inquisitive spectators who have stopped in front of their cage.

"Do you want to eat?"

Carlotta, also settled in a rocking-chair, rocked away, gazing at the town in the sunlight across the other side of the arroyo.

He preferred to help himself, lifting the lids of the saucepans and opening the refrigerator. He found some rice with red pimentoes and goat's meat, heated up a large plateful, and went and ate it on a corner of the table where the others had already eaten their meal, but which they hadn't cleared.

It worried him to see that it was already two o'clock, for no special reason, possibly because he would have sworn he hadn't slept more than an hour. Carlotta came in to him, hands on hips.

"Are you going back to bed?" she asked.

Sometimes, when he worked nights, he slept all day, getting up with just enough time to eat.

He shook his head.

"Are you going back to the hotel?"

He said yes. He had been wrong to leave, to have given in to a second's tiredness, to a momentary depression.

"Just now," she went on, "I thought they were coming to fetch you."

She referred to it as if it had no importance, as if she were simply making conversation.

"It was about eleven this morning. Eugenia hadn't yet arrived. I was out on the verandah, when a large black saloon passed slowly by, braking in front of every house, and the chauffeur looking at the numbers as if he was trying to find someone. He stopped completely in front of ours and I saw him reading the name on the letter-box. I made my way over to the pavement to ask him what he wanted and he saw me coming. When I was only a couple of yards away from him, he put his foot on the accelerator and the car disappeared round the end of the street."

"Was there anyone else in the car?"

"No. Only the chauffeur in uniform, black like the chassis."

It could only have been Dick, Zograffi's chauffeur.

"Didn't he stop in front of any of the other houses?"

"No. I thought you must be wanted at the hotel and they'd come to fetch you."

He went on eating, but he was in still more of a hurry to be away.

"Why do you think he came and looked at the house?"

"I don't know."

275

He thought he understood. The previous day, hadn't Zograffi asked the manager how much Elie earned and how long he'd been living in Carlson City? He was still gathering information. He no doubt wanted to find out how he lived and had sent along his chauffeur.

But why, when it would have been so simple to ask him himself?

"Will you be coming back tonight?"

"I don't think so."

"You'll be spending another night down there?"

They watched him walk away, and only started gossiping again when he was out of hearing distance.

The streets had more life than usual, and groups of men in white shirts were standing in front of the company offices, waiting for news. Zograffi's car wasn't at the hotel entrance. Three technicians, who worked for Craig, were slumped in the hotel arm-chairs, hats on the back of their heads, smoking cigars, and a few customers were visible in the bar.

Elie couldn't see the manager and went over to the desk. Emilio was at his post behind it.

"Any news?"

"They've been on the go all morning."

"Have they gone out?"

"An hour ago, with Craig and two other engineers. Apparently, they went to look at the mine."

"Has anyone asked after me?"

"No."

"Where's Chavez?"

"He's just gone up to his wife."

"You can go. I'll take over."

"What, until tomorrow?"

"Yes. There's no point in your coming back tonight. Only, I'd rather the manager didn't know it was me who suggested it. You can tell him your wife isn't feeling well."

She was often sick. Emilio didn't dare refuse. Delighted at having some free time, he was, all the same, worried by Elie's attitude. It was the first time that anyone had offered to work for him, and he tried to make out why, guessing that it had something to do with the new owner's arrival. But what was the connection?

276

"Two guests have arrived from New York," he said, pointing to the forms.

"No women?"

"No."

"Hasn't a woman phoned from New York?"

"Yes. At a quarter past eleven, to No. 66. They talked for over ten minutes. The two new guests, they look like lawyers or business men, are in Nos. 22 and 24. They went up to No. 66 for an hour and came down again for dinner. Now I suppose they're having a sleep, because they took the night plane. That's all. No one's left. No reservations."

He winked to indicate that Chavez was coming downstairs.

"Shall I really tell him?"

"Yes."

"Mr. Chavez, I'm very sorry. My wife has just phoned me to say she's had one of her attacks and . . ."

He lied well. Even so, the manager looked at Elie suspiciously, and asked him:

"Do you intend to do the night, too?"

He didn't understand any more than Emilio did. On the other hand, he had been impressed that Elie had known Zograffi before. Not quite sure what their relationship had been, or what it would be in the future, he preferred to remain discreet.

"Please yourself."

Emilio went off, first slipping into the cloak-room. Elie examined the forms, and copied the names and figures into one of the books, while Chavez stood there leaning his elbows on the desk in his usual way.

"Didn't you ask me yesterday when he arrived in the United States?"

"I don't remember."

It was true. So many thoughts had passed through his head since the previous day that he could no longer tell what he thought from what he actually said.

"He landed in 1939, two months before Hitler invaded Poland, and England and France declared war. You could say he foresaw what was to come . . ."

Elie didn't dare ask any questions, but remained in suspense, hoping the other would go on.

"He was rich even then, owning among other things,

277

interests in the Belgian Congo copper mines. His mother and he settled in the St. Regis and he has always kept on the apartment, even when, later on, he bought a property on Long Island."

Elie couldn't help asking:

"Did he tell you that?"

"I found out through Hugo. One of his customers, who has mines in Mexico, forty miles from here, was in business with Zograffi. He reckons he's more of a gambler than a business type. The first thing he did, when he'd hardly arrived in America, was to acquire a big block of shares in a Canadian mine which couldn't find a buyer on the market at ten cents a share. Eight months later, they found pitchblende there, and today the shares are quoted at eighteen dollars. Since then, it's been the same with everything he's gone into."

"Is his mother still alive?"

"I think so. She's presumably on Long Island."

He hesitated, then finally asked: "Is he married?"

"No. It's not that he doesn't like women because, in New York, Miami and Las Vegas, he's always surrounded by fabulous girls. One of them phoned this morning."

"I know."

It had slipped out. He had admitted that he had already questioned Emilio.

"He's talking about modernizing the hotel for next winter, and we're expecting the contractors from Tucson tomorrow. Mrs. Carlson will probably sell her ranch, if she hasn't already. Craig's to remain director of the mine and Jensen will supervise the work during the first few months."

Chavez was excited by it all, his only fear being that the new owner had someone to put in his place. He kept watching Elie.

"Do you want to talk to him?"

Elie blushed. He couldn't help it. He always blushed when he felt he'd been caught out, even if he hadn't, and the manager became more suspicious, to the point of laying, to some extent, his cards on the table.

"I don't suppose you intend to make sure of your previous acquaintance to . . ."

It was too direct. If Elie hadn't already had the idea, it was, anyway, unwise to put it into his head.

278

"Would you like to change your job?"

"Certainly not."

"Are you sure?"

"It's the truth."

This time he added, with feeling:

"Even if I was offered a job ten times better, I'd ask to stay on reception."

Chavez hadn't dared ask why. He obviously couldn't understand. After their conversation, he prowled round Elie, trying to make him out. Elie sensed it and, each time he felt he was being observed, began to blush guiltily.

Zograffi returned at five o'clock and there were two men with him, besides Jensen and Craig. He stopped, as he usually did, in the middle of the hall. The men waiting in the armchairs got up. Craig moved forward to introduce them one after the other. Elie, from where he was, was unable to hear what he said. They merely seemed to be exchanging polite remarks.

When Zograffi turned round, as Jensen went forth to fetch the key, his eyes met Elie's, and he frowned as he had on the previous day, suddenly seemed to be in a hurry and walked rapidly towards the lift.

Elie felt he had just made a discovery, but he was so dumbfounded, he refused to believe it.

Was Zograffi really afraid of him?

He recalled in the minutest detail, as if it was a slow-motion film, the movements he had made, crossing from the middle of the hall to Gonzales' lift, the set of his shoulders and the look on his face. It was the look of a man who has suddenly noticed a vicious dog and has hurried away, a man who had already, for instance, been bitten by that dog.

It wasn't credible. Michel knew that Elie was harmless. He had seen his face, immediately after the shot, and knew that he would have been incapable of pressing the trigger a second time, even if he had been begged to.

Michel was wrong. Elie was just a fat man, with no ambition other than to live peacefully in his hole. Chavez was wrong, too, if he imagined he wanted to take his place.

He didn't covet anyone's place, not even Zograffi's: he wouldn't have known what to do with it.

He had to tell him, let it be known, so as to put an end to the misconceptions they had about him.

There must surely be a moment when Zograffi, as important as he was, could spare him five minutes of his time. Even three minutes!

"Forgive me, Michel. I'm sorry. I've suffered as much as you have, more than you. I won't do it again."

Was it absurd? Perhaps not all that absurd. Michel would understand. If he hadn't been capable of understanding, he wouldn't have looked at him like that when he lay at the foot of the fence and, afterwards, he would have denounced him.

He had no need to be scared. Elie felt neither hatred nor envy inside him, even after what Chavez had said about his former companion's luck. You had to expect that sort of luck. Michel went on playing, the only difference being that, today, it was with mines and the futures of thousands of men.

Everybody used to like him, then, and now everyone trusted him. They hurried from all over the place so as to follow in his wake, and soon Carlson City would come to life again, some people had arrived from New York, and others were on the way, awaiting his good pleasure.

It was fantastic that Michel should be scared of him. Scared of what? That he might kill him a second time?

Was it, by any chance, to spy on him that he'd sent his chauffeur roaming round his house?

Elie was surely mistaken. It wasn't fear. He wasn't playing the part of a vicious dog, more that of some bothersome fly.

It annoyed Michel, every time he crossed the hall, to see his red face and his popping eyes. From a distance, Elie must have looked like a beggar. What exactly was he waiting for? For Michel to shake him by the hand, saying that he bore him no resentment, that he had long since forgiven him, and that he was delighted to see he was working for him?

The truth is that Michel despised him, always had despised him, enough not to give himself the trouble of condemning him. It was contempt which, when he was in the garnet room with Louise, made him shoot an occasional glance at the keyhole, behind which a wretched little Jew from Vilna was kneeling.

Now he had come across him, he frowned, impatiently. That was it. Elie's presence made him impatient. He had other things to think about. He was busy trying to recreate, on his own, through his own energy and self-assurance, a town which, without him, would be dead, which, two days earlier, had been dead.

He had the power to sack him. All he had to do was pick up the phone and say to Chavez:

"Show the receptionist the door."

Elie would have to go away, leave the town, because no one there would give him work after that, or be willing even to shake hands with him. Carlotta wouldn't follow him, because she needed her sisters and their brood more than she needed him.

The phone rang. It was No. 66. Jensen's voice.

"Will you ask Mr. Kahn to come up?"

It was one of the New Yorkers who had arrived that morning.

"Hallo! Mr. Kahn? Reception here. Mr. Zograffii's expecting you upstairs."

The three men who'd been introduced to Michel shortly before were celebrating their newly assured futures, for no reason other than that they had gone up to him, and he'd shaken them by the hand.

All afternoon, people came and went. Hugo, across the way, slumped in his armchair, looked like an information bureau. Scores of people came for news, waiting their turn, including the company doctor, who was the last to be told what was going on and glanced up at the sixth floor windows which concealed his new master.

Zograffi and Jensen didn't come down for dinner, but had their meal served in their apartment which must have stunk of Turkish cigarettes. At eight o'clock, Zograffi came down alone and crossed the hall, without glancing towards the reception-desk. His car wasn't there. He was taking advantage of the comparative coolness of the evening to go for a stroll, and people stared after him, not daring to speak to him.

As soon as he came in, half an hour later, Elie, even though he was in the middle of dinner and had his mouth full, got up, hurried so fast round his desk that he banged his hip, and took three or four steps forward. He didn't care if he looked ridiculous and his cheeks were stuffed with food.

Michel saw him. It was impossible that he hadn't seen him approach but, like that afternoon, he hurried off and disappeared into the lift, and Gonzales closed the door.

Then, without even finishing his meal, Elie seized a sheet of paper and wrote in Polish, not even pausing to search for his words:

I must talk to you.
Elie.

Jensen had just come down to the bar and joined Craig and several others there. Michel was alone upstairs, in the apartment no doubt, reading the papers he had bought at Hugo's and had been carrying under his arm when he came in. For about a quarter of an hour, Chavez had been back with his wife, who hadn't left their apartment all day and whom he didn't want Zograffi to see.

To Gonzales' surprise, Elie, holding his letter, entered the lift.

"Sixth floor!"

"Don't you want me to take it up?"

"No."

Then, up there, he asked:

"Shall I wait for you?"

"It's not worth it."

The passage was feebly lit. No. 66 had double doors. In the middle of the left-hand one was a letter-box.

Finding himself alone in front of the door, Elie's courage deserted him and he let his hand, which he had extended towards the bell-push, fall and, not moving, he listened and tried to make out what Michel was doing inside.

It never occurred to him to stoop and look through the key-hole. He couldn't have done it. Slowly and regretfully, he slipped the envelope he had prepared through the letter-box and heard it drop to the floor on the other side.

A few seconds, maybe minutes, went by. The springs of an armchair or sofa, gave a slight creak. Then he heard the letter brushing against the parquet floor and the sound of the envelope being ripped open by a finger.

If Michel had heard him come, he must have known that he hadn't gone away. Only a yard separated them. He was reading, he hadn't returned to his armchair straightaway, but was standing as still as Elie.

Was he going to refuse him the kindness of opening the door to him?

Elie stammered, so quietly that he could barely hear himself:

"Michel!"

He waited a bit and repeated, hardly any louder:

"Michel!"

As long as there was silence the other side of the oak panel, he kept hoping and his blood kept on pulsing hard. Michel still hadn't moved. He was going to reach out and turn the handle. Elie didn't say another word but held his breath and, in the silence, could hear his temples throbbing.

Finally, just as he was full of hope, footsteps moved away, becoming softer as they went from parquet to carpet, the armchair creaked again and someone turned the pages of a newspaper.

He didn't ring, didn't persist, didn't say another word. He had to remain some time where he was, so as to reassume a more or less normal expression and, slowly, his head bowed, he made his way towards the door of the lift and pressed the button.

He avoided turning to Gonzales, who was observing him, aware of his peculiar expression. In the hall, he felt sure he was lurching. Chavez, who had just come down, watched him approach, a question on his lips:

"Have you been up there?"

Elie, turning his back on him, murmured:

"I was taking a letter."

There was no delivery at that hour, but the manager didn't object on that score, merely asking:

"Did you speak to him?"

"I didn't ring."

What did they want him to explain? There was nothing he had to explain to Chavez. He had gone up, he had slipped the letter through the box, waited and called out:

"Michel."

And he hadn't opened. That was all.

If he hadn't sent Emilio away and if he hadn't forced him to lie, he would have gone home and tried to sleep. Michel wouldn't come down again that night. Unless, suddenly, he had remorse.

He wasn't the sort of man to have remorse. He was innocent. He had no need to feel ashamed and he had almost certainly never asked anyone's forgiveness.

Could he ask forgiveness for being himself?

He was scared of Elie, no longer daring to look him in the face. Or else it was contempt. Or pity. It all came to the same thing. Someone in the world existed who made him frown and walk quicker and, not being brave enough to go there himself, he had sent his chauffeur to see what his house and his wife were like.

"Do you mean to stay the night?"

"Yes."

"Please yourself. I can't stop you if, as Emilio makes out, his wife's not well. I should like you to resume your normal hours of work tomorrow."

It was beginning. Who knows, it might be the last night he was allowed to spend at the hotel. It's so easy to get rid of a man like him! All you have to do is show him the door and he goes off without a word, even if he has nowhere to go.

Whether it was the last one or not, he lived through that night with as great intensity as the previous one, the only difference being that the bar stayed open till midnight, and one of the New Yorkers, who had gone out, came back a few minutes before one.

Elie worked the lift, and the other stared at him curiously, as if he had a spot on his nose, opened his mouth as if to say something, and then closed it without a word.

Elie asked, in his most professional voice:

"What time would you like to be woken in the morning?"

"At eight."

"Good night."

"Good night."

He went down to the kitchen to eat, and found in the refrigerator a piece of cake which had been specially made for Zograffi.

He ate it. He was eating Michel's left-overs. Like a dog!

Do you give a dog who has bitten you a chance to explain himself? Dogs don't explain themselves. A wall of silence arises between them and men. You try to understand them. They bite because they're bad-tempered. Or else, as they say, because they're vicious.

He sated himself with food and humiliating thoughts, not having to look far for grounds for humiliation.

The other was asleep, high up there, with the chirping of the crickets coming through the open windows and, in ten thousand years' time, the same stars would be twinkling in the sky. He had once been taught how to calculate their speed. Nothing stopped. The world seemed motionless, yet it was whirling round, going God knows where, with tiny creatures like Elie clinging on to the smallest ledges.

He was asleep, his mouth open, because a man always falls asleep in the end. You cry, you shout, you make a fuss, you despair, and then you eat and sleep as if nothing had happened.

When he opened his eyes, at dawn, and looked at himself in the mirror which Chavez never failed to glance in as he passed, he saw that his face was puffy, and his eyes looked as if they were going to pop out of their sockets.

Who knows? Perhaps he could manage to look like a vicious dog? Whatever happened, he wouldn't go away, he would stay there, whether they liked it or not, clinging on to his desk.

Emilio wouldn't be there till noon, as he'd proposed the previous day. There was nothing Chavez could do about it.

Michel hadn't come down during the night. He hadn't dared. And, later on, when he crossed the hall, he would be flanked by the massive Jensen, who was there to protect him.

He wouldn't look at Elie or speak to him, that was certain from now on.

Was it because of what Elie had to say that he was so scared? Because he'd seen him naked within, turned inside-out like a rabbit-skin, pale and spattered with blood?

"Are you still there?" said Gonzales, in astonishment, when he came on duty.

He shrugged and went down to the kitchen to get some coffee. They were just taking the rolls out of the oven and he stood there, as if to defy the chef, and ate as many as his stomach could hold without bursting.

He felt better. He could face up to them now.

It wasn't quite eight o'clock when No. 66 rang for breakfast.

They would probably go to the mine again or buy some ranches. What difference did it make? There was only one thing Zograffi wouldn't do: spare the alms of five minutes of his time to Elie who needed it, in order to find peace inside himself, at last. He didn't know what it was like. He never would.

The chauffeur was ready and, a quarter of an hour later, the black saloon stopped at the door.

Maybe they were going a long way that morning? Maybe Zograffi had finished with Carlson City and was leaving for good?

It all happened very quickly, while the boy was sorting out

285

the newspapers on Hugo's stall. No. 22 phoned for his breakfast, then No. 24. Two of the regular guests went and sat in the dining-room and asked for eggs and bacon. They were in a hurry. Everyone seemed to be in a hurry.

Gonzales was standing in front of the door of his lift. There was a ring from upstairs, and he shut himself in and went up to the top floor.

For a few seconds, Elie was alone in the hall, then he heard Chavez's footsteps on the stairs from the first floor. The lift was coming down, too. It could be heard nearing ground level, and it gave a kind of wheezing noise as it stopped.

The door opened just as the manager appeared round the bend in the stairs. Zograffi, wearing a panama hat, was first out, took a few steps across the hall, and stopped in the same place as before, not looking towards reception, while Jensen walked over to leave the key on the desk.

He didn't notice anything. Elie, with a natural movement, had opened the drawer where, ever since the hotel had been the object of a hold-up, ten years earlier, a loaded revolver had been kept. To avoid hitting Jensen, he had to step to one side, and four shots rang out, Zograffi twisted round as he fell, and the two cartridges left in the chamber only failed to go off because the gun jammed.

The blue vase on the table was blown to pieces. The other three shots had hit their target and Michel, lying on the floor, in almost the same attitude as he lay at the foot of the fence, stopped moving.

This time he was dead.

Shadow Rock Farm,
Lakeville, Connecticut.
October 30, 1953.

286